LUCKY BABY JESUS

Peter Bradshaw is the film critic for the *Guardian* and writes regularly for the *Evening Standard*. He has also contributed to the *Modern Review*, the *New Statesman*, *Tribune* and the *London Review of Books*. His second novel, *Dr Sweet and His Daughter*, is also published by Picador. He lives in London.

'Peter Bradshaw is fast becoming the best comic writer of his generation'
Jonathan Ross

'A splendid novel'
Charlotte Raven, *New Statesman*

'Tender in the romantic moments, with a great supporting cast, this is a fine and funny piece of work'
Independent

'There are passages of tremendously careful, sensitive and illuminating writing, particularly those involving Sean's mother. These manage to combine the genuinely sad and the genuinely funny . . . Put it this way: to review it, I had to put down another book I was struggling with . . . After the enjoyments of this book, I found it impossible to pick up the first again'
Euan Ferguson, *Observer*

Also by Peter Bradshaw

DR SWEET AND HIS DAUGHTER

PETER
BRADSHAW

Lucky Baby Jesus

PICADOR

First published 1999 by Little, Brown and Company

This edition published 2004 by Picador
an imprint of Pan Macmillan Ltd
Pan Macmillan, 20 New Wharf Road, London N1 9RR
Basingstoke and Oxford
Associated companies throughout the world
www.panmacmillan.com

ISBN 0 330 42683 4

1 3 5 7 9 8 6 4 2

A CIP catalogue record for this book is available from
the British Library.

Printed and bound in Great Britain by
Mackays of Chatham plc, Chatham, Kent

For CSH

1

The conversation restarted as soon as they were out of the tunnel, as if they were all listening to themselves on the car radio.

It was Ysenda speaking, the director of the Sacred Heart Institution, a radical Catholic research foundation and think-tank; yet again, she was criticising Sean's cat.

'And the *name*, the *name* of this cat is an affront and an abomination. Tell us again, Sean, what is your cat's name?'

'Pussy Fwed. Fred.'

'*Pussy Fred*. Pussy, fucking, Fred.' Ysenda drank deep from an Evian, and made a *moue* of disgust which dovetailed with the suction slurp as she disengaged the bottle.

'And the cat is so *ugly*, you know? It's so *fat* and it's got a *nasty* squashy little face; it's the sort of thing a drug dealer would keep instead of a pit bull.'

Ysenda looked around briefly at the other occupants of the minicab. 'And Jesus, it *farts*; it *farts* like some sort of old man in a hospital bed; when I was round at Sean's apartment tonight I walked in through one door and Pussy Fred walked in through another door, and then it *farted* and I thought, Jesus, did I just step on Donald Duck's foot or something? And then the smell was something under licence from Porton Down, I felt like checking the relevant clause in the fucking Geneva Convention, Sean's disgusting flatulent cat is not allowed to *blow off* within seven hundred metres of Dag Hammarskjöld.'

Sean tried protesting or just interrupting, but no good.

'Sean, don't tell me you're one of these fucked-up bachelors with a creepy T.S. Eliot thing about cats?' she jeered. 'You're in your little study working late on something and then Pussy Fred stalks across the page and you have to stop and stroke it or something because Pussy Fred is just so *a-dor-a-ble.*' She gave it the full derisive four notes. 'No, pardon me, "Pussy Fwed"? Don't tell me: "Pussy Fwed" isn't his full name. Really he's Pussington Frederick Albemarle III, and you've got, like, some kind of stupid family tree showing how he's descended from Pussington Frederick Albemarle I, and when you were eleven you wrote creepy little poems about how he felt when a bunch of experimental scientists took his brothers and sisters away to be connected up to the fucking mains.'

'I've got a cat.'

For a second, all four of them in the minicab – Sean in the front passenger seat, Ysenda, Wayne and Nick in the back – could not work out who exactly was speaking. Then with an uneasy start they realised it was the driver: a balding man with glasses who wore a V-necked jumper over an open-necked shirt; some sort of laminated ID on a rubbery thong hung around his neck.

What was the form about minicab drivers taking it upon themselves to join in your conversation? And revealing, as they do so, that they have taken a close and uninvited interest from the outset? There was no glass partition to be closed. They are right up there with you, in your face.

Instinctively, and with the unquantifiable speed of thought, the four of them reviewed their conversation since getting into the car from Sean's flat in Highgate, and if they had said anything about all minicab drivers being Tories or kiddie porn enthusiasts.

But it was nothing like that. They had had the usual conversation about 'driving' their credit cards; Nick as usual hadn't taken his for much of a spin; it had a pitiful acceleration and terrible suspension. It was the Trabant of credit cards. Wayne, now that he was making the big time, had traded up to a sporty convertible little Amex which was cornering very nicely and last weekend he had taken it into the Giorgio Armani store, put the top down, and floored the accelerator while he felt the credit-rush whistle deliciously through his thick, layered hair. Ysenda, however, had pranged her little Visa horribly in Harvey Nichols on Friday, and suffered multiple credit abrasions and unpleasant phone calls when she crashed through her spending limit and her driver-side airbag failed to inflate.

Nothing nasty about minicab drivers, though. Nothing about their pathological unpunctuality, and a lack of spatial awareness so awe-inspiringly profound that you just want to take the wheel and drive them over to Oliver Sacks's house as quickly as possible.

'I have a cat,' the minicab driver continued. 'And he is called Henry. And a nicer beast you could not hope to meet.'

The studied blankness with which this observation was delivered made it impossible to tell if some sort of rebuke was intended. A silence descended on the vehicle.

Sean was responsible for the gathering to which he and his friends were headed this evening. He was editor of a conservative magazine for gays called *Somdomite*, which since its foundation by Sean with a capital sum of £9,500 from Sean's family (also £500 from Ysenda, who owned five per cent of the shares) had been a wild success. Daringly, Sean's magazine argued against special recognition for gays, and accepted and even embraced their marginal status as a political expression of 'the erotics of liminality'. It commissioned articles from off-the-wall 'inverts' – as *Somdomite* provocatively termed them – largely from the United States, who would say that pre-Wolfenden homosexuality in Britain, being forbidden and underground, was preferable to its current blandly progressive context, and so was the more thrilling and authentic sexual experience. *Somdomite* pertly harked back to the days when a policeman would chase a 'cottaging' homosexual down a back alley and the quarry would be unsure if he would be arrested or taken back to the policeman's own little semi in Colindale for an erotic and liminal seeing-to.

Sean was twenty-nine, and every magazine and newspaper editor, every television producer, wanted him to voice these stunningly radical views. His bullet head, with dyed blond hair, receding, cropped close to the skull, was to be seen on every television screen. He had even been hired as a deadpan demi-celebrity, photographed in flattering matte, to advertise a new unisex scent called Ambiguity. Sean had had to acquire an accountant (an urbane man recommended for his willingness to go 'off the record') to cope with the extra income.

Life was sweet for Sean, as he cheerfully assured his acquaintances and himself, no doubt about it. But something was strange – none of Sean's friends from university could remember him being gay. In fact, they couldn't remember him having much of a sex life at all. What they remembered, or thought they remembered, was him squiring girls about the place. But none of them liked to voice these doubts – if *doubts* they were – as they regarded it as good taste to salute the courage with which Sean had 'come out', and the canny way he had formulated a career-building way of doing it. He and his three friends were heading for a party to launch the latest issue of *Somdomite* at a club in Frith Street called The Ranch.

Directly behind him sat his friend Wayne, a direct contemporary of Sean's from university, and enjoying a promising measure of success himself. Wayne was an actor; attractive, with muddy, not-blond hair, coming down over his forehead in carefully cultivated little tendrils which he occasionally swept back over his head, revealing the beginnings of a widow's peak. He was wearing longish shorts: something none of the other men there could carry off; they extended just over the knees. Also, he wore a loose, short-sleeved shirt with a big check design, unbuttoned enough to show his tight, and entirely hairless torso.

Wayne was praised for a crucial ability to 'do' both English and American voices. He could switch between a floppy-maned drawl and a tight, whiny *schtick;* he rode horses and motorbikes; he learned lines; he took notes; he was flexible and available. Wayne had just made something of an impression with his portrayal of the footballer Peter Beardsley in a surreal work disturbingly evoking an erotic and psychotic subtext to his career with Newcastle United, called *Killing Zebras,* which had just concluded a triumphant West End run. Wayne's performance was described in the *Financial Times* as 'triumphantly bizarre'; *Time Out* called it 'thrillingly menacing' and the *Evening Standard* praised the professionalism with which Wayne submitted to the necessity of assuming such heavy prosthetic make-up for every performance.

Between them, Sean and Wayne had drawn up a Beaufort Scale of Fame.

THE BEAUFORT SCALE OF FAME

No.	Description	Specifications: on land	mph	Specifications: at sea	knots	Specifications: in public and the media
0	Calm	Smoke rises vertically	0	Sea like a mirror	0	You are completely unknown. You live with your mum and dad, and you mope around the public library reading *The Stage*. You have to travel on public transport and your fellow passengers look right through you
1	Light air	Direction of wind shown by smoke drift, but not by wind vanes	1–3	Ripples with the appearance of scales are formed, but without foam crests	1–3	You get small roles in fringe theatre, and some voiceover work on local radio. You scale down your day job at Sainsbury's Homebase to just working Saturdays. You have saved enough to start looking for a flat
2	Light breeze	Wind felt on face; leaves rustle; wind vanes move	4–7	Small wavelets, still short but more pronounced. Crests have a glassy appearance and do not break	4–6	You play Macbeth in a touring production to good reviews. You draw double-take glances from members of the audience when you appear in the theatre bar after the show, and you seem mysteriously to have become better-looking; girls laugh at your jokes more, and call you by your first name before it's occurred to you to call them by theirs

3	Gentle breeze	Leaves and small twigs in constant motion; wind extends light flag	8–12	Large wavelets. Crests begin to break. Perhaps scattered white horses	7–10	Your production of Macbeth has a short run in the West End, you have a small part in a BBC2 sitcom. You draw double-take glances from members of the public when you appear on the streets. Your parents forward messages from school and university acquaintances – some of whom you never really liked – wanting to get back in touch
4	Moderate breeze	Raises dust and loose paper: small branches are moved	13–18	Small waves becoming longer: fairly frequent white horses	11–16	Sitcom goes to a second series, with your part expanded. You move from rented flat in Holloway to buying a maisonette in Ladbroke Grove. You are now really very good-looking, copping off with girls you could never have dreamt of even talking to 18 months earlier. You appear on the front of *TV Quick*
5	Fresh breeze	Small trees in leaf begin to sway; crested wavelets form on inland waters	19–24	Moderate waves, taking a more pronounced long form; many white horses are formed. Chance of some spray	17–21	You are short-listed for an award. You get drunk at the ceremony, and take a swing at a footballer, getting you on the front page of the tabloids

No.	Description	*Specifications: on land*	*mph*	*Specifications: at sea*	*knots*	*Specifications: in public and the media*
6	Strong breeze	Large branches in motion; whistling heard in telegraph wires; umbrellas used with difficulty	25–31	Large waves begin to form; the white foam crests are more extensive everywhere. Probably some spray	22–27	You found independent production company which produces your sitcom and 'develops' other projects. For the first time the status-ratio of Your Calls Returned to Calls You Do Not Return tips in your favour. Your fan mail includes three serious stalkers who each require court orders. You are receiving at least 3 A-list invites weekly, each of which has 'star-fuck' opportunities as routine
7	Moderate gale	Whole trees in motion; inconvenience felt when walking against wind	32–38	Sea heaps up and white foam from breaking waves begins to be blown in streaks along the direction of the wind	28–33	You are invited to take part in Comic Relief and present a segment from typhoon-ravaged Turkmenistan and excoriate the British Government for doing nothing. *The Daily Mail* publishes an article attacking you, but you become a hero to young people, and you cannot leave your house in Holland Park without a small riot developing. You become engaged to a 17-year-old American pop star
8	Gale	Breaks twigs off trees: generally impedes progress	39–46	Moderately high waves of greater length; edges of crest begin to break. The	34–40	Your fiancée introduces you to American film studio executives who have become familiar with your work from cable TV. You film a screwball comedy over the summer about a

				foam is blown into the spindrift up into well-marked streaks along the direction of the wind		pair of twins, English and American, with you playing both parts. It is a medium-sized hit. You break off your engagement
9	Strong gale	Slight structural damage (chimney pots and slates removed)	47–54	High waves. Dense streaks of foam along the direction of the wind. Sea begins to 'roll'. Spray may affect visibility	41–47	You are nominated for an Oscar. There is no restaurant in which you cannot get a table, no public gathering in which your appearance does not cause a ripple of excitement. You change your agent to a formidable American, who places a sensitive interview about the traumatic end to your engagement
10	Whole gale	Seldom experienced inland; trees uprooted; considerable structural damage	55–63	Very high waves with long overhanging crests. The resulting foam, in great patches, is blown in dense white streaks along the direction of the wind. On the whole the surface of the sea takes a white appearance. The rolling of the sea becomes heavy and shocklike. Visibility affected	48–55	Seldom experienced in the United Kingdom. Three consecutive Oscars for Best Actor. You now do not admit anyone to your acquaintance who is not A-list famous. Your staff all love you and agree with you. You have homes in London, Geneva and Los Angeles. When you meet members of the public, they quake with reverence. You marry a member of the Royal Family and you are knighted for your charitable work in Turkmenistan

No.	Description	*Specifications: on land*	*mph*	*Specifications: at sea*	*knots*	*Specifications: in public and the media*
11	Storm	Very rarely experienced; accompanied by widespread damage	64–72	Exceptionally high waves (small and medium-sized ships might be for a time lost behind the waves). The sea is completely covered with long white patches of foam lying along the direction of the wind. Everywhere the edges of the wave crests are blown into froth. Visibility affected	56–63	Very rarely experienced anywhere. You own a global conglomerate controlling 65% of the world's cinemas, TV and radio stations, magazines and newspapers – all of which promote you. You are recognised by tiny children in shanty towns in Romania, Rwanda, North Korea and Wellington. You entertain Presidents, Popes and Imams
12	Hurricane		73–82	The air is filled with foam and spray. Sea completely white with driving spray; visibility very seriously affected	64–71	Your private corporation and private army controls the world's security and its economy. Judaism, Christianity and Islam are recognised as mere forerunners of the one true religion: i.e. worshipping you. No one may look directly at you or say your name. You are invited on to *Desert Island Discs* with Sue Lawley

Like all actors, Wayne had become a connoisseur of fame, a great judge of the total-stranger-pupil-dilation. He savoured the gradations of fame and calibrated its nuances with passionate attention to detail.

He considered himself to be somewhere between 2 and 3 on the Beaufort Scale – light breeze and gentle breeze. Sean's breeze was perhaps fresher, but as he was a journalist, Sean could never be really famous because he was not in showbusiness, at least not properly. Sean's fame-weather was illusory, it was like the winds on one of Jupiter's moons.

Ysenda was fairly interested in Wayne's Beaufort Scale but she believed that the experience of becoming more famous was not perceptible in this gradual sense: rather, it progressed, if it progressed at all, in a series of quantum leaps. One of them, she believed, was how you gave autographs. Any journeyman, any footsoldier in the army of fame, could give an autograph at some official meet-the-public gathering. The key autograph moment was giving one 'on the street'. The *al fresco* autograph was given in the supermarket, in the railway station, in the pub. It involved a member of the public disturbing your privacy and humbly petitioning you for your name written on the back of a beer mat, a till receipt, their left breast. Giving an autograph in these circumstances, she considered, had raw authenticity.

Of all the car's passengers, Ysenda was enjoying this ride the least: she loathed being bunched up in the back and keenly resented the rule announced by a strange padded little disc suspended from the driver's mirror, showing a lighted cigarette crossed out. She had a small, intense, pretty face, framed by a short haircut whose spikiness had softened and mellowed in the six weeks since she had had it done. Her hair was very dark, a kind of blue-black, darker than her eyes, dark brown, darker than her black leather jacket, the small black bag containing her cigarettes and lighter whose arm strap drooped away from her shoulder, and the black eye-liner which she wore on the very rim of the upper and lower eyelids.

She really didn't like sitting next to Nick, the fourth passenger in the car, an old friend and contemporary of Sean's and Wayne's. Just at this moment Nick had offered to give Ysenda a neck-rub, on the grounds that she had complained of stiffness – owing largely to the cramped conditions of the mini-cab.

'No way! No fucking way! Jesus, it's like being touched up by Boris Karloff with his hands of death, ugh, get *off* me.'

Nick took this hard. For the last year of his college degree course, and for many years since graduating, Nick had been a masseur, and now ran his own clinic.

It was a variant of shiatsu massage of which Nick was a practitioner, called Complete Shiatsu Massage. He had been attracted by a notice advertising free training courses from the University Complete Shiatsu Massage Society pinned up on the wall of his Student Union, which had a row of little tags along the bottom, each with a telephone number. One or two had already been detached; Nick took another.

The voice on the end of the phone told him to report to a small room above a pub in the city centre called The Bailiff's Farewell. There was a miscellaneous collection of people there: largely students and unemployed local people. Nick stood out in one particular respect: he was the only man. Nervously the group were standing around a large table in the middle of the room, on which a small selection of drinks had been thoughtfully prepared for them. They were nervous partly because they did not know each other, but mostly because the drink selection was not the only thing on the table. There was also a very fat man lying there, face down, quite naked except for a blue towel around his waist. This was the person on whom these massage neophytes were expected to try their hands later in the evening.

Extraordinarily, Nick had been rather good at it. Though all the girls, giggling from the immoderate amount they had had to drink, became almost hysterical when they had to plunge their hands up to their wrists into the vast pink doughy flesh,

Nick had demonstrated great reserves of stolid calm. Under the guidance of Ros, the Society's President, he had massaged almost every square centimetre of the fat naked man, from his wrinkly scalp, down past his flabby breast-like pectorals with great grey nipples like huge sightless eyes, guts, thighs, calves, soles of feet, even palms.

Nick was a natural! Everything was going swimmingly, and Nick had been such an excellent student and, indeed, getting on so well with the pretty, dark-haired Ros, that they hardly noticed that all the others, bored or irritated, had drifted away and it was now just Ros, Nick, and the fat, naked man who had been lulled to sleep by Nick's inspired manipulations.

Ros and Nick's eyes met over the flabby man-mountain. Their faces were very close. Gently Ros pulled Nick towards her and they kissed, but as they did so, the door to the private room banged open to admit Mr Derry, the landlord of The Bailiff's Farewell who – unaware of the exact nature of this particular University club – had arrived to inform them that it was last orders and he must now close up. As he did so, the fat man woke up with a great grunt and the towel slipped off to reveal his large buttocks over which the young couple were spooning.

'Perverts! I ought to call the police! Out!' he screamed.

Ros and Nick left the pub, the fat man only half dressed. Together, they made a tableau oddly similar to the pub-sign which was branded on to Nick's memory: the bailiff and his men jeering and sneering at the impoverished family as they drive away in a truck full of repossessed furniture.

Something about this traumatic circumstance had introduced a tiny drop of poison into the well of Nick's Complete Shiatsu Massage. His relationship with Ros was, as he broodingly confided to Wayne later, 'shafted' – he accepted that. But it was not just this. Something seemed wrong, from the outset, with his massage technique. After graduating, it had seemed to offer a heaven-sent answer to the desolate question of his professional future: he would be a masseur, but, more than that, he would be a carer, a healer. He would make people well.

Or would he? Something in the movement of Nick's hands seemed to introduce tiny twinges and aches into whatever body he happened to be manipulating with the elaborate flourishes that came so easily to him. Nick established his business, or, as he loftily termed it, his 'practice', in one of the rooms in the house he shared with Wayne in his first year in London.

Often Sean would meet Nick and a departing client on the stairs, the unfortunate outgoing patient bravely wincing and flinching as Nick cheerfully helped him on with his coat. It was not unusual for the patient to let out a cry of discomfort or even pain at this point, at which Nick would smoothly assure him he had got up too quickly from the table after the massage was finished, or that the patient had failed sufficiently to 'warm up' before coming to see him. (Part of what distinguished Complete Shiatsu Massage was this baffling and spurious 'warm up' requirement.)

Whatever his shortcomings, Nick had a perfect genius for convincing each massage subject of their own 'psychic' responsibility for the treatment's success, and implying therefore that any problems were their own fault. Many was the subject whose involuntary yelp of pain was followed immediately by a frown of guilt and self-reproof.

Despite, or perhaps because of this distinctive approach, Nick's practice flourished. He grew his hair slightly longer, and now affected a goatee beard. He pitched his voice a little quieter and made it measured, more centred, when he was with clients, and sometimes even tried to introduce a faint hint of an American accent – to make him sound a little more guru-like. But he did not try these mannerisms on his friends. Nick soon moved into a new, special 'clinic' on Highgate Hill, which advertised in the local and London Press. It had a sleek consulting room, an elegant reception area staffed by Inge, Nick's enigmatic blonde helpmeet and junior colleague from

Helsinki who would assist him with some of the radical and experimental two-on-one massage techniques he was developing. Daringly, Nick would incorporate actual psychotherapy into his massage. It was not unusual for a subject tearfully to unburden himself of his feelings about his mother while Nick and Inge worked aromatic oils into his solar plexus, before packing him smartly off for a vigorous step-class in the mini-gymnasium next door. It was here that bewildered, middle-aged clients were occasionally brought in to do twenty press-ups followed by a number of star-jumps, while Nick and Inge enjoyed a discreet Silk Cut in the adjoining Observation Suite. Then, wheezing and sweating, and strictly forbidden to take a shower, the client would be ushered into a Seminar Room and seated, where Inge would appear in a clinical white lab-coat and smoothly produce – a pack of tarot cards.

Nick bashfully withdrew his healing hands from Ysenda's neck to the usual jeer of laughter in which poor Nick did his sophisticated best to participate himself. But actually he was rather upset about the way his massage skills were habitually slighted by his friends, and indeed was very worried about the way his practice was developing.

2

The minicab pulled up outside The Ranch club in Frith Street, and Ysenda, Nick, Wayne and Sean alighted – Sean having paid the driver the £42.50 he requested, on account of the waiting and the 'stress'. Their arrival had been delayed by about twenty minutes owing to the fact that the minicab driver had got lost at almost the exact moment that his passengers sighted the Frith Street sign.

He had become upset, he shrilly complained, by Ysenda's bad language, and started to become aphasic with distress, yelping and humming strangely as he brandished his stained hardback *A–Z*. Soon he was driving at 10 mph past the Centrepoint building on Tottenham Court Road, suppressing racking sobs. So many more people one met were like him now.

Gently, Wayne coaxed him back to Soho.

Eventually, Sean, Ysenda, Wayne and Nick made it into The Ranch; it was a club that *Somdomite* had hired to promote the new issue, together with a mini-paperback-sized manifesto, which the publisher had prepared in a shallow pyramid next to a generous selection of drinks, into which the guests had already made very considerable inroads.

Now that Sean and friends were here, the party could be said officially to have started. The guest-list seemed to most of the people there oddly heterogeneous. It did not seem 'gay' in any obvious sense, and Sean's magazine was so strongly pitched to fellow-travellers, and so stridently apolitical, that it could have been a launch for any book, and indeed many of the faces were wearisomely familiar from just this sort of event.

The conversation was about only one thing: The Sighting, which had occurred last night in Tallinn, in Estonia. It was being reported on the Live Channel, to which the television over the bar was now tuned. Many of those at the party, as they collected their drinks, gazed raptly at the news footage, though they had all seen it many times before. With the 'live' logo winking insistently in the bottom left-hand corner, the camera panned over a desolate configuration of high-rise apartments, constructed in the Soviet era, and now evidently in a more scandalous state of disrepair than ever.

The shot cut to one of the apartments inside, and the camera took in the fibrous, seething damp on the bulging walls, the colonies of cockroaches and silverfish that did not bother to disperse when the electric light was turned on in the grim winter mornings. The interviewer was speaking to the family – this was obviously taken from some Estonian broadcast, and the Live Channel commentary superimposed on it – that lived in the apartment. A mother, father, three boys and a girl: their cramped, narrow beds were squashed up against each other in the tiny, squalid sitting room. But there was yet a seventh person in the flat, absent from the picture; the grandfather, father to the children's father, who for the past four years had suffered from skin cancer, a condition that had converted most of his skin into a hideously discoloured carapace. That is: he *was* suffering from it until last Saturday night, when he was watching the subtitled American soap opera that was one of the very few remaining pleasures in his life. The old man's voice, accompanied by the running translation, told of how he had been alone in the apartment, watching the blaring TV drama, when he was suddenly aware of an ineffable sweetness flooding the air, an overwhelming sense of female beauty and goodness. The man could not describe it in terms more concrete than this – and here the spectators at the bar, still avid to hear the story again, leaned forward – a strange and transcendental blonde shimmering, an elegant Princess-like bearing, combined with a somehow exquisitely fragile loneliness, a lovely off-centre smile, some bewitchingly hesitant words of benediction, spoken in English. And then it was gone, and a visit to the state hospital the next day disclosed that, quite against all clinical precedent, the old man's condition was not merely in remission, but cured. Within just a few more days, the grotesque lesions had been shed like the skin of a snake.

This was not all. The camera panned left in the old man's direction, in an apparent attempt to *show* the remarkable transformation, and the image broke up, crackled in bonfire hues of orange and black and red. For some reason, it was impossible to capture the miracle on videotape. The same went for film, and every kind of photography. Photographers from all over the world groaned with dismay in their darkrooms as roll after roll was a dud. So The Sighting bypassed electronic media of communication entirely; to witness the miracle, it was necessary to do it in person and supplicants from every neighbouring town did exactly that. Catholic and Orthodox alike arrived to gaze upon the old man who charged them for the privilege, and they left offerings and libations in the apartment block's reeking stairwell. Most of these were crucifixes, but many were secular tributes. The supervisor of the building, a man not noted for his devotion to duty up until now, was forced to clear the gifts out of the vertical stairwell every two days, because the previous day there had been a nasty incident. One of the votive offerings had come with a shallow, scented candle, and a plump nylon Snoopy, which the pilgrim had succeeded in laying right up against the old man's family's front door. The candle had set light to the Snoopy – an illegally produced non-trademarked approximation – which could not have been more profoundly unsafe if it was stuffed with Semtex.

Subsequently, the old man had actually suffered a nasty burn on his left forearm, as he attempted to extinguish the flames. This, in fact, was the only part of the man's body that would show up on any television picture. If the producer attempted to pan back to take in the renewed flesh, the televised icon would disintegrate once more. Finally, the filmed report ended with a shrugging piece to camera from the Live Channel's on-the-spot reporter in the apartment-block forecourt.

As the news item ended Sean got up and gave a languid and urbane welcome, in which he did not neglect to emphasise his profound contempt for any disempowering and obsolete notion of a separate gay 'identity'.

Sean's speech went down well with everyone but Ysenda, who, as ever in large crowds of unfamiliar people, had become shy and withdrawn and her natural gregariousness utterly failed her. (It had been like this since childhood. She was actually Canadian; born in Britain, she had left with her parents as a small child and returned with them to London when she was thirteen.) She felt like a student again, shuffling uneasily into the kitchen at parties, staring glumly down into her beer. She failed to respond to any of the eligible men that Wayne introduced her to. This was a familiar pattern. But there was another, particular reason tonight.

Ysenda's younger sister Catherine was coming to the party: Catherine, who worked in television; Catherine, who looked very similar to Ysenda in some important respects; they both had this rich blue-black hair, though Catherine's was worn longer, almost down to the shoulder. As children, they had both had absurdly large freckles, almost as big as coins; they had faded almost to invisibility with Ysenda but not Catherine – the summer brought them back stronger on her younger sister. They were both quite tall, Catherine a little taller, both with brown eyes. But with two differences: Catherine had lost her Canadian accent, where Ysenda had not. And Catherine was beautiful and Ysenda was not.

It was impossible to say why exactly. But it was certainly possible – even a human and intellectual duty – to say that it was indeed the case. Many was the time that Ysenda had entranced men, or at any rate cowed and impressed them with her volubility. She had a knack of using their remarks as feeds to set up punchlines of her own, yet without completely intimidating them. It would work satisfactorily – until Catherine showed up. Then the light in these men's eyes would dull in her company and relight in Catherine's.

Ysenda had had to live with this now for almost twenty years.

Catherine had called her earlier that evening to say that she 'might be coming'.

'You *might* be coming?'

'Yep,' said Catherine, lightly. 'I got an invite. I'm calling from the office.'

'The office got an invitation and you're coming along?'

'No, Ysenda, *I* got an invitation, personally, and *I* am coming along, and I really—'

'OK—'

'—don't need this attitude from—'

'OK, fine—'

'—you on the few times I actually manage to get invited to one of these parties—'

'I said OK—'

'—you don't seem to realise that I get invited somewhere nice slightly less frequently than the appearance of *fucking Comet Hale-Bopp*.'

'Fucking language!'

'You can fucking *talk*!'

Ysenda frowned at the memory of the row, which had run on lines as traditional and unvarying as the State Opening of Parliament. Airily, Catherine had declined to say when she was going to be coming to the party, and Ysenda was considerably chagrined to note that she had arrived at a party before her beautiful and desirable sister. Once again, she feared, she was to be the warm-up before the main event, the perky balloon-folding act before the arrival of Frank Sinatra.

At a quarter to midnight, Catherine entered the party with a boy from her production company, though nothing – as Ysenda knew of old – should be read into this 'walker' arrangement. It would be brutally dispensed with as and when the need arose. She was wearing a little black dress, no, actually a midnight-blue dress, which immediately made Ysenda in her leather jacket and jeans – she rarely wore dresses or skirts – feel like a roadie for a support band. Catherine looked flushed and strangely animated. Ysenda's eyes met her sister's, and having briefly pondered the possibility of procuring the means to become flushed and strangely animated herself, she ostentatiously declined to greet Catherine straight away, and continued her conversation with an older man she had just met.

'So where do you think you'll be going?'

'Oh, well, my wife and I and some of our friends have hired this enormous old World War One zeppelin and we're going to hover directly over Berlin and when midnight comes, we're going to switch this enormous laser display on to the Brandenburg Gate saying: "Happy New Millennium, Love Keith, Hazel, Ken and Lesley".'

They were having the What Are You Going To Do On New Millennium's Eve conversation, a topic which now obsessed Ysenda and all her friends. They fretted that they had nothing suitably visionary planned, and that there was now less and less time to plan something sufficiently extravagant. Everywhere was booked. New Year's Eve was deeply depressing enough as it was. But a new *millennium*. Jesus. You couldn't just stay in and watch TV and then come in through the front door with a lump of coal and go straight to bed. Not with a new millennium on the go. Could you?

Annoyingly, Catherine crashed straight into the conversation.

'So where's the drink?'

'The *drink*, Catherine? The *drink*,' said Ysenda archly. 'You want to know where the *drink* is? What *is* this?'

Catherine's walker hung back. Ysenda's older man also shrank infinitesimally from this exchange.

'I just wanted to know where the drink was.'

'Like some sort of fifteen-year-old. What have you done, brought a two-litre bottle of *cider* with you?'

'OK, well, I can see, the drink's over there.'

'And who's this?' Ysenda had, fractionally, lowered her voice.

'Who? That's James, from the office.'

'And?'

'And what do you mean *and*? And nothing.'

'Come on.'

'I'm telling you, nothing, and get off my case anyway.'

'Give me the number.'

'Oh *please*.'

'Between zero and ten, where zero is a cold handshake and ten is full penetrative sex, what is the number?'

'Oh . . .' Catherine had an exasperated look, somewhere between a scowl and a smirk. '. . . four.'

'Four!' Ysenda gave a great whoop which caused James and the older man to become even more uneasily interested in the conversation that they were so patently excluded from. *'Four*. Snogging and some hand-in-sweater action. Mmmm. So what's the final ratio figure?'

'Shut *up*, Ysenda, you don't seem to realise that a nice man comes into my life slightly less frequently than the appearance of *fucking Comet Hale-Bopp*.'

'Fucking language!'

'You can fucking *talk*!'

This 'ratio figure' that Ysenda mentioned was a mathematical equation designed to quantify, objectively, how exciting a sexual relationship is. It was as follows:

$$\left(\frac{f}{t} + a\right) \times m$$

(where m is greater than zero)

. . . where f is the fanciability factor, an integer between one and ten usually arrived upon without too much acrimony in discussion between Catherine and Ysenda. t is the amount of time, expressed in months, that the relationship has continued – here it is in the denominator position, as the excitement of a relationship diminishes with time. a is the age difference expressed in years, as it becomes scarier, riskier and more exciting to have sex with someone the older or younger than you they are. m is the length of time, also expressed in years, the man has been married or in a serious relationship to someone else. This multiplies the ratio figure, because m, like a, is considered to be a greater danger factor the higher it is. That is: the longer a man is married, the more likely he is to leave his wife, or *want* to leave his wife. Ysenda had mildly wondered if the equation should not be amended so that m could be added to, and not multiplied by the rest, but Catherine outrageously claimed that a sexual relationship was not truly exciting *unless* it was adulterous – that is, where *m* was zero, the whole relationship's ratio figure was also zero.

After a while, Ysenda found Catherine prodding her in the side, a means of attracting her attention which had irritated her since they were children.

'What?'

'Ysenda!'

'What?'

'Ysenda!'

'What, for Jesus' sake, what?'

'Who's *that*?'

With her hand on her heart, Ysenda couldn't see who she meant, although she saw, peripherally, James already being sulkily marginalised and going on a pointless second trip to the drinks table.

She couldn't see past Wayne, dearest Wayne, who, with a broad smile on his face, was approaching her carrying two drinks.

Ysenda had had a thing for Wayne ever since their romantic interlude five years ago when they kissed in the back of a taxi on the way to Ysenda's flat in Marylebone.

Kissing in the back of a taxi, late at night, has an abandon, a what-the-hell quality that teenage snogging could not devise and could not afford. There is something exquisite about the hoist and turn of a taxi propelling your tongue further into someone else's mouth as you both swing and slide and sway and giggle on the smooth back seat while your cab, as if borne on heavy seas, pitches and rolls. That dull black canopy of a taxi's interior, the flapping extra seats for those facing backwards, the mute traffic lights, the silent carousel of Georgian houses and striplit shopfronts – are you doing it in public, or doing it in private? As they rushed down the Marylebone Road, Wayne had sturdily braced his right leg against the opposite door of the cab and pinioned her into the corner and kissed her yet more deeply, his left hand round her waist, his right on her breast. Ysenda had gasped and moved Wayne's hand between her legs and up her skirt. It was all achieved with a lurch and a shudder, as the cab braked and accelerated and nosed out into traffic all unseeing. The cab's ID number and the Hackney Carriage conditions of hire seemed to bespeak some occult message of love. Kissing in a cab! That stateless, weightless urban sense of being in transit, where you could do what you *liked*.

Wayne did want to put his hand up her skirt; he wanted to a very great deal. And as he did so, Wayne did the most erotic thing of all. He removed his tongue from Ysenda's mouth and said: 'I love you.'

Unfortunately, at that moment the cab arrived at Ysenda's flat and the driver, while enigmatically not appearing to see what was going on – some vow enforced at the Carriage Office? – tactlessly snapped on the light in the back. Hastily, Ysenda alighted first, followed by a sheepish, self-conscious Wayne. Negotiating the bikes and old gas bills in the hall and the timer-light that seemed to go off just before the key was in the lock, was an anti-aphrodisiac of the first order.

Ysenda had fixed coffee and brandies and so on in her open-plan kitchenette, while Wayne had settled down uneasily on the great sofa. She had brought them to him and tried to inaugurate an urgent kiss. But it was no good. They didn't have that old black cab magic. The sofa did not rev up or lurch away from oncoming traffic. There was no red handle to hang on to for dear life, no maritime romance. Perhaps if Ysenda could quickly redecorate the flat in a kind of fuzzy matt black and soften the rectilinear corners of floor, wall and ceiling. Perhaps if she could chuck a few old copies of *Cab News* about the place, or if she could just ring up the cab company and get one of their drivers to position himself outside the window with the back of his head to them, and declaim his personal idiomatic translation of the collected speeches of Jean-Marie Le Pen. They were on the second floor, so he'd have to sort of crouch in the window-box or something.

Eventually they gave up and Wayne slept on the chaste and stationary sofa. But Ysenda thought of him fondly nevertheless and smiled to see him advancing on her warmly now with the two drinks. He obviously still liked her, and – who knows? – perhaps tonight would rekindle something. She craned to see past him.

'Who?' she asked. 'You mean the guy behind Wayne? Isn't that your *date*?'

She turned back and to her horror saw Wayne give one of the drinks to Catherine, keeping one for himself, the two looking grinningly into each other's eyes.

'There!' said Wayne roguishly to her, entirely ignoring Ysenda. 'I'm not one of these people who says "I'm going to get some drinks" just to terminate a party conversation.'

'Thank you,' said Catherine. 'I'm Catherine by the way, but who are you?'

'Hasn't she told you?' *She*. Not Ysenda – *she*. And still not looking at her either.

'No, I was just trying to *get* her to say while you were coming over.' This with a little playful slap of rebuke, slightly too hard, on Ysenda's arm, while Catherine's gaze remained locked on to Wayne's.

'I'm Wayne.'

'Ah!' Catherine did her eyes-wide-opening act, that Ysenda bitterly recognised and knew made her even more irresistible. 'You were in that Gianluca Fibionacci movie about Cardinal Newman.'

'That's me.'

'I thought it was a really challenging film, although my mum was kind of upset about the bad language.'

Grimly, it dawned on Ysenda that her chances of rekindling her romantic situation with Wayne were quite extinguished.

At this moment, Sean, who was having a lugubrious

conversation with Nick about the rocketing price of still mineral water, had been interrupted by Steve, a video-journalist with the Gay Cable Channel.

'Sean, it would be really great if we could have your views for the Gay Window On A Gay World discussion programme.'

'Uh.' Sean pushed the heel of his right hand up into his eye and rubbed it distractedly, as if he had just got out of bed. 'I don't know; I don't know if I feel that I want the, uh, *gayness* to be pre-packaged and ghettoised on a gay cable TV channel.'

'Ah, but why not? That would be a very interesting discussion topic for us.'

'Oh . . .' Sean's voice rose into an unbecoming whine. 'It's really not something I feel I can get into now . . .'

Just at that moment, Sean saw something very like his own face grimacing and wincing from the TV screen over the bar. Wait a fucking moment. It *was* his face, and it was as unglamorous a moment as catching sight of yourself in the TV monitors outside Dixon's.

'Don't tell me this is going out *live*?' he saw the ugly head over the bar say.

'Well yes, actually,' said Steve, disconcerted, shifting the weight of the camera on his shoulder.

Nick, who had been drinking heavily, adjudged this to be the moment to plunge into the situation's tricky personal and sexual politics.

'Poof,' he said sullenly, half under his breath.

An H.M. Bateman-type gasp-plus-silence ensued in the group immediately around him, for the remark was clearly audible.

'What did you say?' asked Steve coldly, swinging round to face him and bringing Nick's pale and goateed face into framed view over the bar, its every feature revealing very clearly indeed how profoundly he regretted saying that, and with what reverent cowardice he anticipated being punished for his bigotry – live, on the Gay Cable channel.

'Nothing, mate,' he leered, unconvincingly.

'Bollocks,' said Steve. Sean saw that Nick's ashen and now vividly sober face remained on view on the TV screen, and was now accompanied by an urgent commentator's voice alerting viewers to late-breaking news, brought to you live, of a homophobic situation developing at a late-night media party in Central London.

Nick tried to brush the situation aside by wheeling around as if to go and get another drink, but his way was barred by Steve and a number of other men at the party, frowningly disapproving. Sean saw that he would have to step in to defuse the situation, using every ounce of his prerogative as host.

'Uh, no, no, Steve, you don't understand,' he drawled softly. 'Nick is using the word in its radical sense.'

'Excuse me?'

'He was using *poof* in the way radical street groups use *queer*. It's kind of like using the ideologically inflected terminology of the oppressor and flinging it back in their face, sort of thing.' Sean was aware of how plaintive and thin his voice sounded, although redoubled in volume from the TV. He felt the desperate need to carry on talking. 'When he was at university, Nick himself used to be the lead singer of a wonderfully challenging band called Poofs With Attitude. Argh!'

Steve's clumsy blow caught Sean harmlessly and quite painlessly on his shoulder: it was more of a shove or a jostle, as his ability to punch anyone was restricted by his video camera. And in any case, the situation's temperature cooled all but immediately; not more than two or three people could have seen it anyway, largely because the TV programme had already cut away to the news. Steve backed away, maintaining truculent eye-contact with Nick, who was gaining his confidence as he sensed the possibility of serious physical contact receding.

Sean sighed with relief as he saw Steve moving away.

But then Nick incautiously said: 'Wanker,' which caused Steve's face to snap back round to face him. He stepped forward again:

'. . . er, in the sense of liberating and empowering sexual self-gratification, a meaningful male *jouissance* . . .' But Steve had now turned away.

Sean was making a mental note never to invite Nick to one of his parties again, perhaps never to talk to him ever again.

During this time, Catherine was having a conversation with Wayne – a conversation which, as Ysenda had noted from afar with a connoisseur's eye, Catherine seemed keener on having than Wayne did.

'It was really great.'

'Thanks, that's – thanks.' Wayne accepted Catherine's tributes redundantly.

'I never thought Newman's life could be so exciting, did you really film it all in Oxford?'

'Yeah, we had to, like, do it really early in the morning so there wasn't anyone around, and the set-dressers had to cover up all the double yellow lines so the roads would look strictly authentic . . .'

'. . . and I thought Fibionacci's own performance as Pusey was *really* cool. That scene in the Sheldonian with the severed head, I mean when I saw it the entire audience *jumped*!'

'Yeah,' laughed Wayne lightly, 'Gianluca said he was really proud of that moment . . .'

'I think he's really got a comeback on his hands,' said Catherine earnestly, 'I mean, I know it's a sort of camp retro thing to "like" Fibionacci now . . .'

Sean was spending some time in one of The Ranch Club's severe aluminium lavatory stalls recovering from the panic attack the near-thing with the reporter from the TV Channel had induced in him. The place was really crowded, now. He knew from experience that a resentful queue would be building up for the stall he now occupied. The Ranch was like this, every night, all night. Thoughtfully, Sean inspected his reflection, submerged as if in soup in the dull, cloudy, matt sheen of the aluminium. He looked pretty good. Emerging at last, he ducked past the line of frowning male lavatory applicants and headed gratefully to where Wayne appeared to be talking to someone. He was aware that this person was Ysenda's sister Catherine whom he dimly remembered from his childhood. Then he saw Catherine's face.

It was upturned in frank adoration towards Wayne, a deflection of attention which allowed Sean in his turn to adore the blue-black hair, the wide eyes, the full, plump prettiness of the face which God, deploying his slightly intrusive, but masterful head waiter's way with the pepper grinder, had dusted with freckles. Freckles!

Sean was falling in love, at first sight moreover, with Catherine. So perhaps the time has come to admit it. The time came long ago for Sean to admit it to himself: Sean is straight. Sean is heterosexual. Sean wants to do it with girls. Sean *does* it with girls. And only girls.

Not that there's anything wrong with that. But how has Sean got landed with a public role as the daringly revisionist spokesman for a gay generation? How has he got trapped in this false position, from which there now seems no way out?

It happened when Sean was doing his PhD at Cambridge into radically Foucauldian readings of the Renaissance emblem poet Francis Quarles. He had given a paper on the subject in professor George Watford's rooms in Nevile's Court, Trinity College. The seventy-four-year-old professor was delighted that Sean had undertaken post-graduate research into Quarles, a favourite of his, but quite untouched by the fashionable academy for many a long year.

Sean himself had been shrewdly advised by a lecturer at

the University of North London, where he did his first degree, that a PhD proposal on a figure like Quarles would be more likely to gain him admission to Cambridge University. This proved to be quite correct. After eighteen months, however, Sean was quite beside himself with boredom with Quarles and with Cambridge.

Sometimes now, at the end of the decade and his youth, Sean would marvel at those long, torpid spaces of Cambridge; they were not languid or elegiac exactly; rather, they had a queer underwater directionlessness. He decided he was going to shake up the English faculty with a stridently, and perversely, 'gay' interpretation of this supremely obscure poet, whose minor and neglected status was in his view so richly deserved. He was going to advance a challenging and dissentient account of Quarles which would take into view the whole concept of the canon, and the bourgeois, heterosexist idea of the university. That morning, he left a note in Professor Watford's pigeonhole to the effect that his paper that evening would be entitled simply: 'Fisting Quarles' and that he wished to show slides. Puzzled but trusting, the professor prevailed upon a college servant to set up a slide projector in his tasteful, panelled room, where various dons, old and young – together with a dozen earnest research students – assembled at 5:00p.m. as they did every other Wednesday in full term, for the latest in Professor Watford's series of informal Renaissance seminars.

They had never been quite this informal. Professor Watford had fondly imagined that Sean was going to show slides of various emblems, or the fruits of some intriguing bibliographical work: some close-ups of water-marks perhaps, or some variant transcriptions. Instead, it was fifteen plates from the work of Robert Mapplethorpe, graphically depicting anal sex – the relevance of which to Francis Quarles seemed difficult to detect, even for the most liberal and open-minded members of the seminar.

Certainly it was difficult to detect for the professor, who then and there succumbed to a massive heart attack, and soon after died. Professor Watford was carried with horrible indignity out of his rooms and down the narrow staircase by two brick-faced bowler-hatted porters, one with a hand under each armpit and the other with his arms locked around his knees – like a *pietà* by René Magritte or Vic Reeves. Sean conspicuously failed to join in the ineffectual crowded fuss that succeeded them out into the corridor.

The story got into the papers. Sean was interviewed about why he did what he did, and started to write for the newspapers himself on the subject of explicit gay imagery and gay rhetoric, generally undermining the tolerant, liberal consensus. He was a fluent writer, and seemed to have a natural knack for combining the flippant and the provocative with the ostensibly serious. He was offered a contract to write a weekly column for *The Harbinger* newspaper at £90,000 a year. Almost overnight, he turned from being a dull, unregarded graduate student into a media star with attitude. But he could not help noticing that all the editors and television producers who now so expensively procured his services were clearly assuming that he, Sean, was gay. It was never said out loud, of course. Nobody had the poor taste to say to him: 'Sean, you *are* actually gay, aren't you?' And indeed, nothing Sean wrote was explicitly premised on his own, personal homosexuality.

Unworldly as Sean was, he realised that his 'conservative gay' persona was his USP, his Unique Selling Point. There seemed no obvious stage at which he could come out and say that he was straight – especially as he had in any case developed all this catchy new post-liberal line about sexual 'identity' being obsolete. In any case, did Sean want to go back to being a PhD student, poring over Francis Quarles's *Emblems* (1635) and *Hieroglyphikes of the Life of Man* (1638)? He did not. So he convinced himself that all sexuality was ambiguous, that he had vague feelings of desire for men and, God alone knew, he had had few enough girl friends. His friends were surprised at this new eminence, and a strange new sexual identity that they had not dreamt of, but – awed by his sudden new status – accepted it mildly.

With what agonies of heart, therefore, with what sweet torture of the soul, did Sean now accept Catherine's hand on his arm, and the pleasing tribute of her exceptionally pretty face turned up smilingly to his as he breezily interrupted her conversation with Wayne. It had been a long time since he had actually met Catherine; she had been working in Manchester and unlike Ysenda, whom he had seen pretty regularly since they were in their mid teens, Catherine had been a stranger – until now. But he knew from long experience of gratefully savouring this sort of thing, that she was excited by his modest fame. But hold on. Hang about. He was famous for being *gay*. Damn!

Moreover, Wayne, the veteran of hundreds of sexual conquests, had once urbanely told him of the strange Physical Contact Paradox. Surely, if a girl places her hand on your arm, it means you're *in*, doesn't it, he once asked him. Not necessarily, Wayne sagely rejoined. It could mean that she doesn't feel sexually threatened or excited by you. It could mean you're a cuddly big teddy bear or a big brother, a pillow, a cushion – or some other object not in possession of a shockingly erect penis.

Or, in this case, it means you're a famous yet unthreatening radical gay writer and broadcaster. Catherine was talking to him about the latest in Sean's TV series on Channel Six about gay writers, last week's on Henry James being entitled: What Maisie Didn't Want To Know. She absolutely hung on Sean's every word, and Wayne, momentarily grateful for the interruption, promptly went off to find Ysenda, a retreat that Catherine registered (Sean noticed) with an eye-flicker of displeasure.

Catherine was really very pretty. Adorably, she was wearing a *cardigan*, but a cardigan of some thin, sheer, expensive stuff, like cashmere, Sean supposed, with some slightly eccentric decorations of tiny pearls woven into the fabric. She had boots. Boots! Her eyes were very slightly unfocused, as if she was short-sighted.

'I thought it was really great.'

'Thanks. Thanks a lot.'

'I mean, using the Mapplethorpe photos like that really kind of threw Henry James into a sharper perspective.'

'Thanks. *Thanks.*'

'Obviously *superimposing* his head like that was a bit cheeky, but it was really funny and ironic, and humour is an important critical tool.'

Catherine's face became heart-stoppingly earnest, like the very prettiest and cleverest undergraduates he had briefly taught at Cambridge.

'Yes. Right. Exactly.'

There was a short pause, while they both drank bottles of pointlessly expensive imported Estonian beer.

'Where do you work again, Cath . . . Catherine?' (Sean pulled away at the last second from the presumptuous 'Cathy' – she might not like it, she might not like him saying it, all sorts of pitfalls.)

Catherine named her independent television production company.

'Oh *yeah.*' Sean physically bobbed into this urgent affirmation, gesturing slightly with his pricey Baltic beer, making it a gesture simultaneously of recall and emphatic admiration. 'God, I know a guy there who was *really* singing your praises. Now who was it?'

A classic attention-grabbing ploy. Sean could pretend to be trying to remember the name of this person for five seconds, or five minutes, and he knew he would have her rapt, undivided and quite silent attention for all this time. Usually, this was a bit of gamesmanship he deployed in conversation with a male rival whose stream of conversation he wished to disrupt and undermine – as he knew that his victim could not help but hush up and wait for the name, thus crucially and fatally conceding a high-status position to Sean.

With the timing of a great musician, Sean was thinking of making this pause a minim, but at the last moment brought it back to a dotted crotchet, and said: 'Mark Harris.'

Well-regarded producer, but not *outrageously* senior, young guy, good-looking, but married with a baby daughter. Perfect feel-good candidate, unthreatening, someone whose approval Catherine would naturally seek, yet by invoking his name Sean had also managed indirectly to imply that Mark Harris *fancied* her, and that Catherine could somehow return the compliment at one remove by *fancying* Sean, as the privileged custodian of this gossip. This was Olympic-standard flirting, a ten out of ten Nadia Comaneci performance.

'Oh, *Mark*. How is he?'

Sean judged this to be the time to shift into suggestive mode, to signal as clearly as possible that this was no ordinary conversation they were having.

She obviously understood the truth about Sean. They were getting on *very* well. She had absolutely no problems about talking to him this way. At the corner of his field of vision, he could see James, Catherine's date, talking to some other girl, but clearly nothing was going on, and he was looking in their direction.

He took a step towards Catherine, glanced down at his beer and then up at her with the up-through-the-lashes effect, in the efficacy of which he had placed great trust since his adolescence.

'I suppose he's all right. But *you*, Catherine. How are *you*?'

Catherine grinned roguishly and intimately, stepped forward a tiny pace herself, placed her hand on his forearm – this is Mission control, Houston, you are looking good – 'Oh, I'm feeling great.'

There was a distant bang of The Ranch Club's heavy zinc door as James was making his furious exit. `Houston, do you copy, Houston, we are clear and ready for lift-off.`

'You know, Sean, when I saw you here, I was really nervous about talking to you . . .'

'Shall I confess something? I was incredibly nervous about talking to *you* . . .'

'Oh *no* . . .'

'Oh *yes* . . .'

Conversation now down to a murmur.

'Look, I think I just saw your boyfriend leave . . .'

Little laugh. 'James isn't my *boyfriend*.'

`Houston, we are clear and ready for countdown. Ten. Nine.`

'So what is he?'

'He's just a friend.'

'Oh, a *friend*?'

'Yes.' Hand on forearm pressure reapplied, further up. `Eight. Seven.`

'Should I be worried about this friend?'

'Worried? How do you mean, worried?'

'I mean . . . *jealous*.'

'Oh no' – little giggle – 'there's absolutely no need for you to be *jealous*.'

'Are you sure?'

'Of course I'm sure.'

'I mean *really* sure.'

'I'm really *really* sure.' With this, Catherine waggled her head and brought her face snugglingly close to Sean's. `Six. Five.`

Sean couldn't believe how fantastically well it was all going. His heart rate had trebled. At last. Someone who wasn't hung up on this whole stereotypical 'gay' thing. Someone who wasn't pigeonholing him. At last he could put it all behind him. He placed his empty beer bottle down on a nearby table. It was about 3 a.m. His car and driver, he knew, should be waiting for him outside the club. `Four. Three.`

'Listen – I really have to get out of here.'

'I know what you would like to do . . .' said Catherine roguishly, her hand resting lightly on his hip.

'Oh yes?' said Sean, heart pounding, hardly able to breathe.

`Two. One. Lift-off!`

'You'd like to find James and give him a good old seeing-to in a public lavatory; I know what you gays are like!' Catherine laughed indulgently. 'Outrageous! But really liberating as well.' Her face became very earnest again. 'Well, you can if you like; like I said, there's nothing to be jealous of in my relationship with him, we're just friends, and I think he might be gay. I think you two would be really good together.'

`Houston, we have a problem.`

Sean and Wayne sat glumly in the back of the minicab on the way back up to Highgate. Sean was silent, Wayne almost asleep.

'Have you noticed all these homeless, or should I say so-called homeless, or supposedly vulnerably housed?' asked the minicab driver querulously. 'Look at them all.'

They looked. There were a lot of homeless people. In fact, it was a rum old shop doorway or commercial property forecourt in London these days that did not, at dusk, play host to at least one homeless person and his sleeping bag, and after nine o'clock the same went for the cheerless threshold of every Underground station in Zone One. 'They're just wasters. A burden on the taxpayer.'

Sean felt it incumbent on him to communicate to Wayne his liberal distaste for these sentiments.

'Some day a rain's gonna come,' he murmured archly.

The minicab driver leaned forward on to his steering

wheel and squinted up through the curved top of the windscreen at the dark and cloudless sky, and the orange sodium glow glinted off his maroon sweater, his suede-encased, laminated ID, and his middle-aged skin.

'Do you know,' he said, 'I don't think so.'

3

Wayne and Sean's conversation was running on this incident as they walked up the long path to the Parliament Hill Lido in Hampstead Heath three days later, their towels and swimming costumes rolled up and tucked away in little bags, as if they were both eleven years old.

After some deliberation, Sean had confessed to Wayne about his reaction to Catherine, though without going into his fraudulent professional life. Wayne had accepted this intelligence with his habitual relish for gossip, disconcertingly combined with his basic lack of curiosity about other people. With a shrug he'd agreed to keep the whole thing a desperately important secret. It was a Sunday and the Lido was going to be crowded. Actually it was always crowded, with the weather the way it was. These days, an aerial photograph of any public swimming pool in London would show not an azure rectangle, but a dense, almost oval mass of bodies, like a bee-hive or the Black Hole of Calcutta.

'What the hell am I going to do?' Sean whined again.

Wayne shrugged. 'I really don't think it's such a big deal, such a problem. It really doesn't involve a big public crisis. I mean, look at Tom Robinson.'

'Who?'

'Tom Robinson of the Tom Robinson Band in the 1970s. You know: Glad To Be Gay, and all that. *He* ended up going straight.'

'Did he?'

'Well, living with a woman anyway. I'm not sure. Whatever, it wasn't a big deal. Everybody still loved him.'

Sean did not reply, and they padded on in silence. Two fourteen-year-olds ran up to Wayne, obviously fans.

'Yo! Newman! Apologia! Fuck you!' they shouted and swept away.

Wayne accepted this boisterous tribute to his latest screen performance, smiling graciously. Other people, people in their twenties, were looking round at him.

'How can I tell her? *How* can I tell her I'm heterosexual?'

'These labels, Sean,' Wayne said airily, as they approached the entrance. 'You know how meaningless they are.'

'Well, yes, that's true, of course that's true,' muttered Sean resentfully as they joined the short queue.

Sean was extremely tense: a tension in addition to, and in excess of, the normal stomach-muscle-tightening tension induced by any visit to the swimming pool. The harsh, tactless smell of chlorine, the endless sound of whistles like a convention of referees, the shallow pools of water underfoot everywhere, the pointless *shouting*. What is it about swimming pools that makes everybody – from eight-year-old tykes to fat, bald eighty-year-old guys who swim in the sea on Christmas Day – start shouting at the tops of their voices?

Sean and Wayne were always going swimming together these days, and Sean enjoyed it: enjoyed the reading, the sunbathing, the hanging out. He even quite enjoyed the swimming itself, this being the only form of exercise he did, now that he had given up going to the gym. Doing that had given him an impressive physique. But now he wished to jettison this approach; he wished to blur and obscure the sharp lines of muscle definition with folds of fat. Having muscles was a gay thing, wasn't it?

It was for this reason that Sean had this morning put away a tube of Pringles after a hefty cooked breakfast accompanied by two brick-red cups of sugary tea, but had ascetically waved away the Fuse bar that Wayne had offered him. After all, he didn't want to get *obese*, and Catherine might be seeing his body this afternoon.

The idea was that Ysenda and Catherine might be coming swimming at the Parliament Hill Lido as well. *Might* be. Later on. Possibly. We don't know yet.

That was a nice touch. It was something he had discovered almost by chance yesterday afternoon, when he had finally nerved himself up to try Catherine's answering machine and found that she had one of those old-fashioned ones – almost museum pieces – that gave a beep for every message she'd received, before condescending to allow him to record his. The beeping seemed to go on for ever. Sean actually held up his watch and started *timing* it: it was going on for over a minute and a half! Suddenly, when there seemed no possibility of the beeping finishing by nightfall, Sean slammed the phone down and said out loud: 'Oh fine! Great! You've got one of those special girl answering machines that you've had customised by a team of scientists so that when I ring up it gives one beep for every different man you'd prefer to *shag*!' His voice rose to an unmanly and unbecoming screech on this last word, and Pussy Fred, curled up on his lap, ran clumsily away with fear and knocked over half a bottle of white wine in the kitchen.

'Oh *bloody* hell,' said Sean crossly, as he went to get a cloth. 'Pussy Fwed, why are you like this? Cats are supposed to be *enigmatic* and *elegant*, with a silky, serene physical grace.'

Pussy Fred gave no indication of having heard this, but

attempted to jump up on to a new table that Sean had bought the previous week, missed the ledge by a whisker – which is to say missed it by about three inches – scrabbled frantically at the edge with his claws and then pulled a cafetière off the table, which had been resting on a little cloth. The cafetière landed on his head, which made Pussy Fred scowl with irritation like Oliver Hardy.

'Jesus,' sighed Sean, and cleared the mess up. Having calmed his irritation and paranoia by soothingly reading the Canadian Netball results on Ceefax, Sean called Catherine's machine once again, grimly determined to sit out the beep-insult. When it was over, he was astonished to hear Catherine's voice actually saying his name:

Hi, I'm not here, but if this is Sean, could you call Ysenda sometime this afternoon?

So after he'd slammed the phone down he called Ysenda, who had told him that the two girls might be joining them on their weekly trip to the Parliament Hill Lido today, where summer opening times had just begun again this month.

Just as he was on his way out of the door to meet Wayne, already a little late, the phone rang. Sean shot back to it, and paused. It *had* to be Catherine! Should he do what every fibre of his being demanded and snatch the receiver up from its cradle – or should he be just a little bit more cool than that? Just let the answering machine get it, screen out the call and show that he could be laid back as well? With a terrible inevitability, he lost his nerve, rushed into his bedroom where the answering machine was, and picked up.

'Hello?'

'Sean.'

It was his mother. Sean experienced the familiar lurch of exasperation followed by a kick of guilt and self-reproach.

'Mother. Hello.'

This is Sean, if you have a message you can probably get me at the Somdomite *offices, or on my mobile . . .*

Both Sean and his mother knew from bitter experience that once his answering machine had juddered into life, they had no choice but to let it run its course, and then Sean had to endure hearing the conversation amplified boomingly throughout the flat as the first minute of it was recorded.

'Sean . . .' His mother's low, sibilant voice reverberated eerily around the walls.

'Mother – how are you?' His own voice echoed reedily, nasally.

'How am *I*? How are *you* is more to the point.'

With a great effort of will, he remembered that the last time she had called him, about ten days ago, it had been in the middle of a terrible migraine attack, which combined visual disturbances that were the equal of a stadium light show with one of his 'reggae' headaches, headaches which throbbed at the off-beat. It was like Bob Marley playing his own Jah version of brain cancer live at the Hollywood Bowl, while the drummer used his head as a snare, and his mother's voice, amplified through the PA system way beyond the (already low) bearability level, made hectoring arrangements to visit his flat next Saturday with a builder friend of his late father's to fix his kitchen unit.

'I'm fine, Mother, I'm just fine. I'm sorry I couldn't really speak to you when you rang before.'

'Well, I was *worried*. I knew that you had to be in a bit of a bad way because of all the *language*.'

The tone of plaintive reproach hung in the air. Sean knew he could only evade the charge of swearing in his mother's telephonic presence by exaggerating the mitigating circumstances of his illness. But this, he knew, would provoke a torrent of nagging at him to see a specialist. Only an undertaking to come for lunch later in the month – Sean had gone through the quite inappropriate business of checking in his 'diary' – had brought the conversation to an end, but it continued to weigh on his mind.

Now Sean paused with Wayne at the entrance to the

Lido where a young man was selling the *Sunday Big Issue*, the new Sunday version of the homeless magazine, and he was groaning under the weight of them, each issue being distended with sections and supplements, including a full News Review section, a City section, Arts and Review, Travel and Property. He bought one, and read that the Parliament Hill Lido was actually going to be the site of one of the Millennium Parties. Apparently, the pool itself was going to be lit, and covered in transparent Plexiglas for people to walk on and then it was going to be filled with dolphins.

'That doesn't sound bad,' said Sean. 'How much are tickets?'

Wayne told him.

'Well, that's OK. Do you think Ysenda and Catherine and everyone are going to want to go?'

'I don't know. Do you think walking around all night on top of dolphins is going to be all that good? I mean – good enough to see in the *millennium*?'

'I don't know. Perhaps not. When do we have to apply for the tickets?'

'Tomorrow lunchtime.'

'Oh no. Imagine trying to get them all to agree to going there. Let's forget it.'

Wayne folded most of the *Sunday Big Issue* into his bag, throwing away the Rare and Valuable Stamps supplement. 'Sean, if you don't book something up soon, everything will be taken, and we can't just do sod-all on Old Millennium's Night.'

Sean and Wayne had arrived at the ticket window. Wayne paid for both of them, while Sean looked uneasily around for Ysenda and Catherine. Still no sign.

Once inside the Lido's great brick portals, it was the work of a moment for Wayne, unselfconscious and quite at ease with his body, to change into his brief swimming costume and hand his clothes in at the locker section. For Sean, it was the work of twenty laborious minutes, as he decanted his keys and change from his pockets into his bag, and fastidiously changed into his own floppy swimming shorts, his every movement crippled and curtailed by a wish to avoid revealing his naked body. Finally, he joined Wayne by the pool, his large plush beach towel and extensive selection of reading matter clutched to his chest.

As ever, the pool looked magnificent. That glorious expanse of 1930s' open-air architecture, the *mens sana in corpore sano* feel of the place. The Lido was filling up, with couples, with families, with tiny wizened old men with cloudy grey chest hair, suntanned the colour of an autumn leaf. Sean and Wayne toured the pool's glittering perimeter, scouting locations, while Sean anxiously scanned the area for the girls – had they *already* arrived? – and Wayne graciously accepted the tribute of shrewd glances of those who, looking up from their paperbacks and supplements, clearly recognised his face.

They settled on a spot near the north-west corner, opposite the springboard. Spreading out their towels, Wayne immediately lay back with his sunglasses on, and his Discman earphones in. Sean sat up and slightly hunched over, creating two plump little rolls of fat at his waist, while he massaged sunblock into his upper arms.

Where *were* they?

'Where *are* they?' he asked Wayne plaintively after a while.

Wayne squinted up at him, and detached one earphone.

'They'll be here,' he said. 'Any time in the next hour or so. Relax.'

'Oh *Jesus*,' exhaled Sean. 'I can't just hang around here for the next hour or so, pretending to be casual. I want them to turn up right now.'

'Well,' said Wayne, impassively, from behind his sunglasses, 'we're talking about a lovely young girl whom you want to impress, and whom you furthermore want to convince that you are not, in fact, gay. Just as the only way to make a bus turn up is to light a cigarette, the only way to make Catherine materialise is to plunge both hands down the trunks of the nearest teenage boy.'

'Thanks,' said Sean bitterly. 'Thanks so much for the helpful, morale-boosting advice. Look, I think you should realise that I might be in *love* with Catherine, passionately in *love*.'

'Are you sure?' asked Wayne.

Sean paused. An extremely corpulent sixty-year-old woman in a blue one-piece and bathing hat jumped into the water, and they both shrank from the spray.

'I don't know. How do you know? How can you tell if you're in love? *Is* there a way of telling?'

Sean's face briefly assumed a dreamy, poetic quality, which was, however, immediately cancelled by Wayne's brusque response:

'Wank, thinking of the alleged beloved, and then afterwards, if you still feel like calling her, you're in love. I've tried it dozens of times. I never called anyone.'

After that, they did not speak for a while, while the extremely fat lady in the blue one-piece scrambled out of the pool and noisily re-entered it, this time in the company of her tiny granddaughter who was wearing vivid yellow water-wings, and who stayed at the surface with the effortless ease of an angler's float, while the fat lady disappeared to the bottom like a U-boat. Some beautiful girls walked past, in the company of ugly men, some of them glancing occasionally in the direction of Sean and Wayne – because they recognised Wayne.

Sean sighed and cracked open his copy of Nietzsche's *Also Sprach Zarathustra*.

The pool was a great and enigmatic blue mass at whose brink the young supplicants of North London tottered and hesitated, with their sunglasses and industrial-strength sunblock, their Discmen, and their palmtop TVs, their novels and their towels. The Lido was the Ganges for the faithless; the Lido was Lourdes for people who did not want to be made well, people who moreover weren't too fastidious about the odd verruca. The Lido was a village, with its beadles and its scamps, its old folk and – in the form of the refreshments shop before which huddled and dripping customers waited in a queue, its *Sunday Big Issue* operatives and its lurking drug-dealers – it was a market. It had its tradesmen, its entrepreneurs, and its retail outlets. As the time went on, and it came closer to midday, the heat became almost intolerable; the Lido's customers huddled under the parasols that the management had lately inserted into its concrete, or under covers of their own; they gratefully received the ministrations of the Lido's newly constituted Melanoma Patrol: people whose job it was to douse people with sunblock from specially adapted spray guns. No one could look up at the sky.

'So do you fancy going in for a quick dip, then?'

Sean had long since laid aside his Nietzsche, and was looking again at Wayne, trying to guess if he was asleep or not.

'Oh, *please*,' said Wayne derisively. 'A quick "dip"? Please.'

'Just a dip,' persisted Sean faintly.

'Please,' returned Wayne shortly, once more, and this question seemed to be at an end. Sean looked disconsolately around. An extremely beautiful girl was enjoying a long, slow kiss with a young man who could pass for Sean's poorer, less intelligent and uglier elder brother. One of the old brown guys was strutting past in a thong, extremely *fat*. All these old guys were fat. A lifetime of swimming – in the Serpentine, across the Channel, up Mount Everest – had done nothing for his ballooning weight problem. Does swimming make you *fat*, or something? The presence of a number of long-term fat old swimmers at the Lido was undermining Sean's body image morale. The fat old brown person was smiling at someone. Waving. Suddenly a beautiful girl appeared from the right of Sean's field of vision, smiling and waving back. His daughter, obviously, *grand*daughter. She approached him. They enjoyed a lingering kiss and an embrace.

'Wayne?'

'What?'

'Did you shower before you came out here? In the Lido's showers, just now, I mean?'

'Of course not,' said Wayne, after a pause. 'Who does?'

'You're supposed to,' said Sean with no particular note of rebuke or complaint in his voice.

'Yeah, but nobody does,' said Wayne.

After a moment, Wayne said: 'You know that time I did a shoot in Reykjavik? Well, there's a pool there for the University students and the showers are unisex. And you're not allowed to stay in your costume either. Everyone does it. It's quite an accepted thing, like saunas and birch twigs and so on.'

Sean was galvanised by this new information. He tried to picture it: the blond, careless Nordic youth, showering together in the Reykjavik University swimming pool changing rooms, beautiful young Ryvita men and women showering naked in a state of pre-lapsarian Scandinavian grace. Then he stopped and bethought himself.

'Did you just make that up?'

'Yes,' said Wayne simply.

A sharp burst of sound from the portable television next to them alerted Sean and Wayne to the fact that an urgent newsflash was just being transmitted. They looked over at the 12-inch screen that the family next to them had erected just by their sunbed. It showed a ramshackle store in Kinshasa, the capital of the Democratic Republic of the Congo, formerly Zaire.

The Live Channel reporter was doing a piece to camera, but his tone was quite unlike the concerned and unruffled manner of his report from the suburban apartment block in

Tallinn. Now he spoke rapidly, frequently, breathless with anxiety, perpetually glancing over at the cameraman for some indication of whether it was safe to continue. The ordinary viewer would conclude that the answer was no. For behind him was taking place a demonstration so disorderly as to constitute a riot. A sea of faces, some jeering, some snarling, all contorted with great emotion of some sort, crowded behind him and rendered him all but inaudible. Already some bottles had been thrown; some missile had evidently hit the reporter before taping had begun, for a thin trickle of blood along his temple showed up scarlet on the screen. In the store, stacked up in various makeshift and ramshackle display units, were postcards, newspapers in various languages, fruit and vegetables, each encrusted with a crackling layer of flies, and also a separate *guichet*, like an old British Post Office counter, which sold tickets for the new Congo State Lottery. It was at this counter the previous week that a young man, whom the reporter identified simply as 'Louis', had arrived, tremulously holding a US dollar bill, with which he hoped to buy one Lottery ticket. After some negotiation, the elderly, frizzily grey-haired woman presiding over the Lottery counter condescended to sell him one – and it was at this stage that Louis fell victim to what he thought was simply one of the minor epileptic episodes to which he had been a martyr from early childhood. But as he wincingly bent to the ground, he was aware of a vivid light, and a strange, ineffable sense of sweetness, of goodness, so heartbreakingly intense that Louis thought that his adored late mother had returned from the dead to be with him again. Then he became aware of a blonde presence, a wonderful off-centre smile, a sense of overwhelming beneficence, of something caring and compassionate, with surging love and grace – then, specifically, he became aware of six numbers: 3, 9, 15, 28, 29, and 41. He recovered himself in a few minutes, and shrugging off the concerns of those helping him to his feet, Louis repeated the six numbers to himself fanatically over and over again so that he would not forget them. These were the numbers he checked off on the rough pinkish card; these were the numbers announced as the winners on the state radio channel that evening. Louis announced the reason for his victory to all and sundry, and solemnly added that he would be spending the money on an operation for his infant daughter who suffered from curvature of the spine. At any rate, he returned to the store the next week, along with thousands of superstitious others eager to see if the Lottery miracle could be repeated. Louis took his position in the enormous and excitable line of people quietly, humbly, his bashful demeanour belied by the brash and shiny suit and the jaunty new trilby he now wore. Finally, he got to the head of the queue, and faced the frizzy-grey-haired lady who he had only just prevailed upon last week to accept his single US dollar. Now he had another one, which he produced with an airy flick from a gold-plated money clip. But again, the same thing happened. Louis flinched from an internal stab of pain, and doubled up in apparent agony. Those around him looked on speechless with reverence. Louis was aware, firstly, of a terrible, insupportable pain in his head and chest, which then cleared and was replaced by the same overwhelming sense of love and warmth, a warm bath of goodness in which Louis felt he could repose his entire being. He had the same spectral sense of blondeness, the same off-centre smile – and then, six more numbers: 19, 28, 33, 38, 39, 48. Louis awoke with a start, again repeating the numbers to himself, but silently, so that his choice would not be copied and his winnings split between him and a crowd of plagiarists. He tried his best to conceal the numbers as he checked them off on the rough, pinkish slip, but inevitably three or four other people discovered his choice. When he and the other jubilant winners turned up to collect their rightful prize that morning, they found that the Lottery outlet had been closed down on suspicion of fraud, and guarded by three or four ferocious members of the Congolese National Army. That was earlier this morning. Now the Live Channel was reporting on the growing disorder in Kinshasa, and the rumours of the miracle. Having manfully attempted to summarise the situation, while being prodded and jostled by the crowd, the Live reporter attempted to interview Louis himself. But as the camera swung round to picture him, the screen fizzed and crackled and became a shimmering rhomboid within the monitor's dark rectangle.

Bored and irritated, the television's owner retuned his set to Channel 11, and Sean briefly saw Wyle E. Coyote crouched down by a desert highway with his fingers in his ears, his eyes tight shut, while a fizzling noise went on in the background.

'So what about a dip?' said Sean again.

Wayne did not reply, and was repositioning his sunglasses and Discman.

'We'll just go to the middle.'

This last remark was something of an error of taste on Sean's part. It indirectly alluded to the fact that neither Sean nor Wayne were all that good at swimming. They could manage a few exhausting strokes of front crawl, some prepubescent breast stroke, occasionally some alarming and frankly dysfunctional butterfly. But they both had a tendency to veer off to the side, to bob pointlessly around by the steps, and certainly never under any circumstances to go further than the five-foot-eleven mark halfway up the pool. Wayne and Sean shared a morbid fear of getting out of their depth, both in terms of swimming and relationships. Since his father's death, Sean was scared of getting somehow *out of his depth* with his mother, whose demands on him were becoming more and more overt, and Wayne of getting *out of his depth* with women in general. The Parliament Hill Lido had become a vivid metaphor for both fears:

THE EMOTIONAL LIDO

Depth	*One's mother*	*One's girlfriend*
3'6"	Seeing her occasionally, with other siblings, at your house or at extended family parties at Christmas. No regular time planned	Seeing her occasionally, at work, or with mutual friends. Flirting, and jokey conversation
4'2"	Taking her out to lunch in restaurants on weekdays, after she has been shopping in the West End. No regular time planned, but averaging once every three weeks	Seeing her for light-hearted lunch, at restaurants near the office. Develops into dinner, and sleeping with her at her flat
5'11"	Getting locked into an arrangement whereby you have to phone her every week, at a certain time, and if you don't she phones you to see what the matter is or if you're in hospital	She starts sleeping over at your place, and leaving toothbrushes and intimate female bathroom stuff there as well, along with T-shirts and sweaters etc. Leaves lots of non-essential voicemail messages at the office
6'2"	OUT OF DEPTH	

Having to go round to her for lunch every Sunday, during which you and she will go through old photos, ostensibly to sort them out for some new scrapbook, but really as the pretext for a terrible emotional scene, generally centring on the lack of interest you took in your late father	Talks obsessively about her friends who have got married. Becomes testy and defensive on the subject of her parents' divorce. Buys *Brides, Brides Monthly, Brides Quarterly, Goin' To The Chapel* (US publication) and *Doing It Properly* (Australian publication) and *Anything Else Means He Doesn't Respect You* (Canadian publication)	7'8"
Converting part of your house into a flat for her, with a connecting door, so that she can come through on Sunday mornings, unbidden, with breakfast on a tray for you and your new girlfriend	Becomes unsteady and emotional at the sight of small children in parks. Develops interest in EU laws on maternity leave and childcare allowance. Bursts into tears at the sight, sound, or textual description, of a ticking clock	9'11"

Perhaps to forestall any further discussion of going in swimming, and in view of Sean's recent confession, Wayne inaugurated a languid discussion of what women did that was heartbreakingly beautiful without being overtly sexy. Sean nominated chewing the inside of their lip while they were concentrating on something, which because it artlessly redirected the viewer's attention to their lips, made you feel warm and protective.

Sean suddenly had another idea. 'I think it's what they do with their swimming costumes.'

'And what's that?'

'Well, when they are walking towards the water, with one hooked forefinger they pull out the material that's been riding up their bottom.'

'And that's supposed to be a *good* thing, an attractive thing? You're kidding.'

'No, no, no,' said Sean. 'It's the *unthinkingness* of the gesture that's important; it's the knowledge that they would be . . . embarrassed to know that anyone else had noticed it . . . and yet also the fact that it *makes no difference* to how you feel about them.'

'How you feel about them? And how's that?'

'You *love* them.'

Ysenda and Catherine arrived, having not yet changed into swimming costumes, or more probably wearing normal clothes over them, but sporting arch expressions of amusement which indicated that they might well have heard every word of the preceding conversation. Wayne and Sean reflexively reviewed it, and satisfied themselves that there was nothing in the transcript to shame them.

Here Sean was, face-to-face with Catherine for the first time since that disastrous meeting. Important to get it back on to the right footing.

'Cath— Catherine. How, how are you?'

'I'm fine,' she said, with a slow and easy smile. 'I think your reading matter looks a bit heavy for poolside.'

Sean did not have the slightest clue what she meant.

'Nietzsche,' she said.

'Yes, well, cool guy,' said Sean, 'cool moustache, cuddled horses . . .' He was babbling.

'I would have thought Alan Hollinghurst was more appropriate. We're just off to get some Volvic. See you in a minute.' They left. Sean exhaled heavily, mouth closed, flaring his nostrils.

'Oh Jesus. Oh very funny. Oh great. With that supercilious bloody remark, Catherine has just *shafted the entire afternoon*. I'm so upset. I'm not even sure I like her that much any more.'

'Will you stop it?' sighed Wayne. 'She was probably just nervous. It just slipped out. Just give this a chance.'

'Fuck giving it a chance. I'm going swimming.'

Sean stalked over to the side of the pool, and assumed the ungainly 'dive' position, bending at the knees, arms straight out, diagonally away from the body, palms facing backwards, looking like Thunderbird One. Then he straightened, and with some dignity walked back to where Wayne was lying, removed his sweater, his T-shirt, and his expensive watch, and laid them out on the towel. Then he went back and assumed the dive position once again, and entered the pool.

Sean did a couple of widths with a laborious anthology of strokes: crawl, breast stroke, crawl, drowning, breast stroke again, and then an unlovely mixture of treading water and doggie-paddle which brought him ingloriously back to the side as fourteen-year-old girls in sleek black one-piece suits overtook him as effortlessly as if they had been attached to the far end by a piece of taut elastic. But once he was there, once clinging to the sturdy aluminium strut of the steps, the real Lido experience could begin. He immersed his head under the surface, where the sound of the pool was immediately replaced by the strange sonic rush of underwater silence.

The great blue soup of the pool revealed itself: that secret vault with its mysterious sloping floor which twinklingly disclosed a lost 5p coin, a discarded rubber ankle-band, a scrunched and semi-vegetable BandAid. From this great blue asymmetric fog did the swimmers questingly and slowly emerge, sentient amphibian forms all unaware of Sean's rapt and covert glance. He was the Jacques Cousteau of swimming pool eroticism. Boys did athletic and expressive racing turns while Sean watched, their great haunches tensed against the Lido's limit. Girls arrived and lingered while Sean surfaced, puffed and ostentatiously ran his fingers over his scalp, with the preoccupied air of a businesslike 20-lengths man, concerned solely with cooling down. He would bob down again for some more swimming pool voyeurism, regarding a girl's seal-like beauty as she disappeared off into the azure mist. Many a time Sean made an afternoon of it right here, sometimes availing himself of a fag, a makeshift ashtray and a paperback on the ledge as the sun climbed up; a sip of mineral water here, a diagonal fragment of Fuse bar absentmindedly detached from his teeth.

While Sean semi-emerged from the Hockney deep, his eyes peering along the surface of the water, like a sexually conflicted hippo, Ysenda and Catherine had returned and were settling down next to Wayne, having removed their clothes to reveal swimming costumes. Ysenda, unwisely, had chosen to avoid her habitual black and opted for a bikini in pastel colours. Catherine had on a sleek black one-piece that was immeasurably sexier, something that Ysenda noted with shrewd annoyance.

They settled down either side of Wayne and the empty towel space left by Sean; Catherine got the one immediately adjacent to Wayne, and Wayne shifted his body language so that he was marginally facing Catherine more, a nuance of body language that was not entirely lost even amidst the heat and the carnival Lido chatter.

'Jesus, we thought we were all going to *die*, I mean *die*. But somehow it didn't *frighten* anyone, or make them pray or take out photographs of their children or cry or scream or anything. It just seemed to make everyone sort of *pissed off*.'

Ysenda was talking about her plane journey back from Iran, a country she had visited many times since becoming research director of the Sacred Heart Institute four years ago, her mission being to promote links between Islam and Rome. This time she had been composing an in-depth field research report for the Institute on the newly inaugurated erotic film and television trade fair in Teheran, a city whose approach to public morality had loosened in line with continental Europe and parts of North Africa. The plane had encountered turbulence, as the pilot blandly revealed to his fractious passengers, lost altitude – and almost crashed. Everyone went by plane now, *everyone*, and the deregulated skies were full of aircraft of questionable provenance, design, safety. Air journeys were as commonplace as bus journeys, and far less pleasant. There seemed to be a major plane crash every fortnight, and it seemed to Ysenda that they had become as unremarkable as horrific car crashes. Just as the latter were only alluded to indirectly in terms of motorway 'hold-ups' or 'bottle-necks', the sudden unscheduled presence of thousands of tonnes of twisted flaming metal in the middle of some traffic island or garden centre, together with teddy bears and fragments of bone, would be described in news broadcasts only as an unspecified 'drain' on paramedic resources which occasioned longer waiting times at the local hospital. Soon aeroplanes would be dropping from the sky like rain; all over Europe, damaged and poorly maintained aircraft buzzed and growled feebly at the margins of cracked and weedy runways like wasps on window panes at the end of summer. Going on planes was something that middle-to-low income groups did; they were crammed in tight in economy class and got candidly drunk, accepting with sour indifference the fact that previous commercial airlines and their customers had conspired to ignore for almost sixty years: that there was no such thing as passenger 'safety'.

Ysenda was talking about her journey from Teheran to London: a first-class flight, but still affected by the other new symptom of plane travel: a shocking increase in rudeness from the airline stewardesses to the passengers.

'They were more like *McDonald's* employees, but so much less *charming* and *attentive,*' complained Ysenda, gracefully surrendering to the attentions of the Lido's sunblock patrol. Unlike Catherine, she did not have her sunglasses, so her face was in a kind of wince or scowl. 'I asked if I could possibly have another sachet of dry roasted peanuts from the great mound they had on their stupid trolley and the stewardess told me to *piss off*; those were the exact words. It was like we were all on some Indian train journey, with people with goats and pigs and grannies all hanging on the roofs and the wings and no one, *no one*, gives two shits about fastening your seat-belts any more. I was literally the *only* one doing it. I leaned across and reminded some lady executive that she had "forgotten" to fasten her safety belt and it was like telling some skinhead on the Northern Line that he'd "forgotten" to put out his cigarette. Not of course that there's any stuff about no-smoking on airlines any more. Everyone was smoking. Cigarettes, joints, one guy even had a Meerschaum. I read about a flight from Algiers to Las Vegas, where they didn't even notice the starboard engine was on fire because everyone was smoking so much. And everyone was so *drunk*, you know,' Ysenda cranked off the top of her Snapple with a hefty elbowy movement, 'really hogwhimpering *drunk*, and not happy drunk; they were like these Icelandic guys or these Eskimos or Scandinavians from places where it gets dark at two thirty in the afternoon and they drink litres of Pernod and then put a pickaxe through someone's head at the end of the evening. And the *take-off* . . .'

Catherine was positioning herself face-down on the warm concrete slabs, a distinctively sensual Lido experience, and took down the armstraps of her swimming costume, though it could not have been to get a tan; all three of them were under one of the Lido's big parasols. She had a copy of Karachi *Vogue* which she was flicking through, trying to find the big profile of Wayne that he'd said was in there somewhere. She propped herself up on her elbows slightly, causing her breasts to swell up discreetly from the towel; Wayne noticed. Ysenda noticed him noticing.

'What about the take-off?' he smiled to her.

'Well, they got this thing called take-off surfing. The drunkest person on the flight, usually the stewardess or one of the co-pilots, gets one of the food trays and positions it at the top of one of the gangways nearest the cabin. Then one or maybe two other people try to stand on it with them and then they all sort of crouch down. Then when the plane accelerates for take-off, they all make this sort of low moaning sound crouched down on the tray like this,' Ysenda pursed her lips a little and made a kind of low 'Wagons roll' call: '"Hooooooooo." And all the other passengers do the same thing; *I* did it as well: "Hooooooooo." And then when the plane inclines upward, these people surf down the gangway, two or three people hunching on to each other like a bobsleigh team. And we all did the low moaning call higher and higher as these mad bastards slid down to the back of the plane, until they end up in a heap by the rear exit, with cuts and bruises and one of them was actually *crying*, no one seemed to be really enjoying it as such. And then when it came time for us to land in Iran, they did the same thing in reverse, from the back to the front of the plane, and we all did the "hoooooo" sound on a falling tone, only at the end most of us were chanting *Crash Crash*. It just sort of comes over you.'

They stopped talking and Wayne and Catherine briefly squinted up through their very dark sunglasses at the unbearably bright blue sky and the dozen or sixteen planes that seemed to be criss-crossing their way over it. One of them seemed to swoop low out of their range of vision. They listened for a moment, but there was no sound.

'How *was* Teheran?' Wayne asked, after a moment.

'Oh, you know,' said Ysenda. 'The usual.'

Sean came back. He was still dripping a little, carrying a massive four-litre bottle of Diet Coke. He had figured out a way of re-opening the question of Catherine understanding the *nature* of his interest in her. This was simply to suggest, or get Wayne to suggest, an old-fashioned 'double-date' with the four of them. Ysenda and Wayne would obviously be the other pair, and this would make a clinch with Sean seem the most natural thing in the world for Catherine. Sean was counting on his reappearance being the cue for both women to pay him some of the attention that he now felt was his due, so it was to his considerable chagrin that his cheerful 'hi' was obliterated by a great *whoop* from Catherine as she discovered the profile of Wayne in *Vogue*.

'Wayne!' she said. 'Here you are.'

'What's it say, then?' he asked dryly.

'Yeah,' said Ysenda, grinning and shaking out the match with which she had just lit a cigarette. 'What *does* it say?'

Sean just stood there, with his great four-litre bottle of Diet Coke, so big it had a special handle, while these three people crowded round the bible-thick copy of *Vogue* as if doing a mime in a game of charades, acting out the phrase: 'Sean is utterly insignificant.'

He had no choice but to sit down at the margin of the group – his own towel seemed to be being used as a lectern for the magazine.

'Wayne Darblay is one of the rising young hot-shot Britpackers of his generation,' read Catherine reverently, while Ysenda snorted, and Wayne exerted every facial muscle in order not to break out in a grin. The magazine article took the reader through Wayne's wandering childhood: his father in the Navy, his time in Gibraltar, in North Africa, in the United States when he was fourteen. It went through drama school, the stage work, and his burgeoning movie career. It slyly touched upon Wayne's recent friendship with a well-known French movie actress, renowned for her gloomy and saturnine screen presence. The interviewer asked him if he ever wanted to settle down with anyone and Wayne had replied with a line in which he had been schooled by Sean himself: 'The thought of marrying, and of being married, flashes afresh to hold and horrify.' It got a small laugh from Ysenda, nothing from anyone else, certainly not Wayne who was still tensely straining every fibre in the cause of looking cool and unconcerned. A mobile chirruped and all four of them reflexively reached for their bags; but Ysenda, Catherine and Wayne sank back as they realised it was Sean's phone. Sean listened, and heard the sound of Nick's hesitant voice addressing his voicemail message. Coldly, he clicked the phone shut.

There was something strangely enjoyable in the cultivation of this displeasure; something comforting. This shade of cruelty to an old friend gave him some awful and unmentionable solace in moments of pain, moments like these as he watched Catherine's tanned and freckled face looking at Wayne. With a sinking feeling, he believed he was about to have a migraine right now: he felt the strange light-headedness, the tunnel-vision, the shimmering firework effect, the sense of Catherine's voice being very far away.

He turned around and sat on the edge of the pool, and trailed his feet in the water. Slowly, like an old man putting on reading glasses, Sean put his goggles back on and, tensing his right hand on the ledge, he corkscrewed his way back into and under the water.

4

Nick snapped shut his own mobile, sitting in his sleek creamy office in Highgate Hill. He frowned once, sharply, like a wince, and then took the mute off the TV on which he was watching Channel 11. Sean was obviously still a bit cross about the fiasco of Wednesday night.

Oh well.

Idly, he gestured at the screen with a remote control as big as a skateboard. It was covered with keys on which were inscribed improbable runic symbols, mysterious icons of which he knew he would go to his grave without ever discovering the meaning. Nick increased the volume slightly, and the fizzling sound stopped with a splutter, and Wyle E. Coyote opened his eyes, blinked broadly, removed his fingers from his ears and walked over to where a stick of dynamite was lodged inside a large box, marked 'Candy'.

Nick pressed the key at the top left and Wyle E.'s face vanished, and the screen was filled instead with the continuous live colour TV relay of the vigorous physio-psychotherapy session currently going forward in Recovered Memory Suite Four. A man in his early forties was doing press-ups, talking, and crying at the same time, while Inge stood over him with a stop-watch. He and Inge had been experimenting with new variants of Recovered Memory, and what a very successful new line it had proved to be. They had had a shaky start, when they tried encouraging patients to recover memories of satanic abuse, while doing circuit training. One man had been so traumatised that after only seven 'burpees', they had had to call a minicab to take him to the Maudsley Psychiatric Hospital. So now they had hit upon a new, and more gentle, Recovered Memory technique – a technique at once so popular and so successful, Nick wondered in delirious moments if he should not receive some sort of medal or Nobel Prize for dreaming it up. At the very least, he should be marketing a video in America to convert the idea into millions and millions of dollars.

The memories that his patients were invited to 'recover' were not memories of abuse, but ones of kindness. It was as simple as that. After much meditation, ten lengths or so in the clinic's small pool (built last year at ruinous expense), a session on the rowing machine and some massage, the patient would dredge up a lovely and hitherto unremembered sunlit summer's day when he was four or five, when his mother had kissed away the dreadful hurt of some playground mishap. Or perhaps his father would enter the picture, usually at a later age, maybe making him a delicious bacon sandwich to celebrate some school sports victory. Last week they had had a fantastic school-related RM: one in which an elderly lady recovered the memory of deliberately losing in a running race on her school sports day to a girl who had been a bit simple, so that she would have something to feel good about in her life. By the end, she had been crying; Nick was crying, warm-hearted soul that he was; even Inge, flinty-hearted Inge, sniffed a little – Inge, whose face generally only betrayed emotion of any sort when she spanked Nick's exposed buttocks at the end of the evening in his flat over the clinic with a reinforced wooden paddle.

It mattered not one jot that these recovered yarns were about as real as the ones with which the apple-cheeked bairns of Orkney or whey-faced pre-school shoplifters of Middlesbrough had once regaled their social workers: the ones about them dancing in a circle around their tumescent scout-master in his front room with the curtains drawn, dressed up in little Dennis Wheatley outfits his wife had run up.

This lady, for example, had clearly read her own story in a film director's serialised autobiography in a magazine that Nick kept in the waiting room: four patients in fact subsequently recovered the same memory. The point was that his patients had felt *good* about themselves, morally good, and that was why they were prepared to return for more treatments, week after week. Smiling gently, with the air of a man who has once again done his good turn for the day against extraordinary odds, Nick turned to the Mac on his desk, with a keystroke dispelled the animated pornographic screensaver of Botticelli's *Primavera*, and then prepared to print out the hefty invoice for what was obviously going to be an extremely satisfied patient/customer. He grabbed the remote again and cranked up the volume:

(Puff), that's when I saw that little Adrian, poor simple little bastard (puff, sob) would never achieve anything else in his life (sob, sob, puff) so I knew I had to let the poor little sod win (puff, sob) oh Christ, I think I've got a stitch.

Not another one. He really would have to change that magazine. Idly, he picked up the bass guitar that he had stowed in the corner of his private office and, unplugged, ran through the opening bars of The Beatles' 'Day Tripper'. Nick was actually in a band now: Filipina Brides, and he was preparing for another gig that he had lined up for them soon.

That was going to be really fun. Would Sean come? he suddenly thought to himself, with a frown. Of course he would. Sean and he would have made it up by then.

Nick put aside the guitar and went out into the reception area to throw away the magazine, this month's copy of Karachi *Vogue*. It was already twenty past five and his two reception staff had gone home, leaving him and Inge in sole charge. He flopped down on a low-slung leather sofa and idly flicked through the newspapers piled there. The property supplement of the *Hampstead and Highgate Express* always particularly pleased him. This week, there had been weird and unpredictable flooding in London. Drains had spewed bile and the Thames had burst its banks. Elegant apartments and commercial property in Chelsea Harbour had been flooded. The value of property anywhere near the river was in free fall, and parts of South West London were extremely low – but houses and flats in the high ground of North Nineteen were on the up and up. Here was an article about an elegant house in Cheyne Walk owned by a sleek, silver-haired barrister, his beautiful second wife and their two lovely children, pictured standing in their drawing room, up to their ankles in brown, sewagey water which lapped at the Conran sofa. He can't *give* that house away. But one-bed flats on the Holloway Road, moments away from Archway tube station? Millionaire's row, mate! High ground, that's where you wanted to live as you prepared to breast the London millennium. High ground.

Then something extremely strange happened. He heard a knock on the front door of the clinic. Not a buzz, as he would expect from a patient, with an appointment, who would be smilingly admitted to the reception area. In any case, he did not have any patients scheduled this late in the day. And this was such a heavy knock, the knock of a policeman, the knock of his father when Nick was a long time in the bathroom, a little more rapid and it could have been the knock of a fireman on a locked bedroom door in a blazing house, behind which sleeping toddlers were about to expire of smoke inhalation. But this was a knock with not so much urgency as massive moral authority, a knock that demanded to be answered. With a strange feeling of foreboding, Nick approached the door.

Knock, knock, knock. Nick came up and was about to bend down and check out the visitor through the fish-eye lens in the door – never normally needed – when another loud knock brought him guiltily upright. Slightly off balance, he opened the inner door with that air of expecting imminent dismay, just as one might open the door of a train lavatory at the end of a Saturday night journey from Euston to Inverness.

What he saw was this: a rather fat and seedy man with pink, mottled skin and long, dark hair streaked with grey, casually dressed but wearing one of those heavy, fleecy anoraks that film directors wear on location. Nick smiled uncertainly, as he thought he recognised the man from somewhere. But he could not make up his mind if he had seen him on television, or some time in the past treated him as a patient. Then, with a sick lurch of horror, he realised that it was both. The man was carrying a microphone which he shoved into Nick's face, and there was a man with a video camera standing just behind him.

'Mr Stewart, what do you say to the fact that your psycho-physiotherapy sessions are *extremely* damaging, that you have no qualifications, and that you forced me to do fifteen squat thrusts, twenty overhand pull-ups and encouraged me to talk about satanic abuse while you gave me an enema?'

It was Aldo Popp, once-feared investigative journalist who spent the 1980s and 90s lifting the lid on all sorts of scandals and abuses on his programme *Popp's on Top*, but succumbed to a nervous breakdown when he himself was doorstepped by Candida Albigens, a radical up-and-coming young Turk who fronted her own rival investigative programme: *Candida's Camera*. For three fraught weeks beforehand, he had actually been sharing a production office with Candida in Soho, the result, he was given to understand, of the merest happenstance. One day Aldo had gone over to her to complain about the length of time she was taking to use the photocopier, when she suddenly whipped round to reveal a video camera, and started demanding answers to questions about his mother's alleged tax evasion. After that, Aldo Popp, the man who fearlessly strode down the Falls Road under heavy fire with *World In Action* in the 70s, lost his bottle – or rather found it – completely. He now presented a low-budget travesty of his original ground-breaking programme for the local cable channel entitled: *Popp! That Surprised You*, investigating absurdly minor misdemeanours. Nick had actually watched it last week, when Aldo had exposed alleged overcharging at a corner shop in Tufnell Park, and he had been impressed by the affronted yet cogent way the shopkeeper had defended himself on the doorstep against Aldo's litany of charges, which were in any case undermined by the fact that he was slurring badly, in the end mumbling something about having 'possibly got the wrong shop'. The man himself used to begin his old show with the boast that you had to get up pretty early in the morning to catch out Aldo Popp. Nowadays, that wasn't true. You could get up at three in the afternoon after an all-night drinking session and still be in good time to catch him out very comfortably indeed.

Aldo swayed uneasily, narrowed his eyes, as if trying to focus on Nick's face, and then took an emphatic drag from a reeking, damp cigar, the colour of which matched his skin so precisely as to resemble another digit. His full lips parted; his body tensed, and for a moment he seemed to be on the verge of a passionate denunciation of Nick, perhaps some form of stylised, scandalised *Sprechgesang*. All that issued forth was a belch of window-shattering volume, culminating in a deeply intestinal gurgle and a retched obscenity, and at the same time Aldo Popp's head, his crinkled eyes shut in pain, lurched over and clinked against his cameraman's lens. The cameraman in question batted it back with a furious swipe of his left hand and said: 'For Christ's sake, keep your head out of shot!'

Aldo wheeled around with disdain, as if he had forgotten for the moment that the cameraman was there.

'What do you mean, keep my head out of shot, Kenneth?' he wheezed. 'My head isn't *in* shot.'

'Yes it is.'

'No it bloody well isn't.'

'Yes it fucking well is, it *always* is.'

'Fuck . . . arghh . . .'

Nick remembered now.

Aldo Popp had come to his clinic about three weeks before, under the false name of Aldred Bang, wearing sideburns and long hair, like Jason King – in retrospect, an obvious disguise, especially as Popp was continuously pressing the left side of his moustache to his upper lip with the heel of his hand, as if he had toothache. In a curious, unplaceable accent, he had asked to be 'cleansed' (his term) of an abuse memory he said he was certain was floating just below the surface. So Inge had shown him into the changing room and asked him to shower, and to then come through into the Initial Treatment Unit, wearing just a towel around his waist. This Aldo Popp had done, but insisted on carrying with him a large, oddly bulky case, which he said contained documents so precious that he couldn't let it out of his sight. He set it down on a table facing the massage table – and Nick now realised that it had contained a concealed camera. He had just arrived back from a long and convivial lunch with a publisher who had convinced him of the desirability, indeed the virtual necessity, of his writing a profitable series of coffee-table-sized books entitled 'Massage And The Zodiac', about the various types of massage appropriate to each star-sign, 'Massage In History', about the types of massage which would have helped various world leaders – Napoleon, Hitler, Henry II – and 'Massage And The Bible', about all the various hidden encoded messages about massage in the Bible.

So he had been in a terrifically good mood. Nick actually came through from the Observation Suite into the treatment unit and affectionately hugged Inge from behind just as she was beginning to place her hands, complete with long painted fingernails and elaborate Mexican jewellery, on Aldo Popp's pudgy neck.

'Mmmmm,' Nick had said warmly.

'Oh!' she had gasped in exasperation.

'Agh!' Aldo had gasped, as her talons cut his skin.

'Carry on, carry on, nurse,' he had said gaily, stepping back, and producing a cigarette and lighter, out of sight of Aldo, but not his discreetly whirring hidden camera. 'I shall retire briefly and join you on the treatment deck.' Here he evaded the camera's eye but Aldo's recording equipment caught the flaring of a match.

'Who was that?' Aldo had asked, speaking very clearly in the direction of his case. 'And why was he behaving in such an unprofessional manner?'

'Oh, that is Mr Nick Stewart, the clinic's director,' Inge had said, loyally assuming the subdued, sing-song tone that Nick considered appropriate for use with patients. 'He is well known for his colourful approach to therapeutic and diagnostic techniques.'

'Those shampoos and conditioners on sale in the entrance,' said Aldo, crossly, as an afterthought, 'have they been *tested on animals*?'

'Oh yes, don't worry,' said Inge brightly, 'you won't get a rash or anything.'

Nick had gone back into the Observation Suite, poured himself out a generous *digestif*, and plugged in the tiny Karaoke machine that he had had installed there to practise his vocals for Filipina Brides. Briefly, he had programmed in a light rumba and launched experimentally into an upbeat, Latin-American version of 'Heaven Knows I'm Miserable Now' which he abandoned quickly enough.

It was no good. He could not concentrate. Something about

that silly little man irritated him profoundly. He poured another half-inch of his post-luncheon *digestif* into his tumbler, and with his remote once again took the mute off his viewing monitor. Silly little Jason King was whinging about his inner sense of dislocation. Inge distracted him by massaging his chest and subtly working her way downwards. With a dispassion born of long experience, Nick noticed a thoughtful silence pervade the massagee's face like the shadow of a cloud over a sunlit hillside. It was, unmistakably, the thoughtful expression of a man who cannot quite see if, or how, he can ask for 'extras'.

Nick's policy was that they were strictly not allowed, by the way. But he allowed Inge a certain amount of leeway on this, and indeed together they had built up a *piquant* and richly varied video library of the exceptions.

But somehow, this fellow shrank from asking – natural pusillanimity, undoubtedly, but also he seemed to sense that he was being watched, though he turned his head not in the direction of either of the concealed cameras, but towards the briefcase that he had positioned with such elaborate care next to the table on which he was being manipulated. Nick turned the volume up, and his concealed surveillance cameras followed as Inge guided him into the 'steam room' and placed Popp, who again insisted on bringing his bag with him, into one of the big steam units, like a cross between a meat safe and squat vertical coffin, with a hole for his head to poke out of the top. Nick had wanted to install these in his clinic because they reminded him of the health farm scenes in *Thunderball*. Popp was positioned in one of them, and the steam turned on, while Inge whimsically indulged in some more 'facial massage' on the now helpless subject: this basically involved simply pinching his cheeks as if he was an enormous baby. Something about this man nettled Nick deeply. He had conceived an irrational dislike of him. His silly red face was sweating immoderately, even for someone undergoing the steam part of his therapy, and his moustache seemed to be wilting, as if it was glued on or something.

Nick thought he would have some fun with him.

Grabbing the brandy bottle, he heaved himself from his chair in the Observation Suite and jogged down the corridor and into the steam room.

'Let's have him out of there, nurse!' he called out sharply.

'But, Doctor Stewart,' said Inge – and for a tiny moment, neither of them could forbear to smile at the 'Doctor' – 'his steam therapy has not yet run its course.'

'Never mind that, nurse,' insisted Nick, unlocking the heavy front doors, 'I think Mr Bang' – Nick had consulted the case notes that Inge had left at the entrance to the room – 'could do with some intensive one-on-one.'

Inge assented with a thin, uneasy smile, glancing at the bottle-shaped bulge in Nick's white coat, and left the room.

Nick smartly chivvied Aldo Popp and his briefcase into the gymnasium, and prevailed on him to do some overhand pull-ups from the bar – something which he'd said would be no problem in the application form that he had filled in. With an air of keen alertness and critical severity, Nick watched the wretched man in his shorts trying to heave himself up to do at least one pull-up.

'What did you say your name was again?' asked Nick at last.

'Bang!' gasped Popp.

'Oh! You scared me there,' exclaimed Nick, and laughed long and hard, with a crazed and alarmingly vindictive look in his eye. Popp had lowered himself to the ground and was staring reprovingly at Nick – but also with an air of triumph. Here was evidence of the unprofessionalism he had been waiting for.

'Squat thrusts now, I think,' said Nick, and Aldo gingerly got down on the floor and managed two or three with Nick facetiously counting them out as loudly and theatrically as a boxing referee over a recumbent heavyweight.

After four, Aldo Popp collapsed wheezing on to the mat. Gently, Nick led him over to a kind of chaise-longue. Ruminatively, Nick watched Aldo as he fought to get his breath back, his shattered lungs sounding without euphony.

'I think you should now try some of the clinic's vegetarian nutrient cordial,' he said. 'It replaces a lot of vitamins.' Behind Aldo's back, he poured him a homicidally stiff brandy and ginger-ale, which appeared before him in an anonymous plastic beaker. Popp took a generous gulp and, empurpled, retched it up and was still coughing while Dr Stewart said smoothly but with the tiny tremor of a giggle: 'Some of the Chinese herbal element is a little strong for some people. Perhaps we could get on to your recovered memories now.'

Livid, but reassured by still more evidence of unprofessional behaviour, Popp took a few moments to collect himself and then started hesitantly to speak.

'Well,' he said, and cleared his throat convulsively. 'Well, I seem to have this memory of abuse, it's just out of reach, it's as if it's just around the corner of my mind. It's troubling me profoundly . . .'

'I'll bet it is, Mr Bang,' said Nick blandly, seated on a small chair just by the chaise-longue, and sipping some of his clinic's vegetarian nutrient cordial. 'I'll bet it is. Nothing like the half-buried memory of abuse to trouble a man profoundly or even shallowly.' He sipped some more cordial, and then looked up sharply at Popp, as if some dire and unmentionable thought had just struck him. 'Nothing *satanic* about this abuse is there, Mr Bang?'

'Sorry?' Aldo Popp had clearly not anticipated this.

'Satanic abuse. There's a lot of it about.'

'Well,' said Aldo Popp thoughtfully, doing a very bad impression of a man being encouraged by an unscrupulous and manipulative therapist to imagine things that had not really happened, '. . . yes, *yes*, I think I can remember images of satanic abuse from my past . . .'

'What sort of thing?' said Nick coolly.

'Ah, robes, inverted crosses . . .' said Popp hesitantly.

'Chanting feature at all?'

'Oh yes. Chanting. There was chanting, definitely.'

'Goats?'

'Mmm, yes, I should have thought so. That is, yes, they did.'

'Ah ha.' Nick now made a great show of making notes in a laptop that he had produced from somewhere. 'Well, Mr Bang, I can definitely say that there is indeed a substantial possibility that you are suppressing memories of satanic abuse, and this may well, in turn, be causing you distress and the various psychosomatic symptoms you detail in your application form.' Nick stood up and walked into the small kitchenette that led just off the gymnasium, and continued talking. Aldo Popp could hear the rushing sound of hot water being emptied into some sort of receptacle. Nick's voice could continue to be heard, the tone slightly bottled from being in this small room. 'Satanic abuse is one of the most distressing things that I have to encounter in my job,' he continued with insolent blandness, and Aldo Popp could hear him return to his seat just behind him. 'But your memories of satanic abuse are rather special, and particularly disturbing, Mr Bang.'

'Are they?' said Aldo uncertainly.

'They are indeed. Because, you see, you are suppressing memories of being not the victim of satanic abuse, but its *perpetrator*.'

'What?' said Popp, sitting up in the chaise-longue and twisting round to face Nick.

'Yes, Mr Bang,' he said. 'You have committed these appalling acts, and there is only one way for you to cleanse yourself.'

With a spinal jolt of fear that sent pins and needles of panic into his cheeks and the backs of his hands, Aldo Popp saw that Nick, his cigar clenched in his teeth, was carrying an enormous jug of hot soapy water in one hand, and a long rubber tube in the other.

'Help!' Aldo Popp panicked. Aldo Popp – the man who had once single-handedly faced down the angry 'Troops Out H-Blocks Out' demo of 1982 armed only with a microphone, the man who had exposed the 1998 Dalston fibreglass draught-excluder racket – panicked. Scooping up his bag, he ran for the changing room down the hall, while Nick whimsically affected to lumber after him with the soapy water, like Arnie in *Terminator* – laughing grimly the while. Aldo found his clothes, struggled into his trousers, headed for the front door, and ran off down Highgate Hill, his waddling progress decelerating as his trousers settled around his knees.

This was the scene that Nick remembered from about three weeks ago. Dimly, fragmented, it swam back into his consciousness, and, urgently, he tried to edit it into some sort of cogent narrative. This was in fact the work in which Aldo himself had been earnestly engaged since he last saw him, interspersing the footage from his hidden briefcase camera with his own solemn addresses to the viewer, and now all that was missing was the final reckoning with the hateful 'Dr' Nick Stewart himself.

Only Aldo Popp now seemed far more interested in the furious, and indeed violent row, with his own chief cameraman.

'Christ. *Christ*,' said the cameraman, hoisting his camera heavily down on to the pavement. 'Why in God's name can't you keep away from the drink before six o'clock? Or five o'clock? Or even four-thirty?'

'Kenneth,' he said with massive and ostentatious calm. 'Haven't I been good to you?'

'No. *No*,' said Kenneth passionately. 'You've been crap to me. I have not been paid for thirty-one days.'

'I can do your job,' sneered Aldo. 'I could use that thing.'

Very unwisely, Aldo made a move to handle Kenneth's camera and Kenneth gave him a forthright shove on the left shoulder which sent him, not directly backwards, but spinning round almost three hundred and sixty degrees so that he was facing somewhere off between Nick and Kenneth.

'You've been a bastard,' said Kenneth quietly. 'A bastard to me and a bastard to my mother.'

'Your mother and I are friends now, Kenneth; we've worked through our feelings for each other,' said Aldo, turning and rallying a little.

'You used her,' spat Kenneth. 'Used her to get to me and my audio-visual editing facilities at the university TV production evening class for this programme. Then you threw her aside.'

'We mutually agreed to scale down the physical side of our relationship, Kenneth. You must understand that.'

'How dare you? How *dare* you talk about my mother like that in front of me?'

As they quarrelled, Nick's mobile cheeped. Leaving Kenneth and Aldo Popp to their domestic dispute, Nick answered it, and was astonished to hear Ysenda's voice, tense and gulping. She said: 'Nick, listen, you've got to come right away. It's Sean. I think he might have drowned.'

5

Under the water the blue is as bright as the sky and just as hot, but there is no weightlessness; he drifts downward as if with a parachute towards the pitched floor, with its tiny blue shadows and blue cracks and its blue geology. He speaks, but the brief sputum trail of bubbles has its own meaning like birdsong or the call of a laconic dolphin; his hair, growing out a little, shimmies up away from his scalp and waves and ripples like the flourish of a 99 ice-cream on its cone while the wobbly honeycomb of swimming pool light traces and retraces itself on his body and he wades and falls through the empyrean treacle and traverses the great glass light and above him the water ceiling, pocked and flecked and upended like the cloud-floor seen from an aeroplane, sags and bags and bows, the great marquee tent of heavy water; his cheeks bulge away from his nose and his shorts bulge away from his thighs, inflated with chlorine; he leaps, he moonwalks, he Neil Armstrongs back from the deep end but makes no headway; he meets the old fat lady and her granddaughter passing him on the left as they arrive from the shallow end; the little girl is crying but the old lady is laughing and so are the teenage

Speedo girls and he follows their glistening seal rumps and feels the lean and unforgiving pectoral muscles of submerged boys with no interest, and remembers putting his stockinged feet up inside his father's giant shoes and walking up their leathery ramp, gaining the prow of their arch but unable to proceed past the tongue and rope configurement of laces, and his father is easy and indulgent, and floating is always his idea, not swimming, floating, in the pool, with an occasional frogleg thrash to keep the lower half from drifting down, and in the salty sea he lies back still and gets flipped up and over an incoming wave, insouciant human driftwood, all smiling, unconcerned and he swims through his legs like Gulliver; his father appears before him in the deep end in the rippling convulsed lozenge of blue and tells Sean he is as old as his own father, and more cynical, slower and more suspicious, arthritic where his father's joints are free, sclerotic where his father's body is ripe; his father is tensed for the starting gun where he is arguing about his disqualification with a track official; his father is up with the lark and he is down in the mouth; his father swims towards him with his friendly hand extended and the other in the calliper walking-stick that never leaves his side, and Sean reaches out and catches it.

6

'Sean!'

'Sean!'

'He's—'

'Sean, can you hear me?'

'He's got hold of my throat.'

'Sean, let go of Nick's throat.'

'This is a good sign. This is a *wonderful* sign.'

'Not necessarily. He might be like one of those catatonic L-dopa patients that can catch a tennis ball if you throw one to them and clap at the same time.'

'What the *fuck* are you talking about?'

Nick, Ysenda, Catherine and Wayne were gathered excitably around Sean's bed at the Whittington Hospital in Highgate, where he had been brought in a black cab (no ambulances) having been fished out of the pool by a blond lifeguard.

Sean had seemed to splutter back into consciousness as he was laid down by the side of the pool, but his eyes remained closed and as yet he had said not a word. Deeply shaken, Ysenda had palely explained to the doctors that Sean was occasionally subject to fits of migraine-type disturbances, though very rarely this bad, and she supposed that, while under the water, Sean must have had some kind of 'episode'.

'Yeah, an episode of *Baywatch,*' said Wayne without thinking, and then immediately regretted sounding heartless.

It had been Ysenda's idea to call Nick. It was while the lifeguard was pumping away at Sean's chest and periodically giving him the kiss of life. Panicking, she had badgered Wayne to call Sean's mother, and when they had only managed to get her answering machine, she insisted they call Nick, believing, *in extremis*, that some kind of massage might just help. Nick had turned up pale and sweating, having run all the way down the Hill to the hospital, and discovered them in a group around the bed – by which time, there was no question of Sean having drowned. Nevertheless, they all believed that some sort of alternative therapy might awaken him from this weird trance. The doctor had said it was a post-traumatic reaction, and had staggered back to deal with his legions of other patients, leaving them to it. It was a miracle that Sean was allowed a bed at all.

Cautiously, Nick loosened the bed gown around Sean's chest and began to knead the neck muscles with his fingertips, working out sideways to the shoulders, while the rest of them watched, the situation causing them to suspend their usual derisive scepticism. For a moment, there was silence while he worked in this awkward position. Sean did not respond, but breathed evenly.

'Well?' said Wayne after a while.

'He's very tense,' was all Nick could think of to say.

'*Tense?*' said Ysenda acidly. 'He almost drowned, and now he's in a coma and you're telling us he's *tense*. Not half as tense as we are.' She was on the verge of tears; Catherine was just very pale.

Nick kept massaging. Then he asked: 'When did you first notice that Sean was in trouble anyway?'

'Well, that was the weird thing,' said Wayne. 'He didn't start shouting or splashing or anything. He just disappeared under the water and we just noticed he didn't seem to be moving.'

'*I* noticed,' said Ysenda quietly and, with a sudden tenderness that even these circumstances could not entirely explain, she reached out too and placed her hand on the top of Sean's head, and ran her fingertips backwards from his forehead towards the crown, against the grain of his fuzzy cropped hair. With an aching heart, she was feeling for the abrasion or contusion that she felt Sean's head must have received from the bottom of the pool – but it was not there. His poor body had never looked less manly to her as it had been trolleyed through the lino corridors. And now he looked as slight and vulnerable as a child, wedged into the uncaring hospital linen. Ysenda had helped a nurse remove his clothes except for the pale modesty of his underpants and had coaxed his thin arms forward into the position in which the back-to-front hospital gown was to be eased up and over his shoulders, the position in which, twenty years before, he might have attempted a sitting dive from the edge of the pool. Now frowning at Nick's clumsy massage, Ysenda let her own fingertips travel along Sean's collarbone, as prominent and visible as a bone for a cartoon dog, and enter the shallow recess below his neck. Sean's eyelids seemed to flutter, and Ysenda could feel thousands of goosebumps, almost feel them separately, as they were raised on his skin.

'Did he say something then?' she asked Nick, who simply widened his eyes and tilted his head a little to the side, to indicate that he had no idea.

Ysenda leant forward and tried to listen. She heard nothing. She looked up at Nick, who looked straight ahead, and then back down. She leant a little further, so that her face was close to Sean's mouth, and then a little closer still. She could hear nothing but the thin wheeze of his breath, voiced tinily, an all but inaudible hum. Being close to him reminded her, disturbingly, of being close to Wayne that night – except that the feeling of loss of control, of prostration, was now evidently the man's prerogative. Was Sean sleeping? Could he sense what Ysenda felt?

Nick was saying something.

'Ysenda, could you – look, could you stop that?'

'Stop what?'

'Stop touching his collarbone, and listening to him breathe. You're disturbing the integrity of my massage.'

After a moment, Ysenda shrugged and withdrew her hands.

It was at that moment that Sean's hand shot up and held Nick's throat in a remarkably secure grip. Maintaining some professional poise, Nick attempted to continue massaging Sean's neck as Sean, otherwise perfectly still, held Nick in a kind of SAS choke position, while the others gabbled and panicked all over again, just as they had by the swimming pool, but now strangely reluctant to pry Sean's fingers away, as they would shrink from awakening a sleepwalker.

'OK, Sean,' said Nick calmly in a throttled squeak, 'you might want to think about letting go of my throat now.'

At this point, when the surrounding group had fallen silent, Sean's mother appeared in the ward. Beautifully turned out, in a discreet navy-blue outfit that went exceptionally well with her thick dark hair which had a Susan Sontag skunk-stripe of grey, she carried an elegant leather clutch bag in which her fingertips made visibly tense indentations. Her court shoes sounded crisp and sharp on the linoleum floor, as, with energy and decision, she walked over to the bed and took in the curious tableau: Sean's three shellshocked friends standing solemnly by, while a fourth in a position of ministration sat on the edge of the bed, his face puce, being strangled by the recumbent patient.

'Sean,' said his mother, and Sean's eyes immediately opened, startled. A tiny moment passed.

'Yes, Mother, what is it?' said Sean.

'Stop strangling your friend Nick.'

As quickly as if she had snipped a tendon in his arm, Sean's fingers opened, his arm remaining upright, fingers star-shaped; and Nick, whom Sean had been virtually holding upright, collapsed to his knees, his face by now the colour of a Turner sunset. His wheezing and gulping continued, while Sean stared at the ceiling's neon strip lights with an air of slight puzzlement, his hand still raised, and fingers spread. Sean's mother remained impassive on the edge of the group and his friends stirred uncomfortably, unsure whether somehow they should apologise to her for the state he was in. There was, for a few more moments, silence – or at any rate no one spoke, while Nick's coughing and retching became progressively less serious-sounding, and he straightened up, his face beginning to look normal.

'Are you all right, Nick?' Sean's mother finally asked.

'Yes, I – yes, thank you, Mrs Cunningham.'

'*Don't* call me that.' For the first time, a lack of composure manifested itself. Sean's mother still spoke with preternatural calmness. But her habitual vexation at being addressed in this way by Sean's friends, instead of by her first name, Gillian, which she preferred, was not accompanied by a smile, but glacial coldness. Her large brown eyes, the most striking feature of her face, brimmed and glistened under her heavy arched brows.

It was time to leave.

As Wayne, Ysenda, Nick and Catherine were walking out of the ward the harassed-looking doctor appeared and asked if everything was all right – directed the question to them, in fact, as if they were the patients. They mumbled yes and disappeared.

The last to go was Ysenda, who found an excuse to linger at the hospital swing-doors, made of a special thin bendy rubbery material, notional doors, clearly incapable of excluding anything, but which presumably opened quickly when stretchers and trolleys had to go through at the double. She looked at her reflection in the right-hand door's round plastic window, and the pale sharp face and the short hair encircled the distant scene of mother and son. Placing her palm up to her cheek, she could smell chlorine minutely transferred from Sean's skin to her own. Then she too had to leave.

The doctor glanced up at Sean and his mother who was positioning herself by the left-hand side of the bed, where the chair was. Sean himself was looking over to his right, his eyes fixed straight at the door. Like his mother's, they brimmed; his mouth was set tight in the downward-turned semicircle, the bottom lip hunched and quivering in the time-honoured, deeply humiliating way. As with so many things, crying was something that did not suddenly enter into a new, mature, adult genre at the age of eighteen, or twenty, or twenty-one. Part of the dispiriting thing about tears was the undignified lower-lip-trembling thing that did not recede with advancing age. It was the thing that everyone on television and films seemed to be able to avoid, the thing that he associated with weakness, with childhood dismay and playground cataclysm; the ruinous sense that one was crying *like a baby*. But that was the point. Everyone cries like a baby. Why fight it? Why cause the lower lip to tremble in the first place, that awful finger-in-the-dyke moment of everyday physiognomy? Why is it that every time it happens, we clench the mouth and the fists and the poor, neglected heart and try to stop ourselves crying? Why do we defer the inevitable with that first, terrible tremor? Has it ever really worked, in the history of tears? Perhaps it is because we forget what crying is, like binge drinkers who forget the punitive hangover, we do it so rarely that in the intervals we forget that there is no point trying to stand up to it. Some day soon we must cultivate the art of spontaneity in crying, bypassing the pointless lower lip phase, and cry as immediately as sneezing or laughing.

Sean cried. And his mother did too, in her more tired, aged way. She was the first to speak and, as much as she tried, she could not forbear to do so with a note of reproach. 'I was worried before, now I don't know what to think.'

Sean did not reply.

'I've tried to talk to you before; I tried talking to you on the phone just today, only today, to talk to you about your headaches. But no, you won't listen, I can hear what you think in that tiny pause between recognising my voice and starting to speak.' Here Sean stirred, as if he wanted to say something, but his mother effortlessly imposed silence on him by raising a hand.

'I know,' she persisted, and tilted her head backwards fractionally, raised her nose and looked down it, a haughty-looking action which her son knew would bring him into slightly better focus. The reproach had suddenly gushed through her voice, like water from an air-locked tap. 'I know how you respond when I call you up. I know because I did it to my own mother. I can hear it in your voice, the disappointment that it's only your mother, and nobody interesting.' Now Sean gave great, dry, silent gulpy sobs, face still turned away. 'It's somebody you've taken for granted, someone whose mortality you fail to understand.' She paused, but only for a moment. 'What do you think that's like, Sean? What do you think it is like to have children in their twenties?' More dry sobs from him. 'I'll tell you what it's like.'

She leaned forward a little. 'It's like *unrequited love*, Sean, that's what it's like. That's what they don't tell you when you're about to become a mother. And it's the worst, the very worst secret thing about it. Accidentally voiding your bowels at the moment of birth isn't the worst thing; having sore nipples and involuntarily lactating isn't the worst thing; seeing you get chicken pox when you're four and thinking you could die isn't the worst thing; and you being a tearaway teenager isn't the worst thing either. The worst thing is when your children are in their twenties being young and having fun and their parents are the most boring, taken-for-granted thing in the universe and they *don't really love you any more*. How do you think that feels? How do you think any of us feels when we realise that this is the awful, terrible thing about our children?'

Sean was still now, not crying, but rocking a little bit, urgently, still looking the other way, his fists drawn up under his chin.

'So try to imagine or remember what it felt like to be in love with someone who just wants to be your "friend". That's what it's like, Sean. And when I call you up on the phone I have to manufacture some silly little reason, some little thought that's just occurred to me just so I can speak to you, just so I can *talk* to you, and I have to ignore that little twinge of disappointment in your voice. That's what I have to feel. And I know that you'll only really love me again when you're in your thirties and forties and I'll be dying and it'll be too late.'

Sean's eyes flicked as he heard the click of her chunky gold lighter. She lit a Marlboro Light. There was a breve rest while she took one gasp.

'And all I ever want to do is tell you to be careful about these headaches. And of course you ignore me, *of course*, and you almost kill yourself.'

Sean's mother twisted round to the left in her chair, and then to the right, her crimson thumbnail indenting the filter, looking for somewhere to flick the ash. In doing so, she caught the eye of a nurse, a heavy-set woman with her hair tied back into a loveless bun, whose duty it partly was to police the no-smoking rule, while the flinch of her glance betrayed a crying need for one herself. With much institutional practised ease (in fact she had had to do this next to a hospital bed many a time) she extinguished it against the side of a metal wastepaper basket near the fire door at the other end of the ward, with a fizzy flare, and returned to his bedside.

'Shall I tell you something, Sean?' was her rhetorical request, as she slid back into her seat, the skirt of her dark Jaeger suit riding up her stockinged legs. 'Shall I?' Sean mouthed it along with her, just loudly enough for his weak and sibilant whisper to amplify what she was saying:

'We are not meant to bury our children.'

She leant forward and gently folded aside the hospital gown and placed her right hand carefully on his chest, just above the right nipple, and squeezed it a little. Sean looked down and for a moment they both took in her hand: deeply tanned, the veins standing out like a river map, a grey liver-spot the shape of Madagascar at the very centre, all this on top of Sean's pale pink unblemished chest, on which each tiny fine hair was equally visible, the flesh differentiated only by the lines at which Gillian's hand was squeezing.

'We just are not meant to do this thing, Sean,' she said, and his eyes rolled up to the neon strip lights and tried to read the tiny writing on the filaments as Gillian's hand began to work on his chest a little.

'We are not meant to do it. It is not meant to be. Burying our children, seeing them die before us, is not right. Sitting there in the funeral director's showroom, and selecting which kind of coffin and which kind of lining and which kind of handles; that's all right for your *parents*, it was even all right for your father, but for your children?'

The hand still worked.

'Your children? No, Sean. No. It's like winding a clock backwards against the mechanism, or trying to enter a supermarket through the exit door and fight your way up past the lines at the checkout. Burying your children is something we're not built for, not made for. Having to come to a place like this and identify your body is something I can't do.'

The hand still worked. Sean still said nothing, but stayed staring at the ceiling, keening just slightly. The skirt had ridden up fractionally higher.

'We can't write all those letters to the relatives, Sean, telling them what's happened. We can't sit there and write them out. We can't invite people to the funeral of our children. We can't sit there at Golders Green Crematorium after we have arrived with the hired limousine to bring our children's coffins over from the undertakers, we can't sit there singing "Abide With Me" about our children. We can't sit there while some uncomprehending vicar gives some stupid fatuous sermon about our deceased children, because that's what *our children* should be doing for *us* – much later on. We can't sit there and listen to that terrible soft organ music as our children's coffins roll backwards into the flames. We're not meant for that. We're not built for that.'

The hand worked harder, fingers splayed out, nails scratching a little while Sean rocked rhythmically, audibly whimpering.

'And then we can't go back to an empty house, because apart from everything else it was empty in the first place, empty from the moment our child went off to university, and never called home once.'

Gillian leaned over and now put both hands on Sean's chest, and stilled his rocking.

'You must not do this to me.' Her voice did not crack, but simply gained in intensity. 'You must not kill yourself. You must go back to the specialist. You must not ruin both our lives.'

'Mother,' said Sean. 'Are you trying to make me feel guilty or something?'

Ten minutes later they were playing knockout whist with the pack of cards that Gillian was carrying in her bag.

Sean was sitting up in bed, with his gown done up again. Oddly, he looked about ten years older, brooding and squinting over his cards (usually he would have had glasses) while his mother, now in a tremendous good humour, looked ten years younger, almost girlish, shrieking with theatrical glee or dismay over her cards, and sometimes outrageously grabbing Sean's hand to see what he had, the occasion of much petulant and tactile dispute between mother and son. With them was the nurse with her hair in the puddingy bun and a nineteen-year-old boy from the next bed whom Gillian, now in her uproarious and garrulous mood, had invited to join them. All four of them were smoking, now apparently heedless of the imagined strictures that caused Gillian to extinguish her cigarette before in the metal bin which had now been dragged over to Sean's bed. The other patients on the ward were either too comatose or indifferent to object to the noise, which had grown considerably since the bun-nurse, an Irishwoman named Bridget, had produced from nowhere a quarter-bottle of gin to mix with some fresh orange juice that Jonathan, the nineteen-year-old boy, had got. The whole occasion was extremely congenial, but Gillian had just told Bridget what Sean did for a living and suddenly, and to Sean's dismay, the conversation turned to what it was like for mothers to discover that their sons were gay. Bridget, it seemed, was in this situation.

'He wasn't going to tell me of course,' she said sagely, scrutinising her cards. 'He wasn't going to "come out" to me and his father. Jesus, he must have thought we were *stupid*.'

Gillian looked archly over at Sean, who reddened, and stared at his cards.

Bridget continued: 'He just went on living at home, treating the place like a hotel, going out every night with a bunch of young lads, going on about bloody Donna Summer and getting his hair cut really too short, dyed the colour of straw – and didn't that look stupid with his dark eyebrows? – and bits of bloody steel through his face and God knows where else. It wouldn't have been so bad but he had the cheek to keep complaining about my cooking. One morning at the breakfast table he put his fork through a bit of slightly underdone bacon I'd got ready for him, held it up and said: "What the hell is *this*?" So I got out a magazine

I'd found under his bed with two men, naked except for leather masks, facing each other, with erections so they look like feckin' Tower Bridge at midday and I says: "Kevin, it's a bit of bloody bacon, now what the hell is *this*?" So he's a bit more bloody civil to me now, though his father still doesn't know.'

Sean was hoping for some urbane detachment from his mother at this point, counting on her to distance herself from the general tone of derision.

But no. She was looking at Bridget very seriously and doing an awful lot of supportive nodding.

'They don't understand, do they?' she said, to Sean's suppressed fury, with a curt little nod at him. 'They will go on about how we don't understand, but *they* don't understand what it means for *us*. Heterosexuality is the foundation of our relationship with our children; they owe their existence to heterosexuality; without heterosexuality they would not be here. They whinge about how we should just accept that they've come out, but how would they like it if their father told them that *he* was "coming out" – do they ever think about that? – and they don't understand how *selfish* it is of them to deny us *grandchildren*.'

Perhaps Gillian was a bit tipsy from their impromptu gin-and-orange cocktail party, or perhaps she only realised halfway through this little speech how absurd her pedantic repetition of the word 'heterosexuality' sounded, or how upsetting it was going to be for Sean, so she tried to carry it off by turning to him with a slightly defiant look. He returned it, and they both sensed that a recurrence of their previous emotional scene was on the cards. But they were interrupted by Jonathan, the nineteen-year-old, who had remained thoughtfully silent throughout this exchange.

'Actually, I don't think the actual act of anal intercourse is all that important any more,' he said.

'*Any more?*' said Gillian. 'Listen to him!'

'I mean to one's gay identity.'

Sean nodded to him cautiously, encouragingly, sensing that here was an ally.

The boy stopped, and gulped, and flushed unbecomingly. Sean realised that he wouldn't have fancied him even if he had been gay. He continued: 'I mean the act itself. It . . .'

Sean helped him out, now feeling marvellously lucid and fully recovered.

'It's only homophobes and the self-loathing idiots who are so hung-up about . . .' He paused, reviewed the various official and Old Testament phrases available to him, and rejected each as too pejorative, too redolent of the magistrates' bench, the National Service exemption assessment, the Book of Leviticus. Why on earth wasn't there a *modern* word for it, free of all that nonsense?

He had lost his thread. 'What I'm saying isn't all that old Gore Vidal stuff about there being homosexual acts but no homosexual people; I'm saying that sexual identity has become displaced, and fractured; displaced from the genital act,' (Bridget frowned and tutted) 'and displaced from a societal sense of repression, displaced from its own comforting sense of alienation, even driven down from the moral high ground of victim status.' He stopped; reached for the gin-and-orange, started again. 'Now, the experience of being gay is an experience of *Diaspora*: an expulsion, a sense that what it means to be a homosexual emotionally, physically, and socially is up for grabs. Which is why . . .' he took a breath '. . . is why that when I say I am *gay*, it does not mean, it *cannot* mean, what it used to mean.'

Bridget leaned forward, gesturing towards him with the hand in which she was holding her glass, the index finger pointing at him, and with the middle holding in position a cigarette which bore the lipstick's trace. 'Either you're a poove or you're not,' she said sagely.

Gillian gave a tiny laugh, like a light snort or a cough, then looked sharply at Sean. His face had resumed its pallor of an hour ago, and for him the straight lines of the ward had begun to drift, shift, settle and flicker like the Lido's lanes in their shimmering blue habitat. The electric-blue smoke from Bridget's cigarette fanned and thinned and dissipated just inches from his face and he curiously watched it withdraw and disseminate its smoky presence into the flat air. Sean leaned over and looked at the floor, a little dizzy, caught the faintest chloriney swimming-pool smell from the backs of his hands, and for a moment imagined himself at the showers at the Lido, his palms up against the tiles, head drooping, taking the shower point blank on the back of his head, hair flicked forward into tiny liquid dreadlocks, spattering droplet ropes grouping circularly around his feet. He blinked and held his eyes shut long enough to review the retinal residue of darkness, of the heavy gloop of lungs filling with water.

Bridget and Jonathan said nothing, but Gillian collected up her bag, her cards, her overcoat, and prepared to drive Sean home to his flat.

7

When Sean next came into the *Somdomite* offices – a two-floor walk-up in a new purpose-built block in the Pentonville Road – it was to a warm and almost motherly reception from his staff: two young women, a young 'intern' from Salt Lake City and his deputy, the fat and slow-moving Alan. He had been away for two weeks, at Gillian's iron insistence, and everyone knew the reason.

Sean had somehow not been able to prevent himself developing various invalid mannerisms over the past fortnight: a certain timidity in his gait, a way of keeping his spectacles on, even when he did not need them, allowing them to slide down the bridge of his nose, and then wrinkling it to keep them up with a toothy, Bugs Bunny expression. It was partly to rid himself of these that he had come into the office today, although his presence was not strictly needed.

His staff were indeed solicitous, and greeted him in an absurd line at the door, in a way that reminded Sean disturbingly of the final scene of *Kind Hearts and Coronets*. They cared about him. They were worried about him.

But there was another, specific reason for their nervy attentiveness. One of them was going to have to tell Sean that while he had been away, a rival American group had launched a radical, conservative gay journal which could not be anything other than a direct competitor to *Somdomite*. Called *C.C.3*, its first issue lay waiting on Sean's desk as he was being ushered into the building. Unlike *Somdomite*, it evidently could afford full-colour photographs, and on the cover it sported a picture of Michel Foucault, apparently at some kind of nightclub in 1960s' Paris, with a drink and cigarette in one hand, and with his left arm around the French actress Simone Signoret. The legend ran: MICHEL FOUCAULT'S SECRET VICE.

As Sean came into the main office, took off his jacket and placed it on the hook by the door, it was Alan who, in his maladroit way, took it upon himself to alert Sean to the existence of this interloper, gesturing feebly at it. Sean said nothing. He simply eased himself into his accustomed seat, booted up his computer and opened up the journal's website: www.somdomite.com and then placed his own palmtop computer, open, at a pleasing angle to it, and to the mobile phone he had also placed on the desk.

Then, and only then, did Sean condescend to turn over the pages of *C.C.3*, which, like *Somdomite*, was the provocative mix of arguments for a bourgeois assimilation into, and duplication of, the heterosexual world, and a disconcerting undercurrent of opinion that gay identity was something which could not, in fact, be said, properly, to exist. Sean pored impassively over each article in turn, a process which took about three minutes, and then turned back to the front and gazed at Simone Signoret. His staff waited for some weighty assessment, some groan of dismay, some explosion of anger with them for not having forestalled this in some way.

It was not forthcoming. Sean's reticence filled his staff with the most profound sense of disquiet. Alan gave the three of them a discreet nod, as if to say that they should busy themselves in the normal way, and he would bring it up with the editor over lunch – habitually, a Diet Coke and ham and smoked cheese bap. Alan knew that unless the traumatic swimming pool episode had radically changed his personality, it could not be long before a display of ill temper would erupt from Sean, with whom his professional relationship was uneasy at the best of times.

But Sean's mind was not on the job. He could not concentrate on the upcoming turf war with *C.C.3*, and the imminent bloody contest for the hearts and minds of those various intellectuals, bachelors, university lecturers and journalists for whom the need to reconcile gay sexuality with conservative politics was a live-wire issue. He was not gearing himself up for the fray. He was not preparing for the radio phone-ins, the performances on TV panel discussion programmes, the arch, 800-word appearances on the comment page of the *Harbinger*. The armour lay unregarded in the corner.

Sean was thinking about Catherine and how beautiful she was. It was a weakness that he simultaneously indulged with wanton excess, and despised in himself with Spartan severity. Already he had laid on top of *C.C.3* and the various research papers and learned journals that cluttered his desk, the current copy of the glossy magazine *Smart* in which Catherine had been identified, in the context of a whimsical and mischievous list, as one of London's top twenty 'smartest' young people, an announcement which ignited in him an assembly of emotions amongst which hysterical jealousy, chest-busting pride and swooning adoration came only slightly behind pique at not being included himself. Sean had been nursing a poignant little hurt that Catherine had not contacted him since the Lido affair, and he was brooding about whether to call her. But how? Wasn't it up to *her* to get in touch with *him*, merely to see if he was all right? Nick and Ysenda and Wayne had all got in touch – Ysenda three or four times – everyone but Catherine. There again, despite the slight, the *insult*, implied there, his poor heart leapt like a salmon. Perhaps Catherine's silence was emphatically significant. By not ringing him up, was she not shouting her love from the very rooftops? Was she not signalling that she was actually *afraid* to contact him, afraid of the Niagara of passionate emotion that such contact would unleash, and afraid that Sean might (huh!) not be all that interested?

Sean looked again at her photograph in the magazine. Catherine was turned slightly sideways on to the camera, a trellis of wispy hair adorably obscuring her right eye. The effect of this – apart from making Sean clench and unclench his fists and clasp the material of his trousers into tight little bunches under the desk – was not coquettish, nothing so trite, but sly in an artless and innocent way and it made Catherine's face a little less broad and diminished its trace of girlish chubbiness. These were qualities that Sean cherished, and he bitterly resented the impertinence of the photographer and picture editor, who, with their soulless professionalism, their philistinism of the heart, had presumed to *notice* these things about Catherine and to *expunge* them.

Sean became aware that the American 'intern' from Salt Lake City was looking up at him from his proof-checking duties, evidently in some alarm. Sean realised that he had been mouthing what he had been thinking, and had said the words 'expunge them' quite audibly. He smiled weakly, aware that the day's first rivulet of cold sweat had materialised, defying gravity to travel *uphill* from the crown of head and over, down towards his forehead. He looked down, and it fell like a teardrop.

Catherine. Her photograph had also failed to represent the freckles on and either side of her nose, but here Sean felt, in all fairness – although this was a consideration he was deeply reluctant to extend to somebody for whom Catherine had agreed to pose for *photographs* – that he should not rage impotently at the magazine for what might have been another vulgar desecration. With fanatical attention to detail, he had also noticed that there were some tawny *highlights* in her hair when the picture had been taken, a detail with which by dint of elaborately casual inquiries made to Ysenda he had been able to fix the timing of the photographs at about late November, a wintry time at which her freckles, like hedgehogs or flowers, would have hibernated beneath her snowy skin.

Sean looked up nervously at his 'intern' from Salt Lake City, in case he had been shouting any of the hibernating-beneath-the-snowy-skin stuff. Nope. 'Intern' still peering down at the proofs, with a tubby blue pencil in his hand.

Good boy.

The time had drawn nigh when Sean was going to have to abandon his adolescent pride and call *her*. He picked up the phone and went into the well-worn, little-loved routine of dialling six numbers out of the seven, waiting in agony over the last one, and then hanging up violently enough to attract more attention from the 'intern'.

Shit. He folded away *C.C.3* and *Somdomite* and *Smart*, placed them to one side of his desk, and produced his mobile phone in the hope that its differing shape and keypad configuration would dislodge his telephone block. Sean weighed the phone experimentally in his left hand, and allowed his right to play sportively, ruminatively, over the surface of the keypad, like a fly-fisherman. Just phone her up, for heaven's sake!

He laid the phone down on the desk. He decided that he had not done enough work on his answering machine message. He decided, with statesmanlike caution, that without sufficiently exhaustive rehearsal of this speech, he was, as they say, going naked into the conference chamber of relationships.

Basically, Sean had two versions ready for transmission. One was the brutally casual 'Hi-this-is-Sean-talk-to-ya-soon-bye', delivered with maximum speed, casualness, who-cares attitude and hefty receiver-down. Sean had practised it for about forty-five minutes the previous night, and got it down to about 4.5 seconds. His personal best for this approach was actually 3 seconds, but it sounded quite unintelligible, in fact it sounded as if some perfect stranger was shouting something abusive into your answering machine and having a stroke at the same time. The point was to sound intriguingly cool, but not so brutally, terrifyingly indifferent that Catherine would be too overawed ever to call you.

Tricky. The other approach was to go completely in the opposite direction, and to enunciate a painstakingly clear introduction in an elaborately clear voice, with a long and protracted preamble to the main message, something which had one purpose and one purpose alone – to give the addressee ample time to pick up the phone. (Obviously it was not acceptable to call up and say: 'Hi. (Pause) It's me. (Pause) Pick up. (Pause) Pick up the phone for *Christ's sake, I'm so inadequate.*') This approach – with its option of moving smoothly on to the message in hand – gave the caller a get-out clause, a way of appearing not to mind, indeed not to notice, whether or not his call was being humiliatingly screened, assessed and spurned.

So what does he do? Sean had done a fair bit of work on Approach Number Two, developing a winning and yet non-committal technique, in which he exaggerated the importance of Catherine getting Nick involved in 'massaging' him back to life. This he refined and planed down like a master craftsman, only feeling able, at 1:30a.m., to phone his own answering machine from his mobile and practise his message and review the results. At 2:40a.m., he popped out to the phone box round the corner, finally to judge the message from a landline.

Hi, Catherine, it's me, Sean. I'm not drowning any more, (little laugh) how are you? I'm on 263 3731. Call me.

The little laugh had been a big logistical problem. He had to prevent it from sounding as if somebody had just jabbed him in the ribs, or as if in the middle of a charmingly yet broodingly romantic message, he was suddenly moved to do a shrill and effeminate impression of Joyce Grenfell. He had to make it sound toughly ironic and yet adorably vulnerable. Was this a winner or what?

Once again, Sean dialled six numbers, paused, gulped, smashed the phone down and tutted. This was the moment at which Alan, heavy, stupid, *irritating* Alan, found it necessary to lumber over to Sean with some hard copy. Alan was undistinguished of face and had the kind of sagging, portly stomach that can be carried off with sufficient height and a double-breasted suit. Alan was short and wore a cardigan. The copy was a series of testimonies – in the article they would be called 'emotional depositions' – from American gays about their first *significant* sexual experiences. Diffidently, he placed them on the corner of Sean's desk. Despite being only in his early thirties, Alan exhibited the signs of extreme mental debility associated with advanced age. These manifested themselves largely in the symptoms of a heavy cold that Alan had had continuously since the age of eleven. His nose, his great red conk, was no stranger to the Vicks inhaler, indeed was on terms of uxorious intimacy with it. His desk was awash with packets of Lemsip which he added to hot water and slurped noisily throughout the day, not scrupling to let it fall in warm sticky quantities into the crevices of his computer keyboard. His cardigan pockets bulged with Strepsils. Alan's supremely exasperating presence made Sean draw back his lips from his teeth and pant with dislike, like a thirsty dog on a hot day.

'Sean,' snuffled Alan. 'I'm afraid our *friend* is back.'

Oh my God, groaned Sean internally. This was all he needed. Apart from everything else, Sean had recently acquired a stalker. A strange, beefy, hairy middle-aged American who was always hanging around the office and lurking near the flat. Sometimes he called Sean at home, and Sean panicked and hung up. Who was this man? Why was he obsessed with Sean? Did he have a manky flat of his own somewhere, converted into a creepy shrine with candles, and thousands of photographs of Sean, clipped from newspapers and magazines?

It was possible. The lowest grade of celebrity had stalkers nowadays. Local newsreaders, stand-up comedians, people who demonstrate makeovers in department stores – they all had stalkers. Even stalkers had stalkers, unable to go about their business of harassing and scaring celebrities without being bombarded with dozens of menacing phone calls a day, an irritating distraction when you're knocking out another 125-page letter to Trevor McDonald, saying that you love him, but he must die.

Or was this guy some sort of *bailiff*, some hideous, implacable creditor? God knows, *Somdomite* was in awful financial straits.

Sean couldn't go on like this. He was clearly having some sort of breakdown. Just at the moment, his thoughts of Catherine, however rapturous, weren't making him feel very sexual. His ears were beginning to hum with pain and his migraine-meteorology was clouding and darkening. He'd have to walk around nude in the Antarctic for a couple of hours to get his penis any smaller than it was now.

A breakdown. Something about that thought pleased him, and calmed him. Quite without thinking about it, Sean leaned forward, and caressed his computer terminal monitor; he cupped and fondled its heavy, curvy, semi-transparent shape. Hmmm. Felt good. He had got into the habit of doing this before his swimming pool episode, and if caught doing it usually managed to carry it off as some kind of absent-minded, abstracted habit. For some time, now, Sean had suspected that his real habitat was the office, not the home. Nothing excited his contempt more than reading about 'sick building syndrome'. Sean suspected that he *loved* the office; he derived physical pleasure from its warped and rancid environment. Some people said that no one died wishing they'd spent more time at the office. As far as Sean was concerned, that was rubbish. On *his* death-bed, his grizzled old face would undoubtedly crease with terrible rage and regret that he had frittered away precious time on, say, having sex on the beach in the Caribbean, or getting to know his grandchildren – when he could have been reorganising his filing cabinet or walking back and forth to the water-cooler. The office was rational and efficient; it was intelligible. It was designed for him to be in. Not like his flat, an irrational higgledy-piggledy affair of chairs, tables and television sets separately bought, and placed in a series of mean-minded 'rooms' notionally differentiated from each other with a series of chipboard partitions.

The office was all sussed out, and Sean was a connoisseur of its sensory pleasures. Many was the time he had allowed a heavy-laden Tippex brush to linger at his nostrils, and mentally swooned at the lance of purple highlighter, flecks of biro ink winking at its brim. It was a rum old day when Sean did not casually stop by the stationery cupboard and unscrew a phial of Pritt, the non-sticky sticky stuff, and delicately, thoughtfully transfer some of the malleable, quasi-vegetable matter from its protuberant knob on to his fingertips and roll it into tiny strips and balls. He did not share his colleagues' mystification at the symbols that would light up on his photocopier indicating one of its many reasons for refusing to co-operate. He was steeped in photocopier culture, in Xerox lore. Sean would be there well ahead of the engineer with a plastic bottle of toner, the fine black powder which he delighted to decant into one of the machine's unlocatable drawers. The Xerox's faint hum reverberated in his blood, and the flash and sweep of its reproductive mechanism was a treasured stimulus. Sean could hear it now, somewhere in the background, like windscreen wipers.

Right. He would *delay* the phoning Catherine thing. He would make a tactical, if hasty, retreat from that front and regroup. The next advance there would have to wait until lunch-time. He felt a kettledrum roll of nausea and disorientation – the warning signal, according to his specialist, for a homeward retreat – but manfully waited for its thunder to recede over the flashing horizon.

He bent his energies towards the American gays' emotional depositions. Quickly, he flicked through the pile. Boys' clubs, summer camps, intimate brotherly walks in the fields, the euphoric embrace in the locker-room, the bedside visit in the sick-room. Is there some deadpan mid-American *genre* that all American same-sex encounters have to go into?

Sean knew very well that he was expected to contribute a testimony of his own: his own, very English account, and so provide the minor chords and grace notes of self-reference and irony that were missing in these American tales of buttery-haired, golden-skinned young men bending over and getting their first epiphany.

But could he do this? Sean rather feared not. He had never had a gay experience. His first sexual experience, like the rest of them, had been with a woman: the twenty-eight-year-old classics teacher at his school. It sounded fantastic when he said it like that, and indeed it had been an absolute show-stopper of an anecdote on the rare, late-night occasions on which he had regaled his friends with it. Wayne in particular had thought it was absolutely marvellous, but Ysenda had jeered, pouted, thought it was 'stupid' and been, finally, furious with both of them for becoming so gigglingly hysterical.

What had happened was that when he was fifteen, Sean had played a walk-on part in a grotesquely awful production of Shaw's *Caesar and Cleopatra*. His costume, mortifyingly, was a sort of cross between a mini-toga and the kind of Roman centurion's uniform that extras wore in films. Every night, about one hour before 'curtain up' at 7:30p.m., he was expected to apply a gungey brownish body-make up to his face, his arms and his legs. Normally this would happen in one of the dressing rooms behind the stage, but these would sometimes be too full, and so some of the cast principals would be required to come around the corner to the girls' gymnasium, just next to the cupboard in which the fencing foils were kept. Usually there would be three or four people there, dotted around the walls, having their body make-up briskly applied, generally by other members of the cast, already in full costume. On one evening, however, the last night, he had been directed into the gymnasium to find that he was the only actor there, and that the person waiting to apply his body make-up was Mrs Kenny, the classics mistress whose contribution to the production had thus far been confined to attending the dress rehearsal and making acidly uncomplimentary remarks afterwards, the majority of which, Sean remembered, had been directed at himself. But it seemed that she personally was to apply his body make-up this evening, an imposition on her time and social status she registered with an air of impatience and severity that could hardly be missed. Sean stood straight up against the parallel bars while she curtly and wordlessly applied the make-up to his face, and the rudimentary eyeliner was drawn with a casual brusqueness that made his eyes water. Then she said: 'arms' and Sean had to hold his arms out straight in a cruciform position while this was smeared on. After that, she said:'legs' and Sean dropped his arms, and spread his legs slightly apart, although it had not in fact been necessary at this stage before now. Mrs Kenny smoothed make-up on his shins, calves, and thighs. Her application went further up his thighs than the limit of his preposterous skirt – a perfectly acceptable precaution, of course, as from the auditorium a visible 'line' would have been absurd. Sean stared straight ahead and reddened under his pancake layer while Mrs Kenny's long fingers massaged make-up into the tops of his thighs like suntan oil. After some minutes of this, time stood still. Sean forgot about how far away his first entrance was. Mrs Kenny's fingers snaked around the back of the legs and foraged at the limit of his buttocks. He hardly dared look down to see exactly what expression was on Mrs Kenny's face. He was sure that it would be some kind of vexation, and indeed he was quite right. Sean concentrated on the trampoline at the far end of the gym, and felt the cold metal of Mrs Kenny's wedding ring on his right hip. Then, after some more minutes, she cupped his penis with both hands and held it perfectly still. Then, after about twenty seconds (it could have been years, for all Sean knew by then) she let go with a tiny 'mmmmm' sound, and walked out.

That was it. Apart from the fact that he was late for his first entrance, could not remember any of his lines, and was personally reprimanded by the headmaster the next day. Sean had tried re-casting it as an encounter with a male teacher, perhaps in the swimming pool changing room. But somehow this involved a completely wayward *generic* shift, the heavy, gloomy weather of sexual abuse. Sean had also tried shifting it back to the school play format and trying for something with Antony and Caesar, and still it wasn't right, now it was overlaid with Rupert Everett, public school stuff, all homoerotic *victor ludorum* Browning Version sodomy – it just wasn't the right style. Just what, in the name of God, *was* the right style?

Despairingly, he put the file aside and called up the latest version of the e-mail to Catherine that he had been working on obsessively over the past thirty-six hours, a text now so delicately nuanced that in Sean's eyes it made *The Golden Bowl* look like an episode of *Are You Being Served?* Just reading the opening line induced in him a nauseous anxiety attack, and he was forced to resort to his own private, and deeply dysfunctional, manner of allaying the symptoms – it was another of his sick building syndrome things. He would have to stand by the air-conditioning vent, breathe in deeply and imagine that he was thereby ingesting fatal spores of Legionnaire's Disease. On a good half-dozen occasions, this had done him an absolute power of good. Who knew why? About a month ago, Sean read of tiny motes of poisonous matter emanating from the backs of computer terminals and, under the pretext of recovering a yellow brick of Post-it notes from behind his desk, got his nose up against the small grille where the terminal was plugged in, and had a covert sniff – in which position he was discovered by his mother, whom he had quite forgotten was coming to take him to lunch.

It did not seem right to ingest that stimulant this morning, with the office so keenly on the lookout for signs of aberrant behaviour from him, the invalid. So he strolled frowningly over to the vent, knelt down, and untied and retied his shoelaces repeatedly, breathing deeply the while, his nostrils flaring. He looked up and saw Alan approaching, holding a length of computer print-out. It was difficult to tell if this was just another of Alan's tiresome look-busy ploys or if he really was going to have to talk to him about something. Time to get back to his desk. Puffing a little, and aware that he looked pale and dizzy from all the getting up and kneeling down and standing up and walking around, Sean made it back to his phone and checked the remote answering machine facility at his flat, merely for something to do. Any messages would of course be far more likely to be on his mobile's voice-mail, and his terminal would also alert him to a message there with three of the violin screeches from the soundtrack of *Psycho* that Nick had downloaded and put on to his office computer. But nevertheless Sean idly called his home number, heard his voice begin its message of desolation and then pressed the digit 1 three times, in order to activate any recordings. He expected nothing at all, and so was electrified to hear the rhythmic *be-doop, be-doop* that meant the tape was actually winding something back. The sound virtually caused his heart to stop beating. But what if it was just his mother?

It was Wayne. *Sean, it's me. Do you want to go see Nick's band next Tuesday? If you do, Ysenda said she might want to come as well.*

There was an odd pause.

With some people. I don't know. What do you think?

Pause again.

Call me, bye.

Three beeps, end of final message.

What the hell was that all about? Other people? Did Wayne mean that Catherine wanted to go as well? In which case, why did he not just say so out loud? Who else would Ysenda want to bring? Why did Wayne sound so shifty?

That really had torn it. There was no way he was going to be able to give his mind to the long think piece that Alan wanted him to commission on the inheritance rights for the adopted children of gay couples, as legally constituted in Chile, Paraguay and Western Australia. His concentration was all shot to hell. He was all over the place. Savagely he twisted ninety degrees in his swivel chair and looked out of the window on to the Pentonville Road.

The glass in his building was tinted to keep out the unbearable summer glare, a fact he would often forget and momentarily wonder at the weather's apparent capricious turn to gloom, or the possibility that it was later than he thought. The fact that the chill of the air con was always more detectable made this melancholy illusion more credible, and in this permanent dusk, this darkness-at-morning-noon-and-night, Sean would often just watch the immobile line of cars hunched stoically in a military column on the stagnant Limpopo of the Pentonville Road, past the prison – that Dracula's castle that none of the North London villagers could look directly at – past the Scala with its smutty all-nighters, past the second-hand jazz record shop with the Mole logo, the strange stench of boredom, and the Blue Note record sleeves in the window, bleached almost white by the sun and all but peeling like old paint, past the sinister 'Fish Bar' which sold chips that seemed to be made out of cre-osote, and whose hopes for passing trade took a terrible knock from the tramp who habitually stood outside shouting and drenching his trousers. This was the river, the great tributary of North London sadness that led to the sea of pain: King's Cross. Perhaps, in some ancient former life, some London sovereign, some leering cockney monarch, had been crucified here by Celts or Visigoths or Germans or Koreans and his bad karma lingered on, was obscurely inscribed in the design of the food courts of King's Cross and Euston, was encoded in some occult form in the sadness of the First Class lounge, and in the men's style/porn magazines carelessly stacked upside down in the W.H. Smith retail outlets.

Every day, Sean came through this manor. Generally he rode the Northern Line, the carriage pushing a hot shaft of halitosis across the platforms of Tufnell Park and Kentish Town. Or sometimes he availed himself of a minicab on the *Somdomite* budget. Mostly though he would generally linger at the great confluence of King's Cross. He would pause at the bookstalls, peruse the *Frankfurter Allgemeine Zeitung* and a representative selection from the new Janus erotic imprint for bisexual fiction, a series of paperback novels with their distinctive black and gold spines and soft core covers: this morning he had flicked through the opening chapters of *Contraflow*, *Both Ways*, and *Vivien Is My Darling*. Then occasionally he might stop by the Pleasure Palace, a video arcade. Places like these alienated Sean now, and pained him as well, because he had been such a fan of the post-Space Invader games he played when he was twelve: Galaxian Invaders, Missile Command. Modern games, with their naturalist representations of violent kung-fu contests and football matches were supposedly such an advance on these earlier games that asking these emporia if they had a Defender machine would be like asking to play Nine Men's Morris or Shove Ha'penny. To Sean they seemed like the crudest and most displeasing regression. And anyway, they had made him feel very unwell this morning, and the naked Princess Xena from the Sex Kombat machine (each three-minute game: £5) had reminded him too much of Catherine.

Now he really *was* going to send this e-mail to her. With a *tsk* of vexation he swivelled around from the Pentonville panorama and called it up on the screen. To his dismay, he realised it was virtually a word-for-word transcription of his proposed phone message:

```
Hi Catherine: You'll be relieved to hear
that I am now not drowning, not waving,
in fact not doing anything much, in fact
pretty bored. How are you? Sean.
```

So he couldn't really do both. It would have to be one or the other: e-mail or phone. He decided on the e-mail as the more non-threatening medium, and his mouse paused timidly over the Send box. He clicked, and watched the grey bar sweep from left to right, closing off other avenues of decision, of progression. Now there was nothing to do but wait.

Sighing, he went back over his sexual deposition and a toxic shower of pale stars obscured his vision for a moment, just as a metallic taste of nausea surfaced briefly in his throat. He suppressed it, then jumped as he realised that Alan was just by his chair, snufflingly leaning over to talk to him.

'Sean, have a word?'

'Yes, Alan. What?'

'Fancy grabbing a sandwich? Then I thought we'd have a chat about that big profile of Sir Frederick Ashton.'

'Oh. Oh yes.' Sean looked at the top right-hand corner of his palmtop which told him it was 12:50. He really didn't want to watch Alan brood over a choice of orange and mango juice and avocado mousse in a sesame seed bap while discharging his sinuses into a Handy Andy. It was a downer.

'Alan, could you be a real mate and pick something up for me, and bring it back?'

'Of course, Sean, of *course*,' frowned Alan. 'I just thought the walk might be good for you, of *course* I'll get your lunch.'

It was only when the office was empty at one o'clock that

Sean felt he could telephone Wayne and press him on what he meant by his enigmatic references to Ysenda, and who she was and was not bringing to Nick's concert. He dialled his mobile, and Wayne quite oddly answered straight away. He sounded strained and, for some reason, strangely guilty.

'Sean, how are you, matey, and how are things in the post-poove socio-political world?'

8

Naturally, Wayne answered his mobile straight away, as it was just by the bed. He sounded strained and, for a very obvious reason, guilty.

'Sean, how are you, matey, and how are things in the post-poove socio-political world?'

At the word 'Sean', Catherine rolled over sharply in bed and hoisted herself up on one elbow. The submerged sense of guilt that sex in the day induced in her came up for air at 'Sean'. The mention of Sean made her feel guilty, though she couldn't say why.

Wayne was wrigglingly getting himself up the bed, in order to sit halfway upright, the mobile in one hand, and with the other giving the fat and fuming joint to the expressionless Catherine. He was listening.

'Ysenda? Yes, I think she wants to come, yes.'

There was a pause, while Wayne's glance flicked sideways to Catherine.

'Yes, I – yes, Catherine wants to come. I think. I guess. I mean – we'll all go. I don't know.'

Another pause.

'I'm, I'm at home. Where are you? You *are*? I thought no way were you supposed to go back in there so early. Sean, listen, you're breaking up.'

Wayne bit his lip and blushed at his transparent and palpable lie.

'Look, Sean, you're break— You're break— I'll talk to you— Bye.'

He clicked off, slapped the phone down too hard on Catherine's little bedside table and snuggled down again.

'Sean. He's back at work. He sounds pretty well OK.'

Catherine did not snuggle, but stayed soberly upright.

'I should have got in touch by now. Are you sure he's all right?'

Wayne was not sure, in fact if anything he was pretty sure of the opposite. But he did not care to dispel the pleasant post-coital torpor with this difficult and disagreeable subject.

Earlier that morning, Wayne and Catherine – that same Catherine concerning whom Sean had been spilling out his romantic hopes and fears – had had sex at her flat. Neither of them had planned it that way. But they had got on so very well at the Lido the other day, before Sean's great crisis, and one of the things they had talked about was the TV comedy that Wayne had been involved in, a sketch show called *Laugh Track*. Wayne had promised to show her a VHS copy of the pilot programme, and after a series of rather coy telephone conversations, he had archly proposed to bring the video round to Catherine's flat on Monday morning, a day which her enlightened employers had allowed her away from the office as part of her ration of American-style 'personal days'. He had arrived at half-past eleven, bearing the videotape. She buzzed him in and greeted him at the flat door. Their faces had loomed uncomfortably towards each other, unsure whether the cheek-kiss allowance was two, one or zero. She was wearing a dazzlingly white and vaguely diaphanous T-shirt and wasp-striped leggings, her hair bunched in some sort of catch or clasp which made it swoosh out at a zany angle. In answer to her first question he replied that he did indeed want a cup of tea, and she retreated into her kitchenette area, and Wayne, with what he considered to be a charmingly presumptuous air, instantly treated the place as his own, located the VCR, brusquely ejected the new BBC adaptation of *Mansfield Park,* and inserted his own offering. The time-clock was ticking down as Catherine settled down next to Wayne on the sofa, having presented him with his mug.

The first sketch featured Wayne prominently. Five or six Japanese actors, in brown and sweaty army fatigues, were apparently playing Second World War fighter pilots. They were being harangued by a senior officer played by a Chinese actor Catherine vaguely recognised. Amongst the pilots was Wayne, dressed identically to everyone else, though a good foot taller, and with a floppy English RAF haircut. The first cut was a close-up on Wayne's face, which showed his hair had been dyed jet black, and eyes drawn back at the corners to produce the studiedly offensive 'Oriental' effect.

'We, the noble Kamikaze warriors, will smash the American imperialist devils and their warships!' shouted the Chinese actor.

There was a guttural and incomprehensible shout of triumph from the assembled troops in which an enthusiastic English drawl of 'Jolly good!' could be heard from Wayne. Medium-sized studio audience laugh. Watching from the sofa, Wayne mouthed the line along with himself on the screen.

'We,' shouted the actor, 'will crush the American imperialist scum with our Kamikaze fighters!' Another guttural shout, into which Wayne's character intruded an earnest '*Bloody* good show' as the shouting-volume declined, a piece of workmanlike timing which the studio audience had rewarded with a bigger laugh, and Wayne, from his sofa, with a little conductor's-baton approval gesture with his thumb and forefinger pressed together.

'May I ask a question, sir?' drawled the on-screen Wayne gormlessly.

'What?' snapped the officer.

'Well, I'm afraid I've never volunteered for one of these Kamikaze raids before . . . how long do they normally last? You see, I want to get back here by three o'clock afterwards because there's a radio play I want to listen to, and then I'm keen to get a bit of shopping in before they close.'

At this moment, the screen freeze-framed on Wayne's face, which was bisected by two fizzing white lines; it was not immobile, but flickered between two infinitesimal phases of movement, the face caught in a sleepy-lidded moment of half-closed eyes and a thin red strip of tongue caught unflatteringly protruding from the lips.

Wayne turned around to ask why Catherine had stopped the video and walked straight into a kiss.

This was an hour and a quarter ago. Now Wayne could not entirely disguise the dismay he felt at having taken Sean's call, and his annoyance at having left his mobile on in the first place.

'Would you like some lunch?' asked Catherine lightly.

'Sure – right,' assented Wayne.

They both leapt out of Catherine's double bed too quickly, and absurdly, stayed stock still and naked for a moment, before they did a little laugh in unison, and Catherine made for a Chinese dressing gown hanging behind the door, and Wayne wrapped the duvet around his middle and padded behind her to the kitchen.

As she loudly sluiced a vivid green lettuce under the cold tap, and Wayne sat swaddled and jammed in at the table, she enquired: 'Do you remember James?'

'James?'

'James. The guy you and Sean met at the *Somdomite* party at the Ranch.'

'You mean your *boyfriend* James?' said Wayne archly. 'I don't think either of us actually met him, Catherine.'

Catherine insisted: 'He's not my boyfriend; he was never my *boyfriend*; that's such a terrible bloody word.' There was a pause, with more lettuce splashing. She cleared her throat with a tiny *hm* and continued: 'I just wondered if Sean had seen anything of him, that's all.'

Wayne looked shrewdly at his joint, which, in tune with the post-coital mood, had gone out. This was the first time that Wayne had ever had sex with someone so early in the day, and his overwhelming desire was to drift into a deep and contented sleep, at least two feet away from Catherine, or more probably to get back to his own flat. Now that was impossible. Was he going to have to spend the *day* with her? Were they going to proceed immediately to the uncomfortable daytime second date stage with daytime talking and daytime intimacies? He could not suppress a lacerating yawn which extruded deeply unattractive tears from the outer corners of his eyes. What time was it anyway? Just as he was manoeuvring his watch into the surreptitious downward-glance position, Catherine turned around, and her colander began an irregular little drip on the floor.

'Wayne?'

'What?'

'Are you listening? I was thinking about Sean. I am quite worried about him, and I wondered if he had seen anything of James.'

Wayne widened his eyes and pushed his lower lip out, shrugging and shaking his head slightly in the universal 'you've-got-me' fashion. 'No. I don't think so.' This expression was replaced with a puzzled frown. 'Why, should he have?'

'Well, it's because I think James is actually gay, and I was thinking that he and Sean might be really good together. You did say Sean wasn't with anyone, didn't you?'

With a start that Wayne suppressed into his intestines, he now remembered Sean telling him about Catherine's grotesque offer to set him up with James, her rejected suitor. This activated his long-suppressed guilt at having seduced the girl with whom he knew Sean to be deeply and helplessly in love.

'No.'

'No what?'

'No, he's not with anyone. You've got to be joking.'

'Well, d'you think he might like to go out with James?' Catherine brought over two very tasty-looking ham salad sandwiches, prepared as neatly as in a shop. Wayne did not feel particularly hungry, but affected a great interest in the arrival of food.

'Mmm, brilliant,' he said, lunging for the one nearer to him.

At that moment, a little *ping* was heard from the direction of the front room.

'What's that?' asked Wayne.

'It'll be an e-mail for me,' said Catherine vaguely. 'It doesn't matter.'

'Oh no, come on,' said Wayne with an odd decisiveness. 'You must see who it's from, and *answer* it.' He skipped lightly into the front room, and with a sigh Catherine followed him, picking up the plate with the sandwiches on. The atmosphere was beginning to sour.

They walked past the TV, where Wayne's freeze-frame image with the half-closed eyes and poking-out tongue was still shimmering and flickering. Catherine had a big Power Mac with as much computer power as, in 1969, Cape Kennedy had used to guide Apollo 9 safely down to earth. She used it mainly for word-processing, and occasionally logging on to the Net. Its screen was completely dark, except for a tiny figure of Postman Pat, who lurched miserably across the screen under a huge mailbag, occasionally flicking a V-sign at the viewer, or giving the finger with a snarl, or wrenching down his blue serge trousers to show his bottom or wheeling round to give his black and white cat an almighty kick. Every so often a strange strangulated voice would say: 'You have new mail.' Catherine clicked once on her mouse, and her mail window appeared: a long column of icons showing open sheets of paper, with a sealed envelope at the top, denoting an unread message, with the word SEAN.SOMDOM.NET next to it. For different reasons, the hearts of both Catherine and Wayne sank to see it. She clicked twice on the icon and read:

> Hi Catherine: You'll be relieved to hear that I am now not drowning, not waving, in fact not doing anything much, in fact pretty bored. How are you? Sean.

Pretty bored. Wayne could hardly keep himself from snorting at Sean's transparent attempt to be cool about this. Bored, indeed. And yet in the next instant, he again grasped the enormity of his own betrayal, and fell silent.

'Well, this sounds pretty hopeful,' said Catherine after a moment. 'He's cheerful enough to go for a little literary reference.'

Uncomprehending, Wayne gave the breathy sound which came ambiguously and non-committally between a *huh* and a *yes,* which he used when taxi drivers shouted some inaudible question over their shoulder and he wasn't sure if it was racist.

'Are you going to reply?' asked Wayne at last.

'*Yes*. Yes,' said Catherine, as if he had reminded her of something she had forgotten.

She clicked on the Compose icon, selected his address from her Personal Lists, and began to type:

> Dear Sean

Then she changed this to:

```
Sean hi.
```

Then, after a few moments more:

```
Hi Sean, I
```

Then Wayne kissed her again, for a long time, and she was twisted round at an awkward angle in her swivelling chair; she placed her left hand on the side of his cheek and the other, negligently, on the keyboard, which gave a sudden, loud chord – the one that begins The Beatles' 'Hard Day's Night'.

Catherine's lips snapped back from Wayne's.

'Oh *shit*!' she gasped.

She had transmitted the incomplete message. It was folding itself up into an envelope icon, and then Postman Pat came trudging resentfully across the screen, swearing and booting his black and white cat out of the way, coming to get the letter, now folded into a neat rectangle.

'Stop, stop, stop,' hissed Catherine, clicking on it frantically. But no good. Pat swept it into his bag and then trudged off into his little van, which drove off into the distance – graphically suggested by perspective lines – honking, and running over a number of small cartoon children.

'Now what do I do?'

Wayne shrugged, a little petulantly. He knew nothing about computers, and the secondary kiss moment seemed comprehensively gone. Suddenly he felt really quite exhausted. He walked around the sofa, holding his sandwich and teenagily ignoring Catherine's proffered plate. He flopped down in front of the TV which still showed his flickering, shimmering face. Wayne picked up the video remote, debated for a moment whether to press Play and watch the end of the sketch; then he did indeed press it, but at the same time pressed the button which switched the screen back to the TV mode; the screen reverted to television transmission and there was simultaneously the most almighty explosion, which made both Wayne and Catherine jump.

The screen, which had the 'live' logo flashing in the bottom left-hand corner, showed a rich and verdant landscape, which somehow was made to look parched and undistinguished on screen; the camera wheeled around a little to the right, and rays from what was evidently the late afternoon sun caused picture interference. In the medium distance, a cottage could be seen, with a great hole gouged out of it, evidently by a bomb, and now the roof seemed to tilt over at a crazy angle, about to collapse. It made a strange and jagged silhouette against the gorgeously blue sky. A caption announced that this was Treyarnon Bay, near Padstow, in Cornwall, and the announcer reminded the viewer that this was the latest outrage from the Cornish Separatist Movement, an extremist body which had been radicalised by the failure of the recent devolutionist vote to reach the majority needed to bring in its own assembly: that is, sixty per cent. Now it had taken to blowing up holiday cottages in Cornwall, after informing the live TV channel so that it could cover the event. The cameraman gingerly approached the shattered cottage, along with members of the emergency services, knowing that a secondary detonation was not an impossibility. Quite silently, the picture wobbled up to the front door, which, as if in a horror movie, swung back with an absurd creak to reveal a beautiful, golden-haired thirteen-year-old girl staring back into the camera, quite unscathed by the blast. But *was* she unscathed? Were we about to witness some spectacle of unspeakable mutilation? For a second, the scene cut away from the live outside broadcast, and switched back to the studio, where the two presenters, an avuncular silver-haired man and an attractive woman in her thirties, were quite lost for words. The woman looked down at her notes; the man stared straight ahead, receiving urgent instructions through his earpiece from the gallery. After this silence, the coverage cut straight back to the live scene without a word from these two, and the cameraman and reporter had evidently summoned up the courage and the presence of mind to enter the building, despite the angry shouts of the emergency personnel that they had no business doing anything of the kind. The girl was standing in the middle of a blackened, charred pit in the middle of what was the sitting room, there being nothing resembling a hall in these cottages. This seemed to be the epicentre of the blast, and the girl had been standing right in it – or at any rate right *by* it. How on earth had she survived?

'You have to come out of there, love,' called out the strong, competent voice of a fireman. 'That is an unsafe structure. You have to come out.'

'No, I'm all right. I'm all right,' said the girl with a strange, spectral serenity. 'I *saw*.'

'What did you see, love?' called out the fireman after a tense, baffled pause. 'You've got to come out. Is there anyone else in there? You've got to come out.'

'I saw her; she was *here*. And she picked up the baby and made her all right; she's all right now.'

The camera followed her tiny pointing forefinger towards an old-fashioned wooden cot. Its edges had apparently been singed, and it was possible to see a tiny yellow tongue of flame just tickling at the edge of the worn mat on which the cot rested. The sound of a child's crying came from the cot, interspersed with a high, wheezing, yelping sound. The steadicam came over and attempted to look down into the cot's great yawning mouth, decked about with fleecy blue woollen blankets. But here the picture cut suddenly to the chromatic key: strips of vivid headachey colour running down the screen and an ear-splitting high signal which lasted for some seconds, and which seemed to continue and refine the child's distress. They had lost the transmission.

Catherine was transfixed by this news, and gazed raptly at the scene, but Wayne somehow could not concentrate. For the past few minutes, he had become transfixed by the LCD video counter which ticked round as the unwatched tape played through. He was always like this when the arbitrary number reached the date of his birth: 1970. From then on, it was as if a bland machine was briefly ticking off the milestones of his life: it was always the same; he was mesmerised; he could not stop watching. 1974, 1975, 1976 – his sixth birthday party, and earliest memory, knocking over his little beaker of orange squash – 1977, 1978 – his mother dying of pancreatic cancer, funeral, father crying – 1980, 1981 – his first day at secondary school – 1982 – liking first pop record, Spandau Ballet's 'True' – 1983, 1984, 1985 – losing virginity, not enjoying it – 1986, 1987, 1988 – going to university – 1989, 1990, 1991 – drama school – 1992, 1993, 1994 – first TV break, cameo on *The Bill*, as man beating small dog with stick, overpowered by plucky trainee WPC – 1995, 1996, 1997 – snogging Ysenda in the back of the cab, almost having sex with her, 1998, 1999. And then the numbers ticked inscrutably, remorselessly on: 2000, 2001, 2002, 2003, 2004, 2005, 2006, but after 2000 they lost the static charge. They became meaningless again, until 9970 video units later Wayne would be born again. Like Hardy's Tess, he was dimly aware that the date-number of his death must be ticking round on the video counter with a psychic *ting* every time, but could not quite compel his mind to speculate on the number's identity. Wayne's idea of the future failed here utterly, but he dimly thought of his life flashing by in little scenes, his hopes and moods and happiness rising and falling like telegraph wires seen from a train.

'Gosh,' said Catherine quaintly at last.

'Yeah,' said Wayne absently, and then, pulling himself together, '*Yeah*.'

'Mm.'

Now Wayne made no bones about looking at his watch, while Catherine looked back at the screen.

'Catherine, I've – I've got to be getting back. Home.'

She turned around, widening her eyes prettily in dismay and disappointment: 'Oh.'

'Yeah,' he smiled, as if manfully bearing the weight of these terrible impositions on his time. 'So you're coming to Nick's concert with me and Ysenda?'

Catherine frowned, feeling that it was an error of taste for Wayne so readily to mention her sister at this point. But she nodded, a little coolly: 'Yeah, I guess.'

'Sean will be there, I'm sure.'

'Right,' she said blankly, a little upset now that Wayne had not said a single tender thing to her.

Small pause.

'You know,' said Wayne awkwardly, 'I really think that you would get on with Sean.'

'I will. I do,' said Catherine, abruptly, getting seriously irritated that Wayne wished to discuss her relationship with Sean and not her relationship with him.

'Because he really likes you—'

'—yes, I . . . I suppose I liked *him*.' Catherine got up from the sofa, put the TV on mute and stomped crossly off to the kitchen.

Somehow Wayne said: 'I think you and he would be really good friends. You'd be . . . good together.' With the last two words, his voice halved catastrophically in volume.

'Oh well. That's great, isn't it,' Catherine called fiercely over her shoulder as she clattered the plates into the sink.

Wayne could no longer affect to ignore her mood.

'What do you mean?' he wheedled.

'Well, you know, great, marvellous. Your dearest wish is apparently for me to be "good together" with Sean. Like as if I'm some sort of fag hag or something . . .'

'Catherine . . .' Wayne came towards her with palms beseechingly outstretched.

When she was upset, or talking to Ysenda (often the same thing) Catherine started oddly *sounding* like Ysenda: 'Like I'm some sort of inadequate woman without ovaries or secondary sexual characteristics whose main claim to social status is that she can provide TLC to a gay guy, a homosexual, who feels absolutely nothing, absolutely nothing for her . . .' Wayne was about to say something; his tongue affixed itself behind his top row of teeth ready, and Catherine sensed it, pausing expectantly. Nothing happened. There was silence. Then he said, quietly:

'I've got to go.'

Catherine did not ask why, but said simply: 'OK.'

Wayne said: 'Bye' and 'I'll call you' and left, almost without meeting Catherine's eye.

As she heard the clunk of the front door, Catherine, deflated, looked at Sean's wan message on her computer screen. Then she extracted a cigarette and, unlit, tested its papery tobacco texture against her mouth, an old habit. Then she put her lips around the filter.

9

That night, Ysenda had a dream about Sean.

They were in the garden of his mother's house: the house where they played as children. It was a brilliant summer's day and she was hanging upside down from the little climbing frame in the yard, the way they used to when they were young. (Catherine always refused to do it, because she wore a dress which would drop down and show her knickers; the tomboyish Ysenda wore jeans and so didn't care.) Sean himself confessed to her as a child that he was scared of dangling from the frame as he was afraid of dropping on his head on to the frame's concrete base. Ysenda was doing it now; she was dangling with her knees bent over one of the frame's bars – only she was a grown-up; she was the age she was now. She could see the garden and the kitchen window upside down, the way she used to, with the green canopy of the lawn above, and the blue sky beneath her knees, and Sean's old toy trike upside down. Catherine was there, too, peripherally. Sean appeared in front of her, his grown-up face upside down. He was asking her if he could join in the game. *'I want to play it now,'* he said. Sure, she said and Sean came up very close and kissed her lightly on the lips; then in a moment he was dangling beside her. Giggling, they took sidelong looks at each other. Then disaster. Sean lost his grip on the frame and fell up into the concrete overhead. Panic-stricken, Ysenda unslung her legs from the frame, swung the universe around one hundred and eighty degrees to get down and help Sean, half jumping, half falling. Sean had banged his head and bruised his shoulder; Ysenda had skinned her knee. But as she tried to go forward to help him, she felt herself unable to move. She was quite helpless. At this moment, she sensed she was wearing not her tomboyish jeans, but a dress, the sort of dress that Catherine would wear. Now Sean was coming to help *her*. He was limping, but placed his left arm round her neck and his right under her knees. He lifted her up, and again her face was very close to his.

'But you're the one that's hurt,' she said out loud, as she woke up.

The dream was not completely dispelled with her trip to the bathroom. After she had been to the lavatory, Ysenda stood in her faded nightie, looking at her face in the mirror: the night had poked her short hair into spiky little peaks and knots around her unmade-up, morning face. Had her face changed *that* much since she was child, she thought, wonderingly, touching her cheek? What did Sean think of her face? With a stab of shrewd annoyance, she noticed again that her right eye these days did not seem to open quite as wide as the left. With her finger and thumb in a stiff little pincer formation, she pulled at the skin above the upper and lower lid, and then the eye seemed a little more open. Sean's face, it seemed to her – snapping out of it a bit, running the bath – had hardly changed at all. Cutting his hair so short gave it a kind of babyish look.

By the time she had arrived at the Sacred Heart Institute in

Shepherd's Bush, the dream was fading, and by her habitual quitting time of half-past five, it had almost vanished.

Her own working environment here – a cramped rabbit-warren of offices leased from the Church – could not have been more different from the gloomy and joylessly high-minded ambience of *Somdomite*. A half-full bottle of Moët on her desk, together with a box of expensive chocolates, bike-messengered round from Fortnum's, testified to her warm and self-congratulatory good humour in having completed a dashing polemic, intended for the Institute's quarterly journal, denouncing the works of the Human Fertilisation and Embryo Authority. Now, it was the end of the working day, and Ysenda had got on to her mobile phone – it was a professional mannerism of hers to use her mobile a good deal, and not the office-phone, in order to remind her staff of her smart, stylish existence which had simply nothing to do with the office routine around which *their* lives rotated. She was doing this in order to buy drugs.

'Size? Size!' she said loudly, her pupils flickering slightly in disquiet because Father Brendan Sparkbrook entered just at that moment, a kindly and urbane man who was on the managing committee of the Institute. Ysenda correctly divined from his sad smile that he wished to discuss her budget over-run. 'Size!' she continued to banter on the phone.

'Yes, I'm . . .' She swept some paperbacks off one of the chairs so that Father Sparkbrook could sit down.

'. . . I'm good, Size, I'm well, and how are you? Sizey, listen, I've actually got to hang up now and call you back but what it is, I need you to get something *organised* for me again . . . yes, like last Tuesday . . .'

Suddenly Ysenda's face fell, and Father Sparkbrook was genially baffled, as ever, by his editor's abrupt and capricious changes of mood.

'Don't tell me that, Sizewell. Don't tell me that. Oh dear . . . Well, if there *is* anything you could do in that line, I'm sure recompense isn't a problem in the *medium term*. Right. I'm going to talk to you soon.' Ysenda clicked off and gave Father Brendan her most dazzling smile.

'Brendan, how are you? This is rather late in the day for you, isn't it?' Ysenda looked at her watch. It was 5:30p.m.

Sean was supposed to be coming at 5:45. Father Sparkbrook was settling himself down rather comfortably in the chair opposite her. He was holding, as Ysenda feared, a sheet of A4 paper with columns of figures on it, the ones on the bottom having brackets around them. At least he didn't have his *pipe*.

'Ysenda, I've just had this memorandum from the accountants.'

'Uh huh . . .' said Ysenda uncertainly, on a rising note.

'Things don't look – well, they could look healthier.'

'Uh *huh,*' said Ysenda again, this time on a falling note.

'For example, Ysenda,' Father Sparkbrook ventured, nodding at the Fortnum's chocolates, 'did you *really* have to have these brought round here by motorcycle messenger?'

Ysenda went into her most Marilynish my-heart-belongs-to-Father wide-eyed routine; it had worked before, though she knew that it was more ineffective with each outing.

'Oh, but, Father . . . it was just a little *treat*, I figured I *deserved* it. And it's not as though I wasn't going to hand them round to the rest of the staff. I was gonna come to your office and make sure *you* had one.'

Father Sparkbrook broke into the smile he had been suppressing.

'All I'm saying, Ysenda, is that we have to be careful now that we're spending so much money on this Millennium Report that you've talked us all into.'

Ysenda pounced, delighted to be given a change of subject.

'That's gonna be big, Father, that's gonna be *really* big and it's really vital the Institute has a presence there.'

'So you say, Ysenda,' sighed Father Sparkbrook, 'but speaking as one who *has* been there, I can tell you Bethlehem is a *very* small place, and I don't see how it can possibly support a world media circus like this. It's going to be very uncomfortable to say the least, and what about hotels? Have you got that organised yet? Have you at all considered where you're going to stay?'

Ysenda was on the point of making a catastrophically badly judged and irreligious joke, but managed to gulp it back in time.

'And this idea about the cake with the two thousand candles,' he continued with a little more severity, 'that's just out of the question; simply transporting it to Bethlehem would be a logistical *nightmare*.'

'Yes, Father, if you say so,' said Ysenda humbly.

Ysenda sneaked another look at her watch. 5:41. Then her mobile went, and Sean appeared palely in her doorway, two factors which propelled Father Sparkbrook away.

'Well, I shall leave you now, Ysenda. But remember, you will have to come to our board meeting on Thursday.'

'Yes, Father,' said Ysenda as he left, unhappily aware that she had failed to re-establish the usual flirtatious rapport.

Sean entered, and Ysenda felt the strange undertow caused by meeting someone you've just dreamt about, the sense of unacknowledged intimacy. Did Sean somehow know? Did her clothes and make-up radiate *déjà vu*? They embraced, more tentatively than when Sean was picking her up under the climbing frame the previous night, with Ysenda still holding the mobile.

'Hi,' said Sean, adding immediately: 'What's this?'

He was holding up a mini-disk, marked simply 'Filipina Brides'.

'It's – you know. It's Nick's band. They recorded four tracks on that. You can borrow it if you like. I'm pretty sure you can play it on your PowerBook.'

Sean gestured at her computer.

'I want to play it now,' he said, using the phrase for the second time in twenty-four hours, and making Ysenda feel, for an uncanny moment, as if they had both re-entered her dream and that Sean must, at the very least, know something of what had happened. Had he dreamt it too?

But Sean was looking round, having apparently lost interest. 'Catherine not here?' he asked.

'Catherine? She's not coming with me,' said Ysenda blankly. 'I think she's coming with – Sizewell!'

Sean looked up sharply at the idea that Catherine was making an appearance on the arm of Sizewell-B, an unemployed rapper, former 'record producer' but otherwise one of the most notorious drug dealers in West London. The realisation that this was not in fact going to happen did not help; he now saw only too clearly that before the evening began, a lengthy and expensive detour would have to be made via the petrol station forecourt near Sizewell-B's unspeakable flat in Percy Road.

'Size, what's the news?' Ysenda converted her grin into a grimace of apology; she knew what Sean thought about Sizewell-B. 'That's *great*. And are we talking Premiership, Nationwide League or Vauxhall Conf?' Sean had never bothered trying to penetrate the coded jargon of these transactions, made even more baffling by the bizarre voice that Ysenda felt obliged to attempt. 'Yeah *sorted*,' continued Ysenda pedantically, 'and the transfer fee is the usual? A bit of a *Don Revie* there perchance?'

Sean held up his watch in an impatient signal.

'OK. I'll see you at the ground, kick-off in twenty minutes.'

She clicked off.

'Sean – you haven't got about £120 on you, have you?'

In the car, Ysenda was unable to tell Sean why Wayne had given him the impression that Catherine would be coming with her, although she had a shrewd idea that what he wanted was for Ysenda to be a 'beard', to bring Catherine along but give Sean the impression that the two sisters had come together. But if that was the plan, Wayne had obviously forgotten all about it, or characteristically messed it all up. She had guessed about Wayne and Catherine long ago, but the truth about Sean and Catherine had not dawned on her. Like everyone else, Ysenda had taken at face value his editorship of *Somdomite*. She found herself thinking about Sean a lot recently, but it only ever tended to one conclusion: that he was effectively celibate, and that his shyness and sexual incompetence meant that a sexual 'orientation' of any sort was purely notional. So she couldn't understand why Wayne should want to keep his new attachment to Catherine a secret from Sean.

'There he is,' she said.

Sizewell-B's 1982 Ford Fiesta was hunched by the petrol station on the Golborne Road, its hazard lights winking superciliously. Ysenda pulled up in the forecourt opposite and wordlessly reached over for the £120 that Sean had been obliged to extract from a cashpoint on the way out to the car, and then went through the pantomime of slouching into the Star Market and buying a pint of milk and a copy of the *Evening Standard*. Sizewell-B was then hailed on the way out, he waved from his vehicle, and then they both strolled with elaborate casualness back to Ysenda's car, in which Sean had deferentially transferred himself into the back seat, next to bundles of manuscript, part of Ysenda's ongoing psychobiography of Monseigneur Alfred Gilbey, the distinguished Catholic thinker and former Cambridge University chaplain – she had been advised by several agents that many of the sexual speculations would have to be deleted.

'All right, Sean, you *fucker*.'

Thuswise did Sizewell-B cheerfully greet Sean. It was a mystery how he fitted into his Fiesta or into any car, or indeed any normal-sized building. He was the biggest human being that Sean had ever seen in his life. His receding hair was cropped savagely close to his ridged, irregular skull, and one of his pupils bled blackly out into the pale iris as if coloured in by a five-year-old. A nylon football replica shirt testified to Sizewell-B's love of the beautiful game, a shirt which he had customised at home using some kind of crude stencil device:

images of dead bodies being carried off a football ground had superimposed on them the legend: 'Two world wars and one world cup, Heysel, Heysel-o.' It was in fact Sizewell's proud boast that as a beardless fifteen-year-old he had put in a high-spirited appearance on the crumbling terraces of Heysel Stadium for Liverpool's meeting with Juventus in 1985, contributing materially to the highly satisfactory outcome. No Shakespearian actor performed the 'Gentlemen in England now a-bed' speech with more tremulous emotion than that which flooded through Sizewell's voice on the very many occasions on which he could be persuaded to discuss this event. At least twice in Ysenda's car, in exactly the positions they were in now, Sean had had to listen to Sizewell-B's choked-up history lesson on the subject.

'Sean, you *FUCKER*, are you all *FUCKING* right?'

Sizewell-B leaned back and grinningly 'tousled' Sean's hair with only slightly less force and vigour than he would need to wrench his head from his shoulders. Before he met Sizewell, Sean had had some absurd notion about dealers never ingesting their own goods. This clearly did not, repeat not, apply to Sizewell-B, who was now rhythmically punching the inside roof of Ysenda's car, accompanying the in-car stereo entertainment system, and causing Sean to wonder if there were any substances left for *them* to abuse.

'So, Sizey, what are we thinking?'

'Hubba, hubba, hubba, *AAAAARGHHOOOO.*' Sizewell-B leaned his head back and howled like a vet-bound dog. Ysenda smiled indulgently and gently turned the music down a little. There was a pause and Sizewell turned and smiled dreamily: 'I'm thinking about giving you something from Serie A.'

'Mmmm, very exuberant, creative play.'

'And not so much worn out by our long Premiership season.'

'Gotcha.'

'Cheers, then, Ys.'

'See you ultra soon, Size mate.'

Sizewell-B turned and this was the moment Sean dreaded.

'Bye then, Sean, you absolute *ROTTER*.' Sizewell gave him the Eric-and-Ernie too-hard punch on the shoulder which made involuntary tears start from Sean's eyeballs, and heaved himself out of the car, a movement that made the suspension groan and shift, and seemed to cause a sudden decline in air pressure which almost gave him a nosebleed. With impossible speed, Sizewell-B had lumbered off over to the Ford Fiesta and was gone.

It was like a magic trick. Ysenda showed him a bag full of white powder and another one with small brown pills. At no time had Sean seen anything pass between them. Then she gave him £12.75 in cash.

'What's this?' asked Sean.

Ysenda sighed.

'Your *change*.'

'Oh.'

Sean reached over for it and put the coins and bunched cashpoint-fresh note into his pocket; movements which made him wince and gasp with the pain of moving the arm that Sizewell-B had so playfully punched. Sean felt the bruise flood his skin.

'So now where?'

'Wayne and Catherine are supposed to be meeting us at the venue.'

'Wayne and Catherine?' asked Sean.

'They're coming, like, you know *severally*. Independently. Meeting each other there at eight-ish. Eight-thirty-ish. And us.' Ysenda was craning her neck to look backwards while she brought her car into a virile reverse out of the station forecourt, which the engine throatily accompanied with a declamatory muezzin whine, and then they were off again.

The club was in Brook Green: apparently called The Product, it was not what Sean had been expecting. So far from advertising itself, it was simply a doorway between a defunct charity shop and a minicab office which underneath its solemn revolving green light advertised an additional service: cheap international cable telephone calls. They would have missed the innocuous door entirely, had not Wayne and Catherine been hanging about outside. But where were all the crowds, the excitable fans for Nick's band, the Filipina Brides?

As she pulled up, Ysenda selected 'hello' from the lexicon of car horn honks – a tiny, clipped single *beep* accompanied by emphatic cheery wave out towards the pavement, as much as anything to show the other drivers that you are not angry with *them* for any reason. Wayne looked up and smiled; Catherine looked up and did not. Sean, after his usual maladroit fumbling with passenger side door handle for which he was cheerfully called a 'spaz' by Ysenda, exited, and the driver sped off looking for a parking spot.

Wayne uncertainly hung back, while Sean approached Catherine. Almost unendurably, she was wearing a leather jacket, over a T-shirt of a kind of dark, beaten-up grey colour, as if it had been washed many, many times, as though to imitate as closely as possible the colour of the jacket. It was stretched with unapologetic emphasis over her breasts, of which the effect, combined with her sublime prettiness, was a kind of belligerent, militant pulchritude, something to make his heart hurt and stomach contract, as though from some kind of intestinal disorder. She wore jeans as well; these were *very* pale, and tight enough to enact a kind of supererogatory crease or fold at the base of each buttock at an acute angle to the square of the back pockets; it was an effect which Sean resolved to store away mentally and ration out for the upcoming week's fantasies, for which a large box of Kleenex had to be within reach – to absorb the flow of desolate tears . . .

'Sean?'

'Sorry?'

'I said how are you?'

'Fine.' Sean said it too quickly, and Catherine smiled at how obtuse he was being.

'I was wondering if you were all right after you were *taken ill* at the Lido.'

'Oh *yes*.' Sean was infinitesimally annoyed that he had negligently all but forgotten to play the sympathy card, and now he had diminished its potential. 'I'm fine. Now. I'm on the, the mend.'

'I was worried.'

'Is that why you've started speaking in tongues?' said Sean, drolly. He was rallying.

Now it was Catherine's turn to look blank.

'Sorry?'

'This.'

He took out of his pocket some print-out. It read:

```
Sean hi, I leajfv yeieenw.kae9uvu
v;avaeiu
```

Catherine was blank, then smiled. 'Oh *that*. I did that when . . .'

Some unaccountable survival instinct, some residual talent for avoiding crises encoded in Catherine's DNA, told her to go absolutely no further than this into the circumstances in which she sent Sean the puzzling e-mail.

'Oh, that was a *cock-up*.' She smiled.

Sean frowned on: 'Have you been here with Wayne long?'

Catherine hesitated, and then Nick appeared.

'Ta-daaaa!' he said, imitating the trumpet clarion.

He was dressed, absurdly, in a leather jacket, not like a *bomber* jacket, but a leather version of a normal suit jacket, with jeans and a denim shirt with great silvery medallions for buttons and a shoelace tie of the kind cowboys wore. The whole effect was execrable, and unbearably mannered. Was it supposed to be a joke?

'What d'you think?' asked Nick perkily. All four of them

now noticed Inge – they hardly recognised her without her white coat, and without her hair being tied up – she was standing near the door, into which people were beginning to stream, lighting a cigarette.

'Yeah, great, Nick,' said Ysenda, back from parking the car, 'you look *fantastic*, not at all like how Bruce Springsteen would look if he wanted a new career in life assurance. What sort of music is this you're playing anyway?'

'It's *crossover*,' said Nick, miffed.

'Crossover from what?'

'Country and metal,' said Inge, protectively, moving in towards Ysenda, and smiling, but not very pleasantly.

'Country and *metal*?' said Ysenda, animatedly enough for Sean to fear for his £120-worth of stock.

'Yes, well, come on, when does it start?' asked Wayne amiably. 'When does it kick off?'

'Brides'll be on later,' said Nick with a shrug.

'Any other bands up?' inquired Wayne.

'Repeat Prescription just finished their set,' said Inge, 'and we're on after Fuck Du Jour.'

'No, we're on now,' said Nick.

'We're on *before* Fuck Du Jour?'

'Fuck Du Jour *cancelled*.'

'That's so *typical* of Fuck Du Jour. Well, we'd better go and set up.'

Inge grasped Nick's elbow impatiently and all but physically propelled him back through the door. Wayne was still thoughtfully absorbing the unsuspected closeness of the relationship between Inge and Nick, when *Hunter Oratorio*, the hot young talk show host, came up to him! Wayne almost didn't recognise Hunter Oratorio at first, because his blond hair had been cut quite short, and he was wearing a pair of Lennon mirror shades, in which Wayne's incredulous face was moonily reflected.

'Wayne, my man,' said Hunter, condescending to stop, and causing the two girls he was with to pause also.

'Er, Hunter,' said Wayne, mindful of the protocol of almost royal strictness that prevailed in situations like these, namely that when a lesser celebrity meets a greater celebrity for the first time, it is the greater celebrity's prerogative to decide whether the encounter is to be on first-name terms. Anything else is grievous *lèse-majesté,* though even at that moment Wayne was wondering with a twinge if he was really *that* much less of a celebrity than Hunter Oratorio. He had been meaning for some time to acquaint Sean with his new theory of fame. He called this:

The Know/Recognise Fame Matrix

There are basically four gradations of fame, and they can be assessed by gauging your reaction to the people who come up to you at social gatherings:

1. UNKNOWN. People come up to you who you *do know* and *do recognise* – i.e. your friends.

2. BETTER KNOWN. People come up to you who you *do know* but *don't recognise* – distant acquaintances with familiar names but unfamiliar faces, journalists, PR people.

3. FAMOUS. People come up to you who you *don't know* and *don't recognise* – fans.

4. ULTRA-FAMOUS. People come up to you who you *don't know*, but *do recognise* – other famous people.

Of course, Wayne anticipated that, once he had told him about it, Sean would identify the weakness of this approach as a total 'unified field' theory of celebrity. Once one had entered into the fourth category, an ecstatic participation in the celebrity community, was it not possible that one had simply been promoted to the bottom of a higher celebrity league, in which one's celebrity status was so low that it once again constituted membership of the first, shaming 'Unknown' category? And that there was, in fact, an infinite regression of know/recognise four-step stages?

Meanwhile, his actual *conversation* with Hunter seemed to have come to a baffling and embarrassing halt. It was as if merely by checking in with Wayne, Hunter had rendered spurious anything either wished to say to each other. The uncomfortable pause dragged on, and Wayne felt like a plucky St Johns' Ambulance Worker at a Buckingham Palace garden party who could think of nothing to say to Princess Margaret. But was there not something he should be saying to Hunter Oratorio, some gaffe, some unspeakable celebrity omission? Just as Hunter, with a whisper of displeasure, was removing the roll-up from his lips, and beginning to wheel back to his two companions, Wayne remembered what it was – in the nick of time.

'Hunter, man, I *really* like the look of your installation.'

His *installation*. Merely hearing the word brought a smile of pure delight to Hunter's lips, conveying, as it did, a tribute to his new seriousness as an *artist*. Hunter's installation was entitled Close and consisted of no fewer than a hundred and fifty video screens in a bare whitewashed room, half of which showed, in real time, a night's growth of beard on Hunter's mottled cheek, the other half showing, in close-up, Hunter shaving what appeared to be the genitalia of a new-born calf. Certainly his friends and colleagues thought they recognised the location: Hunter's farm near Aylesbury in Buckinghamshire. Hunter had been hoping his installation would be entered for a gigantic millennial exhibition of contemporary art in Zürich, but it had so far failed to ignite the controversy considered necessary for a really important installation. To remedy this, Hunter was rumoured to have wished to replace the seventy-five video images of the calf with seventy-five close-up images of Hunter shaving the genitalia of Jon, the twenty-seven-year-old producer of his TV talk show. He was rumoured to have attempted this on the set of his television programme last Monday evening after that night's show had been taped. However, Jon had not been informed, still less consulted, about his volunteer role in Hunter's new artistic vision and some sort of fracas had ensued, which resulted in Hunter sustaining a black eye – the residue of which Wayne could still see – and Jon's trousers becoming badly torn, and a nasty razor gash running down from his right thigh to his shin. Jon was now understood to have accepted a substantial redundancy settlement.

'Yeah, we've got it on at Earl's Court,' continued Hunter affably, 'and I'm hoping to get it on at the Dome in six months' time.'

Meanwhile, Sean was scrutinising Catherine's face in profile, as she turned, aggravated, to face Ysenda. He had not hitherto appreciated the way in which, in moments of emotion or stress her nose – slightly longer than Ysenda's – would incline infinitesimally downwards, while her chin would incline upwards. But not *all* of her chin. The actual bone would remain stationary, but not the fleshy part under the lower lip. That part would subtly fatten and bulge; it would grow plumper, but not evenly so. The accretion of flesh would accumulate at the top, near the lip, delineating an irregular half-moon in contradistinction to the curvature. In an insane access of rapture and enthusiasm, Sean spent a couple of micro-seconds imagining kissing that chin after a night of lovemaking, a kiss in which the gently collapsing impress of his lips mimicked the softness of that chin, a chin which swelled with the onset of Catherine's tears at his departure. An eviscerating pain instantly played cat's cradle with Sean's intestines, and he converted the doubled-up wince of pain into a cough. As he did so, Catherine launched into a furious attack on Ysenda.

'What on *earth* do you think you're doing being nasty to Nick like that?'

'I wasn't being *nasty* to Nick, don't be so stupid.'

'Of course you were being nasty, that nasty crack about Bruce Springsteen, of *course* you were being nasty.'

'Look— look—' Ysenda cast about briefly for a new line of attack, and defence, 'what the hell's it got to do with you, anyway? I've known Nick longer than you have, we all have, and he doesn't need your facile little defence.'

'He certainly doesn't need you undermining him!'

'Don't be such a bloody little prig and a fucking prat.'

'Oh great; you get to ruin the one evening out I've had in months by calling me names.'

'What do you mean your "one evening out"? You mean you're like, staying in and reading Anthony Trollope all evening and listening to *fucking* Radio Four? You're out every night.'

'Like hell I am. I get a pleasant evening out slightly less often than the appearance of *Comet Fucking Hale-Bopp*.'

'Girls, girls, ladies,' was Wayne's insolent, emollient intervention. 'Why is it that sisters always have to row all the time? And while you're arguing, you might want to know that Sean isn't feeling very well.'

It was true. Sean had been imagining Catherine shouting at *him* like that, perhaps in the course of their first row. Then he had rashly shunted this reverie sideways into an explicitly erotic fantasy in which she was obscenely abusing him, while seated astride him naked. On a desert island. Having first tied him up. The resulting fuse overload had caused him to clamp both hands over his ears, double up into a crouch, and all but topple over sideways on to the pavement like a fully clothed anatomical drawing of a foetus. Wayne, Ysenda and Catherine were exclaiming with dismay while Sean stoutly rallied, and was picking himself up off the ground, trying to give little laughs and shrugs as if this was the most unremarkable thing in the world, though his blood-pressure worsened as Catherine made herself the most concerned of the little trio.

'Are you all right?'

'Are you all right?'

'Sean, are you all right?'

No was the answer. Of course he wasn't all right. He was having some sort of very important breakdown. He had appeared to topple over for no good reason in the street, and people were looking at him with that curious, but eminently uncompassionate glance generally reserved for men being sick on Tube platforms. He was passionately in love with a girl whose only interest in him resided in one thing and one thing alone – that he was homosexual. This really was the love that dared not speak its name.

'I'm absolutely *fine*.''Are you really?'

No was the answer. He was having some sort of early mid-life crisis; his life and career were about to slide into some terrible emotional fissure that he was powerless to do anything about.

'Really, I'm OK, I just felt a bit faint there for a minute, and I think I got jostled or something.'

Nobody present remotely believed this explanation. They stood looking at each other in silence, lips slightly pursed, knowing that Sean was having some sort of relapse, the kind that had almost killed him at the Parliament Hill Lido, and now forcing him to enter a smoky and disagreeable club was the worst idea imaginable. Their thoughtful, subdued silence was also due to the fact that this evening, which had taken such time and energy to organise, was presumably at an end.

'Honestly,' said Sean with weak smile and pallid shrug, 'someone just shoved me.'

But Ysenda was very concerned. She was about to offer to drive Sean back to his flat again, in fact thought this might not be such a bad end to the evening, when a miracle happened, an event which convinced one and all that he really *had* just been shoved. Someone came up and shoved him. Sizewell-B.

'Sean, you *card*, you absolute *card*, you absolute bleeding *knave of hearts*.'

Sizewell gave Sean the kind of playful cuff that King Kong might give Fay Wray after a bit of a row; Sean staggered, while keeping his uneasy grin of greeting, and the others reeled back, shocked by Sizewell's sheer brute size, his shaven, oddly uneven-shaped head, which looked as if it had been extruded upwards from the temple like a clay pot on a wheel, and of course the satanic aspect of the pupil of his left eye.

'I didn't know I'd be seeing you here as well tonight, Sean, you *dark horse*, you absolute fucking *cheval noir*.'

'Are you coming to see the Filipina Brides as well, Sizewell?' Sean managed weakly.

'I always come to The Product of a weekday evening,' was Sizewell-B's vacant and strangely haughty response to *that* question. He then clasped him mightily around the chest and hoisted him an inch off the ground, and rubbed his groin mound against Sean's quailing, convex stomach, with the sensuous, unselfconscious enjoyment of a grizzly bear rubbing its itching back against a tree stump. As Sean's poor head perceptibly flopped back and forth, Sizewell shouted delightedly: 'Sean, you are *just toying with me*! You are just making sport with your poor Sizewell! Let me know if there's anything more I can *do for you* later in the evening. You've got my mobile number. Laters!' Sizewell dropped him, and lumbered off into the club, giving the four of them a view of his Toujours Hillsborough T-shirt.

So they went in as well. Having paid a mightily exorbitant fee at the door, they descended a flight of ruined steps which seemed to splinter and disintegrate even as they came into contact with it. This was not like clubbing. It was more like an old-fashioned rock gig combined with some experimental theatre 'happening'. The stage and audience area were weirdly long and thin, as if designed for something quite different: the housing of rolling stock, for example. Dimly perceptible at one end was a bar, which was adjoined by another which sold horrible-looking food. The noise was fairly unbearable, although they had all known it to be more unbearable than this in other, similar, clubs that they patronised, and it at least had the novelty value of being the work of Nick and his band, who were on stage now, apparently well into their set. Nick was on vocals, a responsibility he was evidently able to discharge by wailing in a virtually unbroken note, which had no very obvious relation to the thumping bass provided by a bearded guitarist with a face misshapen in the classic forceps birth manner, who was almost but not quite short enough to qualify for the title 'dwarf'. There was a drum machine.

Inge's role was as follows. She danced about the stage with the airy insouciance of a young Isadora Duncan, making a wailing noise of her own, which became suddenly and fiercely audible as she passed by the microphone of the near-dwarf bass guitarist, and which changed to a kind of chirrup or yelp when she tripped over the guitar lead.

Her contribution did not stop there. Inge would periodically waft, chirruping and wailing, back to a curious device to the right of the stage, which looked like nothing so much as a Van Der Graaf generator, with two short oscillators, and between which passed a vivid and mesmerically blue electrical charge. Inge waved her wands through this, and instantly the machine gave a unique twanging sound, metallic and yet sweet somehow, like the melancholy *cantabile* of the saw played with a violin bow. Sean recognised this rare instrument: a Theremin.

The other thing that should have impressed itself on the audience was that the band were all quite naked – except for Inge, who wore a modest phallus. This should have *struck* the audience in some way, but apparently did not, or the effect had worn off, because it did not distract them from dancing in a state of the most violent abandon, crushed together, whirling around, windmilling their arms, lashing their legs out into what looked like vicious kung fu kicks, madly crashing into each other. The age-range seemed to be from fourteen to late thirties, all utterly given up to the Dionysiac state which the Filipina Brides evidently induced in them, and tolerant of the physical pain and discomfort which this entailed. The band's biggest fan was clearly Sizewell-B, who was lashing his great body around, with a look in his eyes which Sean provisionally labelled 'vacant' in the absence of a less relative term. Sizewell barged into his fellow revellers; he stomped on their recumbent bodies, and flattened four or five at a time when he favoured the assembled company with one of his habitual stage-dives. And yet the wild mêlée continued quite unaffected: everyone was thrashing around epileptically, with one exception: an older man, lounging by the side of the stage, with long hair and a beard, who simply gazed with an expression of shrewd annoyance at the band. Was he a bouncer? A club employee? He had an oddly similarly dressed friend, who looked irritated with his companion and with the whole set-up.

Sean, Catherine, Wayne and Ysenda lingered at the edge of the dance-area, Sean already feeling intensely ill and profoundly regretting his decision to come. It was quite clear that he was not going to be able to *talk* to Catherine at any stage, indeed, he noticed with some puzzlement and chagrin, she somehow seemed to be always standing next to Wayne, and in such a way that Wayne was standing between him and Catherine. Ysenda was the only person who seemed to be getting into the Filipina Brides' sound – something else that indicated that she had made substantial inroads into the stock that they had just purchased. She swayed and bopped unobtrusively on the spot, before saying to Sean – or rather shouting at the top of her voice – 'Do you want a drink?'

At full volume, each of them specified a beer, insisting on the modish new Kazakhstani import, each bottle costing slightly more than a difficult-to-obtain CD. Ysenda made off towards the bar, bopping expansively the while, and occasionally clutching someone who she was forced to barge into, laughing and grinning with them as if she had known them all her life. Sean watched her disappear, and wondered if he could very easily turn back and try to establish some form of mute contact, some mimed conversational transaction, with Catherine. He strictly made himself wait until Ysenda was quite invisible, before turning around, an act of austerity and emotional continence that was rewarded with the sight of Catherine laughing delightedly at a joke which Wayne had just made, evidently prior to signing an autograph for an attractive young seventeen-year-old female fan.

'So what do you think?' he squawked, pitching the question neutrally between Wayne and Catherine. Mortifyingly, they continued their hilarious and intimate conversation. Sean seethed. (Wayne had *better* be talking him up in all this, and generally giving him a tremendous press, or there would be big trouble.)

'Actually, it *isn't* Pusey in the Cadillac in that scene!' said Wayne as the fan left. 'She had it all wrong!'

He shrugged, and Catherine turned to Sean, belatedly aware that he had shouted something.

'What?'

'I said – *what do you think*?'

'About what?'

'Nick's *band*. What do you *think*?'

At that moment, the Filipina Brides' number came to an end, and Sean automatically tensed himself for a mighty roar of appreciation from the crowd. But instead there was an eerie silence, so sudden and intense it made his ears pop like the dropping of air cabin pressure on a plane. Evidently, it was bad form to make a noise between tracks, and this audience would no more think of whooping and hollering than they would applaud between the movements of a Beethoven piano sonata. Suddenly, their conversation became absurdly audible to everyone around them.

'I think they're . . . they're great,' said Wayne, shifting uncomfortably from foot to foot.

'Mmm. Me too,' agreed Catherine, nodding thoughtfully.

'They're top.'

'Can't get enough of them.'

Had they all gone mad? Sean pressed his fingertips to his right temple, and discreetly massaged, under the pretence of scratching. Ysenda returned with the beers.

'Jesus, what a crowd,' she said and added roguishly: 'Your friend Sizewell was holding court up there, Sean – wanted to know where you were.'

They all laughed, and Sean was extremely annoyed. *His* friend? Sizewell-B was bloody *her* friend, and – courtesy of his cash – *her* bloody dealer. But now that he's a colossal embarrassment suddenly Sizewell becomes *his* friend. Sulking, he sipped his lager as Nick began to say something into the microphone.

'OK, yeah,' smirked Nick into the strange, dark rustling quiet. His voice hissed and popped against the mike, and within the cavernous gloom, his pubic hair showed up like a lacuna in the middle of his body, or a badly developed photograph. 'Yeah. Thanks. I'd like to just say something now, please. As you know, Brides have been together now for exactly one year, and we couldn't have achieved any of this' – he gestured modestly about him, the nude dwarf bass guitarist, the nude girl with the phallus – 'without the help of my friends, and there's one friend I'd especially like to mention here and that's my friend *Sean*, who's been very ill recently . . .'

Sean cringed into his clothes with embarrassment.

'. . . and I haven't been as good a mate to him as I'd've liked to have been. So, Sean, if you're out there, mate, sorry!'

'Sorry? What about saying "sorry" to all the poor dupes you've emotionally abused at your so-called psycho-physiotherapy centre?'

The cross-looking man whose irritable demeanour had

so intrigued Sean earlier strode defiantly on to the stage, and with one dramatic gesture swept off his wig and moustache.

It was Aldo Popp.

Nick pursed his lips, and raked the audience with his eyes. The multitude gazed back at him incuriously, as if assuming that this was some form of funky street theatre. The man behind Popp revealed himself as well: Kenneth, the cameraman.

'Well, Mr Stewart? What explanations have you?' Aldo visibly swelled. This *coup de théâtre* was a fantastic idea. Not often did he get to do his act before a live audience, even one as bovine as this. 'What on earth have you got to say to the viewer at home?'

He turned around to see his cameraman fiddling with his camera-case. This remarkable scene had not yet been committed to videotape.

'Kenneth, what in Christ's name are you doing?'

'Can't get the camera out . . .' muttered Kenneth.

'Oh that's great. Fine. I'm producing great investigative consumer television here and you can't get your *bloody* camera out now when we need it. What am I supposed to do when we go on the air, Kenneth? *Describe* the scene? Maybe do a series of pen-and-ink drawings like Rolf Harris?'

'Look, I'm *trying*, all right . . .'

'*Trying* isn't good enough, Kenneth. Look, just keep going, I'll do some more verbals.'

Aldo Popp turned back to the Filipina Brides who seemed rooted to the spot, paralysed by the fact that the audience so plainly expected them to respond in some way.

'So, Mr Stewart,' Aldo returned to his theme, raising his chin a little, 'what have you got to say to those distressed dysfunctional people with multiple personality disorder to whom you have seen fit to give an *enema*.'

The three nude band members remained perplexed and even the drum machine looked embarrassed.

'Look, mate, you've had your say,' said the nude bass guitarist at last. 'Now get off the stage, would you, please?'

'No,' said Aldo, shaking his head emphatically, 'no way.' Aldo's confidence grew as Kenneth's camera finally became operative and its intense little mounted spotlight picked out Nick's flinching face. 'Now, Mr Stewart, I ask you again: is it or is it not a fact that the Certificate of Psycho-Physiotherapy on display in your so-called "surgery" was in fact obtained by means of a correspondence course from an establishment in Bushey?'

At this, the dwarf bass guitarist unslung his instrument, and placed it on a discreet metal stand at the back of the stage. Then he advanced threateningly on Aldo Popp. The audience gave a low bestial growl in the anticipation of imminent action, perhaps encouraged by the sight of the bassist's crooked unveiled penis, in its own unlovely nest of flame-red pubic hair.

'Look, mate,' he said. 'What are you trying to do to our anniversary gig?'

'I am speaking to Mr Stewart,' replied Aldo, with massive dignity. 'Now please stand aside.'

With a lightning-fast movement, the midget bassist unzipped Aldo's fly at eye level and a length of white schoolboy shirt tail instantly protruded, illuminated by the spotlight mounted on Kenneth's camera.

'Get the bloody camera off *me*,' squealed Aldo Popp, his voice climbing an octave and a half as he scrabbled at his trousers. The small bassist had skipped backwards, smirking with satisfaction at his childish subversive gesture. The audience gave – not a laugh, exactly, more a murmur, a sense that the drama was *progressing*. Last month at The Product, at a concert in aid of the British Union to Abolish Vivisection, they had seen the Filipina Brides climax their set by leading on stage a Labrador, a stoat, a collie, and a beagle, each with a lighted cigarette in their mouths and, over each of their faces, a cardboard Steve McQueen mask.

But Aldo rallied. Aldo regrouped. Aldo took charge and once again imposed his personality on the situation, the way he had in the snide HRT clinic in a South Lowestoft industrial estate in 1994, when its fraudulent finance-director-cum-chief-physician had got down on his hands and knees in the car park and bit him on the leg.

Once again, and with Kenneth in his train, he advanced on Nick, who was trying to adopt an attitude of amused superiority.

'When are you going to apologise to the people whom you have shamefully abused?'

This was when Nick decided to do some threatening advancing of his own. It was a moment that Aldo, despite all his years in the foot-in-the-door game, had never been entirely happy with. His comrades exulted in the jostling moment, when an indignant question would be shouted and repeated over the violence, and the camera-wobble. It was the *sine qua non* visual moment of TV investigative journalism. Kenneth had in fact strict instructions to wobble the camera even if he was in no danger and had no physical contact of any sort, and always to keep tight behind Aldo's sightlines, and keep Aldo out of shot as much as possible so that at this vital moment, the viewer identifies with Aldo, and both Aldo and the viewer ideologically fuse and personify the victims themselves.

But Aldo nearly always bottled. He shrank from the violence itself, particularly now that being exposed on television was not actually such a deterrent. In this age of thousands of cable-channels, television could not confer nationwide fame, and neither could it threaten nationwide notoriety. Being on TV these days – it wasn't such a big deal. Kenneth had once captured Aldo taking it over the pate from a dodgy timeshare guy in Ibiza; he gave Aldo two or three good ones with a pool cue and then put his Henri Winterman's out on his forehead. All this went out on the air, on a cable channel readily available all over the EU, and the ratings weren't bad, but it made no difference whatsoever to the man's timeshare business, which continued perfectly profitably, and the guy was even in the local English-language paper the next week doing a parachute jump for charity. Television these days just evaporated.

So Aldo backed away in a classic cowardly playground arc, a one hundred and eighty degree U-turn, and Nick followed him, mimicking the turn as if he were being towed. Kenneth scrambled behind, endeavouring to keep the spotlight beam on Nick's jeering face, which was made a new moon by the shadow cast by Aldo's shoulder.

'What have you got to say for yourself then?' stammered Aldo, trying to pretend that this retreat was *his* idea.

'I think you've outstayed your welcome.'

A small, ragged cheer went up from the audience.

'Huh. *Huh,*' said Aldo defiantly, 'I think you'll find, Mr Stewart' – and here Aldo tripped over the mike lead, in much the same way that Inge had done – 'I think you'll find that it's *you* who have outstayed your welcome with the British public, with, er, your – your clinic.'

'Oh. Good one, Mr Popp, that's *me* told,' sneered Nick, continuing to advance. Now he had Aldo and Kenneth backed almost right up against Inge at the other side of the stage. Kenneth swung around, fearing a collision and, facing the audience, had to film Aldo in profile, which he knew he would hate.

'When are you going to admit that your massage techniques are a grotesque farrago?'.

'I could say the same thing about your hairstyle,' said Nick.

'Now look here,' said Aldo, 'if you don't start giving me and the public some pretty convincing answers, you are going to get a nasty shock. Aagh.'

It was here that Aldo finally toppled backwards, banging against the Theremin, his body apparently passing briefly through the electric field. The instrument responded with a declamatory *cantabile* wail which effectively doubled the volume of his scream of agony. Aldo now fell forward as if he had been punched in the small of the back, and slumped down on his knees, crying quietly to himself. Quite forgetting Aldo's injunction to keep the camera on Nick at all times, Kenneth could not forbear from training his camera-beam on his injured employer's trembling body and his frazzled comb-over quiff.

His audience began to applaud, sporadically at first, and then the ovation grew into a mighty acclaim. Whether they thought these events had been scripted, or if they were complimenting Nick and the Filipina Brides on their resourceful self-defence, was far from clear. But they had the sense of an ending.

In the midst of the uproar, a wincing and cringing Aldo crept away through the wings towards the massive staff entrance doors through which he had spirited himself earlier that evening. Kenneth followed, a grave and grieving Sancho Panza.

The house-lights went up, and Ysenda, Catherine, Wayne and Sean were quite stunned. They had had no idea that Nick's massage clinic was under investigation by the media, though in their hearts they were not surprised. The band had left the stage. The audience milled aimlessly about, unsure of what to do. Then some music came on the PA, and things settled down.

Nick appeared amongst them, grinning helplessly, dressed again in his cowboy outfit, mopping his brow with what looked like a towel mat from the bar and swigging from a bottle.

'What did you think?'

'Absolutely incredible,' said Ysenda. 'Who *was* that guy? You certainly dealt with him effectively.'

Nick shrugged irritably.

'I've no idea. Some sort of wanker. I meant what did you think about the *band*?'

There was a tiny embarrassed silence, resolutely broken by Sean.

'I thought you were brilliant, mate, and I was really chuffed by what you said about me.'

After a fractional pause, they did the male hugging thing, thumping each other powerfully on the back.

The time seemed propitious for Ysenda, and then Sean and Nick, to repair to their respective lavatories to sample some of Sizewell's wares. On his return, Sean found that their effect, though gratifying, was diminished by the sight of Wayne and Catherine once again in close conversation. The time had come to make some sort of bold move. But what?

'Catherine, may I have the pleasure of this dance?'

The look of bafflement on her face was mortifying.

'Sorry?' said Catherine.

Sean swallowed the bile, the bubbling acid of humiliation.

'Would you like to dance?'

Wayne looked away with emphatic tact, as if he was pretending not to notice a nursing mother breast-feeding her baby in a restaurant. But Catherine herself seemed pretty enthusiastic.

'Yeah, sure,' she said lightly, and even took his arm as, skipping girlishly, she led him, to the crowded dance-floor.

The music was violent, loud, uncompromising. It seemed impossible for Sean to see how they could understand it or derive pleasure from it in any way. Catherine caught hold of him around the waist, and wanted to do some sort of close dance with him.

He could hardly breathe for pleasure and joy and delight and doomed, tremulous hope. From somewhere in his memory, the thought of a dire teenage party swam into his head. Close dancing was something you did to classic tracks like The Commodores' 'Three Times A Lady', or 10cc's 'I'm Not In Love'.

But he could not relate that strange teenage lassitude, that helpless adolescent eroticism, in any way to his present situation. Catherine clearly wanted to talk to him as easily and naturally as if they were having tea somewhere.

'Sean.'

'Yeah?'

'When I asked you how you were – you know, at the beginning of the evening.'

'Yeah? *Yeah.*'

'Well, I really meant it.'

'Oh right.'

'I've really been wanting to talk to you all evening. In fact, I've been wanting to talk to you since your illness at the Lido.'

Sean could hardly speak with emotion and pleasure.

'Oh yeah?' he said, trying to be casual.

'Yeah.' She looked up and grinned at him with sudden, heart-stopping candour.

'Why's that, then?'

They swayed to the deafening cacophony, in which the screams of the damned seemed to have been sampled and rhythmically interjected.

'Well, I wanted to talk to you. *Speak* to you.'

'Right. Right. Well, I sort of wanted to speak to you, as well.'

'Really?' Catherine looked up at him again, her wonderful face now transfigured with what looked like joy.

'Yeah. I really liked meeting you that night at The Ranch Club at my opening.'

'Yeah – that was great.'

'I'm glad you thought so.'

'I did. I really did. Listen, Sean . . .'

'What is it Cath— Catherine?'

'All that stuff I said about you and James. You having sex with James in a public lavatory. I'm *sorry*. I'm really *sorry*. It was stupid of me.'

'No.' Sean hugged her closer.

'It was, Sean. It was.'

Sean hugged her close and they swayed around.

'It was stupid because I really wanted to get to know you, and I was being *silly* . . .'

'That's OK . . .'

Catherine looked up at him again, her chin working a little, as if she were nodding, or trying to stop herself crying.

'I felt that I was being so *obtuse* . . .'

'That's OK,' gulped Sean softly. 'I was being really . . . really *uncommunicative.*'

They waltz-shuffled a little more.

'You see,' whispered Catherine, 'I didn't *understand*. I didn't realise what it was that you were trying to *tell* me.'

Sean's heart expanded. He could hardly breathe.

'And what was that?' he whispered, his lips very close to hers now.

She angled her face up towards his.

'Something about yourself, something I didn't *get* . . .'

'Yes . . .?'

Catherine's full, slightly parted lips were within millimetres of his now; he could taste the muted sweetness of her breath.

'. . . that you're obviously having a very rich and rewarding physical relationship with Sizewell-B, and it was terribly insensitive of me to go on about James like that.'

Sean stopped dancing abruptly and loosened his grip on Catherine, though without detaching himself entirely. Catherine toppled a little against this sudden stop, like someone standing inside a sharply braking bus. He was staring, eyes widened, over her shoulder, as if he had seen something startling, and startlingly unpleasant.

'Are you all right, Sean? Is everything all right?'

'Yes. No.'

'Sean?'

'What?'

'Sean, I said *is anything the matter*?'

'I think . . . I think I may have a headache coming on . . . I think I need to be taken somewhere quiet . . .'

'I'll fetch Sizewell.'

'NO!'

Sean ran, in a stiff-legged way, away from the dance-floor, in the direction of the large men's room near the bar. Catherine gazed after him astonished. Then she quickly went back to Ysenda, Nick and Wayne who had found a table near where they had been standing.

'Listen, everyone!' she said urgently.

They all looked up.

'It's Sean; I think he's not well again. But it's more than that; he seems really upset about something.'

Ysenda half rose from her chair.

'Upset? Did you say anything to upset him?'

'No.'

'What did you say?'

'Nothing.'

'It's all right.' Wayne thoughtfully stayed the hubbub of concern. 'I think I know what it— What it could—' He paused. 'I think I can sort it out.'

He left them, and found Sean in the men's room, having just emerged from one of the stalls. His face was hard, and cold and bright, and he was smoothing his hair back with both palms at the temples. Wayne could tell he had just recklessly despatched the rest of the evening's recreational material by the way he placed ten fingertips on the mirror above the washbasins, and flexing them, leant his sweating face up against the reflective surface and repeatedly exhaled with a painful whine, causing a condensation cloud to flare and retract about his mouth like a lung.

Wayne said: 'Sean?'

Sean made a noise like 'Tah!' or 'Dah!', unvoiced, like a cough.

That was it for a bit.

Sean wasn't moving, and so neither was Wayne, who just kept on looking at him steadily, trying to transmit his concern. Someone came into the men's room, glanced at them, approached one of the urinals, glanced at the two men again, and ducked into one of the stalls.

Finally, Sean looked up.

Wayne asked: 'Sean, is everything . . .?'

'Yes. Yes, everything's . . .'

Sean straightened.

'I felt a bit unwell. But I'm fine.' He shook his head infinitesimally, as if dispelling droplets of water. Then he strode purposefully out of the door, his exit briefly but painfully deflected by his shoulder crashing into the doorjamb. Wayne scurried after him.

When he rejoined the group, Sean was to be found questioning Inge about the Filipina Brides, with a strange and unpleasant intensity. Inge was wincing, and most of the group were unnaturally quiet at Sean's manner, as if he were a TV with the volume and brightness turned up too high, and no one could find the controls. Only Catherine seemed unaffected, gazing at poor Sean with bland and benevolent interest.

'Your *phallus*. Your, if I may, your *faux* penis. Your *ersatz* wanger. What was it *saying*?'

Inge glanced at the tote bag under the table, where her stage gear was stowed, as if fearing that the phallus might squeak its own answer like a ventriloquist's dummy in a horror film.

'Well, I guess I think we were questioning the nature of sexuality,' she answered warily, thinking that the wrong answer, or perhaps any answer at all, might be construed as some sort of obscure and belligerent challenge.

'Yeah, mmmmm,' said Sean, nodding and staring like a lunatic, 'the *nature* of sexuality, that's so ambiguous, isn't it? I mean that's just such a problem.'

'Yes?' said Inge quietly.

'I mean: fancying somebody of the opposite genital group, or the same genital group, or maybe both or neither. What a problem, eh? What a terrible universal problem.'

Ysenda's mouth was now set hard; Sean was being boorish and losing sympathy with the group, and with her in particular.

He carried on: 'I mean, the tribesmen of Ethiopia, those noble nomads, or the Afghan horsemen, or the Eskimos, inscrutably frozen under some flickering northern light, do they stop everything, do they come to a dead halt in the rippling dunes or the frozen tundra and say: "Hang about, I think I'm bisexual."'

'Sean . . .' This was Ysenda, trying to sound exasperated but angry and upset at the same time.

'I bet there's some wizened old Cairo merchant, sipping his delicately perfumed saffron tea in some courtyard, inlaid with exquisite Moorish tiles, a fountain trickling in the background, and he's saying to himself: "Well, I have four children and thirteen grandchildren and yet the sight of my twelve-year-old houseboy's pert buttocks swarming in his burnoose doesn't half give me a stiffy. What for gosh sake's does this say about my 'sexuality'?"'

Sean did the rabbit's ear quote mime, with elbows high and index and middle fingers crooked pugnaciously like claws. Inge was pale and resentful from this unprovoked browbeating and no one could blame her. Sean went on.

'And what about Argentina? What about those gauchos, and those proud Buenos Aires menfolk with their tight trousers and their waisted shirts standing up at those zinc bars with tiny cups of coffee, talking about the *Malvinas*, and tangoing, and how very keen they have historically been on the art of *sodomy*.'

'Sean, it's time to go. Let's go.'

'At the magazine today we got a research paper in about rural North Wales . . .'

'Sean . . .' (He was almost shouting by now.)

'I mean, do they have problems up there?'

Inge took Sean's rhetorical question as a genuine query.

'I think *you* have a bit of a problem, and *you're* unhappy,' she said quietly.

Sean was quite still for a moment; then he lifted his chin as if about to speak. Then he lowered it again and without another word headed for the exit. At the beginning of the evening, the rest of the party might have been disposed to follow him to see if he was all right. Not this time. Out of a mixture of embarrassment and irritation, they remained behind, subdued. Then Ysenda went after him.

Not as subdued as Sean, who was now out on the street – in the rain. The rain was thin and warm; it varied in consistency and texture; it was not the rain that Sean remembered from his childhood, not the Monday morning rain through which he had to bicycle to school, the Monday morning English rain that lasted until Sunday night. This was whimsical rain, hallucinatory rain, rain that extended and withheld its physical presence. Only intermittently could Sean identify drops of anything, anything other than his choking and unlovely tears. It was more a pointillist cloud of wetness, an ioniser spray, a peasoup heat-haze of weather.

Sean stood out in the middle of it, staring up at the spongy London sky, glowing and flashing with the sodium lights and the deregulated airlines. It seemed now to be as close as a high ceiling. The first thing he felt was that the temperature of his despair, and of his fear, were in fact lowering a little. Back, once again, from the brink. What now? Walk home?

He had never done that in his life. Black cab? It was a tenet of London life until only recently that rain meant taxis would be as scarce as hen's teeth and not to be had for love nor money. But this sort of rain had a sensory delicacy; it brought out the hedonists who desired nothing more than to expose themselves to it like sunshine. Already he could see crowds of people assembling on the rippling pavements, their faces smilingly upturned to the subtle, aerated spray.

Taxis rolled past, each with its yellow beacon light. No takers. Sean certainly was not eager to climb into the black cab and wince meanly as the driver, in honour of having to work on an unspecified public holiday or sacred religious feast day, activated various mysterious 'extra' fare figures on his meter in different colours and then pressed vigorously down on some button on the top which advanced this basic fee by 40p with each click, as if doing some sort of demanding wrist exercise.

In any case, he did not have that much cash on him. Just as Ysenda came out to look for him, he disappeared into the minicab office with the cheap international cable telephone calls that was next door to the club. Pushing open the door, he walked up the narrow and horribly carpeted staircase that it is compulsory for every minicab office to have – and into its supremely nasty front parlour for 'waiting' customers, with its various, familiar features, without which a minicab firm cannot legally trade: the ripped sofa with the snogging couple, the television mounted on a bracket high up in the corner, tuned to one of the Police Academy films, the harsh single lightbulb, and the controller in his screened-off booth, surrounded by a mysterious posse of mates, the obscure HQ *consiglieri* of the minicab world, who seemed to be neither drivers nor involved in the business in any obvious way.

CONTROLLER (Reluctantly suspending discussion of domestic Algerian politics) Yeah?

SEAN Highgate?

CONTROLLER Fah! (The CONTROLLER and his posse exchange a series of ethnic hand-gestures, crooking the little finger against the eyebrow, pulling the left eyelid up with the thumb, to indicate their inordinate contempt for this request.) This is Brook Green, mate. From here that'll be . . . (the CONTROLLER consults fantastically elaborate directory of prices) . . . forty-seven pounds.

This was the moment at which Sean realised that he didn't have his wallet, the reason being that his wallet was still in his coat – which was still in the cloakroom of the club.

Feeling as if twenty pounds of wet sand had just been placed in his heart, he turned and with a vague shrug and a grimace, a grimace that tried to convey to the cab controller that his sudden change of heart had nothing to do with the price he had just been quoted, began to trudge back down the staircase while the controller called something unintelligible after him, something to the effect that it was still not too late to procure a cheap international cable telephone call. Ysenda had tentatively walked a little way down the street looking for him, and missed Sean's re-entry into the club.

The Product was emptying, and Sean had to fight his way back through the swarm of the outgoing crowds on the pavements outside, a crowd which, however, thinned as he got back inside the doorway, and told the woman at the door that he had forgotten to retrieve his coat, flourishing his dog-eared ticket in proof of this fact. There was no sign of the others.

The cloakroom was a narrow room, bounded at one end by a long bench at which, at the height of its custom, three employees would be busily depositing and retrieving coats and bags at the racks behind. Now there was only one person there, a teenage girl reading a paperback, with a tip saucer in front of her, from which she had cannily weeded all but the £1 coins.

There were two people in the corner just as Sean came in, where he hardly noticed them. Where he *didn't* notice them, in fact. He just went up to the counter and wordlessly presented the girl with the ticket. She placed her book – *Sense and Sensibility* – face down and turned away to find his coat. From behind him, Sean could hear a kind of tiny scuffing or shuffling, but he paid no attention. The girl came back with his coat, returned to her book and Sean anxiously felt for his wallet in the inside pocket. It was still there and the cash was still inside it. He gave a tiny gasp of relief, a gasp which was oddly duplicated and amplified by a familiar girl's voice behind him. It was partly voiced, more of a mew, or an ever so muted, ambiguous squeal. It was like the sound someone might make entering some very cold water, a shivery shock to the nervous system; the sort of little *whinny* he had heard girls make at the Lido as they lower themselves in, the water closing definitively over their waists and shoulders as they push themselves away from the side, lips and chin pressed and set like a six-year-old's as they breast-stroke out. It was a noise that he himself had made, or heard himself making in his head, that noise of fear and pleasure at once.

Or it was like something else. It was the noise of tears. Tears suppressed, tears deferred, tears negotiated away.

The cadence he had heard could have come at the end of tears – or was he mistaken? – it could be the gulp, the valedictory despatch of tears, the drying of the eyes. Then he heard that little sigh again, and knew that he had got it wrong.

All these things Sean thought in the fraction of a second. In what seemed like slow motion, he turned around to see who the couple were behind him, and to find out, or rather confirm, whose the girl's voice was.

What he saw was Wayne, his friend, languorously kissing Catherine, the person with whom Sean was hopelessly in love. Actually, only 'snogging', that porcine word, did justice to what they were doing, and the sound was Catherine's gasp of pleasure, fear and dismay as their mouths briefly parted.

There is a moment in Marvin Gaye's 'Heard It Through The Grapevine', one of Sean's favourite songs, that describes Sean's sudden, massive brooding calm, his icy, shell-shocked self-possession, the sudden coil of discipline. It describes the sudden mood of clenched determination to drain the delicious cup of bitterness dry, and to be seen not to flinch. It is the line where Marvin sings of the terrible moment of revelation: 'It took me by surprise *I must say*.' It is the terrible redundant irony, the sarcasm – *'I must say'* – as if this moment of ultimate devastation means less than nothing, or at any rate less than you all thought, as if at this unspeakable mortification, the most important thing was to salvage some preposterous shred of dignity, to devise some unconvincing dismissive mannerism which affects mild surprise and less than mild contempt, a mannerism which is in some way consistent with the shudder of fear and anguish and utter humiliation which has just trampled your poor unguarded face. Yet, incredibly, you hope somehow to carry it off. Even, you pathetic fool, in your bruised little heart, to derive some sort of swaggering, masochistic pleasure from this moment. Hey, the person that I'm in love with doesn't care about me, and not only that, here she is making love with my best friend, well that took me by surprise, *I must say*, and there is finally the sinister grace note of threat, the menacing understatement of someone capable, flintily, of committing an act of violence. But that act of violence, you immediately realise, can only be directed at yourself. And if you're serious about *that*, well you'd better get on with it, now, while you're in the mood.

Sean stood there, quite still, made of stone, or flint. It was like a dream in which he could not move or speak. But then he did move, twisting back round with his coat bunched in one hand and his wallet in the other and gave the uncomprehending girl a strange, twisted smile, as though to assure *her* that there was nothing wrong.

With a single motion, he shrugged on the coat, and pretending once again to have found the wallet, he had a pretext for audibly saying 'ah' in his recognisable voice and was rewarded with the sudden cessation of the intolerable noise behind him, as sharp as if it had been turned off with a switch. Sean settled the coat on his shoulders, by shoving his hands down in the pockets, and fixed his eyes straight ahead. One tiny compensation that he was not too far gone to feel was a *frisson* of pride and self-congratulation that he was not blushing like a fool or a guilty person, but could feel himself going alarmingly, but not unbecomingly, pale. Soon he knew that one of the two, Wayne, was going to tap him on the shoulder and greet him, and insolently ask if he was all right, and might even have the nerve to pretend not to know what was amiss. It was vital to pre-empt such presumption.

Sean wheeled round, and made as if to walk briskly out of the door, as if he had delayed over some foolish distraction. Catherine had disappeared, and it was Wayne who said: 'Sean . . .'

But Sean looked neither to his left, nor his right, just walked straight ahead, up the stairs and out into the amphibious street.

10

Some months later, Sean was in Nick's office while Nick himself was listlessly going through a sheaf of CVs – applicants for the assistant's job, Inge having walked out in a bit of a huff some weeks before over what Nick himself would only call the personal/professional 'grey area'. This he did purely by means of looking at the passport-sized photograph affixed to the top left-hand corner of each sheet of paper, while he absent-mindedly strummed the opening chords to 'Smoke On The Water' on his non-plugged-in electric guitar. Next to him, slumped on the small squashy sofa, was the happy and contented figure of Aldo Popp, with whom Nick had effected a remarkable reconciliation.

After the debacle at The Product club, *Popp! That Surprised You* was cancelled, mid-series, by the cable channel, on the hallowed grounds of low ratings. Its production budget of £17,500 for eight editions – much of which came out of Aldo's life savings anyway – and its current transmission time of 4 a.m., were considered by the management to be simply too great a commitment. Aldo was given the redundancy notice by bike messenger, an approach the channel judged to convey a considerate note of *urgency* and was also more personal than a fax. The simian despatch rider, with his slouch and his crackling walkie-talkie stood mutely by as Aldo, his lip a-quiver, read how he was being encouraged to develop a freelance career. Any reply? said the rider through his fizzing helmet. No, said the gulping Aldo. No reply. The awful news even made a paragraph in the *Archway Journal*, a local newspaper of unremitting horror, devoted largely to octogenarian sexual assault and step-families burned to death in smoke-alarmless council houses, with a centre spread of TV, satellite and radio. The personal and professional distress of local man Aldo Popp, 45, was given one column width next to news of a middle-aged Archway serial killer who was wont to flit capriciously along the urine-soaked walkways of the Clement Attlee Estate, flashing kitchen knife akimbo, dressed as Delia Smith.

Nick read it – and decided to give Aldo a chance. He got his number from the cable company, called him at home, and then and there offered him a job producing and presenting his new promotional video – a radical, impetuous, impulsive creative gesture that extravagantly confirmed Nick's genius in his own mind. Nick heard no hesitation in Aldo's voice, other than that enforced by a choking sob of emotion. Popp started work the very next day, and was doing a bang-up job from the word go, touring around the clinic's various facilities, and subjecting them to a keen scrutiny through a letterbox formation of index-fingers and thumbs, sizing them up with a sure professional touch: but this time with only extravagant praise in view.

Sean noticed that Aldo, as he was leafing through a shooting script on the sofa, was virtually *purring* with satisfaction. He was a new man. He seemed slighter; he had lost weight since that night at The Product; his hair was shorter and less unruly, thicker too. Aldo was wearing a classic white T-shirt which disclosed, Sean couldn't help noticing, a rather impressive musculature with what were probably wonderful abs. Great. Now he was *fancying* Aldo Popp.

Sean's mobile sounded and he snapped it open.

'Sean? Sean! Is that you, Sean? Look, I have to talk to you. We *need* to talk. You know it. I know it.'

Oh my God, oh my God! Sean went pale with anxiety. It was his stalker: the big, fat, beefy, hairy American who was always hanging around the office, obsessing on him.

'What do you want?' he stammered. 'Go away! I can't form a relationship with you! Please!'

He quakingly closed his mobile, and crept cautiously over to the window. Was that him, standing in the bus queue outside Nick's clinic? He looked down, and thought he caught a glimpse of a burly Jerry Garcia type, skulking with a handset. But he couldn't be sure, and in the next moment he had vanished. Did he want to serve a court order on him for the magazine's many debts? Or shoot him, after getting him to sign a copy? Was it in fact safe to leave the office, or would he end up in the guy's apartment in the pitch dark, imprisoned in some dank hole while a lot of locusts flew about, with nothing to do but sob and nurse the beard-burn on his cheek?

With a deep breath, Sean turned back to what he was desultorily working on: the music and projected order of events at his memorial service. The thing with Catherine had certainly been the occasion for these fiercely melancholy thoughts. But this had been a morbid project that he had been working on intermittently for some years now, ever since discovering the profoundly disappointing and unenlightening programme of readings and music for his own father's memorial service. Everything about the memorial service, he had decided, was an act of existential cowardice. Instead of this flabby humanist 'celebration' of the departed's life, the entire congregation should be forced to confront the terrifying truth of *death*. He worked on it the way public figures with their favourite records hope one day to be invited on Desert Island Discs. The poem he wanted to kick off with was Paul Celan's *'Todesfuge'*, intoned with as much Germanic dreariness as possible. ('Perhaps do it in the original German?' he had noted in pencil in his little notebook.) Then Chopin's 'Ballade No. 17', to be played with the maximum nihilistic violence in the final chords. Having cleaned the palate with this sorbet of melancholy, the next reading would be Philip Larkin's 'Aubade'. He didn't know which of his friends should read this, but maybe it should be someone old, like Uncle Albert, Dad's rather fey brother who lived in Northampton. Then he would have that poem by Hugo Williams about wanting to grow old and incontinent, and *wanting* to have a steel pin inserted – in your penis, was it? He couldn't remember. He couldn't find the poem, now. Maybe there was something about an ileostomy as well. Well, he would check that out later on. *Not* 'Funeral Blues' by W.H. Auden.

It was a promising line-up. It would force everyone to stare, really stare, into the raging black sun of death until their eyeballs melted. Mmmm.

Though Sean could not admit it, there was another reason for his preoccupation, something else to contribute to his post-Catherine gloom: somebody really *had* died. Pussy Fred.

It had happened last Sunday, when Ysenda had come round with the Sunday newspapers and some fresh orange juice that she had bought from the local corner shop, with a view to having some 'brunch' with Sean. She seemed to be always coming round these days, checking up on him. He and Ysenda were talking about another problem with her Visa card: only back from the garage a couple of weeks, Ysenda had driven it into Agnès B at a pretty good lick and lost control; the crumple cage collapsed, leaving her with superficial cuts and bruises.

As they were getting settled, Pussy Fred stalked into the room in a way that Ysenda found horribly familiar: an odd, splay-footed gait. She put down the review section and eyed Pussy Fred tensely, shrinking back into the sofa, as if the cat was about to attack her. His tail shot straight up, the fur frizzing: the usual warning flare. Sean was in the kitchen rustling up some kippers. Pussy Fred's face pushed down against his chest, his paws out, rear haunches bent, but with none of the usual cat languor and cat lassitude. His face now assumed a belligerent double-chinned quality, slightly pop-eyed, like Quintin Hogg answering questions on television about the Profumo affair. Then Pussy Fred assumed an absolutely blank look, the blank look that can be seen at comparable moments on the faces of babies and adults alike.

As Sean came through into the sitting room, carefully carrying a tray with juice, croissants and dinky little cafetière, Pussy Fred seemed to raise his left hind leg in the air and tilted, horribly.

'Sean, is this fucking cat going to—'

Afterwards, Ysenda found she could remember everything about the disposition of the room at this moment; it was seared on to her memory like the outline of bodies on the pavement at Hiroshima: Sean's wary frown, the creases of his loose-fit chinos and the pale blue sailor's sweater, the Moorish chequerboard pattern on the tray he was on the point of setting down on the table.

The sound was somewhere between a loose connection on an old hi-fi, and a medieval sackbut suitable for incidental music in an open-air production of *Henry IV* in Wembley Stadium. Ysenda and Sean found it necessary to adjourn to the dank and dripping communal garden behind his apartment block, there to partake of a deeply uncomfortable and unsatisfactory brunch on the damp outdoor table. When they returned after an hour and a quarter to the apartment, it was to see Pussy Fred recumbent on the carpet, on his side, slightly shrunk, back arched.

He was obviously quite dead, and Sean burst into uncontrollable tears.

He did this first on his own, standing up, with his two palms pressed to his face, like a figure in classical drama. He remained in this position while he felt Ysenda's arms snaking round his neck. Then he crossed his palms between her shoulder blades. Ysenda herself was not immediately aware of how much she had been looking forward to hugging him in exactly this sort of protective way. In the hospital, there had been no opportunity; she was able only to trace his collarbone with her fingertips. But now she had Sean in her arms, a great shuddering bundle. He smelt different; not of the swimming pool, but warmer, with a trace of the coffee he had made. She squeezed him a little bit and let him cry on, without saying anything, and letting a warm feeling of virile emotional pride flood through her. She had never been able to do this for a man before, although there had been plenty of times when she had played the submissive sobbing-it-all-out role in the man's arms, starting with her father, between the ages of five to thirteen. She knew she should *say* something. 'There, there' was out of the question. She tried a soft 'OK. OK' – which sounded good in her American accent. If it wasn't for the ghastly, manky corpse of Pussy Fred on the floor, this would be a wonderful moment.

Sean's tears were not merely for Fred, but they were a trigger for the awful pent-up shame and self-pity that had afflicted him since the beginning of the year. And even as he sobbed, great racking sobs that clenched his face up in a rictus of pain, Sean was aware of the overwhelming relief that he was finally able to cry, and in front of someone else, and that he had a respectable reason for crying, a reason that people would sympathise with: a fat and extraordinarily ugly dead cat.

Pussy Fred had been given to Sean seven days after his fifteenth birthday, a strange extra gift that he correctly assumed was an emotional diversionary tactic to compensate him for witnessing, the previous day, a terrible row between his mother and stepfather and then later barging into their bedroom in search of his stereo earphones and witnessing their reconciliatory love-making. This activity, fortunately for his peace of mind, was being conducted in an unadventurous missionary position.

They froze. Stunned, Sean could only think of asking if either of them had seen his earphones.

'Have you seen my earphones?'

'No,' said his mother patiently, her mouth the only moving part in a static and excruciating tableau.

'Where are they?' he said at last, leaving his mouth gormlessly slack on the last word.

'Will you *please* leave,' his mother had said, softly, with a tone more of supplication than rebuke, while his stepfather buried his head in her neck like a man who wished to avoid identification.

Sean had left, in a light trance, as if he had witnessed nothing more important than his mother in the act of searching for her shoes in the cupboard, or cutting something out of the pages of a magazine. The next day, his stepfather failed utterly to carry off the affair with the candid jokiness that he could see, in retrospect, that the situation called for.

He was withdrawn at breakfast, and favoured Sean only with a pale and wintry smile that seemed to glance and deflect off him towards his mother – who was being extra curt. When he returned from school that evening, there it was, waiting for him. His name was Fred. This name was lengthened, *de facto*, to Pussy Fred, or Pussy Fwed, because this was what his mother used to call him, in that strange baby talk that families and long-standing couples use among themselves, but never to outsiders.

He didn't even like cats. Sean simply hadn't been pestering them to get him a kitten, and that was the sort of thing much younger children did anyway. So he greeted Pussy Fred's presence with the same unease that he felt walking away from his mother's creaking bed the night before. But something in Sean knew that it would be ungracious to refuse him, and

Pussy Fred's continued presence by his side, he guessed, might even give him some obscure advantage over his mother and stepfather in a future argument.

He was right. He took an enormous interest in the kitten, and, curled on his lap like a gargantuan hairy turd, it reminded his mother and stepfather continuously of its origins – that terrible primal scene – and conferred on Sean a strange ability to disconcert them.

The kitten grew in all directions and never lost its puppy fat. From the outset he was an unprepossessing animal, insultingly indifferent to human interest even for a cat. He developed a charmless habit of *biting* his victims; not scratching, but biting. Never Sean though. Pussy Fred was often to be found on his master's lap and would condescend to communicate with Sean in short, petulant little mews that Sean, eerily, could imitate.

He took Fred with him to college, and kept him in all his shared houses, even taking him with him to gigs when he went through his brief eccentric goth phase at university, growing long wiry black hair which seemed to cascade and mingle indistinguishably both with Pussy Fred's gleaming pelt and with the hairs of his dark angora sweater, creating a kind of great semi-organic hairy sheath that ran from the crown of his head to his waist.

Under this, it was possible to detect his great crimsoned mouth, as he affected the mannerisms and the image of Robert Smith of The Cure – though it was really only Pussy Fred who was fat enough convincingly to attempt this pose. Having Pussy Fred with him was a very important part of his personality-capital and character-stockholding as an undergraduate. Sean was always in the kitchen of his many hostels and shared houses, feeding him more and more, and Pussy Fred soon graduated to dog food and then human food, a disastrous habit causing his unprecedented colonic problem, which led on one disastrous occasion to Sean's stepfather having to write out a cheque for £250 to redecorate a veterinary surgeon's waiting room and a further £75 as informal compensation for the nurse's trauma. Now Pussy Fred was dead, but not before age had withered him and custom staled his far from infinite variety.

They had buried him in the communal garden – despite the misgivings of the apartment block's managing agents – in the presence of Ysenda and his mother, who had never looked more striking, in a beautiful classic coat, a little old-fashioned, but becomingly severe. Sean felt that her breath should have been condensing in cinematic clouds as she gravely attended the curious occasion. Instead, it was actually quite warm. Pussy Fred, in a small MDF coffin, was lowered into a hole dug under the plane tree, by a contract gardener hired by Sean himself. As this solemn act was going forward, for reasons she could not quite explain, Ysenda positioned herself to the right of Sean in such a way that she could take his arm and incline her head on to his shoulder in a companionable way.

Now Pussy Fred was dead, and Sean was wondering whether he should use up all his bleak memorial ideas on the cat. A memorial for a cat? A bit camp, he thought to himself. The diary columns would treat it as comedy, and *C.C.3* would make mock.

'What the fuck is this?' asked Nick, arousing Sean from his reverie.

He was kicking a plastic carrier bag of Sean's that was slumped in the corner: it was a tall bag, the sort sometimes given away by dry-cleaning shops. It had something leather sticking out of it.

'Nothing,' said Sean shortly, and moved to pick up the bag, fold it double, and put it by his *other* bag.

'No, no, no,' grinned Nick, forestalling him, and picking it up. 'What is it?'

He emptied it out: *it* was a heavy leather suit, with shackles at the wrists and ankles, a number of zips at mysterious angles all over its surface, and a hood that clearly covered the entire face, with a large zip where the mouth would be.

Nick was stunned and even Aldo Popp looked up for a moment. Nick continued to hold it upright, and for a moment it looked like a fourth, malevolent person in the room, mutely threatening.

'It's mine,' sighed Sean, taking it from Nick. 'Or rather it's not mine. The *Harbinger*'s Style section lent it to me. I'm *reviewing* it.'

'Oh,' said Nick and Aldo at once, and returned to their respective tasks, as Sean started experimentally trying on the jacket, now almost oblivious to their presence.

'OK,' said Aldo at last, to Nick. 'I think we should go for a little informal rehearsal of your intro.' He handed him a sheet of paper which had the text of Nick's opening piece to camera. Nick looked through it cursorily, and agreed briefly to walk through it then and there, to give Aldo some spatial sense of how this introductory sequence was going to look.

'Right,' said Aldo, and together they walked out into the lobby area, just by the front door where only a few months before they had had their first extraordinary confrontation. 'First, music – crashing synth sig composed and performed by the Filipina Brides.'

'Minus Inge,' said Nick sadly.

'Minus Inge,' agreed Aldo. They sang it together, making emphatic conductorish movements with their hands: 'Da-da-DA-da, wumpety-wumpety-AGH, wumpety-AGH, build-up, build-up, build-up, *build-up, build-up, build-up*, quiet bit, quiet bit, quiet bit, BUILD-UP, BUILD-UP, BUILD-UP, a-a-a-nd FINISH!'

'Right,' said Aldo a little breathlessly, staggering slightly with his fingers up to his forehead, having put a bit too much into this impromptu performance. 'Over that, we'll be having an action sequence and the titles: you meeting with the customers or rather patients, shaking hands, nodding thoughtfully and vigorously as they explain their problems, close-up of you examining pulse read-outs, respiration charts, crystals and tarot cards, shots of you and – and Inge's replacement doing two-on-one massage on a client, shots of the client or rather patient in the gym and in the various treatment suites, shots of you doing some psychoanalysis, nothing heavy, just talking, and then maybe another shot of you saying goodbye with them all glowing and invigorated and happy and *centred*.'

'Nothing with the big lymphatic drainage wand?'

'I'm *saving* that,' said Aldo twinklingly. '*Saving* it.'

Sean heaved a shattering sigh, which they could both hear from where they were standing.

'Sounds like your friend Sean is really taking the death of his cat very hard,' frowned Aldo.

'Mm,' agreed Nick. 'But I don't know if it's just that.'

'Perhaps you could give him a reduced rate on your pet bereavement course,' pondered Aldo.

Nick wasn't sure about this. The pet bereavement course had been Inge's idea, and it was something that Nick liked very much in theory, but in practice it had been very difficult to manage the clients' emotions and had not been all that cost-effective. The idea was that the clients would be encouraged to believe that their trauma stemmed from having *suppressed* the normal grieving process – something of which it was very difficult to persuade them, as they were already extremely distraught.

Nick and Inge would nevertheless give them the chance to work through their emotions with a series of workouts and role-playing games in which they would handle and fondle a stuffed toy – usually a purple dinosaur – which would stand in for The Pet Loved One. Unfortunately, they had only done it once, with a man whose pet terrier had been hit by a car, and, inattentive and hungover, Inge had managed to drop the purple dinosaur on the ground and run over it with a trolley on which capsules of the clinic's own brand herbal drink were kept. More unfortunately still, the histrionic rage and grief of the patient at this turn did not find much in the way of sympathy and understanding, still less apology, from the grumpy Inge, who ended up by shouting: 'For fuck's sake, it was only an animal.'

'I don't like to offer therapy to people that I know,' said Nick primly. 'It isn't in keeping with professional procedure.'

Aldo nodded solemnly, without comment.

'Well,' he continued. 'This is the opening piece to camera that I've, er, *roughed out* for you.' Aldo produced a sheet of paper. 'Let me just walk you through it.'

Aldo moved a few paces away from Nick and turned back to him, emphatically, as if Nick were the camera, and gestured with both hands as if doing two mild karate chops, thus establishing the *mise-en-scène*.

'"Hello. I'm Nick Stewart and I want to tell you all about my holistic clinic, offering radical inclusive therapy right here in Highgate, England."' Aldo came out of character for a moment. 'That's for the international market. Perhaps it should be Highgate, North London, England. Or perhaps just London, England. Anyway. "Here we treat the mind, the body, the soul, the id, the ego, the super-ego, and the . . . the super . . . id. We have here one of the most challenging treatment procedures in Western Europe, together with highly trained and committed staff and the most up-to-date hi-tech equipment. Let's take a look."'

Aldo lowered the sheet of paper. 'This is where we cut to you in the first treatment suite. I thought it might be good if you were actually copping . . . er, getting a massage while addressing the camera.'

Nick looked up sharply, the first time he had given any indication of having actually paid attention to anything Aldo was saying. 'I don't like that. In fact, I'm not sure if I like the whole way this is going. Too broad. Too corporate video, Aldo. Too much like one of those people that appear in adverts for their own used car dealership.'

Mortified, Aldo cleared his throat and said: 'Well, there is another approach. It's more a development idea at the moment. More of a treatment.'

'Let's hear it.'

'Infomercial,' said Aldo. 'We hire a studio and fill it with geeks and menopausal women and retired people and transsexual car-thieves and underachievers and just pretty well a *cross section* of British society. Then we get a female presenter with a big mike who will introduce a thirty-minute "discussion programme".'

'Fat woman?'

'I'm thinking possibly drag queen.'

'*Fat* though?'

'Let's come back to that.'

Nick nodded.

'OK,' said Aldo. 'So: titles, sig. Completely different. Not dramatic or in any way wumpety. It's fast; it's light; it's lifestyle; it's *daytime*. It's for the way modern busy twenty-first-century people live their life in the zero-zeroes. House lights up in studio, and the presenter is caught in kind of mid-discussion with some people in the audience; he/she looks up, smiles and introduces the subject of the show. Guess what the title is?'

Nick shook his head, leaning forward. 'What?'

'*Unhappiness*. Unhappiness today. Why are we all so unhappy? What is it about modern life, and our modern consumerist society that condemns us all to a private hell of sadness?'

'Now this I can work with,' said Nick.

Aldo nodded, blushing furiously with pleasure.

'Believe me, Nick' – and here Aldo's face took on a seriousness, a solemnity that it hadn't had before – 'believe me. In the zero-zeroes, unhappiness will be big. Really big. In fact, it's the next really big thing. It will be the time when we finally face up to the fact that human life is anxiously, vaguely unhappy *all the time*, but that it needn't be. And that we must make a really big lifestyle choice to ah, turn the corner . . .'

'Yeah, yeah,' said Nick, a little impatient with Aldo's purely theoretical analysis. 'So what do we see then?'

'The panel,' said Aldo firmly. 'Presenter introduces the panel. Maybe they've been in shadow before this, I don't know. Anyway, lights up and first is a couple: attractive sixteen-year-old girl, blond hair up in bunches or maybe shaven, ripped T-shirt, combat fatigue trousers, body-piercing, tattooing, branding, whatever. With her is her stepfather, a forty-eight-year-old systems manager with angina. They're in love. They're shagging. They feel no guilt. But her mother has put a tremendous downer on the idea.'

'The uptight cow. Where's she?'

'In the audience – in disguise. Big sensational eruption for after the commercial break.'

'Commercial break? But isn't *this* an infomercial?'

'Related products, Nick, related products. Branded merchandise. We shift units there, plus the commercial break kind of establishes the meta-seriousness of the main programme.'

'Right.'

'Anyway, she's in the audience. Or maybe she's in a side room with the camera on her, and we do a split-screen. I don't know yet. Whatever, next are two vivacious young career women in their late twenties. They dress exactly alike. Their hair is exactly alike. Their bodies are exactly alike. Their *faces* are exactly alike.'

'So they're twins?'

But Aldo was already shaking his head, smiling.

'Nope. They're triplets. With one of them *dead*. Childhood boating accident, or something. They talk about how part of their identity has been amputated or destroyed, and each of the triplets doesn't know whether to love or hate the other one, because of whether they represent an absence or a presence. I thought we could get a bit of a cat-fight going, ripped clothes, sort of thing.'

'So what do we get, twins to play them?'

Aldo looked affronted. 'Of course not. We get real two-out-of-three tragic triplets. There must be some somewhere.'

'Who else?'

'Lottery winner. Nothing much. Five numbers, bonus ball, seventy grand. Gave it away to local charities, now bitterly regrets it, thinks he should have kept it all. Can't come to terms with what it says about him.'

'All right,' said Nick, 'so then what?'

Aldo fanned his palms out in the air, something like Al Jolson, while assuming a dreamy faraway look. 'All these people,' he sighed, 'are living their normal twenty-first-century life in the zero-zeroes. Just like the rest of us. They thought things would be different once they had crashed through the big 2000 firewall. And it is and it isn't. But they're suffering from PMD.'

'PMD?'

'Post Millennial Disorder. The realisation that things are just the same – only a fuck of a lot worse. But what's different is that they're far more rigorous about unhappiness. They want to manage it away like a kind of emotional inefficiency. They know that prescription drugs don't work, and ECT's too much like banging the TV set and hoping for the best.'

'And that's where I come in?'

'Yes. Or not yet. We take questions from the floor about all the people with all their unhappinesses, and also the viewers at home with ISDN links, and then we introduce you, and you go into a big spiel about the mind and the body and the holistic centre of being. How people go to their analyst twice a week; they go swimming once a week; they go to the gym every day, and see their doctors once a year. All so inefficient! They need an all-in-one holistic one-stop shop.'

'Me!' beamed Nick.

'Yep,' said Aldo, taking out a pack of Henri Wintermans and beginning to cough uproariously.

'Aldo, I don't know what to say,' said Nick emotionally.

'All this time you've been wasting yourself in investigative journalism, when you're more, so much more than that. You're an artist. A visionary. For the twenty-first century. For millennium three.'

Aldo's eyes glistened and brimmed. But then a frantic humming or moaning came from the private office, where they had left Sean, along with a desperate clanking sound, and then a black leather figure pogoed out into the hallway, its legs furled together in a chain and its black leather bullet head seamlessly encased and with the mouth fully zipped up.

'Sean,' said Nick. 'How *have* you managed that?'

11

Actually Wayne was breaking up with Catherine when Sean saw them together. It was in the death throes. Wayne had taken Catherine aside in the cloakroom at the very end of the evening and said:

'Catherine, listen. I don't think we should see each other any more.'

She had said quietly: 'Oh no . . .'

They had pulled together for a kind of consolatory embrace which had, messily, developed into another proper kiss, which was what Sean had seen.

Why was this happening in the first place? It was because Wayne was going to bed with someone else. Someone famous: an encounter with one of the hot young women on the comedy show that Wayne was showing Catherine when *their* relationship had started. The propensity for famous people to have sex with each other without the public ever finding out was something that had astonished Wayne at first. It was how minor provincial businessmen must feel when they arrive at their Masonic induction ceremony and find everyone they know – police officers, clergymen, judges, aggressive beggars, independent financial advisors – already there, in wordless greeting, one trouser leg rolled up.

He knew that, obviously, you could have sex with an attractive, non-famous member of the public if you really wanted, and indeed the availability of such sex was until recently considered one of the unacknowledged perks of fame. But now it was too dangerous. For example: Wayne would be far from home, in a small country hotel bar contemplating a 5:00 a.m. start for location work the next day. Or he would be at a fervid first-night party in the provinces, or perhaps, earlier in his career, at a genteel 'dramatised reading' organised as part of a literary festival in some spa town. All circumstances in which the flirtatious encounter with the attractive girl, the sly and candid offer of 'coffee' in one's hotel room, was Wayne's as of right. Yet now Wayne could not see an attractive girl's smiling face without imagining, superimposed as in a kind of palimpsest, an expression of carefully composed hurt and dismay, perhaps in a dressing gown, posing across the tabloid centre-spread. 'How Wayne hurt me', 'How Wayne made me feel cheap' – that sort of thing. He saw the ghost of that tabloid pratfall in every gesture, every smirk. He saw the embryo of tabloid betrayal within them all. And it wasn't as though his neurosis did not have some foundation.

In the innocent days of the mid-Nineties, girls would package their tales through agents. Now the rumour was that the tabs were cutting out the pricey middle-men and the excitable, unreliable amateurs, the accident-prone game show contestants. They hired professionals – models, actresses – the way they once hired Page Three girls. They packaged various stories around them; they *made the movie* – only with a blank where the famous man would be; and then they set out to find horny, credulous married celebrities to slot into place, sending their girls to roam hotel bars and studio parties to make the entrapment. This was how celebrity journalism was going to work in the zero-zeroes.

So now famous people closed ranks, sexually speaking. Like the farming communities of East Anglia, they were only doing it with their own, thus endangering the gene pool and loosening the already tenuous grip of some of their number on reality. But that was of no account. Theirs was a sexual co-operative arrangement. As the trilingual, high-IQ presenter of a popular science programme once told Wayne, just prior to wrapping her legs around his face on a deserted Sorrento beach at dusk: 'Nobody shags outside the faith.'

Indeed, if Wayne was honest with himself, he didn't need that much persuading. He had actually become a bit snobbish about the non-famous, although to admit as much was a terrible error of taste, even amongst the elect. Wayne had always relished the trappings of alienation from the public. It was an unattractive part of his character, but there it was. One of the happiest days of his life was when he had his telephone number made ex-directory, or 'unlisted' as he liked to say in the American manner. He immediately telephoned directory inquiries and asked for his own phone number, obediently giving the full address, as bidden. And oh, the exquisite thrill of that cold rebuff: 'I'm sorry, the number you require is *ex-directory.' I'm sorry!* I'm sorry you can't come in, mate, it's members only. I'm sorry, sir, we can't possibly find you a table, the restaurant is fully booked.

But then, Wayne's pleasure was immediately clouded by the realisation that the non-famous were allowed to have ex-directory numbers as well. The presumption of it! So he began to pine for a special two-tier system of going ex-directory, one for the famous and one for the obscure. Asking for the ordinary person's unlisted number would draw the usual blank. But asking for the famous person's private number would elicit something colder, something harsher – an extra note of rebuff from the operator's voice. Perhaps she would become very patient: 'I'm sorry, but the number you require is that of a famous and important *ex-directory person*, really they're very tired, look, if you call tomorrow I can give you the address of their record company, now please show some manners and give this person some *space*.' Or perhaps the operator could simply say: 'I'm sorry, the number you require is *ex-directory*, now *piss off*!' And maybe the telephone could be rigged up so that a short, sharp electric shock could be administered over the line. Fantastic!

Oh well. Just after Wayne had had sex with Catherine that time, he ungallantly became involved with the comedienne; it was a party at his producer's tall, cliff-like house in Holland Park; she had tremulously revealed to him the distressing circumstances of her break-up from her last boyfriend and he had instantly comprehended that these were, in fact, precisely the circumstances in which she hoped to take up with her next one – Wayne. Their preliminary kiss in the bathroom confirmed in his mind the necessity of breaking off the ill-advised morganatic shag situation with the non-famous Catherine, with whom his relationship was already a bit uneasy. Might she, in fact, be on the point of chucking him?

Clearly, the last thing he wanted to do was 'hurt' Catherine: this was the troubled male mantra that he repeated to himself silently, over and over, the word 'hurt' pinging in his head like a Buddhist prayer wheel. But hurt her was clearly what he was going to *have* to do. This was the law; the terrible natural law of splitting up. Hurting them was necessary, and in these situations it was mostly because of the ignoble desire to pre-empt any move on her part to hurt you. There can never be any question of 'mutually' deciding to end a relationship. No. You have to decide. Either you dump her, or she dumps you. You hurt her, or she hurts you. Or: you hurt her more than she hurts you, or she hurts you more than you hurt her. In the great cosmic scheme of things, it never evens out until that moment at the very end of your sexual career, when St Peter opens up the great brass-bound ledger of sexual liaison, and you'll find you've given and received the same amount of punishment: the columns are exactly the same. But it's never even with the same partner. So you have to decide. Which is it going to be? Winner or loser . . .

Wayne grimly decided winner, but then could not conceive of a gracious or adroit way of managing it. He delayed for days, sprawled on his sofa, twirling the video remote. It was best to end it straight away but, in the most cowardly way, he shrank from the task, as Catherine's increasingly wan and insistent messages started piling up on his answering machine and voicemail. Moreover, and revealing an unexpectedly mawkish and girly side to Catherine, there were her e-mail messages accompanied with little snapshots of herself that she had digitally schemed in to her PC and transmitted, together with the downloading of some heart-rending audio, little ditties of love, that she accompanied with – for heaven's sake – an *acoustic guitar*, at which she had blushingly confessed some proficiency some way in to their relationship. He had never dreamt she had this tiresome folkie side.

But then something happened that changed Wayne, changed his attitude to the responsibility of finishing with Catherine, changed his attitude to everything.

He was passing the time at the Pleasure Palace, the arcade in King's Cross that Sean had introduced him to earlier that year. A lot of the kids recognised him in there, and indeed there had briefly been an actual computer game there based on his movie which had just opened: sometimes the delicate face of Cardinal Newman was to be seen flashing across the screen on the rare occasions that one of the boys could be persuaded to play it. Wayne liked to hang out there, exchange some banter, and loose off a few autographs. For something to do, he decided to have a go at the Sex Kombat game that Sean was supposed to be pretty good at. He paid £15 in advance for three continuous three-minute plays, and strapped on the virtual reality suit and the wrap-around visor while the usual audience of cool, blank thirteen-year-old arcade connoisseurs assembled, and prepared to view his progress on the 2-D monitor on the side of the eight-foot metal capsule into which Wayne had gingerly stepped.

Wayne felt that he was suddenly in the middle of an extraordinarily detailed alternative reality: a large, sleek bar with various hip young customers, some in animated conversation, some loners staring miserably into their drink, some craning to attract the attention of the huge shaven-headed barman. But everything was uncannily silent, while suspended in front of him, six feet away in cyberspace, as if on a glass screen, were the image of his face, digitally inscribed by an internal camera inside the visor and projected into the 'room', together with the words Prepare To Qualify. Under this were three options: Straight – Princess Xena; Gay – Prince Xeno; Bi – Princess Xena and Prince Xeno. He assumed that Sean had always gone for the second option, but Wayne reached forward and touched the box for Princess Xena, suspended in front of him (as he did so his cybergloved hand motioned forward in real space and pawed the air).

At this, the screen and its choices ripplingly evaporated to a snatch of breathy, saxophone music which Wayne recognised as a recurrent theme from the original Star Trek series, usually accompanying Captain Kirk's encounter with an attractive woman.

He surged forward into the virtual bar, and towards a knot of people apparently clustered around some kind of disturbance. A pushy drunk was there pressing his unwelcome attentions on Princess Xena herself, whose costume was already ripped in the most revealing and provocative way. Wayne silently gasped – she looked almost exactly like Catherine.

'Get *away* from me!' squealed Princess Xena.

'No way, darlin',' jeered the ruffian idiomatically.

'Please help me,' said Princess Xena, directly to Wayne, and then the ruffian swung directly into shot and the screen froze momentarily, while Wayne's cue flashed up in the top-left-hand corner: 'You heard the lady. Now get lost, before I lose my temper.'

This inaugurated stage one of Sex Kombat: fighting Princess Xena's would-be assailant. This was managed with a series of feints and blows with the cybergloved hands, feet and forehead. Connecting blows notched up points in the flashing box in the top-left corner of the screen; where Wayne was hit, he felt a slight painless jolt, and his point-total was diminished. The time in minutes, seconds and tenths of seconds was flashing in a box elsewhere. Occasionally, as he bobbed and weaved in his v-suit, Wayne caught a glimpse of Princess Xena's lovely, flushed figure at the bar, writhing and squirming with desire for the handsome stranger who was defending her honour. Wayne eventually despatched the opponent in 48 seconds, a good time which earned him bonus points. He turned back to Princess Xena who ran her tongue sensually across her teeth – the shimmering pixillated vision was almost unbearably erotic.

'I like your style, *Wayne*,' she said, seamlessly, the machine having registered his first name before the game had begun. 'Boy, am I ever going to *put out* for you later on. But first let's have a walk in the countryside.'

Wayne accompanied Princess Xena's semi-clad form out of the crowded urban bar and – suddenly! – they found themselves in an Arcadian paradise. Beautiful unspoilt countryside. About them were the rich greens and browns of late summer – although these blurred at the edges of the vision field, because the King's Cross Sex Kombat unit, at three months old, was nearing the end of its design lifespan. A splendid hay bale lay in one direction, some cows in another, and just behind him – Wayne's cybersuited body twisted in the video booth while the King's Cross traffic thundered by – he could see a beautiful, babbling stream. All was quiet, except for the digital chirrup of a skylark, far, far above.

'Oh, Wayne, isn't the countryside wonderful?' sighed Princess Xena happily, inclining her face up to the warm sunshine.

Wayne shyly agreed that it was.

They walked across the delightful sylvan scene, as Xena shyly took Wayne's hand, interlocking their little fingers. Emboldened, Wayne presently detached his hand, and placed his arm around her magnificent waist.

Outside, one of the Sex Kombat regulars removed the briefest cigarette end from his mouth as he peered at the monitor, threw it on the filthy floor, placed his carrier bag of purchases from the neighbouring adult store on the ground, and spat. 'I think we could be on here,' he growled shrewdly to his fellow spectators, who nodded sagely.

Suddenly, Xena's lovely face registered dismay and panic.

'Oh, Wayne!' she gasped. 'Look!'

She pointed to somewhere in the middle distance behind him. Wayne could hear the histrionic thundering of hooves. He twisted his body uncomfortably in the Sex Kombat cubicle, and could thus see a gigantic bull pounding towards him. Sean had told him what the correct form here was, and he tensed his body, and his cybergloved hands grasped a thin aluminium bar in front of him, just as, on the screen, he grabbed hold of the bull's great horns. He was now face to face with the huge ugly, cartoon bull – its bloodshot eyes, its farting, steaming nostrils. The aluminium bar pressed against him, he pressed back, the tenacity and force of his response registering in the score-box in the top-left corner of the screen. As before, he could see Xena in the background, panting and squirming with intolerable desire.

'Oh, Wayne,' she whispered in his ear, not scrupling to put him off. 'You're like a bull yourself with your awesome power, aren't you, with your sheer brute strength! Oh, Wayne! Ohhhhhhh!'

Slowly, but surely, he forced the once proud bull to its massive knees and haunches. Its great puffing became an effeminate whinny. Having subdued it, Wayne turned back triumphantly to his companion, who looked adoringly at him, and his points total advanced very satisfactorily with a series of pinging sounds.

'Let's have a swim!' suggested Princess Xena impulsively, and peeled off her clothes, still ripped and wine-stained after the altercation in the bar, to reveal her magnificent body. She dived into the stream, which responded with hardly a splash, and Wayne followed, the v-suit transmitting delicious sensations of wet warmth to his tingling skin. They frolicked in the water, while the angle of Wayne's mounting erection was recorded by a tilting diagram flashing at the top of the screen. Its prompt and continued appearance clocked up a lot of points which presently meant that Wayne and Xena were ready for stage three. They clambered out of the stream, and Xena, in her full, proud naked glory, nipples absurdly erect (it was the only lapse of animation taste that Wayne could detect) led him by clammy hand to a cow byre, whose door stood invitingly open. At its threshold, Princess Xena came close and said breathily: 'I really like your style, Wayne.' Again the join was inaudible. 'Boy, am I ever going to give you a *seeing to* later on. But first, let's go in here . . .' She gestured to the aperture, and a low, homely mooing could be heard from within.

When they went through it, the scene changed utterly. They were in Princess Xena's luxury penthouse apartment, late at night. Wayne could see the twinkling skyline of New York spread out below from the wonderfully broad window that made up one whole wall of the building. 'I'm going to slip into something more comfortable,' purred Princess Xena, sashaying towards the bedroom. 'Pour us a drink and we'll take it from there.'

Wayne's field of vision surged towards the drinks cabinet. Sean had told him that this was the final, and in some ways the most important, test. He would have to pour two cocktails, as quickly as he could, with a steady hand, and spill as little as possible. It was tricky, with the old-fashioned, fan-shaped glasses. He boldly attempted two margaritas, the necessity for salt around the rim earning more points than the more standard vodka martini or maybe just the beer-plus-lime-slice that Sean said he always went for at this stage. (Prince Xeno liked something a little more butch, after they had fenced with foils, rough-housed ambiguously in the locker room, and talked a little about how his parents, the King and Queen, were pressuring him into a marriage which he felt he wasn't ready for.) Wayne did not do badly; only a few drops overboard, and the ticking, tilting icon at the top of the screen saluted his tenacious hard-on. The points box flashed, indicating the final section of the game: The Bedroom.

The screen panned round to the bedroom door, where Princess Xena was in an absurdly brief negligée, the sort with a kind of fluffy fringe around the bottom, and flashing a coy smile while beckoning him with a bicycling forefinger.

'Let's have those drinks, Wayne,' she breathed, and Wayne handed her a margarita.

'Mmmm,' said Xena appreciatively, sipping it, and running her pixillated tongue around the rim. 'What an *astringent* taste. Now let's see what sort of an astringent *rogering* you can come up with. *Not half!*' Wayne registered that the programmer of this game had evidently found it amusing to have the Princess suddenly, bafflingly, do an impression of an elderly disc jockey that he could just about remember from his teens.

It was time to enter the bedroom for the final section: the sex. The more points that the contestant managed to notch up, the more intense the pleasure that the machine would now administer to his penis, via the attachment in his v-suit which was a cross between a cricket box and a jock strap. This was a crotch attachment connected to the rest of the suit via a succession of tiny wires, which held the penis in such a way as to prevent climax. Moreover, the faster and more efficiently the contestant had completed the course, the more time he would have at the end to enjoy this sensation. It was very rare for a player to be rewarded with no pleasurable experience at all, though clocking up a disastrous zero points would result in Princess Xena haughtily slapping your face and leaving as the screen faded to black, and actually going into minus points would result in Princess Xena's psychotic father, King Xenus, suddenly entering the story and chopping off your head with the small hatchet that he kept in his belt: a nasty tingly sensation the v-suit would transmit to the back of the neck.

Princess Xena peeled off her negligée in front of Wayne and the entire male population of the King's Cross and Somers Town areas of North London who had now assembled in the Pleasure Palace, crowding and scuffling in front of the 2-metre monitor screen on the side of the Sex Kombat machine to watch the denouement.

Xena slithered invitingly into the enormous heart-shaped double bed in her sumptuous boudoir, on the walls of which various tasteful erotic prints from Pietro Aretino were peripherally to be seen. Xena now looked incredibly like Catherine, and that thought – and the sense that he was somehow being unfaithful to Catherine, by having cybersex with her lookalike – infused Wayne with an exquisite sense of wrongdoing, a deplorable thrill of evil. She reclined languorously on a bank of cushions and the cloud of dark hair was *exactly* like Catherine's. But just as he was going to make an absolute pig of himself and avail himself of the two minutes and fifty-three seconds of cyberpleasure with Princess Xena – that videoharlot slapper – a very strange thing happened.

Wayne clambered on to the bed on top of Xena, and that's when he felt a third presence in the room. He hesitated at the very point of penetration. Xena groaned imploringly. The seconds ticked by at the top of the screen. Satisfied, he advanced again and squeezed Xena's left breast, an action which elicited a histrionic squeal of pleasure from Xena and a cheer from the adolescent audience outside in the Pleasure

Palace. Then Wayne was aware of The Presence again: a powerfully moral Presence which disapproved, a Presence which enjoined Wayne to think again about his greedy and lustful and shallow approach to life. Again, Wayne hesitated, stunned, disorientated. Now Xena pouted, her lower lip protruded, and then she tilted her head birdlike on one side. One of the audience impatiently banged the outside of the machine; but this impact was quite unheeded. The mysterious Presence had again intruded itself in Princess Xena's bedroom, and Wayne was more aware than ever of its powerful physical dimension. A blonde femaleness was what it seemed mostly to consist of, a slight off-centre smile, a distinct *shyness* and yet the sort of shyness that asserted itself boldly and with an air of command.

'What is it, Wayne?' asked Xena at last, annoyed at this baffling interruption to her pleasure, yet still hoping to salvage the situation.

'I don't know, darling,' said Wayne at last.

Xena smiled roguishly. Perhaps Wayne was shy; so many of her sweetest conquests were. Time was getting on, though. A minute and a half to go.

'Well, come *on* then, darling,' said Xena and reached across and caressed his strong thigh; kneeling on the bed Wayne could feel her hand across each tiny hair. Then he felt her other hand caressing his responding penis. Then he felt another hand, lightly, and yet commandingly, on his shoulder. Jesus Christ. Did she have three hands or what?

'Wayne! Whatever is the matter?' Now Xena was getting annoyed: a minute and ten seconds to go, and she was noting alarming signs coming from the ticking, tilting erection meter.

But Wayne was looking away from the lovely Xena towards the saintly blonde Presence with the off-centre smile on the far side of the room, a Presence which called him away from crass exploitative sexuality and towards a more loving, respectful approach to Catherine, and to all women.

'Wayne!' barked Princess Xena, now sitting, her knees

drawn crossly up.

Wayne turned back to her distractedly.

'What is it, darling?'

'*When* are we going to make love?'

'I, er, I don't think I should.'

'Why ever not?'

'Well, I've, I've already got a girlfriend . . .'

Princess Xena smiled knowingly. 'That's all right, darling. I've got a boyfriend too. It doesn't matter this once.'

'No, you don't understand. If we had sex now it would be an empty experience, an experience devoid of love.'

'What on *earth* are you talking about?' snapped Xena. 'And what is that you keep looking at?'

Princess Xena craned her neck to see beyond Wayne at the end of the bed, and as she did so, she went very pale.

'Oh my *goodness*,' she said, and Wayne guessed that this quaint phrase, so different from the earthy vulgarities of the rest of her speech, had clearly been retrieved from the deepest recesses of her cyberchildhood.

Both Wayne and Xena were deeply awed by the mystery of The Presence. Like small children in some fable, they hopped out of bed and knelt down.

Outside, the chanting of 'Why are we waiting?' from the huge crowds of adolescent boys and young men, had got very ugly. They were banging rhythmically on the outside of the machine, and other machines as well. The proprietor of the Pleasure Palace, a gentle Greek Cypriot, fingered the emergency red button that he kept in the change counter which would (theoretically) summon the private security service he subscribed to. How bitterly he now regretted hiring the version of Sex Kombat (£85,000 per week) that had the spectator monitor facility.

As he looked down, Wayne could see the animated version of his quivering naked knees in front of him. Squinting to his side, he could see Princess Xena kneeling as modestly and chastely as a nun. Having resembled the brashest and most cosmetically enhanced of porn queens, she now looked a little like a cross between Mia Farrow and Liv Ullmann. Then Wayne made so bold as to raise his sightline and gaze directly at The Presence herself. As he tried to do so, the screen went fuzzy; it blurred and went blank – but sprang back into life, the moment he humbly averted his eyes once more. The same happened with the monitor on the outside of the machine. Something, some spectral presence emanated from that grubby glass square as it did so, and the entire company assembled in the Pleasure Palace grew thoughtful and silent. They considered their misdeeds, their inadequacies, their predisposition to treat women as sex objects.

The monitor screen went blank; Wayne's field of vision also, because he had closed his eyes tightly, but within the dark brown soupiness, he could see, like a photographic negative, a lovely female image in which the blond hair, brief summer dress, and the whites of the eyes were reversed into smudges of blackness on his retina, like revelations of the Blessed Virgin at Knock or Medjugorje. Trembling and wincing, he disengaged himself from the sweaty, loathsome v-suit, and staggered out of the cramped Sex Kombat booth in which he had been kneeling as if in confessional. Almost tripping, he stepped out of the trouser-legs, and could hardly bear to fold the suit up and replace it in the relevant unit, as he was strictly told to do by a notice on the sheer aluminium panel next to the door. Wayne was now openly sobbing with dismay and self-disgust. A winking display on the panel then invited him to register his still very creditable points total as a high score, and by keying in his address and the number of his bank debit card, apply to compete in the international Sex Kombat 2000 world cup in Asunscion, an unrivalled forum for Sex Kombat technology and expertise. With a single slap of his outstretched palm on the panel below, he ferociously erased and rejected this offer, and the assembled company honoured this gesture of self-control and moral seriousness with a gasp. His poor face was still bunched and clenched with suppressed sobs, which periodically escaped like hiccups as he gathered up his coat and bag. The crowd stood back respectfully, and the Pleasure Palace owner briefly deserted his post at the change *guichet* in order to demonstrate his proprietorial solidarity with Wayne.

He rushed out of the arcade, glassy-eyed. But once he was gone, the atmosphere of overwhelming moral exaltation diminished almost immediately. The crowd awoke as if from a light trance. They milled around a little, occasionally meeting each others' eyes with a slight laugh or shrug, as if they had all witnessed something rather odd – which, of course, they had.

Wayne was accelerating into a run up the Euston Road. The great sugary sky sagged and rippled overhead. He was approaching St Pancras station and hotel, those great, morose, religiose buildings which inspired in him a need to run even faster, cannoning off people as he did so.

From the great streaming access of the Marylebone Road to the crescent cages of Regent's Park, North London was losing the light, and Wayne, emboldened and maddened by redemption and release, ran on and up into its darkness, while on his hip and thigh his bag smote an irregular tattoo.

12

'Getting Past The Millennium' was a programme that Catherine was producing, a segment of a gigantic European transmission notionally going out live to millions of cable subscribers. A discussion panel would ruminate on the meaning of the millennium. This panel was going to include Ysenda, who would be joining the symposium via a link-up from the Middle East. Her plan to see in the new epoch in Bethlehem was going ahead, despite Father Sparkbrook's anxious prediction that it would be an expensive fiasco. The Bethlehem hotel would only return eighty per cent of the booking fees in the event of a cancellation, and the resulting mess had almost cost Ysenda her job at the Sacred Heart Institute. Another member of the panel was Sean, whose brief was to discuss the dissolution of categories in sexuality in the third millennium, and whose participation had been guaranteed by hints dropped to the effect that the editor of C.C.3 would be more than happy to fill in if he was unable to come. The programme was due to be transmitted from a studio set up in the Royal Observatory in Greenwich, and afterwards there would be a modest 'wrap' party, which happily solved all of Sean's worries about how he was going to see in the New Millennium.

Nick had not been invited to 'Getting Past The Millennium', nor the subsequent party. There seemed no very obvious reason why a maverick psycho-physiotherapist should be invited, and yet he was already keenly aware that almost all of his circle of friends would be going. Since he broke up with Inge, he did not even have a date for the evening. So, humiliatingly, he had had to ask Ysenda if she could get Catherine to get him into the party.

The thought of staying in for the night was intolerable – even though he realised that this was probably the most sensible option for what was bound to be the most hellish evening anyone in the world would ever experience in their lifetimes, literally *two thousand* times worse than any New Year's Eve party. And how he hated New Year's Eve, how *everyone* hated New Year's Eve. Did anyone, ever, enjoy this meaningless pseudo-celebration of nothing? Nick often thought that a way of understanding and indeed respecting the curmudgeonly ill temper of Ebenezer Scrooge would be to imagine that it was not Christmas but New Year's Eve he was objecting to, not 'ho, ho, ho' but 'should auld acquaintance'. That really was humbug. And watching television was somehow out of the question. Inevitably, he would be drawn to the millennium discussion, even though it was bound to be far more austere programming than anything else on the airwaves – not Nick's sort of thing at all. But he would find himself watching it, because all his friends were on it, or involved in it, and there is something about watching one's friends and acquaintance on television that is subtly bad for the soul.

There was another reason why the thought of the forthcoming millennium should dispirit Nick so much, and it was the same reason why he felt so closely tied to Wayne and

Sean and Ysenda. The reason was that it was his birthday: all their birthdays. They were all born on 1 January 1970: it was what brought them together at infant school and what habitually inspired them to have joint parties. But now this was something they did not care to discuss. They were all twenty-nine years old, and the approach of the year 2000 gave the end of their youth a cataclysmic air. It was the Armageddon of their carefree prime. This really was the end of days. When the dreadful hour of midnight arrived, it would bring with it the Four Horsemen of the Apocalypse: Receding Hairline, PEP, Weight Gain, and Not Knowing What's At Number One.

Twenty. What a light, capricious sound the word had, and how hatefully heavy *thirty* sounded, like someone saying 'twenty' with a speech impediment brought about through some debilitating malady like Parkinson's Disease. Come kiss me sweet and thirty did not have the same ring.

Not all of his acquaintances had Nick's horror of becoming thirty years old. Wayne, in particular, had breezily assured him that though it would be horrible at first, once they were through that dreadful and painful barrier they would emerge into the broad, sunlit uplands of realising that a man in his early thirties is more or less the same as the man in his early twenties, only much richer, cleverer, more assured, and much more likely to make it with women in their early twenties!

Nick was not so sure. Wayne was actually coming round to the clinic tonight with a 48-pack, so they could all watch some edited highlights of the secretly recorded Inge massage tapes that Aldo had prepared for him. (Nick had been considering saving this audio-visual treat for himself on 31 December, but an innate sense of generosity and the spirit of human fellowship compelled him to share it, just as someone of his father's generation would not have wished to open a really good bottle of claret and then drink it all himself.)

Ysenda turned up with Wayne, which disconcerted Nick at first. He showed them both into his private-office-slash-video-monitoring-gallery with a distinct sense of dismay that they were not, after all, to sample the video treat that was the whole point of the evening – until Ysenda demanded: 'So when's the *show* start? What, do we have to make *conversation* until you put the *video* on?'

Sheepishly, Nick unlocked the bottom drawer of his desk, produced the VHS copy and inserted it with a plastic clunk into the VCR. Ysenda laughed uproariously throughout, a strident contrast to the blank, poker-faced neutrality that both Nick and Wayne judged it expedient to maintain while watching pornography in the company of another male.

'Oh no,' she said over and over again. 'Oh no! Not again! Oh gross! Oh you're grossing me out; *ich bin ja outgegrossed*! What *is* that? Why do they always want that? Why do *you* always want that? Why don't we just skip everything and just go straight to that? What's going to happen to the human race if all you ever want is that?' Nick did not reply, but withheld a second tape that he had in his desk drawer, devoted to him personally having sex with Inge; if Ysenda had not been there, he would have put it on. Many was the time, watching the tape on his own in a dull half-hour, he realised that this was the only image he actually possessed of himself, aside from his passport photo. No one took holiday snaps or family videos of Nick. If ever he was murdered or abducted and the police needed to jog the public's memory with his likeness, then *this* was the video they would have to show on the early evening news or as part of the 'Crimewatch' TV appeal. His straining face would appear in the videotape's smeared and lilac hues, with the deadpan timecode winking in the corner, while presenter Nick Ross intoned: 'Police are keen to contact anyone with any knowledge of the whereabouts of this young man, Nick Stewart, seen here in a home video, getting a blow-job.'

The tape over – more than enough at twenty-five minutes – Ysenda showed that she did not want to be a parasite, and that she had something to bring to the party. With a flourish, she produced a mini-disk.

'What's that?' asked Nick.

'It is a *treat*, Nicholas, a treat which you have done nothing to deserve.'

Nick inserted the disk, which contained one visual file, and by clicking on a few icons, was able to play its contents on his computer monitor. It turned out to be something that Ysenda had downloaded from the net at one of the alternative Disney sites: covert video recordings from the big, disabled lavatory in the staff section at Disneyland Paris, the real jewels being those emergency visits by staff playing characters, staff who had frantically absented themselves from the daily Main Street parade to answer a call of nature. At an approximate speed of twenty-four silent-movie frames a second, they watched a gigantic Minnie Mouse silently shoehorn herself inside the lavatory stall: a difficult business, even given the fact that the disabled toilet was designed to be big enough to accommodate a wheelchair and companion. With the jittery movements born of urgency and panic, she started unclipping and unzipping her costume, while her great head rolled and bashed against the lavatory wall, and all carried off with Minnie's strange and vacuous open-mouthed smile. Finally the lower half of her costume was detached and shoved downwards, while Minnie smilingly swept up her tail and upper costume above the waist and plonked herself down to take a much-anticipated dump, which proceeded as Minnie's head sagged downwards in little jerks, smiling beatifically. Then it jerked upwards. The door was moving.

Goofy. Goofy was trying to get in. For fuck's sake. Smiling tolerantly, Minnie kicked the heedlessly unlocked door back as it swung open, but to no avail. In a trice it snapped back and Goofy's great grinning snout and the brim of his dumb, battered hat intruded into the lavatory. His little corncob pipe waved at Minnie like a tiny finger. Did Goofy want to use this toilet? Was he registering a principled objection to the fact that Minnie was voiding her bowels in costume, which was strictly against Disney policy, no matter where they were on the site? Ysenda commented that the chat room discussion of this moment could not definitively enlighten the viewer, and the French notice over the lavatory was illegible. For a while Goofy and Minnie conducted a smilingly amicable exchange, the extravagant hand gestures limited to Goofy pointing to somewhere outside the stall and Minnie pointing down at her haunches. Playfully, Goofy at last hauled at Minnie's body; Minnie grinningly stayed put. Then the tape seemed to snap and restart some time later in the next scene. Goofy and Minnie were now standing, facing each other in the same mute, simpering colloquium. At almost exactly the same time, they pushed back their face masks and their giant beaming heads snapped back horribly, like the death of the Elephant Man. Their human faces were still invisible, but what was apparent was the fact that Goofy was now producing a triangle of paper, unfolding it, sprinkling some powder out on the cistern, and cutting it into lines with the hard piece of plastic appended to the end of his tail. Minnie and Goofy ingested this deeply and their great rolling heads nodded forward, back into showtime position. Their smiles now took on a worldly, jaded aspect, as if frozen in contempt, clouded by fear, for what this rush of pleasure could mean or entail. They stayed hunched together in a mysterious sensual association, and the scene played out like some kind of freemasonry ritual or a disclosure of inscrutable movements in a badger sett. Soon there was another movement at the door, a slight shuffle or scuffle and then two more figures entered – Dumbo and the Hunchback of Notre Dame. Now, although still silent, the scene took on a more emphatically dramatic character, like something from Feydeau. Wayne, Nick and Ysenda watched in a trance, as they passed round a medium-sized joint. The four figures on the screen gesticulated at each other, they bobbed and moved around each other, like an experimental ballet of dolphins. They all broke off and consumed some of what Goofy had laid out on the cistern, and presently, the gathering split on Darwinian lines. Whatever their argument had been, Dumbo had evidently made common cause with the two other animals against the human. The hunchback cringed and flinched as the dog, the mouse and the elephant rounded on him, crowded him – and pushed him over. Soon they surrounded the prostrate cripple, kicking him, kicking him, kicking him over and over again, kicking him with massive hoof and paw while the Hunchback's face was set in a mask of agony, and Dumbo's great blue trunk lashed up in the air like a flail, kicking the Hunchback in a Dionysiac orgy of violence. Suddenly, apparently dislodged by all the activity, the lavatory seat fell shut, and the noise (there must have been a bang) caused Dumbo, Minnie and Goofy to stop kicking and look up. The Hunchback looked up also, supporting himself on both elbows, although in truth he was already semi-upright because of having to lie on his hump. That is where the tape ended: the grey bar along the bottom of the frame had extended all the way from left to right, and the screen went blank.

'Right,' said Wayne, at last.

'Yeah,' exhaled Ysenda.

'Mmm,' concurred Nick, narrowing his eyes and looking at the glowing red tip of his joint. In fact, he hardly dared admit to everyone that this entertainment had begun to pall with him. There was a time when hanging out aimlessly with his friends all the livelong day, smoking, drinking and watching trivial or semi-obscene material downloaded from the net would be the very finest pastime life could offer. *It can't get any better than this*, he would often think happily, reclining in front of the screen. Earth has not anything to show more fair. But these pleasures involved a certain lassitude, an extravagant expenditure of time, and at the age of twenty-nine the fabric of life and youth had been pulled a little taut for that.

Twenty-nine. Time was running out for him, and Nick would have to resign himself to never achieving anything of fame or note in his twenties. A bitter pill. The other day he had asked Ysenda's advice on, of all things, a *book* to read: a really good book. Stumped, Ysenda at last recommended *Wuthering Heights*. Nick borrowed it laboriously from his local library, took it home, but before he read a word, he checked the publication date (1847), and the date of the author's birth (1818) which made her . . . bitch! Smug cow! He flung the book across the room, and slumped, sulking, on to the chaise-longue-cum-massage-table in Suite Four. He was fucked if he was going to read it now. Not with Miss Emily Twenty-something Brontë Achiever gloating over him. Huh! Twenty-*nine*. Just under the bloody wire, darling. And afterwards Nick disconsolately showed Ysenda the fruits of some research he had done in the local library and elsewhere to which he had grumpily returned *Wuthering Heights*. It was a table, the purpose of which was to focus his mind on how he should be approaching his Personal Millennium.

29-angst figures

1. ZARATHUSTRA. Sean had told him about this one. Lead character in Nietzsche's *Thus Spake Zarathustra*. Spent his entire twenties sitting up in a cave carved into a mountainside, and only left the cave on his thirtieth birthday to start haranguing the people in that distinctive visionary way. *29-angst approval rating: B+. Only started his career after 30.*

2. NEIL TENNANT. The singer from The Pet Shop Boys. Started recording when he was in his thirties and even going a bit bald. *29-angst approval rating: A+. Excellent.*

3. **JESUS CHRIST**. Achieved nothing of note until His thirtieth birthday; only then did He begin His ministry. Disputing with the doctors in the temple at the age of 12 does not count. *29-angst approval rating: C-. The low score is because of the James Dean career move factor which kicks in almost immediately at the age of 33, which spiritually back-dates Jesus and makes him a youth icon.*

4. **NAPOLEON**. Did not become master of all France until his thirties. *29-angst approval rating: B-. Unlike Zarathustra, Napoleon was striving conspicuously for success throughout his twenties. Also, he was born on 15 August 1769, and achieved supreme power on 9 November 1799. So he might have done a lot of pining in private about just having missed it, and how cool it would have been to be the Emperor in his twenties.*

Inevitably, lugubriously, the conversation veered and banked towards the upcoming youth-apocalypse and Wayne, despite telling Nick earlier that he was not that worried, joined in the general anxiety.

'Jesus,' said Wayne. 'Have you noticed how you can't remember what you did last Friday? Or last week? Or last year?'

'Mmmm,' agreed Nick. 'It's as if you've hit a patch of ice, and you've lost all traction and you're skidding across the line. Being twenty-nine; it's not even properly in your twenties any more, because you can't help thinking about being thirty; you can't enjoy it, it's as if you've lost a year.'

'Yeah,' said Ysenda, 'actually, come to think of it, why can't we *gain* a year? Why can't it be, like, going from British Summer Time to Greenwich Mean Time? You're thinking, hey, well, almost time for my thirtieth birthday, and someone says no, have you forgotten, tonight's the night we turn the calendars back. You get to be twenty-nine again for another year.

And later you pay it back by going straight from thirty-eight to forty, because by then obviously you'll be such an old wreck you won't care about age or time or anything.'

The three of them nodded thoughtfully.

'Really, I'm not too worried,' said Ysenda. 'Twenty-nine isn't nearly as anxious as nineteen.'

'Yeah?'

'Of *course* yeah,' she said. 'Being twenty looked like being a nightmare. But the real horror was before *that*; being *nine*.'

'You're kidding,' grunted Wayne.

'No, that was horrible. I couldn't sleep for thinking or worrying about it. *Ten*. Double figures. It was gruesome. What a horrible quantum leap for a little kid. Not something you face again until you're ninety-nine.'

'But why? Why were you so upset?'

'Because Catherine – my sister, and your girlfriend –'

Wayne shifted uneasily. So Catherine hadn't told her yet. Was *he* supposed to tell her?

'Catherine told me that once I was ten I wasn't allowed to be a kid any more. I would grow a beard and all my toys would be taken away. Although what the hell she thought she knew about it, I don't know, because she was younger than me.'

'A beard?'

'Yep. A great, grown-up beard would suddenly sprout on my little ten-year-old face. Also, I had this little doll called Amanda-Jane and I had lots of really nice clothes for her, and she wasn't like stupid, airhead Barbie, she was a really nice girl, and she lived in this little doll's house and I had little chairs and tables and a little bed for her and everything.'

'So what happened?'

'Catherine said my dad would smash it up with an axe on my birthday. My mother would come into my bedroom at the stroke of midnight on my tenth birthday with a cake with ten candles on it, but my dad would come in behind her carrying an axe and smash up Amanda-Jane's house because it's something that only nine-year-olds can have. Then he would give me my one and only present for my tenth birthday.'

'What was it?'

'A grey school dress. For the special school that I would have to go to with all the other ten-year-olds and have lessons until half-past-nine at night.'

They were silent for a while, and then Nick spoke up with a sudden, passionate sense of injustice.

'Why the hell do we have to stop being in our twenties next year?'

'Because we'll be thirty,' said Wayne.

'But it's so unfair. I still feel in my twenties. I still feel the same as when I was twenty-one, or twenty-four. Look – we were only in our teens for *seven years*. I think we should have an extra three years of being in our twenties to make up for being short-changed on that one.'

'Oh, you men. You guys,' snorted Ysenda. 'You really have got it easy in the getting older department. If you really want to change the numerical rules, there's only one fair way of doing it.'

'Which is . . . ?' inquired Wayne.

'Women are allowed to get older in Base Twelve.'

'Really?'

'Yes. We reach our physical and sexual peak much later than men and we age much more badly than men, who are allowed to be really like *distinguished* and *greying* when they get older, as opposed to women who become boilers and slappers and slags and then when we're old we get to be invisible and nobody takes any notice of us at stuff like bus-stops. What we need is longer decades. So we should stay in single figures until we start our periods, which is usually about twelve. So what we do is invent two new digits for eleven and twelve: # and *.'

'# and *?'

'Yeah. # and *. Then, while you men are ageing from twelve to twenty-four, we are going through our richly mature teens, culminating in #teen and *teen, and then our twenties come while you are going through the hell that is twenty-five to thirty-six. While you guys are creeping up to early middle age, we are in our vigorous prime: twenty-# and twenty-*.'

'But listen,' said Wayne, rolling another joint, this one the approximate size and weight of a rolling pin. 'Listen. How could that actually slow down the actual, biological ageing process?'

'Mmmm,' said Ysenda dreamily. 'You know, the answer's obvious. It's—'

'I've been thinking,' interrupted Nick, who had been gazing broodingly out on to Highgate High Street. 'Thinking about Sean.'

The subject made both Ysenda and Wayne sit up a little. It made them both uneasy, Wayne because of the whole Sean-and-Catherine thing, and Ysenda because she found herself concerned about Sean anyway. Quite involuntarily she raised the back of her hand to her face, seeking that exotic chloriney perfume of Sean's helplessness and his nearness. Ysenda would often tell others and herself that she was *worried* about Sean – but in fact worrying about Sean was just a pretext for thinking about him.

'What about him?' they both asked in unison.

'Well, is he like straight or gay now, or what?'

Wayne frowned and looked down. He didn't know if he could possibly tell them what he knew.

Ysenda quietly offered: 'Well, he had girlfriends. Girls he went out with. But now I guess he's gay.'

Nick frowned even more. 'Why?'

'Well, he's the editor of *Somdomite*, isn't he?'

'But he's never had a, a male *partner*, has he?'

'I dunno. But that's not the point, is it? Sean rejects those labels.'

'Does he? Is that what he does?'

'Yeah. I mean, it could be that he's like a kind of notional

Anglican; a non-churchgoing Anglican. Sean's a gay man who doesn't go out with men or have sex with them.'

'Or fancy them?'

'Then how can he be gay?'

'Well, I don't think he's having sex with anyone. So he's celibate. He's non-practising. It's like non-religious people in Ireland being *cultural catholics*. Sean's a cultural gay. Maybe we're all cultural gays.'

There was a brief pause while Nick ingested this information. 'You mean, like, wearing eye-liner?'

'No, Nick,' said Ysenda, recovering some of her acid toughness. 'That is not what I mean by "cultural" gay. It's more about vacuuming, and wearing freshly laundered jeans and affecting a stupid gooey enthusiasm for each and every talentless American singer and showbiz broad who has ceased to menstruate.'

'I don't do any of those things,' said Nick reasonably, after a beat.

'OK,' said Ysenda blearily, 'so we're *not* all cultural gays.'

'But listen,' frowned Wayne. 'How on earth did Sean get to be this way? How did he see himself as a notional, celibate, cultural, intransitive polyvalent non-heterosexual?'

13

It was certainly a question that continued to trouble his mother.

'I simply cannot credit it,' said Sean's mother heavily, sitting at his dining table, both palms down on its surface either side of a mug of instant coffee on an octagonal cork coaster. She was wearing a burgundy cashmere sweater and a delicate buttery-coloured blouse whose teeny collar protruded around the sweater's neckline like the fashion of far younger women from fifteen years ago. 'I cannot credit it. First the cat dies. First Pussy Fred dies of some intestinal disorder that I simply do not understand. How *did* Pussy Fred die incidentally?' his mother asked fiercely, but then carried on without waiting for a reply. 'I mean how on earth does a cat die . . . like *that*? Was it something he ate? Was it something *you* ate? But this is by the way. It is by the by. It is as nothing compared to *this*.'

Sean had never been closer to shouting at her. Instead, he kept his cool and quietly folded away the copy of the *Harbinger* that she had brought with her, the copy with his review of the leather outfit.

'You're homosexual. I know that. I suppose I've come to terms with that. You're an invert.'

'*Mother—*'

'Let me finish. You're a same-sex enthusiast. This I know. This I have registered. This I have taken on board. I am never to have the sweet pleasure of—'

'Mother—'

'—of grandchildren. No. Not me. Not this lady. Ho no. The older person's prerogative of enjoying the pleasure of young children, yet without the parents' burden, the nappy-changing, the scrimping and saving to educate them privately, and recently in your case dragging their unconscious homosexual bodies out of swimming pools . . .'

She paused a beat, expecting some protest or intervention. None came, and she continued '. . . this I am not to have. I know that you have decided to remain in a kind of sexual orientation that *I* grew out of when *I* was fourteen.'

'*Whaat?*'

'Oh yes,' she said with a supercilious smile, scooping up the mug with both palms in the hot-chocolate-drinking-chocolate position. 'This is just another way in which young people think they invented everything and we old folk fell off the top of a Christmas tree and don't know from anything. So yes, Master Clever Smartypants Who Knows Everything, yes, your old mother used to be a homosexual, but it was just a phase, because men and women of our generation knew that this was just something you went through, and if it took a long time to get through it, well there we are.'

'Mother, are you saying you used to be gay?' Sean felt as if he was going to faint, for the first time since the swimming pool incident.

'Yes. Yes.'

Something in his mother's defensive manner caused Sean to grow suspicious, suddenly.

'Who were you gay with?'

'It was when I was at boarding school with a girl called

Anna. We would do everything together. We would decorate each other's exercise books with flowery patterns in felt pen. We would write long entries about each other in our diaries. We would play tennis together, and we would use each other's racquet presses on alternate days because we felt it would help to entwine us spiritually.'

'What on earth are "racquet presses"?'

'Do please shut up. Our beds were next to each other in the dormitory and, just before lights out, we would have long and drawn-out conversations about what had happened during the day, and if at any time we thought our friendship and our regard for each other had faltered, we would "make up" by writing extra-long entries about each other in our diaries.'

'Mother?' asked Sean heavily.

'Yes?'

'Did you ever actually kiss her or have sex with her?'

'Of course not, don't be disgusting. I only knew her for one term and to be honest I never liked her that much. It was her brother I really fancied. But the point, the whole point of telling you this is that you think you're so big and clever and that your generation invented everything, but it's *not true*.'

'So what are you saying?'

'*This*.' His mother put the mug down and once again opened out her copy of the *Harbinger* at Sean's article, which discoursed at some length about the distinctive role of leather in the fabric of modern gay consciousness: its dark fetishistic quality juxtaposed with its luminous mystery, its associations with manual labour, the sense it conveyed of wearing an alien animal hide – a thoughtful disquisition for which the accompanying light, self-deprecating description of his difficulties with the various straps and zips provided a suitably ironic solvent. All in all, it was an impeccably cerebral piece of writing but, quite unknown to Sean, the *Harbinger* had illustrated it with a photograph of someone else wearing a similar leather outfit; one in which the buttocks were exposed, and this person was being whipped by a naked man in a feather boa. To the unsuspecting reader, it did indeed look as if Sean had been photographed in this position; certainly that was the impression gained by Sean's mother and the various members of her Tuesday morning German conversation group.

'*This*,' she repeated, redundantly. 'We know you're gay, but did you have to be an *abject pervert with no dignity as well*? Or more to the point, did you have to be an abject pervert with no dignity as well and then *shout it from the rooftops*?'

Sean wanted to shout so many things at this point, chief among them was the fact that it was even more shaming than his mother imagined: that he was straight, that he was in love with a girl, a girl who was conducting an affair with someone he had hitherto considered his best friend, and whose only marginal interest in him was that he was supposed to be gay.

'Do you hear that sound, Sean? Do you hear it?' His mother leaned across the table with a piercing glance, her head tilted to one side, like a large, belligerent bird. 'That churning, moaning sound, coming from the churchyard?' She had her hand out; it had insinuated itself between the second and third buttons of his shirt and it was now gently, rhythmically massaging a small area of his chest.

'That is the sound of your father turning in his grave. That rustling, bumping sound you can hear is his elbows banging the side of the coffin as he stirs in his worm-eaten shift, that poor unquiet sleeper—'

'Mother . . .'

'—tormented by the thought of his son being a perve. How I wish in my imagination I could quieten him, Sean, quieten him with a little shake or a pat, the way I used to do when he woke me up with his snoring. But I can't. Because parents never get used to it, Sean. They never get used to it, and there's no use pretending that they do.'

'Mother, that photograph in the paper, it isn't of me,' said

Sean at last, detaching himself from his mother's touch, standing up and moving away from the table, hoping that this mundane point of detail – an issue from which she had long since progressed away – might disrupt her train of thought. To his surprise, it seemed to work.

'It isn't?'

'No it isn't. That silly photograph was of someone else, and was used without my permission, and because of it I have resigned from the *Harbinger*, which I don't think I can afford to do incidentally.'

'Really?'

'Yes, really. The whole thing is an incredible embarrassment.'

Indeed it was. *C.C.3* had run a very big feature about it, in terms wholly unflattering to Sean; a feature whose hostile tone was coloured by the fact that the naked man in the feather boa wielding the whip in the offending picture turned out to be one of *C.C.3*'s contributing editors, a lecturer in gender studies at the University of North London, and the man actually wearing the outfit and being whipped was one of his doctoral research students. The picture had been taken at a party to celebrate this student's successful submission of his PhD thesis about Goethe. The baying, leering mob visible in the murky margins of the photograph was the university's Modern Languages Faculty. The *C.C.3* article itself, so far from sympathising with the way in which Sean's gay identity had been trivialised and marginalised by the *Harbinger*, roundly denounced him for failing to show solidarity with the people pictured and being a bit of an ideological wimp.

'Well . . .' said his mother doubtfully. She was not sure whether she could detach the photograph from the text of Sean's article in her mind, but this was what he now begged her to do. He enjoined her to consider how thoughtful the whole thing was, and how she must not allow her judgement of his views on the semiosis of leather to be poisoned by the photograph. In fact, he asked her to go home and think about it there, because he had a very important lunch date here at the flat in about a minute and a quarter.

Catherine was coming. Her arrival was imminent, in fact. It was a meeting that she herself had proposed, in the course of a phone call put through to him at the *Somdomite* offices which had caused his heart to lurch and leap.

'Mother, I think you had some shopping to do back down in town.'

'Yes?' His mother's voice was light, neutral, a maddeningly obtuse tone she had mastered for the effect of maximum contrast to the histrionic tone of importunate pleading and threat that tended to precede it.

'Well, you remember that someone is coming round for lunch here?'

'You are cooking lunch?' Again the dumb insolence.

'Yes, Mother.' He indicated the glowing oven in his kitchen in which a russet-red casserole dish reposed.

'I myself will be lunching in town,' said his mother, managing to suggest a rebuke for Sean's uncalled-for negligence in not offering to let her stay, despite the fact that at the beginning of her visit she had repeatedly said how much she was looking forward to eating at a restaurant.

Just as she was stirring from her seat, the door buzzer went, and Sean realised with a sinking heart that Catherine was early and that she would now have to meet his mother.

'And who is that?' asked his mother.

'It'll be Catherine,' said Sean distractedly as he went over to buzz her up, and opened his door.

'Catherine. Who is now the girlfriend of Wayne.'

'Yes. No. *Ex*-girlfriend. Listen, Mother, please don't say too much to— Catherine!'

She came in, smiling politely and looking prettier than ever.

'Hello!'

'Hello, Catherine, my mother's here!'

'Mrs Cunningham – it's nice to see you again.'

His mother's appraising glance rested shrewdly on Catherine while she pulled on her gloves and for a paranoid second Sean suspected that she somehow divined the distress of his unquiet heart.

'Catherine, how lovely to see you again,' she said, and stretched out her hand for Catherine to take, and held on to it for just a little bit too long, placing the left hand over it in an oddly mannish double clasp, and then letting go as if she had just remembered something.

'Oh! My mug!'

'Mother . . .'

His mother proceeded to wash up her own mug, quite unnecessarily, a mannerism that Sean had quite forgotten about, designed to show that she did not wish to be in any way a 'burden' on the host and which she was clearly deploying here to delay her exit.

While she elaborately rinsed her mug under the hot tap in the kitchen, Sean's mother called out to Catherine: 'Have you *come far*?'

'My flat is near Goodge Street,' smiled Catherine.

'Ah – Fitzrovia, as Sean's late father would say.'

'Yes!' smiled Catherine with a little laugh. 'That's exactly what my father says as well!'

Catherine and Sean's mother gave a second little laugh of cultural fellowship and then his mother turned to Sean with a smug little nod, as if to assert some obscure victory.

'Now, Sean,' said his mother, upending her mug on to the draining board briskly, as if it had been he who had been delaying her, 'I want you to come outside with me very quickly and give me some advice about my car.'

'What?' asked Sean in a mild state of despair which overruled the elation and relief at her imminent departure. 'But, Mother, I have a guest, and in any case I don't know anything about cars; I can't drive.'

'Ah,' said his mother sweetly, looking directly at Catherine, 'that is another of your absurd homosexual affectations. It may be *macho* to drive, but plenty of homosexuals do it. Drive, that is.'

Sean went purple.

'Mother, please . . .'

'Besides, didn't you write in your magazine that driving cars makes all men look gay?'

That, unfortunately, was true. Last month, Sean had dashed off a little *jeu d'esprit* for *Somdomite* on how the supremacy of European automobile design, with its cramped and rounded form, together with its dullard 'family saloon' concept and effete comfort and safety features, had unmanned the modern driver. How typical of his mother to remember this now.

'That isn't quite what I said, Mother, and that is *not* why I don't drive.'

'Then why not, for heaven's sake? I am ready and willing to buy you a car if it's the money . . .'

'Mother . . .'

'Or is it some fastidious Freudian thing about handling the *gear-stick*?'

'Mother . . .'

'I'll get you one with automatic transmission . . .'

'Mother!' Sean took her arm and all but physically propelled her towards the door. 'Catherine, I shall be back soon.'

'Goodbye, Catherine!' said his mother gaily.

'Goodbye!' said Catherine brightly.

Outside, by his mother's minute and ovoid Japanese car, Sean hissed: 'What the *fucking* hell was all that about?'

Coolly, and without responding to the obscenity intended to punish and upset her, his mother produced her ignition key on a little fob device which caused her car door to unlock remotely with a strange little gulping *bleep* noise.

'Are you in love with her, Sean? Catherine, I mean?'

Crucially, Sean could not regain his composure immediately, but left an incriminating pause before replying.

'With Catherine? What on earth are you talking about? You should know by now that I'm—'

'— gay, poofy, woofy, yes, yes, yes. But are you in *love* with her?'

Again, there was a pause, and Sean managed an unconvincing laugh.

'What makes you say . . . what on *earth* makes you say that?'

'Because you didn't look at her,' replied his mother simply, swinging her bag across the driver's seat on to the passenger seat.

'What?'

'You didn't look at her. Not once. No little glances, nothing. Not even the way you do with your friends when you think I'm embarrassing you.'

She was in the car now, looking up at him from a seated position, a posture which oddly seemed to disconcert Sean more than if she was standing.

'You're not getting any younger, Sean. You're certainly not getting any richer. So you have to work out what you are.'

With that she closed her door, emphatically enough to compel Sean to jump a little out of the way, and then drove off without another word.

Sean stood stunned for a moment before he realised that Catherine was waiting for his return. Then he turned and quickly let himself in at the front door, vaulted up the stairs and back into his flat, the door of which was still open.

Catherine was still in the kitchen, facing the sink with her back to him. Was she fixing herself a drink? Was she annoyed with him, for leaving her alone so long? Either way, he had been remiss, simply in discharging his duties as a host.

'So, Catherine,' he said brightly, and out of breath. 'What can I get you . . .?'

Catherine turned around, and he could see that the corners of her mouth were turned down, like the face of a cartoon character, and that her bottom lip was trembling.

'Oh, Catherine,' said Sean gently. 'What's the—'

Catherine's face buckled into a single, wet sob and she moved forward. Sean got ready for the longed-for hug situation, bracing himself, his feet planted a little apart and at an angle, the way he sometimes positioned them on the Tube when there was nothing to hang on to. It would be a terrible thing if she threw herself imploringly at him, and they both fell over. Surely now she would embrace him, confess that she realised his love for her, and forget all about Wayne . . . Her arms were tightly round him. Perhaps this would be the big one. Perhaps they would now just tumble ecstatically into bed. She's saying something. What is it?

'Oh Sean, you're the only one I can talk to, because you're so wise and also you're gay. Why is Wayne ignoring me? I thought we were in love, I thought we were even going to get married. How can I win him back?' There was a pause in which Sean said nothing at all.

'I'm sorry,' said Catherine, trying to detach herself from the embrace with Sean. 'I didn't mean to dump my problems on you. That's OK.' She gave a little gulpy laugh. 'I'm OK. You can, you can let go of me now. Really, I'm fine. You can let go.'

Catherine walked back to where her bag was sagging on a chair by the dining table, and fished in it for a squishy pack of twenty Marlboro Lights and a chunky gunmetal-grey lighter. For a second, Sean was able to look at Catherine as a brother or room-mate might see her: her face was flushed and her nose even a little red. The perfection was briefly marred by a whorl of hair, a curly *smear* of hair looping round from the right and attaching smudgily to her right cheek with an adhesive mix of tears and a translucent trace of snot: in the next microsecond, Catherine had brushed it away, and blown her nose with a sharp honk into a tissue from a little Cellophane pack. She turned back and gave Sean the brightest of reassuring smiles. The face was perfection again, and this minute sequence of events made Sean's heart ache with tenderness, ache that he had been vouchsafed a glimpse of her imperfection, ache that she would not have let him see it had she not considered him so completely as a non-lover.

She held the cigarette oddly, between her teeth, and was about to light it when she looked up to Sean in distress and alarm.

'Oh, but, Sean, I'm so sorry, is it OK to smoke in here? I know how sometimes gay men have very strong views on smoking indoors . . .'

'I'm not gay! I'm straight and I adore you; I think about you every minute of the day and I want to go to bed with you' is what Sean perhaps should have said. Instead he daringly muttered: 'Really? I dunno. Give me one of those things.'

'Oh. OK. All right,' said Catherine, a little disconcerted, and passed him a cigarette. Sean accepted the light incompetently as usual, the tip of the cigarette being lit unevenly and diagonally, down one side, leaving brown, dry pristine tobacco at the other side.

Sean decided he was going to be a little less obviously sympathetic, and try something more direct, perhaps even a little curt.

'Drink?'

'Sorry?'

'What would you like to *drink*?'

'Oh, yes. I'll have a beer please.'

'Beer. OK. Lunch'll be about fifteen minutes, incidentally.'

With elaborate casualness, he sloped off into the kitchen, leaving Catherine sniffling a little and wondering where she was supposed to flick her cigarette-ash, a question that immediately perplexed Sean as he tried preparing drinks holding a cigarette, something he had not done for about six years. It was making him feel sick and slightly dizzy.

Eventually, he came back with two cans of lager and an ashtray. Catherine had spent the time of his absence brooding on whether it had been a good idea after all to unburden herself to him in this way.

'Sean – it is all right for me to talk about this to you, isn't it?'

'Of course.' Sean kept the note of cool rational detachment, like a psychiatrist being asked in for a consult.

'I feel that I can really talk to you, but then I realise that you might have problems of your own. I know that you were a bit stressed out when we went to see Nick's band.'

Stressed out?

'I don't think I was really focused on you, or anyone else to be quite honest,' she went on blandly. 'You know I was breaking up with Wayne then?'

Sean didn't know.

'He'd told me just that afternoon, when I'd found a message from another . . . well another girl on his voicemail. So we broke up, and it all got a bit heavy, and we were having a real *heart-to-heart* in that cloakroom place and we were both really upset . . . well, I was really upset . . .' She paused and took another rather bitter drag on her cigarette. Sean remembered to do the same, drawing absurdly hard with a finger and thumb grip, like George Cole in a St Trinian's film.

'Anyway, we were sort of hugging in there, and it was really emotional—' just thinking about it made Catherine a little weepy, 'and then we saw you come into the cloakroom to fetch something.'

'Argh!'

'What's the matter?'

'I've burnt my – it doesn't matter.' Sean had burned the side of one finger on his cigarette's glowing tip.

'Anyway, I saw you, and in a funny way it was quite comforting to see you there.'

'Yes?'

'Yes, really,' she smiled, finishing her beer. She had got through that pretty quickly. 'You looked so serene. So above it all. Like as if you didn't have a care in the world. I mean,

I know you weren't enjoying the gig very much but you've obviously got such wonderful inner *resources*.'

Sean acknowledged the compliment, if compliment it was, with a tight smile. They had both finished their lagers, and Sean opened another pair and they both started drinking them, without a break. His oven timer made a little *ding* sound, but Sean was disinclined to break the flow of Catherine's reminiscence. It automatically went on to a keep-warm function.

'Well, anyway we were, sort of *kissing* and everything—'

'We *were*? Oh, you mean you and Wayne.'

'Yes, Wayne and me,' said Catherine, puzzled at his incredulous interjection. 'And we were both suddenly getting so close, like as if we were sort of comforting each other on our break-up, that I thought we might actually kind of rekindle our relationship from that moment, the, I don't know, the specialness of that moment.'

She smiled at him sadly, as if expecting him to interject. 'Does that sound silly?' she asked.

Sean rallied. 'Of *course* not,' he said firmly. 'I think anyone would feel the same way.'

Catherine's sad, brave smile faded away.

'Wayne didn't feel the same way. Wayne still wanted to split up with me—' Catherine's voice cracked, and Sean, lacking any clearer idea of what he should do at moments like this, leaned forward and refilled her glass.

'Well, perhaps,' Sean cautiously essayed, 'perhaps you just have to move on. Progress. You have to make a New Life for yourself. You had the experience with Wayne, and it was great, and you have no regrets, and you've grown as a person; you can never look back in this life; what is that old saying? You can never go home? So now could be the time to move on, and you'll find that your life is richer and fuller because you have opened yourself to new experiences and maybe, you know, opened yourself perhaps to people that you didn't realise you actually love—'

'Oh *why* can't I have Wayne back? Tell me how to get Wayne back!'

Catherine jumped up with her fists girlishly together and walked jitterishly out of Sean's field of vision towards the window. Sean found himself holding his smiley expression of knowing condescension and aiming it pointlessly at the sofa.

'Sean?'

'Yes?' said Sean with a little start, looking up.

'How? How am I going to get Wayne back?'

'Well,' said Sean at last, clearing his throat, and shifting uneasily in his seat. 'I don't know, Catherine, I think before we get on to that, you might want to make sure that you're not just getting involved in a, ah, very disempowering situation . . .'

Something in Sean's manner, something quite new, intrigued Catherine. Slowly she sat down.

'No,' she said carefully, looking at him steadily. 'I'm sure I'm not. You've got something in mind, haven't you? I *knew* it. I *knew* you'd think of something. Oh Sean darling, you are a star. What is it?'

Sean sipped his beer to cover his cardio-vascular system's convulsive lurch at this endearment, and then set the glass back down on the table.

'Well,' he said. 'You could try . . . making him jealous.'

In his head, in the peeling echo chamber of his skull, Sean could now hear a kettle-drum roll whose tone swooped nauseously downwards to a lower, tenser pitch, like the soundtrack of a thriller. Was this, in fact, the sound his heart was making? His lips were very dry, and he felt the urge to lick them, but was restrained only by the knowledge of how irretrievably uncool that was going to look. Sean took another sip from his glass instead.

He had said it, and he couldn't look Catherine in the eye.

'Jealous?' she said at last, with a little laugh.

'Yes,' he said quietly, and tried a little shrug, as if to say, well, you were going on and on about this, so I just said it to shut you up.

'Jealous,' she said again, with a downward tone. 'Jealous.'

They were silent again. Now there was no turning back. Sean felt the way base jumpers must do the moment after their feet have left the roof of the Park Lane Hilton and they are hurtling down, down, down, down towards the long thin flag pole that extends over the revolving door into the lobby, the pole which will snarl around their half-opened parachute, ensuring that their fragile bodies will hit the unresisting pavement by the cab rank at about four hundred and seventy miles per hour.

'How would that work, exactly?' asked Catherine. Something in the directness of the question, together with the fact that her tears had appeared to dry so quickly, disconcerted Sean, and in another way emboldened him. He ploughed on.

'Well,' he gulped. 'You could pretend to him that you were . . . going out with someone else.' His voice trailed off into a squeak.

'And?'

'Well, that would make him jealous.'

Catherine looked straight through him. Her brow became furrowed with a kind of concentrated bafflement, inducing two lines, one a few millimetres longer than the other, to fork above her eyebrows. Sean thought about what it would be like either to kiss them laterally, that is, with his lips along the lines of the creases, or transversely, his lips crosswise against the lines, sipping a fold of slightly tanned skin. Presently, the brow smoothed out once more and was then scored with a more emphatic look of quizzical amusement.

'How, though? Do I tell him that I'm going out again with my old boyfriend? Wayne *did* meet him once, and they didn't get on. I can see how that might really ann—'

'No,' interrupted Sean in a nervous and unbecomingly high voice, which he managed to get down into the correct chromosome range for the rest of the sentence. 'I think it might be better, more effective, if it was . . . if it wasn't, you know, your old boyfriend, someone he associates with a sort of pre-Wayne status quo.'

Once again, silence reigned.

Catherine asked finally: 'So what *do* I do?'

'Well, for it to be credible I think Wayne has to somehow experience or witness it for himself, sort of spontaneously. He sort of has to, ah, see you with . . . with this other person. This other man.'

'You mean: see me kissing him.'

'Er, yes, well, ahem, well, yes, I s'pose *kissing – kissing* him would be good, yes, kissing him at some, say, party to which you were both invited, yes, kissing, yes, with tongues, that, perhaps, you know, a bit *obvious*, but, yes . . .'

'Are you all right?'

'Yes, yes, I'm absolutely fine, I think this lager's a bit cloudy.'

Now it appeared to be Catherine's turn to smile superciliously.

'Sean, this is all very well, but there's one thing you haven't thought of, isn't there?'

'Is there?' he said weakly.

'Yes,' she said. '*Who* am I supposed to kiss, according to your brilliant master-plan?'

'Who?'

'Yes, who! You haven't given a single thought to who it is you want me to kiss, you silly thing!' She gave his knee a playful, sisterly shove.

The kettle drums were now coming back up in tone, a vulgar *glissando* that was accompanied with shrieking Bernard Herrmann violins. Sean managed a chuckle at this stage, but it took it out of him; for that second it felt like trying to talk after a two-and-a-half-hour operation.

'Well,' he said after a while, raising his palms, as if sportively conceding her point. 'OK. So who should it be?'

'Oh, I don't know,' said Catherine severely, looking down at the carpet, and after a moment Sean comprehended that she didn't mean she didn't know who she should kiss, she meant oh, she didn't know about this whole crazy plan. 'Is this a good idea? I mean, who could I ask to do it? I mean, it could get pretty, you know, *messy*.'

Sean nodded seriously in grave agreement, bulging his chin against his chest. Again there was silence, and he finally placed his glass unsteadily on the table in front of him, half on and half off the octagonal cork coaster. He felt difficulty breathing, as if he was halfway up K2. The kettle drums were now like pneumatic drills. The kettle drums were just getting silly. He was getting a headache from the bloody kettle drums.

'Catherine. Look, there is a way of doing this. A way that might not be so messy.'

He had her attention, certainly.

'What?'

'Well, I was thinking – you could kiss *me*.'

Sean could not quite bear to look directly at Catherine when he said this and so looked down into his lap in an odd imitation of bashfulness, and forced the corners of his mouth up into a sad smile. Peripherally, he saw Catherine jumping up and preparing to sit down next to him and hug him. But euphoria had no time to climb into his chest, because in the next moment he saw that the hug he was going to get was the sisterly sideways-on sort, the sort recommended in American offices as the politically correct sort of spontaneous male-female cuddle.

'Oh, Sean, that's so *sweet*.'

No one likes to feel that he is being pitied, and no man especially likes to feel that he is being pitied by the object of his recently declared love. It was the sort of thing that could sour relations very badly. But Sean kept his nerve; and remembered that he hadn't declared his love, and wasn't being pitied. Catherine simply really did think it was sweet.

'I really do think that's sweet.'

Sean coolly managed a jaunty raising of the eyebrows, and turned round to look directly into her eyes which met his candidly. He shrugged.

'Well, think about it. If you kiss me, we can organise the whole thing together. We can get it sorted out. We can choreograph it.'

Catherine looked down. Then she got up and resumed her seat facing Sean. This down-to-business formation told Sean, in his maddened state of secret cunning, that he was getting somewhere. But wait:

'I don't *know*, Sean.' She was smiling, shaking her head, the frown-fork on her forehead reappearing minutely, and yet she wanted to be convinced. 'I feel weird. It feels weird kissing a gay man like that. What would it . . . what would it *say*? I mean, it can hardly be some kind of neutral state for you, can it? You have feelings too, and you can't really put them on hold as far as kissing me is concerned. Kissing a girl, I mean, wouldn't you find that sort of weird? Would it, like, sort of make you feel nauseous? You surely can't do it without feeling *anything*. I'd feel like I was using you. Would we have this long kiss, and then you'd have to run out to throw up or something? And what would Wayne or anyone else think about *me* kissing *you*?'

Sean did a convincing job of smiling and shaking his head throughout the last third of this, as if to say there was *so* much she didn't understand both about gay men's sexuality and the universal nature of male jealousy.

'All that doesn't *matter*,' he told her. 'It's what I've been writing about in *Somdomite* for such a long time. It's just the spectacle that counts. The fact of it being seen to happen.'

Catherine nodded uncomprehendingly, uncertain.

'Besides,' said Sean, and even had the *sang-froid* to take another sip of beer, 'there's a very good reason for you to kiss a gay man.'

He had Catherine spellbound. She just leaned in towards him, lips slightly parted.

'You can make him think you've *converted* me. You can make Wayne think that this thing between us is so strong that you've tempted me over to the other side. That way you'll really make him jealous. You'll make him more jealous than he's ever been in his life. It'll freak him out. '

Catherine took this in, then leant back in her seat. Her lips pursed momentarily in a kind of 'whew' expression, but then were immediately split by a mile-long grin – a grin of sheer pleasure and excitement.

'Sean, that is absolutely brilliant. You are absolutely brilliant. You're a star. You're a superstar.'

Speak on, thought Sean dreamily, speak on and cease not.

'I mean what an absolutely fantastic thing. Idea. Fabulous.'

They smiled vacuously at each other for a moment. But then Catherine's face clouded again, and the little frown-fork on her brow reappeared.

'Where is this going to happen though?'

'Where?'

'Yes, where!' Again, Catherine radiated amused exasperation at the fact that Sean had apparently not given this scheme the slightest thought.

'Well,' said Sean, 'I was thinking we could do it—'

(These last four words caused his face to twitch imperceptibly, an unwelcome addition to the internal spiritual and physiological uproar that he was heroically keeping in check.)

'—at the New Millennium Discussion Wrap Party.'

'Why there?' persisted Catherine.

'Well, you could invite Wayne to it; get separated from him in the crush at the party, and then let him see you kissing me.' Sean realised that he was holding his glass with white-knuckled tightness.

Catherine giggled softly. 'Right,' she said shrewdly. 'I think I see it happening like this. Stand up a minute.'

Sean did as he was told, and Catherine rose with him, her hands raised up to elbow height, fists tensely closed.

'How about . . .? How about if I wait until I know he can

see me and then I come up to you, and it's about twenty minutes after midnight, so he can't think to himself that it's just Auld Lang Syne, so I come up to you with a drink, I give it to you like this' – she handed him her glass – 'and then . . .'

Then Catherine, tilting her head adroitly to the left, kissed Sean with her lips very slightly ajar, and her fat tongue slithered hotly into his mouth while her right hand snaked round to the nape of his neck and her splayed fingers playfully disturbed the fuzz of hair at the back of his head, then pulled away, and a microscopic twine of her saliva momentarily connected their lower lips.

'. . . do that? What do you think?'

Sean pressed his lips together and earnestly knitted a frown on to his forehead. This was an alternative to letting his jaw go slack and dropping with a sob to his knees. What was that his mother was saying about being an abject pervert with no dignity?

'What do you think? Not enough? OK.'

Catherine was chastened, an undergraduate whose work had been gently slighted.

'When we meet at the party, I promise I will really *go for it*. I will come up to you when Wayne is really close to you and then give you a Grade One French kiss that would take the top of your head off – if it wasn't for, well, you know. Honestly, short of actually doing it with you there and then, there's nothing more I'm going to be able to do to show Wayne that I'm totally over him. Do you think it would be a bit too much if we were to grope each other a bit, you know, in that really *infatuated* way, that way that says: look everyone, we can't keep our hands off each other, the way that says to the world: later on tonight we're going to be having *lots of dirty sex*. Do you know the sort of thing?'

Sean nodded dumbly, and even tried to say 'sure' through a cool half-smile but his tongue stuck fast to his traumatised palate and what came out was 'srczk'.

'We'll *really* give Wayne something to think about! It'll do his head in!'

Energised by this wonderful plan, Catherine leapt up and scooped up her cigarettes and lighter.

'I'm sorry, I've got to go now, Sean; I've got so much to organise. It's been lovely having this chat with you. You're always so understanding. I'll love you and leave you and say bye-bye.'

Catherine leaned forward as if to kiss him goodbye on one cheek. In a daze, Sean leaned forward to accept this tribute but at the last moment Catherine coquettishly pulled away with a giggle and wagged her finger.

'No, no, no! We mustn't peak too early! Got to keep you hungry for it! Ha! See you!'

She skipped away, slamming the door behind her. For a second, the room throbbed and spun in a series of little, unbalanced semi-rotations, the way his bedroom did, with his head as a fulcrum, when he went to sleep drunk. Sean ran an exploratory tongue around his mouth and silently checked that he could actually say the word 'sure'. This achieved, he wandered into the kitchen and opened up the oven containing the casserole for which he now had so little appetite.

In the midst of his jittery and dangerous excitement, a thought swam into his head: Sean had recently read of the death from heart failure of a much-loved radio comedian. This man had, about twelve months beforehand, suffered what had then seemed to be a minor and unthreatening 'episode' – sharp pains that quickly dispersed – but which now appeared to have been a 'silent heart attack': a heart attack which sounds like the tree falling in the forest with no one around to hear it. A heart attack which can somehow wreak its mysterious damage and intra-ventricular defects without the patient noticing, until many months afterwards, when everything shuts down.

Sean wondered if he had suffered a 'silent nervous breakdown': a breakdown which he could somehow carry around with him – like the shattered pieces of a tea service inside a dropped gift-wrapped package, squeezed inaudibly within their protective plastic wrapping – until the zero hour came when he would somehow have to open up the package and show the contents to others, and to himself.

Had that zero hour arrived?

14

Ysenda was facing the panel on a large screen, singing Prince's '1999' off key, grinning and gazing slightly off centre at where she could obviously see her own face on a monitor. Behind her was what appeared to be the teeming and anarchic main street of Bethlehem, in which Ysenda and a film crew had set up, having been acrimoniously ejected from the reputed stable itself after Beezer, their sound man, was discovered affixing lengths of heavy cable to the priceless structure with a succession of metal pegs. Beezer assured an apoplectic official that the pegs could easily be removed without any damage; the official insisted that this would not happen without large chunks of wood coming away. On being proved right, and having to witness Beezer's sheepish grin as he held a metal peg with a fragment of wood in it, the official shrieks of rage became as convulsive as a fatally wounded animal and Ysenda, Beezer and Chris, the stoic cameraman, had to retreat in some disorder from the stable, and their exit was not made any more diplomatic by Beezer shouting: 'Christ, I think I've kicked over the manger.'

Through a satellite link-up, Ysenda would be joining the millennial discussion live in the studio which was in fact taking place in the Royal Observatory in Greenwich. It was a quarter to ten, fifteen minutes until air time, and Ysenda was supposed to be testing her satellite and audio link with Gordon, the programme's jittery Scottish chairperson.

'But, Ysenda,' he said laughing uneasily, 'this *is* Nineteen Ninety-Nine.'

But Ysenda was already out of shot, to the studio director's dismay, her head looming hugely against the edge of the screen, and she was shrieking and giggling with Beezer who appeared to be making the *thomp-thomp-thompa* sounds of a funky bass guitar. Had Ysenda and her crew been drinking? If so, there would be some post-millennial scenes once this was over.

'Twelve minutes until we're on the air.'

By the screen, there was a semicircular table and the set of the nightly news discussion programme of which this was a special Millennium edition. Like all sets for television programmes, it looked simultaneously much larger and much smaller than what appeared on the screen.

On the right-hand end of the table, stage right, was Sean, billed as editor of *Somdomite*. All day vaguely, and for the last hour and a half quite intensely, he had wondered where Catherine was, and whether, despite working on this programme, she was only going to be based in the production office and never come on to the set itself. If this was the case, would he only see her at the post-show party? Would he in fact, given that this party was going to be crowded, *ever* see her?

Just at this moment, Catherine actually appeared, wearing a kind of absurd pair of headphones with a little speaker attachment by her mouth, a gadget which evidently did not fit well, and which she kept having to readjust. In spite of himself, Sean inclined his body towards her, realigning himself in his seat like a compass needle, and arched his eyebrows in a pitiful solicitation of greeting. Gallingly, she did not return it, but instead spoke to someone else, a tubby man with a clipboard who had ushered him to his seat on the panel some forty minutes before.

The person to whom he had been speaking, an emotionally unstable historian, registered without comment the fact that their desultory conversation had been terminated without ceremony in order for Sean to receive this infinitesimal snub. Finally, having concluded her important business with Mr Tubby, Catherine turned and smiled in Sean's direction.

'Hi, Catherine.'

'Hello, you two.'

He had called her by her name, and she had not only declined to return the compliment, but lumped him in with this mottled and Scotch-blasted academic, who she seemed to know from a number of publishing and television parties and with whom she now affected some one-of-the-boys banter. Now she was winding this up, and during her conversation with *him* Sean might as well have been inside a soundproof booth for all the notice they were taking of his frantic little jokey remarks and *Ha!*s. The tubby man came round announcing that they were five minutes away from air time. Catherine stopped and now turned directly to Sean.

'Will I see you later, Catherine?'

Catherine affected an air of brisk and polite bemusement.

''Course you will! You've got your "Access-all-areas" laminated invite haven't you?' She shared another little complicit laugh with the emotionally unstable historian, who actually held his up, and then was gone.

Jesus. Sean could feel himself going pale, and hot prickles of dismay and mortification danced across the backs of his hands. Had she forgotten about their arrangement? Had she just casually forgotten all about it, or set it at naught, this little conspiracy in which all his hopes and fears now resided? Or was it all just an elaborate joke, a harmless little fantasy, in which she thought he was indulging her to cheer her up? In which case, how absolutely embarrassing and pathetic of him to have taken it so seriously! How awful of him to have spent hours pacing up and down in front of his phone. How ridiculous of him even to have considered ringing her up. And what would we have said? 'Oh hi, Catherine, look I was thinking about that thing, where you come up and kiss me. I've drafted some notes about when and where I think it should happen.' – 'Whaaat? That was just a joke, you creepy pathetic little pervert! I can't believe you've been thinking about that, get some serious psychiatric help before I call the police! No, actually I *am* going to call the police. Help! Help! Help! Police!'

If he was lucky. So the name of the game had to be: play it calm, play it cool. If she came up to him as arranged, he would ultra-coolly play along. If she didn't, well he would behave at the party as if nothing was going to happen anyway, mingling, chatting with his interesting and intelligent friends in publishing and the media, smiling, laughing, finally going home in the car that the TV company had lined up for him, going into his empty flat, switching the light on, and not at all bursting into tears or eating the duvet in rage and shame and despair.

One minute to go before air time. Sean's other panellists were a rational scientist who had found God, and whose mission as a lay preacher it was to reconcile these two faiths, and also the editor of a major Sunday newspaper who had just published a short book calling for an end to cynicism and for moral, ethical and spiritual rearmament. Along with Ysenda live from Bethlehem, they were the quorum of panellists.

There was a small studio audience too, and on the front row were Nick, who seemed almost to doze with boredom. Next to him was Aldo Popp, who took a keen professional interest in everything that was going on. A lifetime in the business had not lessened his enthusiasm, and he kept brightly asking technical questions of the production staff until he was firmly and politely asked to resume his seat. Also there was Wayne, who had been particularly asked to come by Catherine in her final, and coldly formal, e-mail.

Wayne was clearly not enjoying himself. Coming along to this TV event and the post-show party had solved his (and Sean's) anxiety about what to do on Old Millennium's Night, but he was annoyed not to have got a heftier invitation anywhere else. Moreover, his actor's sense of fame had been severely nettled by having to sit in the *studio audience*, and he had been in showbusiness long enough to know that no other group of people were more patronised and despised than those who, of their own free will, came to sit in studio audiences, grinning bovinely at the monitors above their heads, willing to sit for hours in their place for re-take after re-take.

Nobody was paying attention to him, either. None of his fellow studio audience *Untermenschen* had come up and asked for his autograph; none of them had humbly asked him how his latest 'telly' was going. None of the TV production staff had spotted him and offered to 'upgrade' him to some kind of VIP section at the side. The lumpenproletariat had not collectively realised their inferiority to him and spontaneously organised some round-robin demanding that his celebrity be given formal recognition. Instead, they seemed to think it appropriate that he be grouped together with *them*. Intolerable.

Naturally, revealing any of these thoughts was out of the question, so Wayne contented himself with talking to Nick about whether he had a chance of meeting an attractive future mate this evening. Nick's theory was that it was such a cosmically important evening that it would melt everyone's sexual reserve as in Rio during carnival time. Either that, or they would melt with a kind of existential horror and agree to have sex with him as a way of staving off the dying of the light.

A tiny green bulb winked on each camera and the programme's title sequence raced past on a dozen monitors, while the panel remained in muted, painterly shadow, and then the lights came up fiercely and Gordon urgently inaugurated the discussion: 'This Is The End?'

The Sunday newspaper editor who had published the moral rearmament book began. 'Of course one derides the idea of prophecy and visionary insight –' a nodding rippled round the panel '– but it is extraordinary how naïve our Western culture is about how the present is constituted, how we seem not to realise that every single human society or empire has been temporary, and proceed on the assumption that *this* order of things will be permanent. How incurious we are about our collective future, and, by implication, our collective present.'

'Do you know, it *is* extraordinary,' drawled the rational scientist who had found God, 'but I really think there is a sense as we approach the millennium, not of acceleration – that is quite wrong – but an increased gravitational pull, a kind of centripetal force to which we are surrendering.'

The emotionally unstable historian nodded vigorously. 'That's absolutely right. I just can't be doing with things that take a long time now, like stupid *meals*, I mean whose idea was that, stupid three-course *meals*; ever since I saw the moon landing with Neil Armstrong in sixty-nine they told me about these capsules that were supposed to replace all that, like one capsule for mushroom soup, one for chicken chasseur and one for, I don't know, profiteroles or something. And that was it. Everyone said that was the way of the future, we wouldn't have the drag of eating meals, well the future's here now so where *are* these capsules?'

Gordon interjected: 'Perhaps we could . . .'

'I'll tell you something though,' persisted the emotionally unstable historian. 'You can do it with television programmes. Take them in Neil Armstrong capsules.'

'How?' asked Sean.

'I'll tell you how, mate,' chortled the emotionally unstable historian. 'You find the programme you want to watch, get the Ceefax subtitles up on screen, and then video it. Then you watch it later on fast-forward. You can get through an hour-long feature or documentary in about twenty minutes. It's a fantastic labour-saving device. And you miss out all the crappy emotive background music and their stupid hammy acting. You get the gist? I 888-fast-forward all television now. I mean, who can be bothered actually *watching* any of it in *real time*? It's like selling your tumble dryer and going back to hanging all your washing on the line.'

Catherine was watching on the green-room monitor, rather than from in the gallery, sitting on a low, plump, purple sofa, sipping a Diet Coke, and smoking. She was surrounded by the debris of the modest pre-show reception held here for the participants and their guests. To calm herself, she treated herself to one and a half capsules from the stock of 'Informal Prozac-Variants' that Sizewell-B had prescribed for Ysenda that night at The Product – Ysenda had passed some of them on to her. Now she was experiencing a pleasant, buoyant little buzz.

With some malice, Catherine had arranged for there to be an administration error: invitations for the little *pre*-show party were sent to Nick and Aldo Popp, but not to Wayne. The invitation policy was strictly enforced on the door and Catherine arranged not to be present to sort out the confusion, thus making Nick and Aldo choose whether or not to stay out of the party to be with Wayne. They loyally trooped off with him away from the Elect, to sit in the grim audience area. Catherine had ostentatiously not spoken to him, affecting an urgent need to talk to the guests without acknowledging Wayne in the front row – this was the reason for her eager chat with Sean and the emotionally unstable historian.

Sean wasn't entirely right about Catherine having forgotten about their arrangement. She did have it vaguely in her mind to stage some clinch to infuriate Wayne. But something had happened to muddle up this plan. Namely, that the emotionally unstable historian had made 'a pass' at her – a phrase derived from fencing which wholly misrepresents the clumsy and ambiguous reality. This was a few hours before at the little reception. There were not many people there, besides him and Catherine, so she felt obliged to make conversation.

CATHERINE So, how've you been? How's the book going down?

EMOTIONALLY UNSTABLE HISTORIAN What book? I'm not writing any book, I'm completely barren, I'm a literary eunuch, Jesus, oh you mean the book I've just published about Mary Queen of Scots?

CATHERINE Yes.

EMOTIONALLY UNSTABLE HISTORIAN Oh *great*, thanks for asking, actually what am I talking about, it's *a nightmare*.

CATHERINE (Pause, glance flicks off left and then back to EUH): Oh, what you mean . . . sales?

EMOTIONALLY UNSTABLE HISTORIAN Sales? Sales? What have you heard?

CATHERINE Nothing.

EMOTIONALLY UNSTABLE HISTORIAN Well, the thing about sales is, with a new biography of a Royal figure from history from a reputable publisher – well, if every American university library buys a copy of your book, then you're laughing.

CATHERINE (Brightly) Oh good.

EMOTIONALLY UNSTABLE HISTORIAN (Passionately) They're not though. They're *not*.

CATHERINE Oh.

EMOTIONALLY UNSTABLE HISTORIAN Listen, when are we going to get together?

CATHERINE Get together?

EMOTIONALLY UNSTABLE HISTORIAN Don't *rush* me, Catherine, you know how messy my divorce was. I'm not sure I'm ready for a new relationship.

CATHERINE No.

EMOTIONALLY UNSTABLE HISTORIAN You're right. Just lunch at first. Take it slow.

CATHERINE What? (Another member of the production staff beckons her away.)

EMOTIONALLY UNSTABLE HISTORIAN OK, OK. If you really want to. I could never guess you were so needy, so emotionally grabby. So often, Catherine, that translates into a selfish attitude in bed. But I'll talk to you afterwards. Don't read too much into this, Catherine.

So Catherine was having a hard time concentrating on the discussion, which was obviously failing to live up to the standards of high seriousness that was expected of it, to judge by Gordon's strained and flinching face, his frequent interventions, and the swearing from the gallery filtering into his earpiece.

Finally, at ten minutes to midnight, Gordon judged the time right to cut away to Ysenda in Bethlehem whose face reappeared on the monitors with an expression of exaggerated seriousness, biting her lip, while suppressed snorts from her camera team could be heard out of shot. Gordon winced as an explosive obscenity from the director in the gallery reverberated in his skull.

'Ysenda,' he asked. 'As a Catholic, do you think the millennium has been denuded of its Christian connotations?'

'No, not really,' she shrugged, and the studio director slumped back in his seat and gave up. There wasn't even going to be any proper argument.

'I mean . . .' Ysenda continued, smiling, 'in observing the millennial epoch, we are commemorating the common continuity of Western culture, aren't we?'

'Yes, yes, that's true . . .' said the rational scientist who had found God, but was immediately cut off by Ysenda.

'No one here gives two hoots about the millennium to be quite honest,' she said, looking around her vaguely. 'It's just like any other evening. I think they get a bit sick of it so soon after Christmas. Most people are going to bed quite early, it seems to me . . .'

She trailed off, and with a flash of panic in his studio eyes, Gordon attempted to restart the discussion, but the director was highly reluctant to cut Ysenda off completely, the satellite link having cost them all so very much money.

'You know,' said Ysenda, 'you've got to wonder, haven't you, at this pious cult of sentimentality and pity that surrounds the Jesus myth. Here he is, snug and warm, "away" in his manger, away from what? Away from what? I mean, it's dark and smelly and, like, unhygenic, but newborn infants simply don't register that. Really Jesus got it all on a plate, didn't he? I mean, what a jammy little shaver. He was a product of a stable nuclear family unit, he had a non abusive step-parent who was prepared to work very hard at a low-status job to keep them all fed, and the minute he was born he got all these people showing up, every stratum of Mid-East society just like showed up and gave him donkeys and lambs and frankincense and stuff, what's that all about, it's a Chinese wedding where you pin money to the bride.'

'Yes,' said Gordon. 'What we . . .'

'And then what?' demanded Ysenda belligerently. 'Then what happens? All the shepherds and Orient Kings kneel around the manger, and, I don't know, hum the first few lines of "Once In Royal David's City", and all the while Mary is looking down at Jesus and they've got funny circles round their heads, and then finally Melchior or whoever it is looks at his watch, and says: "Well now, Mary, we've got to be off, the three of us have got to be back in the Orient in about five hours, and to be quite honest it was a bit of a cold coming we had of it getting here in the first place." So then they all stir, and the Three Kings kiss Joseph and Mary on both cheeks, and it's like the end of a dinner party, when somebody makes to leave, everyone else does as well, and the shepherds all catch each others' eyes and say: "Whoa, yes, we should be going too," and then they all do the cheek-kissing thing and the Three Kings say to the shepherds: "Can I drop you anywhere?" so some of the shepherds climb on the back of Belshazzar's camel, and pretty soon they're all gone and Joseph and Mary are stuck with the washing-up and emptying the ashtrays and a whole bunch of very-expensive-to-maintain livestock, which is like *lowing*, and uninsurable jewellery and perfume, so what are they supposed to do with it all? Little Jesus is as happy as Larry but Mary they just irresponsibly encourage to feel an unsustainable post-partem euphoria and then leave her on a tremendous downer and vulnerable to depression. What sort of post-natal care did they call that?'

'Moving on now,' said Gordon, heavily, 'from the specifically Christian aspects of this moment—'

'Do you know,' interrupted Ysenda, 'I often wonder how Jesus felt about that scene when he got into his late teens? Did he even know about it? When I was eighteen, I found this little silver christening mug and spoon that I had no idea about that my uncle had bought for me, in my parents' silly little sideboard, and also a photo of my mother pregnant – all this past, all this history, simultaneously about me and nothing to do with me. It's like when you come home from university and you're rooting around your bedroom and you find some sort of furry pencil case that cost ten pence, full of pens, something you'd quite forgotten, and then you find your exercise books from when you were ten and you realise that all kids' drawings and all their handwriting is all exactly alike, and yet it's like a message from the past.'

'Perhaps we could—'

'Is that what Jesus thought, I wonder? Was he moping around the house at sixteen or whatever, getting under his parents' feet, and then he found this old cardboard box under the stairs, pulled it out, opened the flaps, and – *ugh* – the smell of old frankincense and myrrh, and the tarnished gleam of gold, and the little wisps of keepsake straw. Did the adolescent Jesus slope into the kitchen with the box where his mum was doing the washing-up, and say, *Mum, what's this? What's what, Jesus love,* says his distracted mum, turns round, then goes pale with shock, when she sees what the teenage lad has stumbled upon, and then Joseph staggers in from the shed where he's been doing a bit of DIY on a spice rack and then *he* sees it, and *he* goes pale and drops the spice rack, and Jesus, says *What? What? What is it? What's all this gold and straw and smelly stuff? Is it something to do with me? What? TELL ME!* So Mr and Mrs Christ take Jesus through into the heavily carpeted front room, turn the TV off, and then they sit him down on the sofa and have to tell him exactly what happened when he was born.'

In the gallery, the studio director was mentally roughing out his letter of resignation. The rational scientist had pursed his lips and was saying nothing; the national newspaper editor who wanted a moral rearmament was glancing pointedly towards Gordon in a mute appeal to bring the discussion back on to the rails. Only Sean seemed content, nodding his head gently along to Ysenda's last speech, and smoking a cigarette in direct contravention of the plaintive request that the production staff had made to all the panellists. Something about his present situation had plunged him into a reverie, and he began to think that his life and career path was like a television schedule, and he would have to decide which he wanted to tune into: BBC1 (conservative highbrow mainstream), BBC2 (highbrow alternative), ITV (populist), Channel Four (alternative populist) or Channel Five (idiot).

Television highlights

BBC1

6.00 Business breakfast.
Sean's career begins with a briskly pragmatic doctoral thesis, concluded in three years.
12.45 News and weather.
The headlines: Sean applies for academic job. Outlook – bright.
1.30 Home and Away.
Lively Australian drama. Sean gets a lucrative short-term lecturing job at the University of New South Wales, and forms a number of healthy sexual attachments, concluding with meeting the love of his life, whom he marries.
3.00 Children's BBC.
Sean and his wife have three children, who are richly and adorably talented at music and the visual arts.
6.00 News and Weather.
Sean applies for academic jobs in England. Wife agrees to curtail her career to fit in with his. Outlook – fine.
8.00 EastEnders.
Sean gets a job at Queen Mary College, in London's Mile End Road.
9.30 Panorama.
Report into how Sean becomes a respected, heavyweight literary historian in the Anglophone world, and a much-loved father and grandfather.
10.45 FILM. The Patriarch (Sergei Petrevich, 1931)
Classic evocation of the career of Sean Tobeivich, a much-loved historian, who after a life of exquisite emotional, intellectual, and sexual fulfilment reaches the end convinced of the existence of a beneficent God. Stunning black-and-white cinematography.
1.00 Close down.
Sean dies.

BBC 2

9.00 Daytime on Two.
Magazine programme into how Sean has begun his career with a doctoral thesis on an accessible subject which he completes in good time.
1.10 FILM. Call Me Darling (Nat Clunker, 1961)
Groovy romantic comedy with Laurence Harvey as sensitive Sean, who falls for kooky bohemian beatnik Catherine, played by Natalie Wood.
2.50 News and Weather.
Sean switches from academia to getting a job editing an upscale intellectual magazine. He asks Catherine out. Outlook – changeable.
5.30 Today's The Day.
Undemanding quiz show based on historical anniversaries. On the first anniversary of their first date, Sean asks Catherine if she will move in with him. She says no.
10.30 Newsnight.
In-depth round-table discussion of Sean's uncertain sexual and professional career. Panellists include Professor George Watford and Sean's mother.

Television highlights

ITV

9.25 This Morning with Richard and Judy.
Bright and cheerful look with Britain's top daytime married couple at how Sean has come very close to royally screwing up his life in both professional and romantic terms before it has even begun. Phone-in.
1.30 The Jerry Springer Show.
The controversial, confrontational talk show today has Sean, billed: 'I pretended to be a homosexual to get a job and then I fell in love with a girl'. Ends with a fight with his mother.
5.00 Wheel of Fortune.
Game show returns, and in front of a baying studio audience, contestant Sean loses all his money.
6.30 News and Weather.
Sean ends his life with no prospects. Outlook – cloudy.
8.00 FILM. Dangerous Woman (Tad Urrf, 1986)
Shoot-'em-up actioner with Arnold Schwarzenegger as Sean, a rogue cop in love with Catherine, and Bruce Willis as Nick, a gloomy North London psycho-physiotherapist. Ferocious final gunfight played out with spectacular stunts and effects on top of the Archway Tower. Look out for the elderly Ralph Richardson as the drug-dealer.

Channel 4

6.00 Sesame Street.
Sean's life begins by being hatched out of Big Bird in an enormous egg, a difficult and traumatic labour in which Big Bird almost dies.
7.00 The Big Breakfast.
Madcap presenters Johnny and Kelly humiliate Sean live on the air with questions about who he fancies and what he's going to do with his life.
12.00 FILM. Do Leave Off (Alexander Mackendrick, 1959)
Bittersweet British comedy with Norman Wisdom as Sean, the mixed-up magazine editor, and Janette Scott as Catherine, the smart modern woman with whom he is in love. Richard Wattis is the grumpy accountant; Joan Hickson is Sean's mother.
4.30 Countdown.
Sean is physically thrown out of the studio by Richard Whiteley when the longest word he gets is 'sex'.
4.55 Ricki Lake.
One of America's favourite talk shows today has Sean: 'My problems brought me closer to my family'. Ends with a fight with his mother.
7.00 Channel Four News.
Special feature about Sean's life-crisis and what it says about modern society. Weather – dire.
9.00 ER.
Sean is brought into the busy Chicago Emergency Room in a terrible state, having thrown himself under a subway train. Dr Peter Benton, Dr John Carter, Dr Doug Ross gather round his mangled, bloody body and laugh, uninterrupted, for fifty-five minutes.

Television highlights

Channel Five

6.00 The Banana Splits.
Sean tries to ingratiate himself with the Banana Splits by sympathising with them about how Bob Marley nicked their theme tune. Unimpressed, the Splits drive away from him in haughty silence in those little cars.
11.10 Leeza.
One of America's favourite talk shows today has Sean: 'I cannot come to terms with the futility and meaninglessness of existence'. Ends with a fight with his mother.
2.00 Open House with Gloria Hunniford.
Sean arrives to discuss his problems with Gloria Hunniford, but at the sound of the doorbell, Gloria hides behind the sofa with the curtains closed and pretends that she is not in.
4.30 The Oprah Winfrey Show.
One of America's favourite talk shows today has Sean: 'I keep getting involved in physically violent situations with my mother'. Ends with a fight with his mother.
7.00 The Pepsi Chart.
Happening pop show, which includes an interview with Sean on the eve of his thirtieth birthday; presenters Rhona and Eddy ask him what is at Number One and he realises that he has no idea.
11.45 FILM. Sex Unlimited (Lisa Spirograph, 1995)
Erotic made-for-TV movie about a nymphomaniac Miami air-hostess, obsessed with having sex with any man whose first name begins with S. Sean buys her a drink in a jazz bar, and she explains she doesn't much feel like it tonight.

Sean kept flicking the channels on the remote button of his life, but somehow just kept getting Channels Four and Five.

The midnight hour approached in Greenwich, and Gordon was able to cut the discussion off in favour of some segments of live footage of how this event was being covered throughout the world, on local news broadcasts. In Accra, a group of citizens appeared to be humming meditatively in the middle of a field. In Pyongyang, a display of urban millennial dancing had evolved into a punch-up. In Birmingham, dozens of old ladies were rapping with twenty pence coins on the window of Tower Records. In the Equadorean conurbation of Quito, a human pyramid of dentists tottered. Thousands of excitable Monrovians implored their neighbours to forgive their mendacious tax returns. In Kuwait City, women over fifty Sellotaped the ace of clubs to their foreheads. Everyone in Rangoon simultaneously cracked their middle-finger knuckles and went 'Ow'. A performance of J.B. Priestley's *When We Are Married* kicked off in Ouagadougou. The Archway Tower in North London was festooned with tiny white fairy lights dropped from an air-sea rescue helicopter, entirely transforming its appearance. A new adult literacy project was inaugurated in Los Angeles. In Bogotá, an order of nuns resolved to communicate solely in clicks and buzzes. In Rabat, a lonely Moroccan laundrette proprietor smoked his final cigarette, climbed into the dry cleaning machine and, hunched behind the glass porthole, gave the signal for his tearful daughter-in-law to press the On button. One of the best skiffle groups in Riyadh disbanded, citing musical differences. Lake Nebagamon fizzed with trillions of gallons of own-brand cola. In Hanoi, private property was abolished. In Ndjamena, an astronomer hesitated. Along the Welsh Marches, a quorum of poets sallied forth, sometimes humming, sometimes breaking out into song. The streets of Phnom Penh were glutinous and sticky. County Antrim smelt of almonds. The sands of Porthcothan Bay in Cornwall dispersed marginally, disclosing a tiny discarded flip-flop.

A dyslexic video store operative shot snipe in Guam. In Maputo, an aid worker became evasive during a telephone conversation with his wife. The mission crew of the South African 'Truth and Reconciliation' space project, far above the equator, slept on. In Port-au-Prince, a baby boy was born named *Ansamn* from the Haitian proverb *Ansamn, ansamn, nou se lavalas*, or *Together, together, we are the flood*. A father of two in Carlisle realised that by dint of hard work at two jobs, he had brought his bank account out of the red. In Nijmegen, an actuary climaxed reading the telephone directory.

And in Bethlehem, Ysenda – with whom the satellite link had been catastrophically lost seven seconds before the midnight hour – thought of Sean, and her heart was filled with melancholy and sadness. All her friends were in London, all about to celebrate their thirtieth birthdays together and she would not be with them. She looked around at her camera crew and, like them, experienced an utter cancelling of the party spirit. Now all that was left was the difficult and uncongenial journey home. Euphoria drained out of them like water from a washbasin with the plug taken out.

Back in London, as the millennium was ushered in so uneventfully, Gordon concluded his global satellite tour with a snapshot of the worldwide web stock price of a software company that was producing programmes for counteracting disasters arising from the 'millennium bug' in computer systems throughout the world. But there were no bugs, or at least no active ones, and the studio audience watched as the share price, in which many pension schemes in the United Kingdom had made a ruinously extravagant investment, started to plummet before their very eyes. It was time for the discussion to finish, and Gordon, relieved that he had now one moment in which to reassert his notional authority over the proceedings, thanked every member of the panel in turn.

The national newspaper moral rearmament editor and the rational scientist had the rueful, pursed-lip expression of those who know they have come out badly in any sort of public show. Sean and the emotionally unstable historian had sleepy, dozy expressions; with Sean, this dissolved once again into his everyday anxiety as he entered the mental decompression chamber which precedes one's psychological exit from a television studio. The historian stayed dreamily happy.

'That's it . . . we're clear. Thank you, everyone,' said the tubby man as the closing credits were reproduced on monitor screens all around.

In the studio audience, Wayne and Nick yawned and stretched. They were unmoved by what had happened. Only Aldo Popp had been engaged by what he had seen; he gazed about him with the wide-eyed rapture of a child on his first visit to the circus. They all stirred, and left with the rest of the audience, discreetly to re-enter from another door for the party in the green-room – for this, Catherine had made sure that they were all invited, including Wayne.

The party was an anti-climax, or so it seemed to most of the guests, largely publishing and broadcasting types, and former guests of the programme. Wayne himself was very subdued; Nick stood in the corner nursing a half-pint of bitter in a pub glass with a handle which he had somehow found. Of the three of them, only Aldo seemed to be having a good time; he had managed to corner a well-known novelist and broadcaster and was attempting to interest him in his new idea for an interactive game show called Ward Round. With the correct encryption technology, cable subscribers could guess the illness from the symptoms and the winners could get vouchers for exclusive hospital treatment. Aldo had plans to build the production deal into a private finance arrangement with NHS hospitals, and after an initial period of wondering how to terminate the conversation, the well-known novelist and broadcaster became highly enthusiastic about coming in with Aldo, to the extent of offering to remortgage his Richmond maisonette.

Sean's friends had all secretly bought each other thirtieth birthday presents, which they had playfully secreted about their persons and had arranged to exchange here at the party. Nick approached Sean, who was standing tensely by himself. 'Sean!' he said, cheerfully, and then composed his face into an expression of alarm and concern, pointing into the distance. 'What's that behind you?'

Sean turned around, but could see nothing. 'I don't know, what?'

'It's your *youth*! Ha! Ha! Ha! Here – happy birthday.'

Sean turned around just as Nick thrust a small gift-wrapped package into his hands. Opening it, he discovered it was an old-fashioned hearing aid, the sort that Gert Frobe wore as Goldfinger, designed with grotesquely tactful flesh-pink colouring and heavy enough to rip the ear off the side of your head. Sean did not find it very funny, and was feeling almost as nettled as he had with Nick at the party at the beginning of the year. Nevertheless, he produced his present for Nick – in another cumbersome box. Nick ripped it open with childish haste and greed, entirely oblivious to Sean's chagrin, and discovered what to any lay observer would have looked like a coil of clear plastic tubing attached to some form of electronic equipment. But Nick immediately recognised it for what it was: a rudimentary voice synthesiser designed for use with an electric guitar – a device that made Deputy Dawg sound as if his voice was being played through a Stratocaster – and popularised briefly twenty-five years before by the golden-haired guitarist Peter Frampton in his double album *Frampton Comes Alive*, a recording for which Nick had an enormous reverence.

'*Thanks*, mate!' said Nick, and Sean's chagrin was assuaged in seeing that, as Nick looked up, his eyes were glistening with tears.

Wayne was trying to track Catherine down to give her *her* present. It was not *her* thirtieth birthday, of course; and he had in any case thirtieth birthday presents ready for Nick (a wah-wah pedal) and Sean (a hearing aid for the other ear, a gift bought in gloating tandem with Nick). But this was a pair of small silver earrings with a discreet opal detail – her Libran birthstone – that she had once admired when they went out together for the very first time. He had an elaborate explanation ready, something about the fact that he didn't like to buy all his friends presents – and he had a Billie Holiday CD ready for Ysenda on her return – without buying her something as well.

But Catherine didn't seem to want to know. She evaded Wayne's pointed attempts to make eye contact with her; she even at one stage made conversation with the Emotionally Unstable Historian . . .

CATHERINE Can I get you a drink?

EMOTIONALLY UNSTABLE HISTORIAN *Please*, Catherine, I'm in a vulnerable place and I don't like that kind of sexually aggressive small talk. Where are you going?

. . . rather than become involved. Her plan to kiss Sean in front of Wayne had never been something that she had taken all that seriously, and yet after a few drinks, she quite suddenly decided to put this plan into action after all. A curious complex of moods, something between a desire to cause a stir and a desire to punish Wayne further, was her guiding light. Illuminated by what she supposed to be a wickedly sexy smile, she shimmied over to Sean, who was attempting to place his double set of hearing aids behind his coat and bag in the small cloakroom area in the corner of the room.

'Sean!' she said. 'What have you got there? Presents?'

'Oh!' said Sean, straightening with an uncool jolt and imperceptibly clipping his forehead above the right eyebrow on the hanger rail for coats. 'No! Hah! Nothing!'

'Anyway,' she went on, 'I thought we might . . . we might do that thing we were talking about.'

'Oh!' said Sean, his heart rate accelerating again. 'I mean, yeah, OK. Yeah, right. Sure. If *you* want to, that is.'

'Sean, if you're not into it, we don't have to—'

'No! I mean no. No, that's fine. Sure. I mean – right. Sure. That would be a laugh. I mean it would be, would be fun.'

'OK. Right! Well, if you position yourself just there, in front of the drinks table' – she pointed – 'it's all systems go. We shall put the cat among the sexual pigeons . . .'

There was a tiny pause in which they both considered Catherine's off-the-cuff metaphor.

'The sexual cat among the pigeons. And then we'll really show Wayne something. Ha!'

She waltzed away. Wayne detached himself from Aldo and Nick and started obviously looking for her. Somehow, Sean was able to detect both their presences in the crowd, using a kind of anxiety radar: a mental antenna which did a three-hundred-and-sixty-degree scope every few seconds, reporting back to the central nervous system with a positioning wince.

Having herself established Wayne's position, Catherine moved towards him, intending to cross his field of vision, ignore him, and go for a passionate kiss with Sean. It would make Wayne jealous, and get her talked about. Sean himself was as ready as he was ever going to be. This was it. Soon he would experience the melting ecstasy of a kiss from Catherine. And afterwards? He didn't care about afterwards. Like Faustus throwing away everything on a kiss from Helen of Troy, Sean was now quite heedless of the future. Catherine was approaching, smiling, through a kind of purple air space. This was it. Sean did everything but pucker up.

But suddenly, just as she was passing Wayne, he darted out into her flight path and with an adorable expression of shy self-reproof offered up his present.

'Catherine, hi, I've got you something.'

Fatally, Catherine faltered and stopped.

'You—? Oh. Hi. What?'

'Well, I wasn't sure if I was going to get to see you or talk to you tonight, but I got you something . . .'

Catherine was already opening the box, and smiled at seeing the earrings. After a beat, she looked up.

'Oh, Wayne, that's – well, that's very sweet.'

Sean registered this unanticipated delay. Catherine seemed to be *talking* to Wayne for some reason. Was she sneering at him, rubbing his nose in it? Was she heightening the dramatic impact of her forthcoming clinch with Sean?

Wayne pressed his lips together at Catherine's response, as if to acknowledge that things had not been altogether easy between them.

'Yes, well, I felt that I should . . .'

'Should what?' Catherine asked archly.

'Well, that I should re-establish contact.'

'And now you have.'

'Yes. Now I have.'

They looked at each other for a moment. Sean watched them, awestruck. Catherine was really dragging this one out. When exactly did she propose to come up and kiss *him*? Just standing here like this was a bit tricky. People wanted to get past. Hang on. What's this? They seemed to be moving close together. Was she going to hiss some particularly unpleasant put-down right in Wayne's face? Was she going to make it devastatingly clear to Wayne that he, Sean, was superior in every respect? But if that was the plan, why were they both smiling at each other in that sort of soppy way?

Now hang about. Hang about just one cotton-picking minute. What, pray tell, is with the head-tilting thing? Wayne is tilting his head to one side, and Catherine to the other. What's all that about? Why are they taking such pains for their noses not to meet? Is this some sort of *Eskimo insult*?

Catherine didn't mean for it to happen this way. She just looked into Wayne's eyes and felt her resolve melting and deteriorating like half a pound of butter left out of the fridge on the hottest day of the year. As far as Wayne was concerned, it was going exactly as planned. All the discomfiture and the sense of having been slighted was worth it.

Then something very strange happened. Catherine froze. Wayne saw her gaze fix on something other than him. What was going on?

Catherine hardly knew either. She had thrown away her plan to make Wayne jealous, and without any reflection had embarked on a catastrophic new plan – one that was bound to make *Sean* jealous. But then she was distracted by something: a pattern of bright lights across the room that she momentarily thought must be coming from the display monitors around the walls. Something must be wrong with them, she thought; the light coming from them was more like that from arc lights or klieg lamps – and there were in any case more of them than could be explained by the number of screens. Moreover, it seemed to Catherine that they were not discrete sources of light, but ripples or reflections, differentiations of one single dazzling light right in front of her field of vision behind Wayne's head, like a sort of benign migraine, a rich golden light, a vanilla light. The background noise and music was numbed and filtered out, and she was ultimately aware only of a heavy, engulfing silence and then a sense of having been lifted above the ground, of floating. Then Catherine became intensely and ecstatically aware of a lovely blonde Presence just in front of her.

Instinctively, she averted her gaze from it, but it surrounded her. This was a Presence which understood all, and forgave all, but still questioned, still demanded. She had had to bear great injustice, great insensitivity – and so asked nothing but that these injuries to a basic human sense of emotional injustice should not be perpetuated. Catherine felt awed and humbled by The Presence's appearance in front of her. The Presence seemed to ask if she had done all that she ought to have done, and if she had left undone that which she ought to have done. Catherine was not sure what that meant. The Presence inquired of her if she had paid enough attention to those who were reaching out to her, to those whose feelings and emotions needed to be tended, like delicate flowers – or maybe an intricate herb garden. All this Catherine understood, bathed in the golden glow, which radiated a halo of rainbow threads of light in millions and millions of infinitesimally narrow spokes slowly circling the central source.

Wayne asked if she was all right; so did Nick who had briefly joined them, but Catherine seemed in a trance, looking straight ahead. Nick was baffled by her dazed inattention. Did Catherine, perhaps, have a form of brain-dysfunction, a *petit mal*? (Recently, a large number of his clients at the clinic had sought complementary treatment for this condition, a form of therapy that would be a kindly alternative to the harsh and disempowering world of drugs and Magnetic Resonance Imaging scans. Nick had organised for them a strenuous game of five-a-side football, which had resulted only in acrimony and a final scoresheet of 0–0.)

The Presence then seemed to smile and beckon Catherine to come closer, and Catherine did precisely that with a feeling that the ground was tilting forward, and that gravity itself had been strengthened, subtly deflected, drawing her onwards, like a piece of thread around a loose tooth. The centre of the light then invaginated, forming a central dark recess, into which the millions of rainbow-light spokes now silently plunged and rushed. It was a weir of darkness in the centre of that great fierce nova of vanilla light. Catherine stepped forward, stopped; then she faltered forward again. The black hole expanded in such a way as to blot out this new sun, and then at some unknowable brink, the Presence took its leave, telling Catherine not to forget what it had said. The glow and its dark vacuum centre then disappeared, as if folded into itself; it sucked out, and the background noise and people returned. After a few moments more, Catherine found herself once again aware of her surroundings, and, like a visit to Narnia, the vision had not taken up too much time.

The blackness was not simply in Catherine's mind. A mysterious darkness seemed also to sweep through Aldo, Nick, Wayne and Sean at the same time: the shadow of a cloud passing over their graves. Wayne could not put his finger on it, but had an uncanny sense of the strange otherworldliness that he had experienced at the King's Cross arcade. He was lightheaded, and could not properly reply when Catherine excused herself and headed for where she thought Sean was.

Nick felt strange too – drowsy, inattentive, dislocated, as if the circuits and synapses of his brain were not functioning properly. Then he experienced an awful clarity, in which he could feel every single hair, every tiny filament, all over his body. He felt as if the blemishes and pits of his skin were being illuminated by a passing probe, like the cratered surface of the moon in twenty-four-hour time-lapse. He felt older; he felt more ill at ease; he felt as if some giant invisible cosmic hand with his own dubious talents for massage had insidiously manipulated every joint and organ of his body.

Aldo felt the way he had when he was making a programme exposing a questionable line in chocolate slimming drinks. Available on mail order from a Post Office box address in St Albans, they were advertised as a ten-day course designed to help you lose three stone: three chocolate drinks a day replaced three meals. After ten days of rigorously submitting himself to this diet and losing no weight whatsoever, Aldo travelled on the train to St Albans with his film crew to confront the manufacturer, but he never made it. He started hallucinating on the platform, was bedridden for three weeks and finally had to go for tests at the Royal Free Hospital. These disclosed nothing untoward. But just at that moment, as he passed through that occluded mental caesura, Aldo experienced a combination of the blessed relief he felt when the hospital said there was nothing physically wrong, and the despair he felt clawing at the no-smoking sign at West Hampstead Thameslink.

But Sean felt strangest of all. Looking at the trio of Wayne and Catherine, with Nick a little to one side, he felt a frisson of that dizzy darkness, that slipstream of departing youth. What secret tumour, what fierce, prophetic meningioma had intruded into his mind to gesture at his body's future ruin? It had gone now, but left a brief residual shimmer, like the photo-negative reversal of colour when you shut your eyes. For a tiny moment, Aldo, Nick, Wayne, Catherine and Sean sensed their mortality sloping above their heads like an attic ceiling.

Catherine now was not sure what she was doing. Her plan to slight Wayne had evaporated, and so had her new impulse to smile on his renewed advances. (Wayne was still holding the earrings; she had left them with him.)

She looked for Sean – but he had disappeared from where he had been positioned. Unable to watch the unfolding debacle, and resigned to a new millennium of ruined emotional longing, Sean had turned back to find another drink and was fanatically trying to rewrite the last twenty minutes of history, to convince himself that it had all just been an enormous joke between the two of them which he had forgotten about the minute she had left his side. Fainting in the swimming pool, Pussy Fred dying, resigning from the *Harbinger*, trapped in a career as editor of *Somdomite* – now this.

He was just considering the long journey back to his dour and speechless flat, to face the compressed lips of the bookshelves and the television's averted gaze, when Catherine rushed up and kissed him full on the lips – just like that. It wasn't the way they had rehearsed. She did not just ruffle the hair on the back of his head with one hand. It was more abandoned, but strangely close-mouthed. No tongues. It was as if they were saying a tragically passionate *farewell*.

What a strange sight they made. The editor of a gay style magazine clinching with the female producer. Aldo and Nick stared; Wayne looked down at the floor.

Catherine drew away and asked if they could go back to his flat. Sean stared too and answered: 'Yzyk.' Then he pulled himself together, ran his tongue around his teeth, then around his lips, and then tried again and managed: 'Yes.'

Catherine drove. They both wore their seat belts, which joined them together at the front in a V-formation. They had feared a long, slow drive but there wasn't much traffic. Everyone seemed at home on this momentous night, or somehow herded into parks or designated open spaces from which to watch the fireworks whose reflections swarmed and slithered across the bonnet of Catherine's car.

They arrived at Sean's apartment block. Catherine parked, and they walked together to the door as outwardly calm and matter-of-fact as if they were – well, as if they were *not* going to sleep together. Sean absolutely could not credit this. He had not asked Catherine why all this seemed to be happening; he dreaded breaking the spell. Once inside the flat, Catherine casually threw her coat on the armchair; Sean had it half in mind to do this himself with *his* coat, as Wayne had once told him that this was the way to ensure that you could sit with the girl together on the sofa. But these strategies were unnecessary.

Catherine gave him another kiss.

'I think we should just go to bed – OK?'

'Okzcyzk.'

'You get into bed. I'll join you in a minute.'

Catherine slipped into the bathroom. Sean went into the bedroom and, thanking heavens that the place was in a reasonably unshameful condition, undressed with uncontrollably trembling fingers, and turned out the main light, leaving the small bedside lamp on. He slipped quiveringly in between the sheets. From far off in the bathroom, he heard the bottled-up sounds of water running, then a sort of clink. Sean looked curiously around him, trying to imagine what she would think of the room, when his eye lighted on the answering machine, whose little green light was winking next to the number one.

He had one new message.

Sean had never mastered the art of ignoring a winking answering machine. If he came into the flat to find the whole place a roaring inferno of flame he would pause before phoning the fire brigade to check his messages. So who'd left him one new message for goodness' sake? He wondered, briefly, through sheer anxiety-stricken force of habit, if it could be Catherine, maybe wanting to, I don't know, ask if he wanted *coffee* sometime or something. Fantastic! Oh, but wait. Hang on. Catherine was in his bathroom, about to have sex with him.

So it couldn't be that. His finger hovered above the play button. Should he? It was almost definitely his mother, wishing him a happy new year. But she would not stop there. Catherine would come in to hear his mother's voice echoing about the room going on about Sean's migraines and their possible connection with his irregular bowel movements. So no: he shouldn't listen to his message. No. No message. No way. He was about to go to bed with the girl he had been obsessed with for a year. Surely to God he could put off listening to his stupid message? Catherine was going to come in at any moment. Forget listening to the message. It's out of the question.

He pressed Play.

Almost immediately, he heard Ysenda crying: two classic gulpy sobs and then a great liquid sniff. Then some quiet, and then:

Sean? Sean. Are you there? Are you back yet? I can't believe you hung around at some stupid wrap party. If you're there, pick up. Sean? Pick up. OK, you're not. Jesus, just my luck.

Pause

Oh Jesus, Sean, I'm so depressed. I'm so lonely. Here. It's so lonely here. Beezer and the rest of them have somehow managed to get hold of some people from CNN who say they know the whereabouts of a so-called underground drinking club. In Bethlehem, for Christ's sake. I didn't feel like it so they've gone and I'm left here in this horrible room. And I mean horrible. There's no TV, no nothing. This phone's a dialler. I'm going mad with boredom. And I had such a strange feeling just now; like I was having a blackout or a fainting fit or something. Our flight's not until two tomorrow afternoon. This whole thing has been a terrible catastrophe; I've pretty well bankrupted the institute.

Pause

There's something else I wanted to say to you.

Pause

I can't believe I'm saying this into a fucking machine.

Pause

It's sort of personal.

Suddenly, the fan in Sean's bathroom clicked and stopped whirring. Catherine was coming! Had she heard her sister's voice? He had deliberately kept the volume down as low as possible. Christ, what was he *thinking*? He pressed the play button again, which put the recording on pause, just as Catherine entered the room.

15

Sean had often thought that having sex for the first time with someone was like *driving* for the first time or, to be exact, was like taking the car out on your own for the first time after you've passed your test. It's the same feeling of excitement. The same sense of transgressing, transgressing the dull uneventfulness of your recent life up until that moment and transgressing the mad and preposterous eventfulness of your fantasies. Left hand down. Mirror signal manoeuvre. Keep your thumbs in the grooves of the steering wheel. Or maybe don't do any of that and see how it goes.

Then afterwards he would think, no, it was more like when you audition for the quiz show *Fifteen-To-One* in some regional church hall in Southwold or something and you do fantastically well and you answer all their questions and you absolutely piss all over everyone else who's also come along for the audition, some of whom you know quite well and you're *tons* better than them. And the assistant assistant producer who's come out to do the East Anglian regional auditions makes a big point of telling you how brilliantly you've done and you feel absolutely marvellous. But then, after it's all over and as the days and weeks go by, and you don't hear any more from the production company, you feel, yes I really enjoyed myself and I did superbly well *but not well enough to get on television.*

Or that it was like surfing. Like jumping up and down on your bed when you're a little kid, knowing that you might well land on the floor and it's really going to hurt. It's like . . . come to think of it, Sean remembered something he thought he remembered reading somewhere about how Freud said that when you made love for the first time, your parents were somehow spiritually at the foot of the bed, watching. If that applied to his mother, he reflected, Sean would insist that *Catherine*'s parents were invited to turn up as well: 'It's only good manners, Sean, and they will probably want to bring some relatives, in which case your late father and I are surely entitled to bring some relatives as well and they'll all need something to eat, *hors d'oeuvres* or something, and maybe some entertainment, a little band or maybe one of those close-up magic people that go around from table to table.'

Christ, thought Sean, my mother has appeared in some creepy quasi-Freudian sex nightmare and already she's arguing with me.

All this ran through Sean's panic-stricken mind in the few seconds it took Catherine to come in through the door and pause by the bed. She was not wearing her jacket any more. With a thrilling nurse-like efficiency, perching lightly on the side of the bed and pulling the duvet taut across his legs, she took off her boots, her jeans and her T-shirt. She stood up, and revealed an old-fashioned appendix scar and as she turned around, a tattoo of a, of a *snake* was it? Or a long green serpent? It spanned her left shoulderblade's blunt point, a curvature he presumed wonderingly to trace with his forefinger, and continued up to her spine. Then the green snake tattoo seemed suddenly to shrug, or shrink, halving in length as Catherine reached behind her back with both hands and undid her bra, detaching the double clip. Then she took off her pants and got into bed with him.

This was the first time Sean had had sex for many years, a fact he did not care to admit to anyone, least of all himself. He had had sex with sixteen people in his life, so Catherine would be the seventeenth (he had been detained with this ungallant and unerotic thought as he was undressing). With self-deprecation that came very naturally to him, he assumed that this was a shamefully low number and that he was furthermore not very good at sex, handicaps which could be surmounted by social, intellectual and professional success in the same way that being terrible at sport at school did not matter *too* much if you were clever.

But like all men, his personal number – he saw it flipping over from sixteen to seventeen, like the old scoreboard at Lord's – was now on display at the back of his mind, and like all men he secretly considered it too low. Every man could tell you his number instantly, if he wanted to admit it, but would be very reluctant for the same reasons that he wouldn't tell you his salary. Whatever it is, it's too low. Perhaps even Georges Simenon himself, who famously enjoyed relations with over 10,000 women in his life, felt on his deathbed the same pang of bitterness that tortured John Betjeman when he was asked if he had any regrets: 'Not enough *sex*, old boy.'

Catherine and Sean kissed, passionately. They kissed each other's top and lower lips, an erotic tessellation of hungry mouths which to Sean disclosed the fine downy hairs of Catherine's top lip with their infinitesimally subtle, briny taste – the mean shade of stubble under his lower lip was a poor exchange.

They went on kissing for quite some time. Sean was absolutely delighted with this arrangement. He loved kissing. For him it was the gratification and deferment of pleasure all at once.

He rolled over on top of her, a manoeuvre she countered with judo skill by continuing the roll another one hundred and eighty degrees, so she was on top of him, perilously close to the edge of the bed. It was a sort of old-fashioned James Bond bedroom scene scenario, one which in a film would be punctuated by an immediate edit, a cut that would invisibly reposition the couple comfortably back into the middle of the bed, this being concealed by the substitution of close-up under an unbroken soundtrack. But this was the tracking shot of real life, and so Catherine and Sean were forced to shimmy across, unbunching the duvet, but the sensation was delicious, and Catherine began to kiss his neck, his chest.

It was Wayne's vulgar wont, in conversation with Sean, to call this the Geisha Scenario.

'What do you mean?' Sean had asked.

'Starting,' said Wayne. 'Starting with that.'

'Starting. With that.' Sean was in awe of this kind of sexual riches, and his voice would become involuntarily stunned and small, as if he had just heard that a school contemporary had made billions of pounds on the stock market. Sean adopted the term on the grounds that, like 'crescendo', it encompassed the all-important gradual build-up and it was better than 'oral sex' which was dentisty and horrible. Moreover, he didn't like 'blowjob' because its etymology was baffling, and it did not have a corresponding word for the man-on-woman act, other than the embarrassing Latin.

Since reading about girls who were called in on the set of porn films to carry it out remedially on sheepish leading males who could not, in the industry jargon, 'get wood', Sean was never quite sure exactly how much of a compliment the Geisha Scenario really was. Was some reproof implied? Couldn't be. Just at the moment he had more wood than the New Forest.

Sean cradled and caressed Catherine's shoulderblades (and that mysterious serpent) as she travelled south, and then, with both hands, the back of her tousled head, but felt that manual contact of this sort at the . . . well at the terminus was wrong, and so felt it decorous instead to reach back with both hands to grasp the headboard, while arching his back.

Nothing expressed the power relations between Catherine and the supplicant Sean less accurately than 'Geisha Scenario', but it lasted about two dreamy minutes, during which Sean suppressed his rapture to the extent of wondering if he should swivel round into the *soixante-neuf* (it was Wayne who had influenced him into mentally using Clouseau French) and if this was expected. It looked so effortless in the beardy line drawings in Alex Comfort's *Joy of Sex*, but Sean knew from bitter experience that if the man's torso was much longer than the woman's, then there was a lot of uncomfy neck straining to be done and afterwards your tongue felt as if you'd been doing one of those pop-eyed Yoga facial exercises.

Best not.

So Catherine sucked his straining penis while he stayed at twelve o'clock, sucked and sucked and sucked, using her tongue and her teeth – a wonderful serration – until Sean came like a shaken Jeroboam.

Afterwards Catherine grinningly snaked up to where Sean was gasping and subsiding, his hair plastered to his forehead as if he'd been running through the rain.

'Was that nice?' she asked and Sean was too overcome, and too out of breath to do more than exhale a 'yeah'.

Now she stroked his shuddering chest, swarmed across it and finally sat astride him, towering gloriously above. It wasn't long before Sean was ready again, as Catherine ascertained by reaching behind her. He entered her from this position now, and Catherine squealed as he did it. Sean wanted to sit up, to straighten up and kiss her while they fucked, but she said no, he must do as he was told, and pushed him back hard on to the mattress and let him hold and squeeze her breasts up and together as he penetrated deep inside her. Catherine's head was tilted back, eyes half closed and jaw almost slack as she frowningly emitted a succession of soprano groans, every other one of which concluded with a kind of rising note, as if a question were being wrung from her, and then a lower sound on every third beat, on a downturn, as if in partial unresolved answer. And then one piercingly loud, sharp cry. Catherine rose up and clambered judderingly off him, stilling Sean's moans of confusion and dismay with an urgent and obscene exhortation that he should finish her off from behind.

She got on to her hands and knees in front of him and Sean went eagerly in and her sweet yelp was doubled by his own as he clasped her hips and felt the purchase of his knees and toes twisting the clammy sheets. She spread her hands out wider and raised her buttocks higher, compelling Sean to rise up a little further.

'Say it, say, it,' Sean gasped joltingly. 'Say "I love you",' he pleaded. 'Say "I love you". Please, now, say "I love you".'

Nothing.

'Say . . . "I love you", oh, please . . .'

I love you

The words drew forth from Sean a deliquescent sigh of rapture and assent. He came, and his pleasure was such that he did not quite hear the strange metallic tone to her voice: quite unexpected this.

I love you

again, and this time they both slowed and ceased their rhythm, as if equally startled by the declaration. Quite simultaneously, Catherine thought, and Sean said out loud: 'That sounds like Ys—' both cutting off at exactly the same point. Sean looked over Catherine's glistening back and saw that her left hand had strayed off the bed area and had accidentally rested on the play button of his answering machine. For the first time, he really noticed how long her fingers were, and how her fingernails were painted a thirsty kind of cherryade-scarlet, but that a tiny hairline fault ran vertically up the centre of each.

Why am I saying this to you now? I don't know. I'm not even drunk. Not much, anyway. Stuck with it now. I can't delete this message.

There was a hiss of quiet, in which Sean could faintly hear some kind of plaintive music, and in which Catherine recognised the sound of her sister breathing, a sound she instantly remembered from the days when they shared the same bedroom as children. The quiet was cleft with a tiny glottal gulp and Ysenda continued

I realised I'm so lonely here. Why on earth did I agree to have my birthday here in the middle of nowhere? We always used to have our birthdays together, didn't we? Now I'm thirty. What's that line? 'I'm older now than I ever intended to be . . .'

Catherine and Sean, frozen in mid mount, listened on, like a statue: 'The Distracted Lovers' . . .

What is there for us now? Listen. I know you have a thing for Catherine. I've guessed it. Nobody had to tell me, I just know. I know all this stuff about being gay is bullshit as well. So there. Nobody had to tell me that either. It's just that Catherine . . . let me tell you about Catherine.

Catherine and Sean stirred uneasily, yet remained locked, paralysed in the position. Sean felt his left leg going to sleep and pins and needles swirling dimly in his right thigh. Ysenda's voice sounded slurred to him, as if she were sleepy.

I've seen Catherine impress a lot of guys. Get a lot of guys. I don't know what she feels about you. I don't think she feels anything

about you at all. In fact, I'm sure of it. But the thing is, she might wind up going to bed with you, because of this weird thing she sometimes does, of just doing it with people she quite likes, she just gets this kind of urge or impulse or vision and she just goes with him and they never know exactly why, but of course they've got this fantastic thing for her, so they don't question it . . .

Sean and Catherine both stirred uncomfortably at this point; now their congress was completely removed from sex. They were like two co-workers who didn't like each other much, forced to join a conga line at an office party.

I just don't want you to get into a false position with Catherine. What was I saying?

After this, there was just silence – silence to Sean that is. Catherine immediately recognised the sound of her sister breathing while asleep. She said quietly:

'Could you . . . ?'

'Oh, yes, of course.' They disengaged, and Catherine moved swiftly off the bed, and snapped on the light switch, thus disobeying Bagehot's rule about letting in electric light upon post-coital magic.

Sean began to ask if she wanted anything, anything in the way of coffee or water but Catherine just walked out of the room, and presently he heard the sound of the bathroom fan come on again. Even in these terrible circumstances, he felt a tiny twinge of pride that Catherine felt so at ease in his flat as to be utterly familiar with the bathroom.

He looked down at the answering machine and then realised what Catherine had known straight away. This was not silence he was listening to, but Ysenda asleep, a gentle rhythmic sighing, all the way from the Middle East. He lay back on the bed and stared at the ceiling, listening to the breathing. He felt himself drifting off to sleep, and roused himself with a shake. Then he sat on the edge of the bed, waiting. He wondered what he should say to Catherine when she returned. What *could* he say? The bathroom fan went off and he put the machine on pause again.

When Catherine came in this time, it was quite different from her first entrance. Her slightly round open face was no longer transfigured, but hard and almost blank. Before she had moved athletically, as if on the balls of her feet, but now she sort of stalked and plodded, picking up her clothes from the floor and putting them back on.

Sean tried again: 'Would you like coffee?' It came out completely wrong. Instead of the cool-jazz intimacy voice he was hoping for, he sounded like Sybil Fawlty. Catherine didn't even answer, and Sean was mortified.

'. . . Catherine?'

She looked up.

'No. No, that's fine.'

Sean tried to say: 'Would you like anything else, then?', but a syllable into it, Catherine tried to say: 'Look, Sean, this is weird, I think I really should be going' and then a syllable or two into *that*, Sean abandoned his first sentence and tried to say: 'Look, it's OK, at least it's OK as far as I'm concerned, please stay' and a syllable or two into *that*, Catherine dropped her sentence and went into: 'I know, it's OK, it's nothing to do with you' – so they spoke over each other in a mad gabbling fugue. In a film, they would then have been silent for a moment, caught each other's eye, smiled, laughed, and the moment would be sweetly resolved. But nothing of that sort happened. They just both felt wretched and irritated.

Catherine completed dressing, she was very quick, and soon she was in her coat, car keys actually jangling in her hand, ready to go.

Sean padded out behind her into the hall wearing his fluffy white dressing gown, the sort that really ought to be worn on screen by an early-Eighties, toupee-period Sean Connery. Catherine stood by the door blankly, waiting to be let out. Sean tried again.

'So, I'll . . . I'll call you.'

'Mmm?'

'I'll give you a ring.'

Catherine nodded. Sean released both door locks at once with a *thunk*. Catherine nodded to him very briefly with a thin smile as if they were acquaintances who had just shared a very short ride in a lift. Sean heard her footsteps accelerate as she went down the stairs; then he padded back and lay on his bed. He stared at the ceiling, and from his open window, he could hear Catherine leaving, sounding like a bank heist getaway driver. Now he didn't know what to think, so he listened to the tape of Ysenda sleeping until he went to sleep himself.

16

This is how Sean's mother spent last night.

Repeatedly, Gillian tried calling Sean to wish him a happy new year and a happy thirtieth birthday, but kept getting the engaged signal. Exasperated, she finally called the operator, and wished *her* a happy new year. The operator gracefully and sadly accepted this, sitting in her telecommunications unit in Lossiemouth, and then checked on Sean's mother's behalf that her son had not simply left the phone off the hook or replaced the receiver incorrectly. But no – she reported back that someone was indeed on the phone to Sean – which meant they had been on for a good forty minutes, continuously.

Gillian thanked her politely, wished her a happy new year again, and returned to her immaculately kept sitting room (she favoured 'drawing room', sometimes even the whimsically archaic 'withdrawing room') and sat bolt upright on the edge of the vividly floral couch. In front of her, positioned on a raffia mat, fraying at the edges, was an Olympic-size gin-and-tonic in a tumbler as heavy as a cricket ball. She watched the bubbles detach themselves for their once-in-a-lifetime journey from the side of the glass, and expend themselves at the surface. There was no ice or lemon.

Gin and tonic was supposed to be a light, bright drink, wasn't it? A happy, upbeat drink. During her young womanhood in Claygate, Gillian had often imagined herself drinking gin-and-tonics – her own mother had favoured something impossibly glamorous called a 'gin-and-it' – in tennis or golf club houses. It was a little fantasy she indulged through her early married life with Sean's father: a happy-go-lucky social life after tennis with like-minded neighbours and friends. But her husband's bad leg made it impossible, and he had in any case no liking for sports of any sort, and her fantasy dwindled into a kind of muted expectation that the present state of affairs notwithstanding, she would one day do these things, and even now, at the age of fifty-four, she caught herself thinking that the days of drinking gin-and-tonics in tennis club houses would naturally arrive at *some* time.

This was now her third gin-and-tonic, and she felt that she had penetrated into this drink's essential character. Far from being an effervescent, buoyant drink it was heavy, oily, treacly – sitting on her senses like some kind of industrial residue. Next to the tumbler was a stack of photo-albums. They were the sort that required one to position each print on to the page in whatever design one found most pleasing. Next to them was a number of glossy packets of prints, each packet holding thirty-six, really, a vast number of packets, and the likelihood of ever putting them into the proper books was remote. She knew that. But she carried on with the task, and reserved quiet evenings like this one for it.

As ever, she had become becalmed at the third gin-and-tonic, and at the packet of photographs marked 'Hunstanton 1975' – the last summer holiday they had all taken together as a family on that long, hazy and slightly bleak stretch of beach up in East Anglia. She had taken out the first photograph: a badly composed shot of the five-year-old Sean in the back of the car; they had not arrived yet, had not perhaps got out of London; she could not remember. He was slightly tilting, his pudgy, smiley face too close to the camera and therefore slightly blurred, and twin dots of light in the centre of his pupils the only clear points of definition.

Gillian looked up from this print and compared the face with the one she could see now on the television, which showed the green 'mute' logo – a speaker design crossed out – in the bottom left-hand corner of the screen. Where five-year-old Sean was happy and chubby, near-thirty-year-old Sean was rather gaunt and muscular. Indeed, his head seemed composed of an inordinate number of tiny flat planes. His lips were moving; he was gesticulating with his left hand and smiling in a way that he never did as a child, or an adolescent, or a young man. It seemed to be something he only did on television. She could see Ysenda on some sort of screen at the back of the studio.

Now Gillian took out the second photo. It was a group portrait of the three of them outside a hotel in an area called Old Hunstanton; that was where they stayed. Sean was between the two of them, holding their hands, looking up at his father, and grinning in a way that adults can never quite manage. His father's right hand held Sean's left; his left hand held the ugly calliper-walking-stick that he was generally never without. She turned to print three, following the order of the negatives, and it was still the group portrait, only this time Sean had let go of his mother's hand, and had snaked his grip around her leg. He was looking up at her, but not smiling. Gazing, with a look of anxious entreaty. Gillian could not remember exactly how this group photograph came to be taken. There was no automatic timer device on the camera, and her husband was shy of asking other people to take photographs of them, and certainly not more than one.

She looked up. Sean was not talking, but raising his eyebrows archly at something the Sunday newspaper editor was saying – again, a mannerism quite alien to real life. The fourth photograph showed them on the beach, the next day, the second day of their holiday. It must have been reasonably warm, as they had laid out a blanket on the fine and wispy sand. There was a shot of Sean sitting next to her on the little aluminium foldaway chairs, and then one of Sean sitting next to his father, the calliper-walking-stick lying by the chair.

Gillian was wearing a one-piece black swim suit. On seeing this photograph, she never failed to congratulate herself on how good her figure was, and how attractive she looked. In fact, since The Change, she felt she was actually in much *better* shape than she was then. She experienced none of the bloats or hot flushes or hot flashes; merely a queer internal stillness, and then an extraordinary explosion of energy. She felt that she could challenge her 1975 self to a sprint along those level Hunstanton sands; she felt she could take her on in one of those stately games of beach badminton that she and Sean would occasionally play – and do it with professional fierceness, howitzer serves, line call disputes. She felt she could lift buses. She felt she could take on Jean-Claude Van Damme in a face-slapping contest. She felt she could award-winningly translate the Bible into Creole patois. As it was, these formidable energies had to be channelled into maintaining her hold over her son, and volunteering to push the mobile library cart around her local geriatric ward, inquiring if any of the patients wished to borrow any books, and making light conversation on literary matters. For someone of her querulous and impatient disposition, this was not an easy task. Presently, this position terminated when she picked up a heavy large-print edition of Robert Ludlum with both hands and brought it down with a terrific bang on the head of an eighty-two-year-old male emphysema patient. The hospital volunteer board accepted her explanation that she had simply dropped the book, and the patient himself never regained a sufficiently lucid state of consciousness to dispute it.

Print five showed Sean and his father in the water together: his father still with the walking stick, and wearing a pair of odd knobbly trunks very similar in design to Sean's own. They were in the water up to Sean's thighs and his father's calves. The clear blue sky behind them had the fierce, hormone-enriched Technicolor quality imparted by the printing process, quite different from the washed paleness of the real thing: the colour that she would sometimes try to recall by closing her eyes. The colour of that snatched moment of the past was cyclorama blue, the inorganic blue of the backdrop used by the professionals when Sean had his school photograph taken: grinning implausibly, stuffed into a green V-necked sweater, grey school shirt and tie, and with a tuft of hair unsmoothed. (A number of portraits like this along the side-board tracked Sean's growth from five to nine years old.) In Print five, Sean is looking off somewhere stage left, but his father is looking directly into the camera, and this is her last proper sight of him.

Print six showed two heads bobbing along the surface of the water: they had to get quite far out to get their bodies down in order to swim properly. The heads, quite oddly, seemed about the same size. Looking at them now, Gillian cannot decide at face value which is which.

Print seven gave the answer. The bobbing head on the left had disappeared, leaving the remaining head a large-ish asymmetric dot. Sean's father had told him to swim through his open legs, and little Sean, who had gamely learned how to keep his eyes open under water, had a go. Sean disappeared into the opaque grey-green sea, and after giving him a moment to get through his father turned around one hundred and eighty degrees and waited for Sean to surface. But he did not.

Print eight captured this statue-like moment of puzzlement; Sean's father was no longer a dot-like head, but a chest and waist as well inclining forward. He had his hands down into the water, trying to part it, like wool or tall grass.

No sooner had the shutter clicked on that exposure, than her husband's sudden sense of anxiety and danger communicated itself to her, as if somehow conveyed through the camera itself. Print nine showed nothing but that cyclorama-blue school-photographer sky; she was gesticulating with the camera and asking if everything was all right.

Everything was not all right. Little five-year-old Sean had not emerged, and now his father had crouched down with his knees bent, groping around for his son with his hands under the water, while he stared ahead, sightlessly, like a blind man, suddenly hoping that a suppression of visual faculties at this moment would assist the other senses in feeling for his (drowning) son. For one awful second, his left hand slithered awkwardly against Sean's small shoulder, and then he lost him again, like soap in the bath.

Sean's mother dropped the camera, and waded into the surf, calling Sean's name. Hence print ten: blackness, darkness, face down in the Hunstanton sand.

Sean's father now held his breath and dived under the surface to find Sean just as his mother came splashing up, lurching from side to side through the water, weighed down by her soaking summer dress. She could remember her husband hunched, all but silhouetted against a sky in which he was the sole distinguishing feature between the shore and the impossibly distant, pin-sharp horizon – and then plunging downwards. And then something very strange happened: Sean emerged with a great heave of water, eyes staring wide open; he exhaled a great stream of snot and spume and sea water out of both nostrils, and burst shrilly into tears, just as his mother enfolded him in her arms and did precisely the same thing. The sense of joy and relief was such that some seconds went by before she realised that now it was Sean's father who was not there.

She looked around, keeping such a grip on Sean's upper arm that he had five quite distinct fingertip-sized bruises for two days afterwards. Surely this could not be happening?

The water was simply too shallow for an adult to lose himself like this. Just as she grasped the absurdity, and impossibility, of this, Sean's father emerged as well. Had he really been submerged for all this time? He was evidently down on one knee; the fingers of his right hand splayed against his forehead. He was quite silent, and she could tell from his face that something was terribly wrong.

The events immediately leading up to this moment, Gillian now realised, probably only took a few seconds, or even a fraction of a second. It was just a confused thrashing and splashing in the grey-green water which leant and slid with the tide and the undertow. But over the succeeding twenty-five years, she had repeatedly reduced this event to its constituent elements in her mind, and done so with such exact attention to detail, that they now seemed to go on for hours like an opera, with scene changes and entrances and exits.

Maintaining her iron grip on Sean all the time, and ignoring his renewed grizzling, Sean's mother helped her husband gradually to his feet, and to shore. Repeatedly, she called him by his name, but he gave no indication of understanding, or recognising his name, or recognising her. This strange trio slushed grimly and slowly forward in the water. Sean's father's face was awfully pale, and with a greenish tinge. When they got to their little encampment on the sand – towels, small tubular aluminium chairs, big candy-striped wind-break – she gave him a towel, expecting him to rub his hair vigorously in the normal way. But he simply held it limply in both hands. He was twenty-nine, and it was his thirtieth birthday tomorrow, but just now he looked much older, and frailer, than that.

Presently, she prevailed upon him to sit down on one of their little chairs and one side of it sank alarmingly into the fine white sand, leaving him at a crazy angle. But Sean now took absolutely no notice. He had his little blue bucket with its yellow handle and his little blue spade and he had returned to digging the hole he had started before going out swimming, a hole which had been deep enough to reach a stratum of dark, wet sand and then a pool of liquid dampness. There was simply nobody near; nobody who could run and fetch help; nobody who could advise. Gillian could just see a few other insect-sized families in the far-off haze. (But sometimes, now, she wondered if this memory was right. Was there really *no one* who could help? Or had she been, at that dreadful moment, embarrassed and maladroit, and ignored offers of help? The photographs did not tell.) She took a risk on leaving her stricken husband and son together and ran away up the heavy uphill dunes to where there was a public telephone. She called for an ambulance, and then ran back to where Sean was still digging, and his father still sitting at an odd angle, his eyes lowered as if in prayer. There was no question of moving this tableau from the beach to the road, and so, after a moment's anguished indecision, she picked little Sean up in her arms and ran in that same awkward high-stepping, trudging way back up the dune cliff to the road, to wait for the ambulance. All this time, Sean's eyes never left the water, as his head jounced and bobbed.

Sean's father was found to have had a slight stroke: the reason for which was a mystery. But on being transferred to hospital in Norwich his condition worsened considerably – this being the effect of one of the super-germs that pervaded the hospital through its heating system – and presently he died, at eight o'clock in the evening, while Sean's mother was driving Sean to Northampton so that he could stay with his Uncle Albert. She was given the news when she returned early the next morning, by the youngish doctor in whose charge Sean's father had been. The shock and profound sense of guilt sent her into a depression which needed treatment in a private nursing clinic on the South Coast while Sean stayed with his uncle. From there, the youngish doctor took an interest in his patient's widow, and found an excuse to visit her.

They fell in love, and Sean's mother remarried, and her young doctor did his best to be a father to Sean in London, but there was always an unspoken tension between them, and he felt always that the bond between mother and son was such that he could not compete. Eventually, Gillian discovered that he was having an affair with one of his colleagues at St Thomas's Hospital, and they divorced, just before Sean went up to university.

All these events Gillian could review without difficulty and the long torpid stretches of Old Year's Night tended now to be the most convenient time for this reflection.

She looked at her watch, and then at her clock. It was a few minutes to twelve. She pressed the mute button on her remote again, and the strident voice of Sean's friend Ysenda instantly blared out, saying something very strange about Jesus. Sean seemed to be agreeing with it, and was smoking a cigarette, a sight that triggered off an intense twinge of disapproval and envy, a twinge which elided unpleasantly with the silent sentinel report of arthritis in her right elbow. She drained her third gin-and-tonic down and constructed the fourth from two large bottles placed by the side of the sofa.

Ysenda she could still remember as a little girl, coming round to play, when the children's parents had briefly been friends. In the little yard adjacent to the kitchen, now wholly obliterated by a patio and conservatory extension, she would play as a little eight-year-old with Sean. Dressing up, she recalled (with a shudder) and ball games – playing *catch*. Did children do anything so quaint as that any more? Play catch? Throw a ball from one to another? Or did they need to be bought American baseball catchers' mitts, like her nieces and nephews, all of them robustly certain of their rights.

Ysenda had a younger sister as well; Catherine. She remembered that Catherine would occasionally come round, carrying a stuffed toy lion that she never relinquished, and which Sean and Ysenda would sometimes spitefully punch or throw up in the air. Catherine was always getting excluded from Sean and Ysenda's games, and Gillian would often have to intervene when she burst into tears.

Midnight. Sometimes she had invited friends and neighbours round for a 'drink' on occasions like these, or sometimes, with both husbands, they would simply watch television exactly as she was doing now. This used to mean Scottish country dancing and the White Heather Club and Jimmy Shand and that long haul to twelve o'clock. Now it meant harsh and incomprehensible comedy. In the early years of her marriage, she even tried the 'first footing' with dark-haired men carrying pieces of coal, the way her own mother had liked, until they had to admit they did not have the slightest clue what it was all supposed to mean and they felt stupid and self-conscious doing it.

But now there was no one. All her neighbours seemed to have gone, moved away, and both her husbands had gone and she was alone. She stood up and moved to the window at the other end of the room, to look at the night sky, and found it richly and fitfully illuminated with fireworks. For the next hour-and-a-half, between her fifth and final gin-and-tonic and finally retiring for the night, she was content to watch, across the furlongs of back gardens, the millennium ushered in with the glow of parties and bonfires and, in the recess of darkness, she heard whooping, and the sound of car horns and dissonant car alarms, the sound of ice being emptied into buckets, the mortar fire of champagne, the sound of breaking glass and the sound of shrieks, pitched somewhere between sexual congress and simple surprise.

Finally, she returned to the thirty-six prints, nine showing those strange pale blue images from another world, and the remaining twenty-seven squares of blackness, like playing cards teasingly turned face down, playing cards which can never be turned over, playing cards from which the meaning of her life must be divined from the uniform pattern on the back. The rest of her life now seemed as blank as those twenty-seven empty tablets. And now, before bedtime, she took them and laid them on her table as if about to play patience or some sort of solitaire, and imagined that these were pictures of the night: the strange indigo-blue of that summer East Anglian sky of a lifetime ago turned to darkness.

17

When Ysenda finally arrived at 'London Luton' on 2 January 2000 after an inexpressibly uncomfortable journey with a Bulgarian charter flight whose crew and board of directors should have been arrested on charges relating to health, safety and maintenance, she felt as if her soul had been so bruised and soiled that she could never love anyone ever again.

Getting out of the hotel had been a nightmare. She was first awoken forty minutes after her phone call to Sean by the sound of a loud bleep and then the dial tone. She registered the fact that she was fully clothed and the phone was on the pillow next to her. Blearily, she replaced the receiver, got into her nightie, and got into bed. She went to sleep for about fifteen more minutes before she awoke and sat bolt upright at the memory of what she had said to Sean's machine and the fact that she had been on the phone for over half an hour and been woken up by the sound of his tape coming to its end. The mortification, combined with her fear of the telephone bill which would await her when she tried to check out the next morning, caused her to weep wretchedly for another twenty minutes. Happy thirtieth birthday.

The sickening leer of disdainful pleasure on the desk attendant's face confirmed Ysenda's worst fears as she stood grimly by his splitting apron of Formica, embellished with credit logos. As she handed over her little magnetic key, he called out its number with a shout of triumph which brought six other hotel employees out to watch, porters, cooks, oily-faced mechanics. Ysenda waited as the attendant, with an insolently bland smile, printed out the computer bill which was specified in American dollars, and handed it over to her to 'check'. The actual room charge had been paid already by the Institution, and the sundries came to two items. One cup of coffee, $1.85; one telephone call to London, $723.00.

There was no point disputing it. With an expression of abject defeat, Ysenda obediently handed over her Visa, and the attendant was visibly disappointed, hoping for a pretty good row. This had to be the worst prang Ysenda's Visa card had ever experienced. As the attendant impassively swiped it through a chunky little electronic machine, she heard the squeal of tyres, and her own muttered gasp of horror as the pumping on the footbrake made no difference and her Visa spun wildly out of lane, into the path of an oncoming school bus, which skidded off the road and over a vertiginous cliff killing everyone aboard, as her card clipped the side of a Volvo and turned over and over, the intolerable shriek of twisting and grinding metal cutting into her head like a chainsaw.

$724.85. Sign here, please.

Back at 'London Luton' she experienced virtual toxic shock at her re-entry into British popular culture. As ever, it was the migraine-clamour of the newspapers, racked up in the arrivals lounge, that was the most offensive thing. The shout of some meaningless PR imbroglio on the tabloids, its status reproachfully confirmed by being muted and diversified on the front of the broadsheets, caused her to wince with guilt that she knew nothing about it. As she dragged her giant wheelie-suitcase behind her and looked for the coach link, Ysenda was astonished to see Nick waving to her, wearing a deplorable pair of mirrored sunglasses pushed up on his forehead, and a puffy, pouchy burgundy bomber jacket. She was so glad to see him she almost burst into tears.

'Hi!' said Nick and gallantly took her bag from her.

'Hello, Nick,' she gasped. 'It's lovely of you to come and meet me like this.'

'Oh, think nothing of it, really nothing!' Nick was in a strangely good mood. 'I wanted to try out my new car.'

They reached the car park, and Ysenda gasped. It was a gleaming 280 series Mercedes.

'Oh yeah, very discreet. Very stylish. Just what a single guy and alternative healthcare professional needs to run about town in. A heavily armoured German tank. And how much did that set you back?'

'Oh,' said Nick grandly, hoisting her bag into the boot which opened with a swish automatic motion activated by his bleeping key ring. 'Not as much as you'd think, actually. It's second-hand.'

'But still.'

They settled into the upholstery with a sigh and eased out on to the Approach Road.

'They've never seen anything like this in Luton, let me tell you,' said Nick smugly. 'Out here they're wondering how this can move along without horses to pull it.'

'Second-hand or not, how could you afford it?'

'A new branch, my darling, a new line.' Nick was virtually singing with joy. 'A new string to my therapeutic bow.'

'Like what?'

'Dentistry. It was Aldo's idea. Aldo's a genius. Alternative dentistry. I hack out their impacted wisdom teeth with my bloody great chisel but instead of giving them local or general anaesthetic I read out the *I Ching*. They love it.'

He switched on the radio, and they hummed along for a while to a medley of Mid Nineties Nostalgia.

'And do people actually pay to have that done?'

'Well, to be honest we haven't actually got to the stage of *extraction* yet. It's more counselling. Therapy. Positive image guidance. Dentistry's such a *scam* you know, I wonder I haven't thought of it before. What other consumer business lets you send a little postcard to your customers every six months telling them to come in, let you poke around again and then hand them another bill? We're mixing it in with a whole lot of holistic stuff. Someone comes in with a toothache, you know cheek puffed out, wincing in agony, we sit them down and say: "Well, toothache, yes, sir, mmmmm, toothache, mmmm, ouch, mmmmm, toothache, bad, ouchy ouchy, mmmmmm. Certainly you don't want to be having anything to do with horrible old Mr Toothache. But let's look at the big picture for one moment. I could just pull it out and you'd feel fine. But I'd just be treating the symptom and not the cause. How are things in the *bedroom department*?" Aldo says in the complementary dental consultancy game, you've got to walk before you can run or neither therapist nor patient will find inner peace. Fuck you!'

This last was to a scooter who had cut him up.

'To be honest, the whole "extraction" thing is a bit unreconstructed and outmoded in the kind of radical dentistry I'm developing. I mean, you know – "good" teeth, "bad" teeth, what is "bad" in this context?'

They drove for a long time after that in silence, with Ysenda drifting in and out of a profoundly unsatisfying, unrefreshing doze. She awoke as they were coming into London quite late in the evening and at this moment, she noticed a copy of the *Harbinger* folded out at the 'People' section at Nick's feet and her heart leapt at the sight of Sean, in the notorious leather photograph. Jesus, how *could* she have forgotten about the horror of what she had said to him? How could she walk around as if her whole world had not come crashing down?

She had made this grotesquely embarrassing confession to Sean. She didn't know *what* she had said, or rather she did, and she was blacking it out, suppressing it. She was numb. But surely Nick must know – everyone must know; Wayne, Sean's mother, everyone. They were all laughing at her.

Night was falling; headlights were on. Ysenda scanned Nick's face to see if he was smirking or frowning. But he had started talking again about his new alternative dentistry practice.

'And we don't have any of that crap about a big chair and those big lights and the drill and the fizzy cup with the pink liquid that you're supposed to spit out.'

'No?'

'No. The chair is too disempowering. Instead, the dentist just lies on a special twin-sofa next to the patient and treats them that way. Or they just lie down together on the floor. Or maybe the *dentist* gets down in the chair and the patient leans over him and the dentist pokes up into his gob from there. Oh for Christ's sake!'

This to a smartly decelerating cab in front of him.

'Really, what kind of anaesthetic *are* you using?'

'Chardonnay. It's tons better than morphine or oil of cloves or anything.'

Ysenda screwed up her courage.

'Nick? About Sean . . .'

A sick feeling invaded her intestines as Nick immediately grinned, elevated his eyebrows and sneaked a sideways glance at her.

'Aha,' he said. 'I wondered if you'd heard his news. I sort of thought you *hadn't*.'

News? What news?

'News? What news?'

Nick chuckled, infuriatingly, and nodded briefly downwards at the newspaper. 'I thought you'd seen it. It's only just happened.'

Ysenda looked down again at the picture of Sean in the

Harbinger and for the first time it occurred to her that this must have something to do with him. Had he announced that he was marrying Ysenda? Or that he had taken out a harassment court order enforcing a hundred-yard exclusion zone around his flat, that Ysenda could not breach without being arrested? Had he announced his engagement to someone else? A woman? A man? Tantalisingly, the story was just beneath where it had been folded. She tried to pick up the paper, but Nick adroitly snatched it away with his left hand, causing the car to sway, ever so slightly.

'Does it have anything to do with me?'

'Do you *really* not know?'

'No, I don't fucking well know! I have been in Bethlehem for the past four days, the worst four days of my life, now tell me what it is.'

'Well, Ysenda, we are heading for Sean's flat right now.'

'*Sean*'s flat? But can't you take me home first? I want to change.'

Nick chuckled.

'I'm afraid that's out of the question. This involves you too, you know.'

Ysenda began to feel light-headed. She was queasy from the airline meal that she had been served up, an X-rated fry-up with a mini-portion of black pudding resembling a tumour, which had somehow involved some sort of poached salmon and which had been so bad it had caused a food fight at the back of the plane.

Then there had been an 'unfortunate mistake', in the words of the subsequent rather perfunctory apology. The co-pilot accidentally inserted what the crew called the 'calm' tape: the tape of a calm voice advising the passengers that they were about to crash on water and that they should assume the crash position braced up against the seat in front after refamiliarising themselves with the workings of the life-jacket. So far from triggering panic, this announcement elicited only a derisive cheer from the passengers who had been drinking heavily from the very beginning of the flight. In fact, one or two of them had recited the message along with the prissy-voiced voiceover artist, and Ysenda divined that it was not the first time this mistake had happened.

She realised that her ears were clogged and she was still deafened from the plane's slow descent into Luton. She crossly pinched her nose, and attempted to breathe out with her mouth closed, which caused both eardrums to pop, and at once the car engine became very loud and she was aware of Nick's soft cartoon sniggering.

'What is going on? What, am I being kidnapped or something?'

Nick just bubbled.

'Nick, for Christ's sake. Are you abducting me so that you and your strange new friend Aldo can film me having sexual therapy and dental work in your new all-in-one oral hygiene suite?'

'I can't believe you still don't know.'

Ysenda became very still and she felt cold, all over her body.

'Nick, look. This is – this is serious. Has Sean told you about the phone message I left on his machine on New Year's Eve?'

'No,' said Nick simply. 'What phone message is that?'

'Stop screwing me around. You must know. Sean must have told you. That message, Nick, you *must* understand. You've got to take it in context. It didn't mean anything. I was lonely. I was depressed. I was disorientated. I was in a vulnerable place.'

'Bethlehem?'

'Shut *up*.'

They were at Sean's flat, and someone must have seen them arrive, because just as they pulled up in the little residents' car parking bay, a group of familiar people came spilling out of the building's main entrance: Wayne, Sean, Gillian, Aldo, Catherine (who had her arm round Wayne), even Inge was included, and the rest of the Filipina Brides and a whole crowd of people that she recognised from the *Somdomite* offices including Sean's deputy Alan and the shy 'intern' from Salt Lake City. They all seemed to have been having a party, the sort of party that she hadn't had for a long time: the sort where everyone was enjoying themselves.

Everyone milled around good-naturedly as they got out of the car, seething with excitement and sheer well-being.

'What? *What?*' asked Ysenda of Nick.

'Darling, Sean is rich! A man from an American gay media group called The Well of Companionship is buying out *Somdomite* and saving it from going under. That's him, up there.' Nick pointed to a large, beefy, hairy man of middle age who had come out to greet them as well, and was standing by the door of the building with a glass of Diet Pepsi in his great paw. 'Apparently he's been trying to contact Sean for ages, but Sean just never returned his calls. Anyway, he's pouring in cash and Sean's not going to be *rich* exactly, but he's technically a shareholder, so he's going to make a bit of money. And you're a shareholder too, aren't you? So that means there's a bit in this for you as well, doesn't it?'

Ysenda and Sean were looking at each other without speaking.

18

Neither stayed at the party for very long.

Sean himself was made to feel thoroughly uncomfortable by the presence of the big man from The Well of Companionship, who looked like Jerry Garcia and had a habit of leaning in a little too close when he talked. He could not quite bring himself to tell the man that he'd thought he was a stalker and that in various fantasies directed by Kevin Williamson, he had appeared in Sean's flat just as he was now, only at midnight, with a knife in one hand and a bridle and reins in the other.

Sean's mother had become over-excited at the thought of Sean becoming 'rich' even though the American gentleman from The Well of Companionship repeatedly told her that although Sean would benefit, especially if he wanted to stay on as editor, *wealth*, as such, was not on the agenda.

After a number of glasses of wine, she was now re-enacting, for the benefit of Alan and the Salt Lake City 'intern', her version of the Max Bygraves classic 'No Charge'. In the original, a fond parent recalls exactly how much he has done over the years for the son's education and upkeep and finally tells him there will be 'No Charge'. Gillian recounted with fanatical accuracy the thousands of pounds that her family – not his father's family – had spent on Sean's schooling and holidays over the years but ungraciously concluded that, yes, 'there would be a bloody charge. If he's going to be rolling in a Mount Kilimanjaro of cash, then frankly he can do a little something for his poor widowed mother. It's not as if he's running up a big phone bill *calling* me.'

Wayne and Catherine had arrived together. Catherine hovered in the sitting room with her glass, while Wayne uneasily sought out Sean in the kitchen, as he manipulated a tray of mini-pizzas while wearing an oven-glove shaped like a dolphin.

'Sean, mate.'

'Good to see you, Wayne.'

'Sean, look: I'm together, that is, I'm *back* together with Catherine.'

Sean was perfectly calm. 'Yes, well. I more or less grasped that when you arrived together.'

'Right.'

'Right.'

There was a pause while Sean blankly started placing the mini-pizzas on to plates. He didn't know what to say. Wayne had betrayed Sean by going to bed with Catherine; but Sean had betrayed Wayne by doing the same thing.

'The thing is, Sean, I know . . .'

Sean looked up, eyebrows raised a little.

'Mmm?'

'I know how you've felt about Catherine, and I know that . . .'

Sean kept looking at him.

'I know that she came back with you here on New Year's Eve.'

Sean really didn't mind that he knew. He guessed that

if Catherine had told him, then she would have presented it in the flattest, most matter-of-fact light possible: a one-night stand that meant nothing and would never be repeated. But in the next horrible, intestine-impacting moment, Sean guessed that she had also probably said that it wasn't much good and that Wayne ought really to pity him. For the sake of his sanity, and his happiness, he suppressed this fruitless speculation.

His mother once told him that what happened inside other people's marriages was the most profoundly unknowable mystery. But he thought now that the real mystery was what exactly your former sexual partners revealed about you to their current mates. You can never ask, and so you can never know about all your different lives and anecdotes and reputations, all those hidden images of you, whispered forth in other people's bedrooms.

Sean raised his right arm indecisively, then patted Wayne's shoulder in a resigned and comradely way.

'That's OK, Wayne. It's all over between Catherine and me. I appreciate you coming out with it like this.'

There was a brief and terrible English moment when both men thought that a hug would be appropriate, and positioned themselves for it. But then they allowed their semi-raised arms to subside and grasped and waggled each other's right fist in a manly high-five way, as if they were about to arm wrestle.

That was it. Wayne rejoined Catherine in the sitting room with his drink, and Catherine gazed about her in a studied way, quite as if she had never been here before in her life.

It had been Nick's idea to pick Ysenda up from the airport and bring her directly to the flat. Sean had told him he didn't think she'd want to come, but Nick had been boyishly insistent, and loved the impulsive side to it. And anyway, he said, even if she didn't know about *Somdomite*, she would surely think the idea of a party was brilliant! Aldo Popp offered to come with Nick in the car and keep him company, but Nick thought not. Aldo was becoming a little stout again in his new-found success. His face had plumped back up and his jackets did not do up at the front. He drank neat malt and affected a little frown of connoisseurship when his host suggested mixing it with water. The young radical of broadcast consumer journalism was becoming the sleek media mogul, looking to cut sweet deals across the spectra of video, CD, publishing, television and alternative therapy. He had moved out of his little flat and now had an elegant little maisonette, into which he was currently trying to inveigle Inge, Nick's shrugging, laconic former assistant.

'Inge, how are you? You're looking good.'

'Mm.'

'What've you been up to since you left the clinic? Are you still into complementary medicine?'

'Mm.'

'Are you still playing music?'

'Mm.'

'In a band? Or are you developing – a-ha! – a solo career?'

Inge gave a 'could-be' shrug: 'Mm.'

'I don't know if you know this, but Nick and I are more or less partners now, after I did my, uh' – he gave a gracious little laugh – 'programme about him.'

Inge looked in entirely the opposite direction and drank slowly.

'As a matter of fact,' continued Aldo, 'Popp Stewart Communications could be one of the leading players in the next millennium. I don't know if you are entirely aware of the impact that digital technology is going to have on massage.'

'Mm.'

'Well, we are going to be leading the field on this one.'

Having seen that indirect allusions to his personal success were no good, Aldo Popp tried something more obvious.

'I personally have got a lot of money.'

'Mm.'

Aldo laughed merrily. 'You know, Inge, the thing that's

so fascinating about you is that you are so ambiguous and non-committal. Would you like to come back to my place?'

'No, I most certainly would not.'

'There's no need to shout.'

When Ysenda arrived with Nick it was very late but the strange buoyant mood that infected the party somehow propelled them all out of the door to greet them. The big bear-like man from The Well of Companionship had a theory that all parties in the immediate post-millennial period were going to go this well: 'It's, like, that they've had the weight of expectation lifted from their shoulders, you know what I mean?'

Nick and Ysenda got out of the car surrounded by an amiable crowd, and when Ysenda saw Sean they just stared at each other, and could say nothing. The crowd cheerfully swept them both back up into the party, and Sean and Ysenda kept looking at each other, and catching each other's eye. The same went for Catherine and Ysenda. For the very first time in their lives, they did not spend a good ten minutes bickering and sniping at each other. They greeted each other very warily, and Ysenda kept discovering Catherine taking sideways glances at her, with a strange unreadable expression. Was she right about Catherine? And then a series of thoughts rushed up at her at once: had she been here with Sean? Had he played Ysenda's sad message to her for laughs? She grew cold with fear and indignation at the thought.

It was now really late, maybe three in the morning. The awful plane journey suddenly exacted its toll and she felt all her vertebrae bunching and sagging at the base of her spine like beads on a string. It was time to go. She took out her mobile from her bag with the intention of calling a cab, but discovered that the battery was quite dead. Then Sean materialised.

'Do you want to go out with me?'

Ysenda looked up at him, baffled.

'Sorry?'

Sean frowned and bit his lip. 'I meant *come*. Come out. Do you want to come out with me? For a walk.'

Ysenda thought about the minicab idea for a moment and then put her mobile back into her bag.

'All right.'

19

So Sean left his own party, with Ysenda, quite unnoticed by anyone. They walked down Hornsey Lane for ten minutes and lingered by the Suicide Bridge – the Beachy Head of North London – a viaduct above the Archway Road with its steel meshing along the guard rail to deter people from climbing up and jumping, and the thin withered bunches of flowers tied into the mesh to commemorate the undeterred. They looked first North, upriver, to the dark woods of Muswell Hill, and then crossed over the road to look South, downriver to Holloway and the far reaches of Islington and Tufnell Park.

After a while, Sean said: 'Peter Sellers once talked someone out of killing themselves on this bridge.'

'Serious?'

'Yeah, absolutely. It's true.'

Sean and Ysenda leant on the rail like Noël Coward characters, smoking and looking at the skyline, just distinguished by a muted sodium glow. Near by to the West, they could see the mysterious Archway Tower, that great slab, completely dark apart from the lights on in the stairwells twenty-four hours a day, and the forest of TV aerials on the roof, like a secret ufology research centre. Under the bus stop's kicked-out panel by the Miranda Estate on the Archway Road, a drift of broken glass gave its distant snowfall-twinkle. Further off, they could see the asymmetric stump of the National Westminster building, and further East, the winking obelisk of Canary Wharf, and the coronet of the Dome. Just as Ysenda was on the point of forgetting what they were talking about, Sean went on: 'He was living in Highgate, and he was driving home in his Rolls-Royce, one of those big bulbous old Rolls-Royces they used to drive in the sixties, and he saw someone climbing up here, and clambering on the top, just about to jump. So Peter Sellers pulls over, slams on the brakes and gets out. I see him in one of those dark suits, three-button jackets, all three done up, and that slightly geeky council haircut, jet black, and the Elvis Costello glasses, maybe with the smarmy smile . . .'

They smoked.

'"Hello," he says, maybe doing the RAF officer voice, and then the guy turns round and recognises him.'

Ysenda's cigarette went out and she hunched down below the rail to relight it, and said indistinctly: 'Then what?'

'Well, then Sellers cheers the guy up. Talks him down.'

'Cheers him up? Talks him down? How?'

'By doing funny voices. You know: Bluebottle, Major Bloodnok, Grytpype-Thynne.'

With an effort, Ysenda could remember sitting baffled in the front room of their house in Edmonton, when they had moved back to Canada in her teens, as her father had gigglingly played to her his old Goon LPs.

'Jesus,' she exhaled. 'That would make me want to jump.'

Sean shrugged. 'Yeah. I'd've rather he did something from *Dr Strangelove*.'

They both looked straight down at the road below, and Ysenda fancied she could see the individual facets winking and glinting in the tarmacadam, the dull Quink-blue mosaic that would rush up to greet you as you went down head first.

'Ever think of suicide?' asked Ysenda.

'Of course – it's like those psychological surveys about sex. Once every twelve minutes or whatever it is. Everybody thinks about suicide when they're teenagers and some people never really grow out of the habit. It's comforting, like a security blanket.'

Sean flicked his cigarette over the edge and they watched the little glowing point disappear into the darkness. Then he lit another one.

'Suicide fantasies are always about throwing yourself off things high up. Nobody fantasises about taking a bottle of pills, that's too banal, and you can't fantasise about sitting in your car with the engine running and the hose-pipe, it's too drawn out and ugly. But ceasing on the midnight with no pain and a graceful swallow-dive from the Clifton Suspension Bridge – that's more like it. It's like masturbating; you have to have the right fantasy.'

They smoked some more.

'Actually, though, throwing yourself off something is never that easy. Take this for example.'

They both stood back from the rail with its tricky rounded top and looked at it critically.

'This is no good. You really have to have some sort of stable platform to jump off. You can't just scramble up and sort of fall off the top before you know what's happening, probably hitting your chin or something on the way down, something uncool like that. The only way to throw yourself off here would be with a step-ladder. I've got a lightweight aluminium step-ladder back at the flat that would do very nicely. Put it up to the rail here, stand on the top little platform, deep breath and then jump.'

There was a pause while they both imagined it.

'Actually, no,' said Sean with a frown, 'that's not quite right. The step-ladder can't face the rail head on, you know, perpendicular, can it? The back legs would go over the edge of the pavement and it wouldn't be even, and anyway when you jumped you wouldn't be able to clear that hoopy little aluminium thing at the top. You'd have to turn the steps so that they were parallel to the rail, and then sort of fling yourself off sideways.'

They walked on. Waterlow Park wasn't open yet, so they walked up the Hill and then down twisty, gloomy Swain's Lane and jumped over the fence into Highgate Cemetery to look at Karl Marx's tomb. They stood, mutely, in front of the great black bearded head, which was beginning to loom in the daybreak. This had been Ysenda's idea: for Sean it was too much like dispiriting Sunday mornings when he'd gone on solitary, propitiatory 'walks' down to the Cemetery with a hangover. These 'walks' were undertaken with the idea that fresh air would somehow do him good. Each time, the fresh air made him feel worse. The convention of going out for fresh air on a Sunday morning with a hangover was a purely penitential act, he explained to Ysenda: it could do the hangover no good whatsoever, but the point was to say to yourself that going out for healthy walks was the sort of thing you should have been doing in the first place.

'How are you?' Sean asked suddenly, after a long silence.

'I'm OK. I'm good,' said Ysenda.

'Not too cold?'

'No. I guess I'm beat.'

'Really?'

'Yes, really, Sean,' said Ysenda with a tolerant smile. 'Jesus. I'd only just got off the plane when Nick brought me to your place, do you remember?'

'Oh, yes. Yes.'

'Let's go up to Parliament Hill.'

Now it was dawn, and they could see the condensation as well as cigarette smoke coming from their lips. Crossing Highgate Road, Sean and Ysenda got on to Hampstead Heath, and toiled up the slope, where in a few hours the parents would assemble with their children and their kites. The day after New Millennium's Day, and the place still had stragglers; fireworks were still exploding belligerently on the far reaches of the Heath like gun fire. Ysenda took Sean's hand. At the top, they looked around, standing very close. Sean hadn't been up all night for a while, not since that *Somdomite* party at The Ranch club in the summer. In the cold morning light, he tenderly noticed wrinkles in Ysenda's thirty-year-old face that he'd never noticed before: crow's feet, a second, shorter line on the forehead and two tiny little lines either side of the bridge of her nose. Sean supposed that he looked older too in his new thirty-year-old form: the bags under his eyes were heavier; there were more wiry grey hairs at the temples and dark hair in his nostrils. Gently, he took hold of the lapels of Ysenda's coat and drew her face to his. Their cold chapped lips touched tentatively enough to register only the peeling, serrated surfaces. Then Ysenda moved away.

'Jesus, Sean, look, I'm *sorry*, if that's what I'm supposed to say or if that's what I *ought* to say, I don't know—'

'What?'

'That message, that stupid fucking phone message on your machine, I'm, I don't know, I'm sorry if it upset you or whatever.'

'The one where you said you loved me?'

'No, the one where I read out the fucking football results, yes, the one where I said I loved you.'

A small dog ran up to them with lightning speed; Ysenda shrank away, but it simply shot past them like a dog fired from a gun at ground level.

'*Do* you love me?' said Sean at last.

Ysenda grimaced good-naturedly, as if he had reminded her of a long-forgotten promise, or asked her to perform some difficult feat of mental arithmetic. There were the beginnings of tears in her eyes, and in her voice a tiny quaver not immediately mastered.

'Yes, I guess so.'

'You *guess* so?'

'I guess so, yes.'

'Listen, this "I love you" thing wasn't my idea, you were the one who rang me up with it.'

'Yes, well—'

'What?'

'Well, I don't know; I guess I've had a sort of crush on you from when we were both around six and it never really went away.' Ysenda had gone red.

'I never knew that,' said Sean wonderingly. 'You mean you had a crush on me when we were six, when you and Catherine used to come round to our house to play?'

Ysenda nodded.

'And we would play on those stupid swings and that dangerous climbing frame that my mother had set up in the garden, and we wouldn't let Catherine join in, and all that time you had a crush on me?'

'Yes. Is it so hard to believe?'

'No – but then you went away for years and I never saw you until we were about fifteen.'

'That's right,' said Ysenda simply. 'And I felt just the same way about you that I felt when I was six. Or thirty.'

'What way is that?' said Sean at last.

'Well, you know, Jesus, Sean, why are you being so obtuse, I *liked* you, that's what we used to say over there; I *liked* you. I still . . . I still *have feelings* for you. I never bought all that gay stuff incidentally.'

'It's not about "gay"—' Sean began.

'Oh, Jesus, whatever it is, shut up about that, you can quit it, I never bought it, and anyway, you *know* what I mean.'

They walked on, and now the bandstand and the tennis courts and the little padlocked pavilions and sheds were close, all grim and lowering in the cold winter morning. Sean asked wonderingly, in a quiet voice: 'So that was why you rang me up in the middle of the night?'

'Why are you being so *horrible* about this?'

Ysenda wheeled around into his path and her earrings swayed and bumped against her cheeks. Her voice had cracked and he could see that she was now very close to crying, something that he had never ever seen her do.

'No,' said Sean softly, stepping one pace up to Ysenda, taking her other hand, and inclining his face towards hers. 'No. I'm sorry. I'm so sorry. Go on.'

'I was just alone out there and then I remembered something I'd read somewhere about how when a woman gets past thirty, she never meets anybody new any more.'

'How do you mean?'

'New, someone that she could fall in love with, get married to, move in with, I don't know.'

'That's not true. That's rubbish.'

'Well, I don't know if it is or not, but I remembered this article said that once you were past thirty you had to find your partner from the people you already knew and it was like buying a house; something you'd previously rejected you had to look at again a little more forgivingly if you wanted to make a deal.'

'Thanks a lot.'

'Oh no, I'm *sorry*, I didn't mean it like that, but anyway I thought of you and I realised how, how *fond* I was of you, how I thought about you almost every day and how we'd always been such friends and how I thought I should, well *realise* you as an *asset*—'

'Like I said, thanks a lot.'

Now it was Sean's turn to feel upset.

'Well, it wasn't just that, OK, it wasn't *just* that.'

Ysenda relinquished both his hands, and walked away up to the bandstand, leaning her arms on the rail round the base.

'What was it?' asked Sean, beginning to follow her.

Ysenda set her mouth in a tight little cartoon line and put her hands on her hips, which caused her leather jacket to bunch and her shoulder bag to flip round to the back. She turned to him again.

'I called you up because I was convinced that you were in love with Catherine.' She paused a beat. '*Are* you?'

'No,' said Sean truthfully.

'Well, you've certainly been behaving very strangely the past year or so around her.' Then her eyes narrowed shrewdly. '*Have* you slept with her?'

Fatally, Sean hesitated. That's a yes.

'I knew it; I *knew* it.' Ysenda threw down her bag in a mixture of pique, exasperation and obscure triumph.

'It was just the once. Just once,' pleaded Sean.

Ysenda was shaking her head. 'I know. Oh, I know. Just once. And now of course you're obsessed with her for ever more. Now she's got you in her spell. Just like Wayne. Damn. *Damn.*'

'No,' said Sean coldly. 'No, I'm not obsessed. I *was* obsessed. I was obsessed with Catherine for about a year. It's been a very strange year. And I slept with her once. But then, I don't know . . .' he looked distractedly about. The same dog shot across the middle distance with a stick in its mouth. 'It sort of broke the spell. The fever lifted.'

Briefly, Sean considered telling Ysenda about the circumstances in which he and Catherine heard her message. In the next moment, he decided to keep it a secret for the rest of their lives. In any case, there was something more pressing on his mind.

'What's this about Wayne?'

Ysenda reached for her cigarettes again. Last one. She lit it and confessed: 'I had this sort of thing with Wayne. It was just over a year ago and we'd met at this dinner at Hunter's house. Wayne and me were getting on very well and I was teasing him about a dumb TV ad he'd done three years ago.'

'Really?'

'We made out in the taxi on the way home.'

'You're kidding!'

'Nope. We kissed, and . . . it got pretty heavy.'

'What certificate?'

'I guess a Fifteen.'

Sean gave a low whistle while Ysenda continued sagely: 'Simon Bates was there in spirit, warning about the sexual swear words. It was a pretty adult taxi ride. But thing was . . .'

'What?'

'He said he loved me.'

They were both quiet for a moment.

'Of course, I know boys sometimes say these things and it doesn't mean anything. I don't think it meant anything this time. He came in for coffee but he didn't stay the night. I think it was just the magic of the cab ride. He just left. I mean, I didn't *believe* him when he said he loved me, but I kept sort of waiting for him to call, and then I suspected he had something going with Catherine, and now I see he's turned up to your party with her. Once again, I am pipped by my younger and more attractive sister.'

Sean came very close and murmured: 'No, that's not true. You're much nicer than she is. You're smarter, and you're a better dresser and you're better looking. In fact you're a beautiful, a beautiful . . .'

It was the right thing to say, but Ysenda was not wholly mollified. She turned her face close to his – looked up at him – and Sean saw how at this range her eyes turned in slightly, almost crossing. He turned his face in to hers, but their lips did not meet at first. Delicately, he undid the large middle button of her coat, and inserted his hands, palms together as if praying or diving. They snaked around her waist, outstretched at first, as if measuring her, then allowing his fingers to splay up the small of her back while his thumbs softly pinched her sides as her coat flapped up over his arms. She felt very warm under the coat. This was how he drew her towards him into his kiss.

Her lips were fuller and rounder than her sister's and she entered more fully and thoughtfully into the languid internal rhythm of the French kiss, the rhythm of the nursing baby or the organic pulse of the heart. Her lips were cold, but her tongue was warm. His hands swarmed up to her breasts just as she put her palms up to his pinkly, bitterly cold cheeks. They parted with a little embarrassed laugh. Where was *that* supposed to go?

Gently, Ysenda drew away from his embrace and her coat flapped down. Then she came around and put her hand on his arm. She threaded it through hers and they walked along and down the slope towards the edge of the Heath and could hear the traffic going down Gordon House Street to South End Green. Suddenly they chanced upon a very large, unfamiliar-looking building with high brick walls and what looked like barbed wire running along the top.

'What the hell is this?' asked Ysenda. 'It looks like some sort of municipal concentration camp.'

But as they edged around the side of it, Sean realised what it was.

'It's the Lido! We've just never approached it from this angle before.'

They came round to the front, and recognised the triumphal avenue of Corporation of London flowers leading up to the front entrance, which to Ysenda's astonishment was open.

'But it's the depths of freezing winter for goodness' sake!'

'Lido's open seven till nine-thirty in the morning every day, all the year round, Christmas Day included. It's free of charge first thing. Come on.'

Together, they sounded the clanging turnstile and turned into the concrete concourse between the changing rooms. Nobody manned the cloakroom at this time in the morning; you were just supposed to shiver in the little stone stall and tip-toe out poolside with your clothes in a refugee bundle and leave them on one of the wooden benches. An LCD sign said the water temperature was 51 degrees.

They went out by the pool and Ysenda couldn't believe her eyes.

'Is this where we were last summer? Where we went swimming? Where you nearly drowned? I can't believe it. It looks so small.'

It did look small. In fact, it somehow looked about half the size it was when they were last there. That huge sunlit pool-piazza of last summer had contracted on this cold wintry morning. It didn't look as if it could contain half the number of people they remembered. The concrete around it looked cracked and crumbly and weedy. It was a desperately lonely place, or would have been, were it not for the athletic Kiwi lifeguards who ambled about the place in pairs. Apart from these attendants, Sean and Ysenda were quite alone. They walked around to the right. Ysenda pointed to a spot by their feet in the corner.

'It was here.'

'Here?'

'Here, where we were sunbathing. And it was here where we dragged you out and you got the kiss of life.'

He looked at the little patch of concrete. He couldn't imagine that anything important had happened here. They walked around to the other side where the café was closed. The clock across the way said twenty minutes past seven. They sat down on one of the benches and stared at the water for a bit. A pale sun emerged and their bench projected milky shadows on the ground.

'I suppose I'll end up being friends with Catherine,' said Sean at last.

'It's better than being enemies,' said Ysenda reasonably. 'You should be friends, why not?'

'It's what people do after they've stopped having sex, isn't it? What civilised, decent people do. They become friends. It's the only way forward. I read an interview with Hugh Hefner the other day where he said some rival magazine had published Polaroids stolen from his mansion taken years ago, showing him having sex with a girl. And he said he didn't mind for himself, but the "lady involved is now a dear friend". Why is that so sad?' He turned round to Ysenda. 'Why is that so desperately sad? It's so inevitable. Death, and becoming a "dear friend" with someone you used to have passionate glorious sex with.'

'Sex doesn't last for ever,' said Ysenda. 'It lasts hardly at all. When you start going out with someone, you have sex four or five times a day. And then it's once a day. And then it's four or five times a week. And then it's once a week. And then – whump! – it's twice a year on your birthdays.'

They looked at the water. Neither of them had any cigarettes left. Ysenda spoke again:

'Friendship after sex – that happens inside relationships, too, you know,' said Ysenda. 'Being friends with someone after you've stopped having sex with them: that's the secret history of marriage.'

'In that case,' said Sean, 'let's not get married.'

'No, let's not.'

Ysenda leant back and stretched. The sun was now out and it was actually quite bright; though not warm. She felt pleasantly sleepy, but reasonably alert.

'If we started having sex,' ventured Sean, 'or if we started having a relationship, what would that be like?'

'Round the other way, you mean, first the calm friendship and then the sex?'

'Yes.'

She thought about it.

'It could make strangers of us. Or it might not work at all. I could start laughing in the middle of sex. I have been known to do that, I warn you.'

'That . . . that would be OK. I mean, it wouldn't be a disaster. We could get past you laughing in the middle of sex.'

'Or it could spoil everything. I had a really good friend once when I was seventeen, and we agreed to go on holiday and we ended up *hating* each other, I mean really hating. It would be terrible to do that on a grand scale.'

Sean considered this. 'We needn't live together,' he said.

This was not at all the point, but Ysenda was at that moment distracted by the sight of a swimmer. A hardy soul and evidently a regular, from the severe way he exchanged greetings with one of the lifeguards. He had a big beachtowel with palm trees on it draped around his shoulders and he was holding a black nylon tote bag with the word 'Cargo' on it. This, it seemed, contained his regular clothes because when he removed his towel with a little flourish, he was dressed in only his swimming costume: a stooping, balding figure in his mid-thirties with what looked like a livid appendix scar across his abdomen. The swimmer gingerly started to climb down into the water from the steps and Ysenda and Sean cringed on his behalf as the water clutched at his poor calves. Then they snorted derisively as the swimmer's nerve failed him and he stepped smartly back out on to the side and marched with spurious energy and decision over to another part of the pool as if he had forgotten something. His face burned, and he was clearly aware that everyone was watching him.

'If we had sex, we would both have to keep a straight face about it,' said Ysenda. 'And you would have to promise not to tell your mother for at least six months.'

'We couldn't do it after dinner, though, not in the evening,' said Sean. 'That's too loaded. And we couldn't go on holiday to do it. What about in the afternoon, something like that, something we could agree on.'

'Next Sunday afternoon, at my place?'

'A Sunday afternoon, at your place, would be all right,' said Sean cautiously after a beat.

The swimmer had come round to the deep end and was staring into the pool, biting his lip with dismay, as if he'd dropped his wallet down there. He crouched down and placed his index finger in the water. Sean and Ysenda relapsed into silence, and watched him turn around, walk back and then stand with his back to the brickwork as if he was facing a firing squad.

'OK,' said Sean quietly. 'Next Sunday afternoon.'

Then Sean and Ysenda turned in towards each other; their lips met and their eyes closed and as they kissed they could hear athletic footsteps and then a great and festive splash, a whoop as from one scalded with cold, a cry of disturbed birds on the Heath, and a tribute from the Lido attendants who had briefly set down their styrofoam cups of coffee to applaud.

PETER BRADSHAW

Dr Sweet and His Daughter

PICADOR

What happens when you think your life just can't get any worse ... and then it does?

Dr Sweet's life is largely unremarkable. A recent divorce and ongoing custody battle; a tame affair that's gradually grinding to a halt; a job which seems to have stopped halfway up the professional escalator; friends who are too preoccupied with their own lives to spare much of a thought for anyone else . . . In fact, the only bright spark in Dr Sweet's life is his terrifically talented and terribly precocious daughter, Cordie. With Christmas family hell just around the corner, however, in the shape of his parents and ex-wife, Dr Sweet's life is about to take a turn for the worse. Sent to the local shop for some last-minute supplies, this is the day he manages first to lose his mistress, then his job and, finally, his freedom, as the police arrest him for murder.

An absorbing and sophisticated tale – part-satire, part-tragedy – that reminds me in places of the best of Martin Amis . . . This is a really good read, with abundant wit, some very funny dialogue and a crescendo of sweaty-palms embarrassment and drama in the final scene'

Daily Mail

JAMES DELINGPOLE

Fin

PICADOR

Joe Davenport seems to have it all: a great career and a beautiful woman. But something nasty is stalking his karma and fear is fast becoming terror. Black-eyed killer sharks are after him and what if his girlfriend finds someone better? He is in dire need of solace from the neuroses of modern life, not to mention the endless replays of his own death scene. And then at a party, he meets a girl not like all the others – with her own shark story to tell . . .

'If you like Nick Hornby, you'll like this. It's very funny, blasphemous and blokey. Against all the odds, I loved it'
Carla McKay, *Daily Mail*

'Sharp and enjoyable . . . A clever social comedy'
The Times

'Canny, funny and refreshingly original'
Mirror

JAMES DELINGPOLE

Thinly Disguised Autobiography

PICADOR

As if it wasn't bad enough the first time around, experience the decade of greed, green wellies, pills, thrills and bellyaches all over again . . . This is the book that tells you like it is and like it was.

Josh starts his first year at Oxford bursting with hopes, ambitions and ludicrously unrealistic expectations. *Thinly Disguised Autobiography* is the story of his rude awakening, from the sleaze of Fleet Street to the terror of the LA riots, from clubbing at the Wag to slumming it at Glastonbury, from Oxford to London via Venice, Spetses, Laguna Beach and Bromsgrove.

'A comedy of manners, and a sharp, honest and extremely funny one at that . . . This is a warm, witty novel illuminated by Devereux's youthful optimism, and written with gusto – a hugely enjoyable read'
Literary Review

'Delingpole's journey through the rites of passage that constituted the Eighties for men like him – pills, the Wag, Glastonbury – hits the spot'
Arena

'Crackles with energy and wicked humour'
Mail on Sunday

ANTHONY McCARTEN

The English Harem

PICADOR

Tracy Pringle is a supermarket checkout girl with a lively imagination. In her mind her customers are not bored and tired Londoners with screaming children, but the likes of Princess Leia and Omar Sharif. It's not surprising she turns a blind eye when Queen Elizabeth I pops a packet of Bakewell Tarts into her handbag without paying, but unfortunately the management don't see it that way, and Tracy is forced to find herself another job.

But nothing can prepare her for the new life that lies in wait at the Taste of Persia restaurant, where our heroine falls headlong into dinner plates, Islam, and a rather tricky domestic arrangement . . .

'A sparkling, fantastical tale'
Eve

'McCarten's novel hovers between indignant satire and engaging comedy of manners while sounding a clarion call against the bigotry and intolerance in our society'
Sunday Times

'Anthony McCarten's sparkling new novel manages to deal with big issues – cultural differences, religion, marriage – in a funny and often very moving way'
Dublin Sunday Tribune

EMILY PERKINS

Leave Before You Go

PICADOR

Leave Before You Go is about Daniel, who escapes the grind of his London life to find himself alone, penniless and paranoid on the other side of the world. And it is about Kate, who lives in Auckland, where she works as an usherette. It is a merciless and witty examination of a generation cut adrift: what do people do when they don't know what they want to do?

'A gifted writer, with an idiosyncratic, clear-eyed take on life'
Harpers & Queen

'The funniest, sharpest depiction of post-modern twentysomething life I've read'
Time Out

EMILY PERKINS

The New Girl

PICADOR

It is the beginning of the summer holiday in a town in the middle of nowhere. Julia and her best friends Chicky and Rachel are school leavers emerging from their girlhood, waiting for the future. While they wait, Miranda, an exotically beautiful woman from the city, arrives to teach a summer class. And after her arrival, nothing will ever be the same again.

'A quietly powerful tale of growing up'
Guardian

'Perkins has created an unforgettable narrative of female teenage coming of age: its poetic tenderness and acute honesty will give painful stabs of recognition'
Evening Standard

EMILY PERKINS

Not Her Real Name

PICADOR

With unnerving insight and wit these stories present an essential guide to post-modern romance, to the vagaries of city life and to a chronically self-absorbed generation whose love affairs are never as good as the last movies they've seen. Emily Perkins brings modern life into harsh and comic focus with a cast of young and painfully vulnerable metropolitans.

'Brimming with talent. I can't wait for more'
Esther Freud

'A stunning first collection: addictive, smart, scary, wise and profoundly funny'
Julie Myerson

OTHER PICADOR BOOKS

AVAILABLE FROM PAN MACMILLAN

PETER BRADSHAW		
DR SWEET AND HIS DAUGHTER	0 330 49217 9	£7.99
JAMES DELINGPOLE		
FIN	0 330 48045 6	£6.99
THINLY DISGUISED AUTOBIOGRAPHY	0 330 49336 1	£12.99
EMILY PERKINS		
LEAVE BEFORE YOU GO	0 330 35308 X	£6.99
THE NEW GIRL	0 330 37601 2	£6.99
NOT HER REAL NAME	0 330 34266 5	£6.99

All Pan Macmillan titles can be ordered from our website, www.panmacmillan.com, or from your local bookshop and are also available by post from:

Bookpost, PO Box 29, Douglas, Isle of Man IM99 1BQ
Credit cards accepted. For details:
Telephone: 01624 677237
Fax: 01624 670923
E-mail: bookshop@enterprise.net
www.bookpost.co.uk

Free postage and packing in the United Kingdom

Prices shown above were correct at the time of going to press. Pan Macmillan reserve the right to show new retail prices on covers which may differ from those previously advertised in the text or elsewhere.